Praise for Laurie J. Marks's previous Elemental Logic novels:

Fire

★ "Marks has created a work filled wit[...]ge."
—*Publishers Weekly* (Starred Rev[...]

★ "Marks is an absolute master of fantasy in this book. Her characters are beautifully drawn, showing tremendous emotional depth and strength as they endure the unendurable and strive always to do the right thing, and her unusual use of the elemental forces central to her characters' lives gives the book a big boost. This is read-it-straight-through adventure!"
—*Booklist* (Starred Review)

"A deftly painted story of both cultures and magics in conflict. Marks avoids the black-and-white conflicts of generic fantasy to offer a window on a complex world of unique cultures and elemental magic."
—Robin Hobb

"Cuts deliciously through the mind to the heart with the delicacy, strength, beauty, and surgical precision of the layered Damascus steel blade that provides one of the book's central images."
—Candas Jane Dorsey

"Laurie Marks brings skill, passion, and wisdom to her new novel. Entertaining and engaging—an excellent read!"
—Kate Elliott

"This is a treat: a strong, fast-paced tale of war and politics in a fantasy world where magic based on the four elements of alchemy not only works but powerfully affects the lives of those it touches. An unusual, exciting read."
—Suzy McKee Charnas

"A glorious cast of powerful, compelling, and appealingly vulnerable characters struggling to do the right thing in a world gone horribly wrong. I couldn't put this down until I'd read it to the end. Marks truly understands the complex forces of power, desire, and obligation."
—Nalo Hopkinson

"Most intriguingly, about two-thirds of the way into the book, the low-key magical facets of her characters' elemental magics rise away from simply being fancy "weapons" and evoke—for both the readers and the characters—that elusive sense of wonder."
—Charles de Lint, *The Magazine of Fantasy & ScienceFiction*

"An exquisite novel of quiet charm. *Fire Logic* is a tale of war and magic, of duty, love and betrayal, of despair encompassed by hope."
—*SF Site*

Earth Logic

★ "The powerful but subtle writing glows with intelligence, and the passionate, fierce, articulate, strong, and vital characters are among the most memorable in contemporary fantasy, though not for the faint of heart. Definitely for the thinking reader."
—*Booklist* (Starred Review)

"The sequel to *Fire Logic* continues the tale of a woman born to magic and destined to rule. Vivid descriptions and a well-thought-out system of magic."
—*Library Journal*

"Twenty years after the invading Sainnites won the Battle of Lilterwess, the struggle for the world of Shaftal is far from finished in Marks's stirring, intricately detailed sequel to *Fire Logic*.... Full of love and humor as well as war and intrigue, this well-crafted epic fantasy will delight existing fans as surely as it will win new ones."
—*Publishers Weekly*

"Rich and affecting.... A thought-provoking and sometimes heartbreaking political novel."
—*BookPage*

"*Earth Logic* is not a book of large battles and heart-stopping chases; rather, it's more gradual and contemplative and inexorable, like the earth bloods who people it. It's a novel of the everyday folk who are often ignored in fantasy novels, the farmers and cooks and healers. In this novel, the everyday lives side by side with the extraordinary, and sometimes within it; Karis herself embodies the power of ordinary, mundane methods to change the world."
—*SF Revu*

"It is an ambitious thing to do, in this time of enemies and hatreds, to suggest that a conflict can be resolved by peaceable means. Laurie Marks believes that it can be done, and she relies relatively little on magic to make it work."
—Cheryl Morgan, *Emerald City*

"*Earth Logic* is intelligent, splendidly visualized, and beautifully written. Laurie Marks's use of language is really tremendous."
—Paula Volsky

"A dense and layered book filled with complex people facing impossible choices. Crammed with unconventional families, conflicted soldiers, amnesiac storytellers, and practical gods, the story also finds time for magical myths of origin and moments of warm, quiet humor. Against a bitter backdrop of war and winter, Marks offers hope in the form of various triumphs: of fellowship over chaos, the future over the past, and love over death."
—Sharon Shinn

"A powerful and hopeful story where the peacemakers are as heroic as the warriors; where there is magic in good food and flower bulbs; and where the most powerful weapon of all is a printing press."
—Naomi Kritzer

Water Logic

Water Logic

An Elemental Logic Novel

LAURIE J. MARKS

Small Beer Press
Northampton, MA

Small Beer Press
176 Prospect Avenue
Northampton, MA 01060
www.smallbeerpress.com
info@smallbeerpress.com

Distributed to the trade by Consortium.

Library of Congress Cataloging-in-Publication Data

Marks, Laurie J.
  Water logic : an elemental logic novel / Laurie J. Marks. -- 1st ed.
      p. cm.
  ISBN-13: 978-1-931520-23-2 (alk. paper)
  ISBN-10: 1-931520-23-2 (alk. paper)
  I. Title.

PS3613.A765W38 2007
813'.6--dc22
                                  2007010083

First edition 1 2 3 4 5 6 7 8 9 0

Printed on 50# Natures Natural 50% Recycled Paper by Thomson-Shore, Dexter, MI.
Text set in Centaur MT 12.
Cover art © Corbis: "To Pastures New" by Frederic Cayley Robinson.

For the people who looked after Deb and our pets, made certain we could pay the bills, took care of my students, and literally put my pieces together and got me back on my feet.

Prologue: Seeking Balance

Fire

If it can be imagined, it can be done, said Emil.

Emil, Medric, and Zanja, all fire bloods, had each by an equally unlikely route become governors of Shaftal. Yet only Emil even knew what a government was. He alone had been a minor thread in the vast tapestry of the old government before it unraveled. Children not then born had now borne children of their own—children who expected only bloodshed and oppression, who did not know and could not imagine how it had once been.

The patterns of the past can no longer serve, but people believe that strength lies in tradition, said Emil.

Zanja said, because of tradition they believe in Karis, little though she wants to be believed in.

No, earth is what they believe in, said Emil.

But even earth is unstable, said Medric. For the power of any witch arises from lack of balance. What we must have is the steadiness that comes from balance: the insight and passion of fire, the solidity and fertility of earth, the ideals and intelligence of air, the fluidity and vision of water. When, though informing and contradicting each other, the elements are in balance, then they become stable, and then we have strength.

But how can an entire country be in balance? asked Zanja. How can we do now what we must, while also devising a future?

Oh, it's an impossible task, said Medric. Let us begin it at once.

Water

Ocean stands knee-deep in the future.

The water is warm. The harbor is protected. There is a narrow beach, insurmountable cliffs, a pounding waterfall. These have not been enough.

She is a child when she flees there with the remnant of the tribe. The strangers have come, with their weapons and their anger. Ocean is there, and now she is the leader of the tribe. She finds a haven for them. She is standing there now, but the tribe has gone.

The people have built larger boats, and have learned to grab the wind with them. They have slipped between the rocks and dared the open sea. Ocean returns to the ship, to every ship, in every storm, in every passage. She returns and the sea never takes the sailors, and they find the way back to the harbor with barrels of salted fish. They go out and meet other ships, and they trade for all that their small harbor does not give them. To this chary shore, to toothed rocks, to hungry waves, they return, she returns, the tide rises and falls and she returns, and the pattern is failing.

She stands in childhood; she stands in adulthood; an old woman now, she stands in the future. The tide flows, in and out, and always inevitably there is less. The pattern will be failing, the pattern has always been failing, and it has failed. She will stand in the future, is standing there, and she is alone. The pattern has failed. It must not fail. She returns and again she begins.

Earth

Months had passed, and every night Seth still thought about Clem, a weary, haunted, quiet woman, making a difficult journey in dead of winter. They had made love in the way of strangers who are compelled towards each other—a surprising, strange, unsettling, yet heady business, coming to know each other's skin without knowing each other's secrets.

Later, when Clem returned as Clement, lieutenant general of the Sainnites in Shaftal, leading a company of soldiers, the uniform had changed her into someone else. They had not touched, though Seth's hands had yearned to her: not to the heavy, oil-blackened leather, not to the gray wool underneath, where brass buttons flashed. Her hands yearned to the skin, upon which her fingers had once sensed the scars in the dark, the scars Seth never mentioned and hardly even heeded.

Seth's hands had betrayed her into foolishness, into a stupid mistake that might well make her notorious—a Basdown cow doctor who was such a bumpkin she had mistaken a Sainnite soldier for a Shaftali farmer, even when they lay naked in her bed! Yet at that second meeting, Clem's—Clement's—identity had been a surprise but had not mattered: Seth's hands still wanted that hauntedness, that hunger. She wanted Clem.

No, the lieutenant general had said. No. And she had left with her soldiers, she had slept with them in the barn, though Seth lay awake half the night listening for the sound of the door latch. She is a Sainnite, she reminded herself, over and over. A Sainnite—a monster—a killer—a leader of monsters and killers. She listened for the door latch, nevertheless. In the morning the soldiers had left, Clement among them, walking across the snow, dragging sledges behind them. Seth's family went to the cow barn, fearing the worst, but found it neater than it had been; found that the Sainnites had made their beds in straw and left the hay alone; had molested none of the animals and had not even requested food for themselves. Never before had Sainnites been such careful guests.

Later, there came rumors: Harald G'deon had vested a successor after all, a woman who had been living in obscurity but now had stepped forth. She had reached through a garrison gate and nearly strangled the general of the Sainnites with her bare hands. Within hours, he had fallen ill and died. With a single blow of a hammer, the G'deon had knocked to pieces the walls of Watfield Garrison. The new general had clasped hands with the new G'deon, and they had made peace with each other. Surely such things could not be true!

But then there were broadsheets, carried from farm to farm—and Seth had examined an etched illustration of the G'deon and the new general standing upon a pile of rubble, clasping hands: Clement, general of the Sainnites in Shaftal, and, towering over her, Karis, G'deon of Shaftal. The etching was titled, PEACE BETWEEN OUR PEOPLE. Isn't that—? said Seth's family. Surely not!

Later, a Paladin had come to Basdown, bearing a letter addressed to an elder who had died earlier that winter. Soon the letter also made the rounds of the households, grimy and softened from being passed from hand to hand, carried through wet weather, read again and again at one or another farmstead. There would be a government in Shaftal once again. A person from Basdown must be named councilor and must travel to Watfield, to speak for the people of the region.

The elders of Basdown asked Seth to go to Watfield and speak for them.

Air

Whatever *he* said, she knew it was truth, knew it in her bones, where it transformed to steel the human stuff that broke too easily and never healed right: Meertown folded steel, which no one had seen but everyone knew about, that never lost its edge and never rusted, not even in salt water. *His* truths gave her bones that did not bend, that supported her changeable, fragile spirit in such a way that she was strong. Such strength she had now!

All will be well, *he* said. Now she had come here, fearless in this fearsome place, this city where all that was wrong was embraced, where people went about with their eyes glazed, some bewildered and some enchanted and most waiting in doubt for their hopes to be fulfilled. She had traveled here with the others, Senra, Charen, Tarera, Irin, and Jareth, her brave companions. Her son had left, for he had his own calling. His absence freed her. She had nothing to do, and the empty hours begged her to fill them with her pigments and brushes. So she painted them: her son and *him*, whose name must never be said or even thought, both of them in one face. Not even the others recognized who it was! Yet to her heart the two of them had always been the same.

She painted, in a cramped, dirty room, in this notorious city, where no one suspected her presence. How delicious that ignorance was. The evil ones, the bringers of violence and destruction, here was their center, their ruler, their locus of power. The soldiers, yes—but not only the soldiers, mere animals after all, hardly worth the time and effort required to exterminate them. Their leaders, for leaders they must have—they cannot decide anything for themselves, not even where to dig their latrines, for land's sake. One might almost pity them in their stupidity if they weren't such brutes.

If they hadn't—if they hadn't...

Her thoughts stopped there, as they always did, ever since *he* put a bulwark in her spirit to protect her from the memories. The past did not matter, *he* had said, and it was true. She looked to the future, to the one who was coming, whose way must be cleared, whose pretender must be eliminated, whose beasts must be butchered, so that the true people of Shaftal could see clearly! Their task had seemed impossible, until *he* showed them the simplicity of it. Small actions have massive results. So simple!

She painted. Her companions could not abide the smell and left her alone, which was a relief, though she adored them. The two faces gazed out as one face, and she felt full, satisfied, fearless. She might die soon, and the prospect filled her with gladness. Whether she lived or died, those united faces would gaze at her always: solemn, confident, approving. *You have done well.*

Senra came in, saying, "Phew! How can you bear it?"

She was making a color, a tricky business in the gloom of late winter, when even sunlight looked gray. She did not look up from her palette. Senra, holding his nose (he was always playful, that Senra) went to the painting. From the corner of her eye she watched as his casual glance turn to a shocked stare, a repelled glancing away. She smiled, working carefully with her muller and the precious pigments that *he* had declared must be bought, though she had expected to sacrifice every-thing, even—especially—this joy. And of course her son. But *he* had been wiser than she—there are no sacrifices, *he* had said.

Senra said, "Why does he have no eyes?"

"He does have eyes," she said.

"They are holes! Right through his head! You can see the hills behind him!"

She continued to work the pigment into the oil, and Senra went away, shaking his head, muttering something. He was amusing, but not very imaginative. He might die soon. Well, what of it? His death would rescue them all! She went back to the painting and began putting flames on the forehead of her son-leader, flames in the shape of that ancient glyph, the one that means Death-and-Life. Tonight on her own fore-head that glyph would be drawn with a fingertip in a paint made of grease and soot. But on *them* it burned always, a pure flame, not golden and red like the hot fire of passion, but white and blue, burning with a cutting, clear cold: flames of air.

She thought of the impostor, the pretender, and her hand painted with anger—anger pure and selfless as the flame. In that perverse, degraded town of whores the evil of Sainna had merged with the solidity of Shaftal—that was disgusting. The bastard child had risen up out of nothing and declared herself the G'deon—that was intolerable. Oh, the painter's skin crawled with rage and horror, but her hand painted true. She had never painted so well as she painted now, waiting in this city, where the pretender also waited for the people who were coming from every corner of the land, coming to be infected by her foulness, and then to carry that foulness outward to the whole. But one simple act would mend all.

It had become too dark to paint. She slid the unfinished painting into the case that made it possible for her to transport her work with the paint still wet. She packed her pigments, her oils, her turpentine, corking the bottles and sealing them with wax, for if she did not die tonight she would flee, bringing her paints and painting with her.

Her companions came in, and at last it was time to draw straws.

Part One: The Region of Reconstruction

Chapter 1

By winter's end, the field of rubble had become famous. The new councilors of Shaftal had begun to arrive in Watfield from far and near, and all came to view the remains of the destroyed wall. Seth went there as soon as she and her Paladin companion entered the city, even before they sought a place to lay down their heavy packs and thaw their frozen fingers.

The massive wall had surrounded Watfield Garrison. Now the stones lay in a swath through the city. Seth squatted down, took off her gloves, and with numb fingers broke a small stone loose from its icy mortar. She set it atop a much larger one, the surface of which had been flattened by the stone mason's chisel. The small stone shuddered sideways off its wide base, to impinge upon another, which cracked free from the ice that pinned it down, and rolled away. Now, that stone touched two others, which also hitched themselves sideways. The chain reaction quickly spread, from a few stones to many, until noisy waves of movement rippled ponderously in both directions, between the buildings, out of sight.

Seth had stood up to watch. She felt cold air on her teeth and realized she was gaping. Everyone spoke of this wonder—but she had not truly believed it.

"You'd better put your gloves back on," the Paladin said.

It seemed impossible Seth could still be in her familiar world. Yet she pulled on her gloves, which like her hat and jerkin were tightly knit of unwashed, undyed wool. The grease that repelled snow and rain from her hat and gloves still smelled like dirty sheep, and the busy city continued to clatter, shout, slam, ring, and rattle even as the crack and thud of the supernatural stones faded into the distance. Seth said, "The wall can't be rebuilt. These stones will always refuse to remain one on top of the other—to even touch each other."

The Paladin, as pragmatic as Seth but even less talkative, shuffled her feet, as if to remind Seth how cold they were and how welcome a hot meal would be. "The G'deon lives in the city center, in a house called *Travesty*." She gestured towards a busy artisan's district, where an oversized shoe advertised a cobbler's shop, a normal-sized wheel the wheelwright's, and a gigantic needle and thread the tailor's. Seth felt offended by the asymmetry of these displays.

"You go," she said to the Paladin. "I'll find my own way."

They parted ways, in the manner of strangers thrown together who had never become friends. Alone now, Seth walked along the edge of the rubble, following the mostly obscured road that once had abutted the garrison wall. On the opposite side of the restless debris stood what once had been an orderly group of garrison buildings. Some were fire-scarred, and others were heaps of charred beams and wrecked furniture. Many were being rebuilt. She could hear the carpenters chanting breathlessly as they pulled on the ropes that lifted a center beam. The banging of hammers punctuated the racket of the city. Roofers swarmed over the top of one building, shouting cheerful curses at each other. At another, the carpenters were hanging clapboards as fast as they could drive in the nails. Some of them wore soldier's gray, but most of them wore Shaftali longshirts, several layers, so they could take them off and put them on again depending on how cold the day became and how vigorously they worked.

The main gate lay flat on its face, embedded in dirty ice. There, two soldiers were gathering stone blocks that had begun to clutter the passage. In their wheelbarrow, the stones banged the wooden sides as they struggled to get away from each other, but the soldiers seemed accustomed to this extraordinary behavior.

The woman soldier looked up as Seth began picking her way through the passage. "Carefulness," she advised. "Rocks move much."

The man soldier had stopped his work to watch a grinding wave of movement he had inadvertently instigated in the field of stones. His wave encountered another coming from the other direction, and there was a brief confusion. A raven that had been perched on one of the stones flew up in startlement. The waves separated and continued on, and more rocks rolled into the passageway he had just cleared. The soldier rolled his eyes comically. The raven landed nearby and began preening its flight feathers.

"I would like to speak to the general," said Seth. "Is that possible?"

"The general is in quarters," said the man soldier. "Will I—I will show you the way."

Seth followed the soldier in dumb surprise, feeling as if a door she'd expected to stick had swung easily open, without even a squeak of the hinges. The soldier said, "I am Damon. You have traveled far?"

"I'm Seth, a Basdown cow doctor. Now I'm a councilor."

The soldier said, "A councilor? Your mission will be difficult. I follow orders only—easier, eh?" He gestured meaningfully at the sky.

Puzzled, Seth looked up. The raven she had noticed at the gate now floated overhead. Why did this soldier find the bird significant? She said, "Is that a G'deon's raven?"

"That one has not talked today, so I am not certain. Still, I have been polite to it." He grinned.

When Seth first realized Clement was a soldier, the woman's darkness of spirit, her bouts of formality, and even her ravening hunger had made sense to Seth. But this soldier's friendliness and humor were as surprising as the supernatural raven. Fortunately, the sound of hammers and saws rose around them in such a din that Seth could not have answered the soldier had she been able to think of something to say.

On both sides, new buildings rose up out of ashes and charred debris. Seth had entered the region of reconstruction.

Damon led Seth into a smoke-stained building, down a hall that was being swept by an old, one-legged woman in a ragged old uniform, to a nondescript door that stood ajar. He called out in the soldier's language and received a brisk answer from within.

"We wait," he explained to Seth.

Looking over his shoulder, she could see only a coat tree on which hung a much-worn, felt-lined leather coat, and part of a homely laundry line, hung with woolen stockings and…diapers? She shifted sideways, and now she could see a large window with its grimy upper panes unshuttered to let in dim light from the rapidly darkening sky. Beneath the window, at a scarred table surrounded by battered chairs and piled with dirty dishes and waxed-leather envelopes, sat the ugliest man Seth had ever seen, reading aloud from a stiff sheet of paper.

She shifted sideways again, and now her heart gave a hard thump. Clement sat across the table from the ugly man. She appeared to be

Seth noticed them in time to prevent them from importunately removing the general's clothes.

"So are you here to see if I am still here?" Clem's breath tickled
Seth's mouth. "What can I do—what will it take—to keep you from
leaving?"

The skin of her face was overlaid with a fine grain of wrinkles.
Her eyes, brown like Seth's, were shadowed by blue underneath, like
shadows on snow. Seth's hand, still pressed against gray wool, felt the
woman's thudding heart. She said, "Just give me a small thing: my skin
upon yours."

Seth felt Clem's breath shake itself out of her. She said, "My room
upstairs—it's cluttered with my son's things. The blankets haven't been
aired since autumn. The shutters are open, to let in the light for the
flowers, and it's bitter cold, certainly. The lamp has no oil—the wood-
box is empty—"

"What can't be fixed we will ignore."

"—And we'll be interrupted."

"What!"

"If I post a guard—"

"You can only have privacy by sacrificing it?"

"I am in charge of several thousand terrified soldiers."

Those soldiers were not in charge of themselves? Were they children? Jolted again, Seth drew back.

The door cracked open and a voice said, "General?"

"Gods of hell, Gilly, leave me alone!"

"I did intend to. But a note just arrived from Travesty."

"Cow dung!" Seth muttered. Clement stepped away. Seth jammed
her misbehaving hands into her pockets and glared into the fireplace.
The flare of new flame had burned out.

At the door, Clement and her secretary argued in Sainnese. The
tone of their conversation changed so swiftly from dismay to sarcasm
to mockery that Seth could not imagine the topic. The baby chortled
sleepily, like a bird at sunset. Clem had not been pregnant, last time—
Seth would have noticed that! This was not a son of the body, then—of
course not; women soldiers never bore children.

Seth had congratulated herself for finding it irrelevant that Clem
was Sainnite. But in fact she had not been thinking of her as Sainnite

at all; she had been thinking of her as a Shaftali in a soldier's uniform, as though the clothing were wearing her. And Seth might wish it were true—she might wish it with vigor for the rest of her life—but all that wishing would make no difference. The uniform was Clement; Clement was Clem; and Seth must know her entirely if she was to know her at all.

The door closed, with Gilly again exiled to the hall. Clement approached Seth with an unfolded note in her hand and showed it to her. "Please visit me," was scrawled on it in pencil, in big, awkward letters.

Clement looked down, seeming very interested in the toes of her boots. "The Council of Shaftal meets in four days. My thirteen garrison commanders could arrive as early as tomorrow, and their quarters aren't even built yet. But the G'deon has summoned me, and I must go."

"I should go there also, I suppose," said Seth distractedly.

"Gilly reminded me that if you have no kin in Watfield, you'll be residing in Travesty."

"I have no kinfolk here."

"The people who live in Travesty are always complaining that none of the chimneys draw properly and the floors are all crooked. But it's a massive building. You'll certainly have a room to yourself."

Seth took a hopeful breath—and then she was jolted again, and appalled. "How could anyone's timing have been so perfect? Tell me I have not been following a path without thinking! Like a cow!"

Clement looked up from studying her boots. A wry smile had reshaped her face. "There was a raven—am I right? A raven watching for you to arrive?"

"There was, but—I am no one to the G'deon! Why would she watch for me?"

"Her seer probably dreamed of you."

Seth stared at Clement. Clement in turn observed Seth assessingly, seeming curious to see what she would do now.

"Then she's subtle, for an earth witch," Seth finally said.

"Oh, yes, subtle as a bull in bracken!"

Seth was so surprised to hear this Basdown saying—uttered with a Basdowner's dripping sarcasm—that she laughed out loud.

But Clement said, "Go home, Seth."

Yes, Seth thought, I certainly should—if I expect to ever go home at all. But beneath the jolts and surprises and clamoring confusion of the last few moments, her certainty remained certain as ever. She said, "I gather that your life is intolerable. And you think those intolerable conditions will be mine, too, and perhaps you think that is already happening. But you don't know me, just as I don't know you. So here's a lesson: I cannot be discouraged—if you don't believe me, ask my mother! And don't tell me what to do, either."

Clement looked at her a long time. At last she said, very quiet and amazed, "You have a mother?"

A dead general's lieutenant serves as general for only four months. Then the commanders gather to choose a new general for life. Because Cadmar died in dead of winter, during two of Clement's four months the only communications with the garrisons had been written. Now all fourteen commanders would soon arrive in Watfield, and Clement would need to convince them that without her as general, the Sainnites would not survive.

Clement could strategize, give orders, obey orders, and argue against plans she thought inadequate. But she did not know how to convince a group of people, whose hostility to her decisions had certainly hardened to intransigence, to choose her.

How do people choose? How—why—had Seth chosen to come to her again? She could not explain it.

Clement had gathered some things for the baby, put on her coat, and left for Travesty. Now, the cow farmer walked sturdily beside her, snowshoes dangling from her knapsack, her legs wrapped in grimy oiled leather, her cheeks chapped and red from facing the bitter Shaftal wind. They walked side by side through the garrison. As always when Clement went out, soldiers continually approached to talk to her.

"Good day, General. I am happy to report that your new uniform will be finished today."

"General Clement, have you heard that we're running low on fodder for the horses?"

"A fine day, eh, General?" This was said sarcastically after sleet had begun to pelt Shaftali and Sainnite indiscriminately.

"General! What's going to become of us?" An old one-eyed veteran, whose duties involved much scattering of sand in winter and sweeping it up in summer, limped out of a sheltered doorway. As Clement stopped to talk with him, he gently stroked Gabian's downy head, which poked out the front of her leather coat. Gabian talked to him also, though the baby's comments weren't entirely sensible.

Now a Shaftali carpenter trotted over to tell Clement that the building they were passing could be occupied tomorrow—the garrison commanders, who would be arriving any day to attend the Council of Shaftal, would have a place to sleep.

Sleet pinged on the hard brim of Clement's hat. The carpenters began to chant a loud song about Shaftal's awful weather. Their hammer blows slowed to keep rhythm, and soon every hammer within hearing whacked in unison, while red-cheeked, vapor-breathed, wool-dressed carpenters bellowed their objections to the looming storm

At Clement's side, Seth also began to sing: "Why must it snow in spring? It is not just nor right!" Her voice was rough and homely as raw lumber.

"Ark!" Gabian shrieked, and wriggled joyfully against Clement's breast.

They crossed the fallen gate, Seth greeting one of the gate guards by name. Now, having finally broken free of the soldiers' anxieties, they rubbed elbows with busy citizens trying to finish their errands and tasks so they could take shelter from the storm.

Seth tucked a hand into the crook of Clement's arm.

Clement looked down, and saw Gabian's bright gaze peeking up at her, as if to ask why she found happiness so alien and bewildering. Even through the leather and wool of their heavy winter clothing, Seth was a warm pressure, tucked up against Clement as though they were an ordinary couple taking a baby on a stroll on a typically wretched winter day in Shaftal.

Of course they weren't, and Clement noticed some hostile stares. She also noticed that Seth was staring back. Not easily discouraged? Well, that certainly was true.

In the square fronting Travesty, Seth dragged a little, apparently unable to tear her gaze from the soaring towers and extravagant decorations of the buildings on that street, a rare sight, and a shameful one in this land of extreme practicality. At the ugly, squatting stone monolith at the end of the square, the usual idling crowd had been diminished but not dispelled by the weather.

"What a horrible place!" said Seth. "How hard would it have been to pleasingly balance the windows? And why must the walls seem on the verge of falling onto us? And what idiot decided to build with that hideous stone? Of course they must call this building *Travesty!*"

"Unfortunately, it's the only building in town that's large enough to house a government."

"Will they rebuild the House of Lilterwess?"

"I don't think so. If there's rebuilding, the library at Kisha will be first—these people are obsessed with books."

Having been admitted by Paladins, they unwrapped and unbooted themselves in the vast cloakroom and made their way through a wide, crowded, noisy hall in which every single piece of extremely ornamental furniture was occupied. What all these people thought they were doing here Clement did not know.

In a room beyond the hall, Norina Truthken had set up her domain. There she kept collected the young air elementals who, after causing great trouble to their parents and communities, had been sent to her as soon as word of the Truthken had spread. Through the storms of winter the air children had come, often unescorted, always unannounced, never recommended. Now, an excessively upright twelve-year-old boy demanded that Seth identify and explain herself, just as one or another of the air children demanded of everyone the first time they entered the Travesty. These children must have responsibilities, Norina had said. But a responsibility like this? Well, if anyone were incapable of error, it was Norina.

The Truthken, who had been standing over a desk reviewing a line of text with a rather frustrated-looking girl, now observed the boy's interrogation of Seth. Norina's hair was clipped as close to her head as any soldier's, which signaled her status, should there be someone whose creeping skin were not a clear enough signal. Once, long ago, a person stupid enough to attack Norina had managed to slash her face open, which was an impulse Clement understood well. Every time Clement saw Norina she had this same thought, and the Truthken knew it.

"Well, we are worried about you, General," said Norina to her.

"So I have gathered, Madam Truthken."

"Should I be offended by your resentment, or should I admire the skill with which you mask it? I can never decide."

"Of course I'm skilled—I've had thirty years of practice. How are the governors of Shaftal today?"

"Working—some harder than others." Norina gestured towards a hallway. "Karis is expecting you."

In the meantime, Seth had been permitted to enter. As they started down the designated hall, she said, "What *was* that boy? And all those other intimidating children? And those monstrous books they were reading? I have never seen anything like it."

"They say it's a law school."

"Oh, those are air children. They do make the skin crawl, don't they. But that woman—!"

"That was Norina Truthken. Her duty is to locate and rehabilitate— or else execute—the villains of the world. She seems to think I can be rehabilitated, though being executed would be less painful. Seth, I should warn you—"

They turned the corner, and there, standing in an open doorway, was the G'deon: tall, broad, big-shouldered, ham-fisted, dirt-smeared, dressed in much-mended work clothes, with a massive hammer tucked into her belt. It was Karis who had named the building Travesty, and who had set about destroying and rebuilding it, one wall at a time. When Clement first met her, she had been covered with pulverized mortar, and ever since then it had been plaster dust and dirt. No one would ever accuse Karis of keeping her hands clean.

"It took you long enough to get here," Karis said. "Anyway, you're staying for supper."

She stepped back through the open doorway, beyond which Zanja na'Tarwein sat cross-legged on the hearth—her extinct people had lived without furniture, and she still preferred not to use it. Today she wore a restrained, meticulously fitted suit, as black as the slim braid that draped over her shoulder like a woven cord. Karis could not have chosen a lover more physically and mentally unlike herself: compact, sharp-edged, dark-skinned and dark-haired, quick and mystical, remarkably impractical.

The door closed. Zanja held out her arms and Clement handed Gabian to her, then sat on a footstool that was upholstered in needlework so lovely it seemed wrong to use it for such a humble purpose. "I believe I'm the victim of a conspiracy," she said to Zanja in Sainnese.

"You are—but it's a conspiracy of friends," Zanja replied in the same language, one of at least three in which she was fluent. "Emil advised Karis that some of the tasks he gives you are impossible to achieve; Norina warned her that you are under unendurable strain; J'han confided his concerns for your health; Medric dreamed of your cow farmer's arrival; and Gilly declared that you would only take a day for yourself under duress."

"You are dangerous meddlers, every one of you."

"*Now* you realize this?"

"Oh, I will never doubt your own or your family's ability to achieve by indirection that which cannot be achieved by force. And of course you act in good will. But what did Medric dream? Why is a soldier's dalliance with a farmer worthy of a seer's attention?"

"Our much-beloved madman rarely bothers to explain himself," said Zanja. "You can be sure it's important, though."

"If it's important, then you all should stop frightening her."

"That one? Oh, no, she's not likely to be frightened so easily."

"Zanja—I'm feeling stupid again."

"You have no idea what she is? Look!"

Clement looked, and saw Seth and Karis, clasping each other's hands, speechless, seemingly entranced.

Clement said, "Bloody hell. What is she then?"

"It's in their hands, Clement. My wife's palms are coarse and seared by fire. Your cow farmer's palms look like leather, and I think her grip would not be easy to dislodge. They enter the world hands first, both of them."

Clement remembered how quickly Seth's hands could find the way to bare skin; how Karis's hands had bent the iron bars of the garrison gate; how Seth's hands had clenched the porch post as Clement walked away; how Karis's hand had reached ahead of her as she climbed towards Clement across the rubble.

"Earth in hands, fire in eyes, air in skin, water in voice," said Zanja. "So elemental talent may be recognized. That old saying sounds much better in Shaftalese."

"She's an earth blood?"

Zanja quirked an eyebrow. "What, your interactions with her have not been memorable?"

It was common knowledge, Clement remembered, that earth bloods were excellent lovers.

The trance seemed to have finally broken, and Zanja stood up to greet Seth, and then she handed Gabian to Karis, who declared that she wanted to do nothing but hold him for the rest of the day. It appeared that Clement was destined to spend the afternoon as neither a general nor a mother. The prospect made her feel quite disoriented.

Seth knelt beside the stool and put her hand on Clement's knee.

"She overwhelms everyone," said Clement, "As I was about to warn you. And the others of her family—well, the full strangeness of this household is not easy to describe."

Zanja said, "Greetings, I am Zanja, a fire blood, wife of Karis, Speaker for the Ashawala'i."

"But—" began Seth.

"My tribe are ghosts," Zanja said. "Sometimes I am one also."

The communicating door to the library opened, and Emil, his gray hair tied back with a ribbon to expose his three gold earrings, peered into the room. "Greetings, General Clement."

"Good afternoon, Emil. May I present Mariseth of High Meadow Farm, the councilor from Basdown?"

Seth leapt to her feet. Emil clasped her hand, and the lines that fanned out from the corners of his eyes deepened. "There must be a great deal of earth talent in Basdown, that they can afford to waste it on government."

"They thought I could fix bigger problems than sick cows," said Seth.

"Hmm. Fix problems, you say. Many new councilors seem to think their job is to punish. The people of Basdown are disinclined to punish the Sainnites for what they've done?"

Emil's conversations were often like this, conducted in great intuitive leaps, efficient but sometimes baffling to his listeners. He had been a Paladin his entire life. But his eyes, the liveliest and most expressive part of his face, were nothing like the passively attentive gaze of a good soldier. Paladins *choose*—they make an art of choosing; they study and argue about it their entire lives. Clement's anxieties again began to claw at her.

Seth said, "The people of Basdown are not united. Even those who see no value in punishing the Sainnites argue that our region has not suffered directly from their rule. So they think it might be wrong to prevent others' vengeance."

"It is a good point," said Emil.

"But they're wrong! And vengeance only leads to more vengeance! We should not allow our future to be shaped by anger and loss—that seems even more stupid than what the Sainnites have done to us."

Emil smiled with his entire face now, not just with his eyes. "You'll be making that argument more frequently than you like, I'm afraid. Welcome to Watfield, Councilor."

He departed soon, for even with the aid of Zanja and Medric and numerous clerks and librarians, his work never seemed finished. Then Karis showed the way through the maze of dim hallways, up two hidden stairways, to the dusty and echoing third floor of the monstrous house. As they negotiated the way upwards, Seth and Karis exclaimed at every one of the building's faults: the maze-like hallways, the uneven stair steps, the crooked walls, the creaking floorboards.

Zanja was as indifferent to buildings as she was to furniture. She asked about Clement's progress at learning to read, for Emil wanted Clement to study Paladin ethics and make herself into an example, a soldier who became a Paladin. He could not believe that books had no effect on Sainnites, whether or not they could read.

"Ethics," said Clement. "That's about choices, isn't it?"

"It was about one choice, according to the Paladins. An ethical person refuses to be a conduit for evil."

They had climbed three more steps before Clement realized Zanja was being sarcastic. "Sometimes the evil lies far in the future! How can we possibly know the future effects of what we do now?"

"Oh, that's the hard part," said Zanja, with an edge of anger in her voice. "But sometimes evil is obvious."

When the Sainnites massacred Zanja's tribe, that had indeed been an evil act, and Clement was glad she could say she had argued against it, for all the good her arguments had done. That attack had also been unimaginably stupid, for it had unleashed Zanja—a crosser of boundaries, a hinge of history. The Sainnites, bloody fools, had set that woman loose upon themselves.

They reached the end of the last hall. Karis opened a door, saying what a wonder it was that one room in the building had nothing wrong with it, except for its remoteness. "Can you be comfortable so far above ground, though?" she asked Seth.

"I'm not that sensitive," said Seth. "I can't endure boats, though— or being dangled from ropes."

"Can you cross bridges? I can't—not wooden bridges, anyway. Stone bridges I can manage, if I move quickly." Karis added briskly, "We eat by the clock here—Garland is a military man." Without disturbing Gabian, who had fallen asleep in the crook of her arm, she reached back to clasp Clement's shoulder and push her into the room after Seth.

The door closed, the floor creaked, and then there was silence.

The room was warm and well lit, with a brisk fire in the fireplace and a lamp burning atop a bureau. The rug was extraordinary, woven in a complex pattern of stylized flower bulbs, each one bravely opening its buds. And beside the window, which had a shutter bravely open to the weather, a dish of living flowers bloomed. *Hope,* said the room to Clement.

"Those people act as a family to you," Seth said.

"They do?"

"Prying, interfering, protecting—that's what families do."

Seth was wandering the small room in apparent delight, and now paused at the flowers. "What are these?" she asked herself. "Such an extraordinary blue color! And that fragrance!"

"It's a Sainnese flower which we call *spring-in-winter*. That plant is descended from my mother's bulbs. Zanja declares that a blooming flower is my name-glyph. But I think she must be wrong, for all Sainnites love flowers. I am hardly unique."

Seth was coming towards her, but she stopped now and glanced back at the blooming flowers, and down at the blooming carpet. "I've never heard of that glyph sign. But the G'deon's wife is a famous glyph reader, isn't she?"

"She invents her own glyphs, I think, and then they mean whatever she wants them to mean."

Seth laughed. She had drawn close now and was hardly more than a step away. "Clem—can you come out from under all that brass and leather?"

Of course Seth remained undiscouraged. She was an earth blood—reliable as dirt, persistent as a weasel, and stubborn—like Norina said of Karis—as an old tree stump.

Clement undid her buckles and buttons. She took hold of Seth's strong hands and helped them find the way inside her linen undershirt.

They entirely missed supper.

Chapter 2

Travesty squatted at the end of its snow-glazed square in the lightless winter night. Six ravens slept in an off-center gable, with their beaks tucked under their wings, satisfied like their mistress by the day's work and dreaming hopefully of what might be accomplished tomorrow. The storm had passed, and bitter cold had arrived in its wake.

For six people who walked purposefully through the square, it was not too cold, nor was the hour too late.

Zanja na'Tarwein slept beside Karis, with their daughter, Leeba, tucked between them, and baby Gabian sleeping in a basket near the fire. Lately the ghosts had left her alone; and, unlike Emil, she didn't write letters in her sleep. She slept peacefully, and then she started awake.

She slid out from under the covers and dropped to a crouch on the floor. Her dagger lay there as always, in its sheath, and now it was in her hand.

She heard the twang of a bowstring. An invisible projectile hissed overhead and thunked into the plaster wall. She sprang forward, and with a single blow at the darkness, slashed the intruder's throat. Hot blood drenched her nightshirt and face.

She had not paid attention when it happened, but now she realized she had heard Karis awaken and reflexively grab hold of their daughter to shield her.

"Karis!" she cried. "What is happening?"

"There are strangers in the house. The one here is dead."

"Obviously! How many?"

"Three more—all armed. How could—?"

"Are these three people together in a group?"

"No, separated. Hunting."

"You're the one they're hunting for. And now I will hunt them."

Karis said, "Take a raven with you."

With a loud crackling of ice, Zanja opened a window, and a raven flew in. She stripped off her nightshirt, for her dark skin would make her invisible in shadow. With the heavy bird's claws digging into her wrist, she left the room barefoot.

"The Paladin guards are dead," said the raven on her wrist. "Others are dead, too."

Then the bird said, "Turn right here."

Travesty's hallways were such a maze that people often became lost in broad daylight. But the ravens, like Karis, were never lost.

"Emil is awake," the raven said.

Karis would have sent another raven to tap on Emil's window— Norina's also, certainly. In moments Emil also would be armed and prowling a hallway.

The raven uttered a nearly soundless croak.

Zanja stopped, and listened. She heard and saw nothing, yet she sensed where her prey walked.

She set the raven down, turned right at the intersection, and ran, nearly silent, until the cursed house betrayed her with a creaking floorboard.

A solid shape in the softer darkness turned sharply. There was no light, no shimmer of metal. Only the swift lift of shadow arm and shadow blade. But the assassin could see even less of Zanja than she could see of the assassin.

Zanja struck low. She drove the deadly sharp edge through the flesh of hip and thigh, landed on the floor beyond, and scrambled back to her feet.

The assassin's breath hissed through teeth. Zanja's foot slipped in blood. The dark shadow swung at her. She parried the blow, then her own blade twisted into flesh and scraped bone. The assassin's weapon clattered to the floor.

Zanja leapt out of range. "Yield!"

She heard a strangled sound, like choking. Heels drummed on the floor. Then silence.

The raven, flapping towards her down the hall, squawked, "Take care! Their weapons are poisoned!"

Emil's prey must have also died suddenly and strangely. Zanja touched the assassin's warm body cautiously, found no heartbeat, and then put the raven again on her wrist.

The bird said, "I'll bring you and Emil towards the last one from opposite sides."

The raven gave directions and added, as Zanja continued blindly through Travesty's maze, "Norina wants you to keep him alive. Don't let him stab himself."

Norina was a better fighter, but in darkness Zanja and Emil could fight by intuition, and Norina could not.

"But be careful," said the raven. "Even a scratch—"

Zanja's heart thudded crazily. She breathed too fast and then too slowly. "I understand the danger."

The raven fell silent, except to utter occasional one-word directions, and then to tell Zanja that she had drawn near the intruder, who had entered an unoccupied room. Zanja set down her bird-guide and waited. At the far end of the hallway, Emil also waited: noiseless, a shadow among shadows, a presence so vivid to her he might as well have been holding a lantern.

The man came out of the room—a small man, able to slip silently in and out of doorways, his feet soundless, his shape nearly indistinguishable.

Emil's shoe leather whispered on wood.

The man snapped into tension. Zanja heard the faint hiss of an arrow's flight. She also flew, and tackled the intruder from behind, flinging herself into the center of his body and flattening him, face first, into the floor.

The man's groan as he sucked air back into his lungs was followed by a cry of rage. Zanja pinned him, got her hands around his neck, and pressed the veins closed.

"Emil!" she cried. The man flailed frantically beneath her.

"Don't choke him to death," Emil said. He searched the prisoner, removing and setting aside several weapons. The assassin uttered a shriek as Emil twisted an arm behind his back. "I guess you broke a bone or two."

Zanja discovered she could not speak at all. Emil's hand touched her shoulder, gently. "She's not hurt," he said to a raven, "And neither am I. So stay where you are, Karis—please. Until we can awaken the house."

"She's not replaceable," he added to Zanja. Then he let his breath out in a groan. "Oh, by the land—"

Emil, one knee on the groaning prisoner's shoulder, was probably thinking hours, days, years into the future already. Zanja thought only about the smell of the blood on her skin.

Then Norina arrived with a light, another raven, and several distraught Paladins.

The Paladins took over Zanja's prisoner. She sat back on her heels. Now she began to tremble, and a weakness came over her.

"Emil—that poisoned arrow missed Karis by a hand's breadth."

Emil lifted her to her feet and put his arms around her. "*This* massacre," he said, "you prevented."

"How could he have gotten so close?" she cried. "Who are these people?"

Norina said, "Look—here is your answer." She turned the lantern to illuminate the assassin's face. Upon his forehead was painted three black strokes: the Pyre, the G'deon's glyph.

"You seek to kill the G'deon in the name of the G'deon?" Norina asked.

The man's chin jutted defiantly. "To kill the impostor," he said. "In the name of the true G'deon."

Emil's embrace was also a restraint, Zanja realized. And for just a moment, she let herself feel the anger—at that idiot Willis, who had nearly killed her when they both were Paladin irregulars under Emil's command. At Norina, for judging Willis harshly enough to destroy his ambitions, but leaving him alive. At Clement, for killing nearly all Willis's rebel band, including Willis himself, and yet failing to eliminate them.

"And how do you know which G'deon is false and which is true?" asked Norina.

But the light flashed on Norina, on her shorn head, and the man cried, "Are you a Truthken? Keep away from me!"

Norina turned away from him, as the law required. The scar that crossed one side of her face, from eyebrow to chin, looked as black as the glyph on the prisoner's forehead.

"Saleen, do something sensible with this man," said Emil.

"Yes, Emil." The Paladins walked the prisoner away.

Emil's clench relaxed and became an embrace again. Zanja pressed her face against his shoulder, grateful for him, and then desperate to get away from him. "I am not confused," she told him. "I know the difference between this night and the night my tribe was destroyed."

He let go and took off his own shirt and gave it to her, "Put this on—throw it away later." He turned towards Norina, saying, "Clement killed Willis and so many of his fighters on Long Night—I didn't think anyone of that rebel company survived. Or that they would still refuse to believe in Karis—how could anyone be unconvinced? But they have reconstituted themselves, nevertheless."

Though the assassin was gone, Norina had continued to look down the hall where he had been taken. She said at last, "I'm afraid it's worse than that, Emil. Much worse."

By the time a Paladin knocked on the door to rouse Clement to face the new disaster, the first floor of Travesty had been lit up by lamps and was noisy with grief and anger. Clement's mind, if not her body, still was tangled in the blankets, wrapped in Seth's sweet, steady, generous warmth. Now the familiar dismay and urgency of recent violence surrounded her, but she could not accept it. She took refuge in a shadow.

Nearby, the two Paladin generals, Emil and Mabin, argued bitterly. Their voices rang and echoed against the polished stone. Further in the depths of the monstrous building, a wail lifted, faded, and lifted again. Pots clashed in the distant kitchen, and in another remote wing there was the thumping of a sledgehammer.

Mabin, an old woman grown hard and stubborn in her lifelong hatred of Clement's people, was saying fiercely, "It doesn't matter! Paladins don't kill Paladins! Shaftali don't kill Shaftali!"

A Paladin approached and said, "Excuse me, Emil, the uproar is awakening the city. People are coming to the door, asking what has happened."

"Thank you for this information," Emil said. "Ask Saleen to speak with them, please, according to his judgment."

What absurd courtesy!

Clement realized then how angry she was. How dared they—on this night—the only night she had ever taken for herself alone!

And it was she who was being absurd. She took a breath, a deep one, and the old armor fit itself to her, and her mind cleared, and Seth became distant. Clement stepped forward, saying, "Here I am, Emil. I assure you both: I knew nothing of any attack. I'll say so before your Truthken, though it doesn't even seem necessary—how could I have been admitted by her if I were plotting this thing?"

"Oh, Norina would have known. But I'm afraid you'll have to make the gesture of clearing yourself anyway. For then we could let it be known that a Truthken declares your innocence. People will believe what Norina says, even if they don't want to believe the evidence."

Mabin said angrily, "What evidence? A glyph painted on the forehead? That doesn't make a person Shaftali! The weapons and clothing? They could have been acquired anywhere!"

"Oh, for the land's sake—" Emil muttered.

Clement watched him, curious whether she might finally see him lose his temper. For now he truly was beset, attacked from without and within, and, like Clement, might find it difficult to distinguish between those in his own camp who opposed him, and those outside his camp who did the same. Perhaps he, too, would begin to dread every new development, lest he be forced to take yet another action that he then must justify to friends and enemies alike.

Mabin said, "This must be the work of Sainnites! To the Shaftali people the G'deon's body is sacred!"

"Karis is hurt?" cried Clement. The Paladin who had awakened her had reassured her about Gabian, but she had not even thought to ask about Karis.

"One of the assassin's darts missed her by a few feet—" Emil shut his eyes and took a breath. "Zanja killed the assassin in their bedroom, but Karis is unhurt. The one we captured alive said she is an impostor—why would a Sainnite care if Karis were properly vested and confirmed or merely a pretender?" This comment he directed at Mabin, but he continued without awaiting an answer, "Norina is barred, yet she learned something—something significant."

Mabin began to speak again, but Emil ignored her. He belatedly offered Clement the handclasp of a friend. "I am sorry," he said.

Clement was learning to make sense of these fire bloods, for she understood that Emil was not apologizing for Mabin's vituperation.

He was sorry for something else, for something lost.

Emil led the way down the lamplit hall to a parlor that had often been used for meetings since it had one of the few fireplaces that drew properly. There, frightened people clustered together for reassurance: clerks, librarians, and councilors who resided in that echoing house. Emil sent them all away on errands, and soon only three people remained: Medric, who cowered in a garishly painted chair with a moth-eaten shawl pulled over his head; Leeba, who was asleep on the carpet, curled up like a cat, with one scruffy foot sticking out from under the bright blue blanket; and Gabian, also asleep in a basket.

With a jolt, Clement remembered that the garrison was even worse defended than Travesty, for Karis had destroyed its weapons first and then knocked down its walls. "Emil, you promised my people would be safe, that no one would contradict Karis. But that obviously is not true—and my people can't defend themselves."

"The attackers were *not* Shaftali—" Mabin began again.

"They were," said Norina Truthken. She dumped an armload of weaponry and clothing onto a chair. "They were Paladin irregulars," she said.

Clement said, "Madam Truthken, I had no knowledge of this attack."

"Then what are you afraid of?"

"My people could be the next target!"

Norina said, "As always, Clement speaks the honest truth."

"Of course." Emil sat down and rested his head in his hands.

Mabin allowed not even a pause before she said, "It's the Sainnites' fault, nevertheless! Without their corruption—"

Norina said, "Mabin, must you always waste everyone's time with your character flaws?"

Mabin went white with anger, and Clement almost pitied her.

"Where are the others?" Norina asked.

"J'han is looking for Zanja...no, here they are now."

Norina glanced at the doorway, through which her healer husband was escorting the G'deon's wife, dressed only in a shirt much too large to be hers, gray-faced, her dark skin speckled with darker drops of blood. The bare blade in her hand rang like a bell when she accidentally touched it to the stone threshold, and she glanced at it in surprise.

Norina asked, "Should I fetch Karis? Or shall we let her smash her own house to bits undisturbed?"

Emil said, "I sent a tremulous librarian after her. You know how she hates to frighten people."

In fact, the distant pounding had stopped. Garland came in with a tray and poured tea. J'han took the first cup, mixed in enough honey to make it into a syrup, and began urging Zanja to drink it.

Immediately before and after a battle, a soldier's most essential character is revealed. Clement had long suspected Zanja's lethality—but that the woman had so visceral a reaction to her own violence was surprising. Clement had never imagined they might have this in common.

Karis arrived: the parlor shrank. She picked Zanja up and embraced her. Zanja's teacup and dagger both rang sweetly as they fell to the stone floor.

Zanja gasped, "I pity the wall. And all your other enemies."

Karis set her down. She was shedding plaster dust like snowflakes; her broad shoulders and undisciplined hair were white with it. "What enemies?" she said. "What reason has anyone to kill me—and everyone in my household?"

Zanja, her voice now muffled by Karis's shoulder, said, "Anyone who won't pay the price of peace."

"It's so much cheaper than war!"

"So one would think," murmured Zanja.

Karis let her go. During that embrace Zanja's face had altered from gray to flushed. She scanned the room, pausing on the miserable seer, on Clement, on Emil, and finally on Norina. These governors of Shaftal had raised a child together, and as naturally as they handed off Leeba's care to each other, so also they handed off authority and leadership. Clement, ill-accustomed to such a fluid command, had learned to look wherever Zanja did, for Zanja always seemed to be thinking a few moments ahead of everyone, except perhaps the seer.

Norina said, "The assassins were Shaftali. They were Paladin irregulars. They had the Death-and-Life glyph painted on their foreheads. General Clement, you're certain that their leader, Willis, is dead?"

"Willis bled to death in front of me. And I saw his body burned."

"Then you did us a favor—but too late. Willis may not have known it, but he had already been replaced, by one far more dangerous than he." Norina paused. "An air witch."

Zanja's swift gaze moved to Medric, and the seer came out of his huddle like a rabbit bursting out of cover. "What?" he cried. "Oh, that's very bad!" He snatched off his spectacles and polished them vigorously on his dirty shirt. "You may not know this, Clement—the Order of Truthkens was invented to get the air witches under control. Before that, the G'deons were constantly having to hunt them down and jam spikes into their hearts." He added, "Unfortunately, fire magic can't predict air magic, as they are elemental opposites. So we were taken by surprise." He put his spectacles on, and blinked.

They all had turned to Norina, possibly expecting one of her famous rages, but the Truthken, apparently not insulted by this piece of unflattering history, said, "Air bloods can't understand fire bloods either."

"Oh, I'm a lunatic to you, of course," said Medric. "Now what about this air witch?"

Norina said, "I can't be certain, of course. But I think that he—or she—was young, or not even born, at the Fall of the House of Lilterwess. She developed her beliefs in a lawless land, without guidance. This young witch directly experienced some of the worst of what the Sainnites can do, and now in the air witch's mind the Sainnites are evil, and anyone who thinks otherwise is evil also. Any action to destroy these enemies is justifiable—especially killing Karis, for she's showing mercy to the enemy rather than destroying them as they deserve, and—worst of all—she's half Sainnite."

Clement had gritted her teeth, but held her silence, for Zanja had shifted her gaze to Karis, not to her. Karis stood stock still, but her muscles bulged as though she were wrestling her own powerful self into submission. "I'll forge a spike." Her damaged voice grated unpleasantly on the ear. "Whose heart do I drive it into?"

Norina's eyebrows rose. "I don't even know how to find this air witch, or how to seek the information. When that assassin is put on trial, when I *can* question him, I'll learn nothing more than I know now."

Karis said, "I'll learn something. My ravens are following two people—two who waited outside the building during the attack. And now they're fleeing Watfield on separate roads, in separate directions. Eventually they'll return to their leader, this air witch. And after that she—or he—will be unable to avoid me."

Clement did not know what Karis was capable of—Karis herself didn't always seem to know. But anyone who chose to be her enemy was a bloody idiot. Mabin had once made that choice, and had lived with a spike in her heart for years, and during all that time, each one of Mabin's heartbeats had depended on Karis's will.

Emil said, "Well, at least this air witch has lost the advantage of surprise. Let your ravens be extremely cautious, Karis. No one in Shaftal sees a raven without wondering whether it might be your servant."

Karis was nodding impatiently. Now, finally, Zanja's swift gaze turned to Clement. "I'm sorry for all my people have done in ignorance," Clement said. "We feared that Truthkens could make people into puppets..."

"Oh, but we can," said Norina.

"...and we didn't understand the Order's function. But now, in the present moment, what am I to do about my people's safety? Our truce is composed only of words! Perhaps my people deserve to be destroyed by this monster we've created, but if that's our doom, at least let me go and warn the garrisons."

Karis and Emil began speaking at the same moment. "Tell your people—" they both said, then Emil gestured and Karis finished, "—I'm watching over them."

"Even you must sleep," said Emil. "Tell your people I am dispatching armed Paladin irregulars to reinforce the garrison guards."

It was an outrageous idea—but a good one. While the garrison commanders certainly would resent being ordered to accept the direct protection of the very people they had fought for so long, one more reason for resentment hardly seemed important. Clement's offenses against tradition, honor, and even propriety had begun to accumulate as soon as Cadmar took his last breath. If the commanders did accept her as their general, it would not be because they approved of her, but because they were convinced of what she knew. And if she failed to convince them, then the hostility she had earned would still be unimportant. She would have failed to save her people. She wouldn't experience that self-destruction, of course, for she would be the first to die.

She told Emil she agreed to his plan and left for the garrison. But before she reached the front door two Paladins had been summoned to join her, and as soon as she stepped outside a raven swooped down, then disappeared in night. She did not think to even send a message to Seth, for she did not think of her at all.

Chapter 3

That night, Seth had not stirred from sleep until a chill crept into the vacancy where Clement had been sleeping. She opened her eyes to see Clement at the bedroom door, yanking on her trousers while asking sharp questions of the Paladin who stood there with a lamp. The flame was trembling violently. Thus their sweet night together had ended, and any more such nights soon began to seem beyond possibility.

People die all the time, and Seth had laid a daughter, a son, a wife, and several parents upon the pyre. But she had never before scrubbed puddles of congealed blood from a floor, nor had she helped to lay out the bodies of people she did not even know—seven of them! Paladins, clerks, librarians—people who had traveled far from their homes to offer their services, people like Seth. Now they had died among strangers, and among strangers they would be burned.

Seth could not endure this prospect. In Travesty and in the city, confusion became fear, and fear became anger. Though Seth certainly was as distressed and angry as anyone, she set about making friends, something she had never before done so deliberately. Three days after the assassinations, she knew the names and life histories of at least thirty people, which was the typical size of a farm family. Then she felt as if she could die without feeling too alone; and her desire to return home to Basdown, to her family, while it did not disappear, at least became less desperate.

Her friends included councilors, Paladins, tradespeople, cooks, all the children she could find, various animals in the immediate neighborhood, and even the agreeable soldier Damon, whom she visited when he was on guard duty. Seth brought him and his partner treats from Garland's kitchen. The Sainnites were not starving but were being fed swill, according to Garland, and they lusted after hot bread, fresh meat, and anything with sugar in it. Damon told her that the garrison commanders had arrived from all across Shaftal, and they were in foul tempers. "They are like old horses who only know how to go down one road," he said.

Seth asked her councilor friends if they knew what their duties were to be. No one had told anyone what they were supposed to be doing, but soon they determined that their first duty must be to invent themselves. The night before the funerals, they all went together to a tavern, ostensibly to figure out how making themselves into councilors was to be accomplished. Unfortunately, the tavern keeper was extremely generous with the beer, and more and more people kept arriving, all discussing the same topic in an outraged roar that overwhelmed all else: the attack on Travesty, the attack on Karis. Purposeful, sensible conversation became hopeless.

Seth began to have a headache. When the tavern keeper tapped Seth's shoulder and told her some people wanted to speak to her in private, she stood up, saying, "I was about to leave, anyway."

"I know these," the tavern keeper assured her. "The cobbler's shop is right across the street there, and the butcher has supplied my meat for twenty years." He forged a path through the tavern, and she stuck close enough to nip his heels, for the people kept trying to close the way before she had made use of it.

The tavern keeper took her to a room down the hall, and she heaved a sigh of relief as the door was closed and the racket was shut out. "I'm Mariseth of Basdown," she said to the four gathered there, and also to the tavern keeper, who seemed to have decided to remain. "I don't know what you want of me—but you should speak to the Watfield councilor, shouldn't you?"

"Oh, we did talk to him," said a woman whose big arms and red face made Seth think she might be the butcher.

A man, the cobbler maybe, because he squinted at her as though she were a shoe, said, "You live at Travesty, the councilor told us."

Another, who for no good reason seemed a greengrocer, said, "Is it true that Karis has not slept since the attack?"

It seemed like the kind of question people ask, not because they are curious, but because they want to help. Seth sat down and allowed the tavern keeper to pour her a cup of tea. "No one is sleeping well in that house," she said.

"But we've heard that she won't allow the doors to be locked."

"Is it true there's less than ten Paladins guarding her?"

"And that she sits awake in a hard chair all night?"

"And no one can persuade her to lie down?"

"Is she frightened? Is she heartbroken?"

The people peered concernedly at Seth.

She said, "The doors are not locked, and there aren't very many Paladins. As for the rest of your questions, I don't know the answers. I did see her at breakfast this morning. She doesn't talk—and she looks very tired. But—"

She had intended to explain that she didn't know whether or not Karis was always tired or quiet in the morning. But she could not finish, for the butcher cried, "It is not right!"

"We must do something!" said another.

With the frightening resolve of solid citizens, they rose up and strode out, leaving Seth alone and quite startled. Should she follow them? Should she rejoin the other councilors in that angry din? Or should she go to the garrison and demand to see their hard-working, heroic, desperately lonely general? How did anyone know what to do in such a dreadful tangle of complications? The same way a mess of yarn is untangled, she thought. Choose a strand, and never let go of it.

Clement. But surely that strand led to the hopeless center of the tangle—the sort of place where a person inevitably felt required to reach for the scissors.

Seth put her head in her hands. She could not help but feel driven to fix things, for she was an earth blood. But that did not mean everything could be fixed.

The lamp flame had dimmed, and Seth's tea had become cold before she could convince herself to stand up. Not until she opened the door to the hall did she notice the silence. At the end of the hall, she discovered that lamp flames flickered in an empty public room. The chairs were shoved back from the tables, ale cups rested in spilled puddles, and someone's late supper of bean stew and black bread had been abandoned with the spoon resting in the bowl and a single bite taken out of the bread. Seth's coat hung by itself on the hook.

Outside, the night air had turned bitter cold. Buildings loomed on either side, shop shutters were closed, and only some light leaked through the upper windows, where people were not yet abed. Mystified,

Seth looked up at clear sky, at brilliant stars, at the moon, slim as an apple paring. She heard a distant laugh. She wrapped her muffler around her face and made her way towards Travesty, forging a meandering path between patches of ice and mounds of horse dung. She considered how differently people lived in the city and wondered whether she would ever get used to it. Then she became aware that a low sound she had been hearing was a melody, and as she emerged from the street into the square, she realized the singing came from Travesty. That horrible building crouched in the night like a monstrous toad with numerous glowing eyes where a few windows stood unshuttered. A dark, swaying chain wrapped the base of the building, decorated here and there by lantern light and puffs of white breath that glittered and dispersed in the patches of light. The gathered people were singing an old lullaby.

> Blow, wind, blow—for there is no cold
> when the fire on the hearth burns so brightly.
> Sleep, child, sleep—for your fears will keep
> when the fire on the hearth burns so brightly.

Someone called out in an affectionate, if drunken slur, "Sleep, Karis, sleep!"

Seth stood still, amazed. She couldn't tell how many people had gathered there, but those who had been in the tavern seemed to have collected a number of others on the way to Travesty, so now there were more than enough to entirely encircle the massive building. The people of Watfield were watching Karis's house tonight.

The Paladin at the door was the same one with whom Seth had traveled from Basdown. She had been a somber companion, but she was laughing as she let Seth in. "Is that lullaby working?" Seth asked her.

"Surely it must!" said the Paladin. "Anyway, I hope so. Are you hungry? Garland always sets food out for the night people."

"I've got a headache—I'm going to bed."

"It'll feel better soon," said the Paladin.

Seth doubted it. But she had not even reached the staircase when she felt the pain disperse so abruptly that she mistook the emptying sensation in her skull for a wave of dizziness, and grabbed a doorway to keep from falling over. Someone spoke behind her. "Seth—who are those people? Do you know?"

The G'deon's wife had a distinctive way of articulating—saying each word so cleanly and precisely that it sounded unfriendly to a Basdowner's ears. Seth said, "I think they're just regular people. Should I tell them to go away?"

"Could you?" said Zanja. "Could anyone?" She was laughing.

"I may be responsible—"

"I hope they come back tomorrow night. Karis fell asleep before they finished the first song." Zanja stepped forward and touched her arm. "Let's get some pie."

Another friend, Seth thought, surprised. Zanja was usually closeted with Emil or Karis, but when Seth did see her, usually in the massive dining room, she had seemed distant and preoccupied. Seth walked with her through the maze of hallways, following the route the Paladins kept lit with hanging lanterns. In the kitchen the cookfires had been damped, but the fireplace bricks continued to release their warmth. Suspended over the glowing coals a couple of giant stewpots steamed quietly, giving forth the delicious scent of chicken and onions. Several dried-apple pies were set on a worktable along with a neat stack of pottery plates, and someone had already eaten a slice out of one. Garland's pies were unbelievably good; Seth doubted anything would be left by morning. Zanja cut a slice for each of them, and they stood at the table, eating with their fingers, talking—not about assassins, or Clement, or tomorrow's funerals, or the Council of Shaftal the day after. They discussed the nearness of spring, the way Basdowners thought about things, and Zanja's peculiar life history. It was an enormous relief to have such an ordinary conversation.

Seth eventually remembered the topic with which their conversation had begun and said, "I think the Watfielders will keep coming for a few nights, anyway. They'll get more organized, and work in shifts, so no one stays up the entire night. A butcher, a greengrocer, those are the instigators, and they're organized sorts of people."

Zanja had licked her fingers, licked her plate, and now looked consideringly at the pies. "We'll have a few days of rest, then," she said. "I wonder if those assassins just intended to make it impossible for us to sleep."

"Dogs!" said Seth.

"What?"

"Watchdogs. A couple of good watchdogs posted outside will forewarn the Paladins that someone is coming. Karis will learn to trust them, and to heed their voices in her sleep. That would be enough, wouldn't it? She doesn't need to be protected, does she? Doesn't she just need to know she can't be taken by surprise again?"

"We've never had dogs," Zanja said, sounding rather astonished. "Can you find out from that butcher or greengrocer where to get some?"

"I'll find out from somebody." Seth felt much better, and suddenly quite tired. "But now I'm going to bed."

As Seth located and climbed the building's various oddly located, crazily constructed staircases, she mulled over a puzzle: Was it possible that large problems were just massive accumulations of unresolved small problems? Was it possible that what was needed was just an awful lot of ordinary solutions all at once? A circle of drunken people singing lullabies, some watchdogs, and a slice of dried-apple pie—surely that wasn't all Shaftal needed. Yet she fell asleep in that lovely room, untroubled for once.

Karis had awakened late and then remained in bed for another hour, trying to eat the tea and pastries Zanja had brought her on a tray, while Leeba crawled over, jumped upon, and danced around her. Lately her parents called her "Hay Child" and "Ink Child," nicknames that memorialized two recent occasions of spectacular dirtiness, both of which Zanja had missed due to being dead. After she came back to life again, she found that her daughter had not yet outgrown the old nickname, "Little Hurricane." Leeba could not be still, and never ceased to wreak havoc.

"I hate this bedroom," Leeba declared.

Karis had gotten covered with crumbs without eating anything, and now her plate lay on the floor, filled with bits of shredded bread. She asked, "Why do you hate it?"

"It's blue."

"Zanja hates it, too."

This strategy diverted Leeba's attention to Zanja, who was painting glyphs with an ink brush on strips of crisp linen to make funeral flags.

"Let me help!" Leeba demanded, for the fourteenth time.

"Keep away from this table, Little Hurricane, or I'll tie you up and put you in the storeroom with the kegs of cider."

"You will not!"

"Then I'll send you away to live with the rabbits in the woods."

"You will not!"

Zanja dipped the brush in ink and began the first stroke of a new glyph, watching Leeba from the corner of her eye, poised to stabilize the table with one hand while lifting the brush out of reach with the other. "Then I'll give you a pair of red wings and make you fly away with the birds."

Leeba looked startled. "Karis! Zanja can't do that, can she?"

Karis had managed to take several swallows of tea. "Zanja hates this room, too," she reminded her.

"Why do *you* hate this room?" Leeba asked, diverted back to Zanja again.

"Because there's something wrong with the floor."

Karis said, "The entire house is wrong! Sometimes I wonder if, having fixed everything, it would still be wrong in a way that can't be fixed."

That Travesty was a symbol of Shaftal Zanja did not doubt, but it would not help Karis if she told her so. Karis did not understand symbols, not even the symbolism of her own obsessions.

"What's wrong with the floor?" Leeba asked.

"It doesn't feel right."

"Why?"

"I don't know. I just don't like to sit on it. I'm sitting in a chair, see?"

Leeba sat on the floor, declared that she didn't like how it felt either, and then proceeded to move from spot to spot, testing each one in turn and telling Zanja what she learned: the floor was too crooked, too rough, too creaky, too cold, and the spaces between boards were too wide.

"You can help me fill the gaps with rope," Karis suggested. "Not today or tomorrow, but the day after that."

Zanja said, "Perhaps a carpet would help. An old one, with a complicated pattern. On that I could sit and be happy."

Karis had finally tossed back the blankets and gotten out of bed.

"Emil would say something insightful to you now, wouldn't he?"

"He'd say, 'You've been seeking that pattern an awfully long time, my sister.'"

"Fire bloods—who can possibly understand them?"

Karis snatched Leeba up from the floor and swung her to the ceiling. Leeba shrieked. The seat of her breeches had proven an efficient dust mop, and furry clots of it flew into the air with her. Karis swung her down to the floor and then up again. "Leeba bird, Leeba bird, will you fly away?"

"Come in," Zanja called, for Emil was just stepping up to their door.

"But nobody knocked," Leeba said, not too breathless from shrieking to protest this breach of custom.

"It's Emil, though." Karis put her daughter down as the door opened, and Leeba ran to Emil and wrapped herself around his leg. He obligingly walked around the room with her hanging on his leg like a squirrel on a tree trunk until she lost her grip and fell to the floor with a thud.

"This floor is too hard," she declared.

"Is *that* the problem with the floor?" Zanja set the ink brush aside and hung her finished flag with the others on a laundry line by the fireplace. After a day's work on that fireplace, a chimney doctor had managed to make it stop smoking, but now it burned coal at a tremendous rate without warming the room particularly.

Emil had been about to say something to Karis, but Zanja's glyphs had caught his attention, and he studied them instead. Writing with glyphs was as much an art as reading them was, and Zanja supposed that in the writing she had revealed as much about herself as she had about the people she was grieving: a Paladin who not only had given her three new glyph signs, but also had drawn the illustrations on the new cards she put in her deck; a librarian who had been so unobtrusive that she walked right into him one day; a clerk with extraordinary handwriting, who had devoted much effort to teaching her how to properly trim a pen.

Emil glanced at her. "I wish we had not lost so many glyphs. I'd love to see what you would do with them."

"I'd waste my entire life with them," she said.

"No, no—it's called being a scholar. How many times must I tell you?"

A year ago, Zanja had transliterated some of the poetry of the great glyphic poet Coles, and Emil had been teasingly calling her a scholar ever since. Coles had used all thousand glyphs in his great book of poems, and since they did have a copy of the book, the glyphs themselves had not actually been lost. But the meanings were lost, for neither the study of glyphology nor any glyphic lexicons had survived the first years of the war. Zanja had started her transliteration of the poetry in an effort to discover some of the lost meanings by understanding the context in which Coles was using them, but after a few months of effort had abandoned the task, not because it was grueling but because it was fruitless.

Emil turned to Karis. "You've slept, finally."

"You've shaved, finally," she retorted. "Speaking of scholars, what's wrong with that husband of yours? He hasn't emerged for three days."

Emil said, "Leeba, J'han is looking for you. But I guess you can't go find him by yourself."

"I can too!"

"Oh, I don't think so. You're much too little to find the way by yourself. You should just stay here and wait for him to find you."

Leeba could not resist setting forth on a mission to prove Emil wrong. When she was gone, he commented, "I'm afraid that trick won't work much longer."

He sat down at Zanja's chair, took up the brush, and began painting some glyphs of his own on another strip of cloth. "Something certainly is weighing on Medric," he said while he painted. "But I don't know what it is. I'm sure it's something in the future, not in the past—not even in what happened three days ago. For it may be his business to understand the past, but to be haunted by it is Zanja's job."

"A job, is it?" said Zanja. "Like writing letters is your job?"

Karis said, "And Medric is avoiding us so he won't have to tell us what he knows? What exactly is the purpose of having a seer?"

"Comedy and aggravation," Emil said. Karis folded her arms. "Don't glare at me," he added, without glancing up. "Whatever I do and say at tomorrow's meeting of the Council of Shaftal will be criticized by everyone in Shaftal for the next hundred years. During these final days it was my intention to do nothing but think about how to make that meeting work. Now I'd gladly kill another assassin if doing so would give me back even one of the days I have lost."

Even Karis treated the pending meeting with due seriousness, though without much enthusiasm. "Send Mabin to the funeral instead of you," she said. "That'll give you a free day."

"But Clement's visiting commanders will be attending."

"I promise I'll try to impress them enough for us both."

Emil set aside the brush, having finished his flag. "Then you'll have to try to *look* impressive—and without looking too miserable about it."

Karis didn't reply, and there was a long silence. Months ago, after fifteen years in the nondescript clothing that made him look no different from everyone else, Emil had begun wearing Paladin's black again. Zanja had found his new appearance surprisingly difficult to get used to: in her mind's eye he had always been a shabby traveler, climbing wearily to a hilltop, never expecting that spears of starlight would fly from the heavens and pierce his heart. Now he no longer seemed like the Man on the Hill in the glyph illustration, and she didn't know what he might be instead.

Karis finally spoke, but on an entirely different subject. "I'm having nightmares about this rogue air witch," she said. "I keep imagining a person like Norina, but not restrained by law or custom, and not loyal."

"It's a terrifying prospect," said Emil. "But it's not today's problem."

"I'm going to talk to that prisoner this morning."

"It won't accomplish anything." Emil stood up. Zanja took his flag from him to hang it with the others, but he stopped her with a hand on her arm. "Don't let him hurt her," he murmured.

"If you must worry, worry about likely things," Zanja said. For the prisoner was refusing food, his unset broken arm also was slowly killing him, and even had he been healthy and fully armed he couldn't have harmed Karis.

"I am." Emil left, dressed in pristine black, his ponytail wrapped in black-dyed leather, his three earrings glittering in his ear. Zanja looked at the funeral flag he had written and saw there what she had also read in her own flags: *Fear*.

Karis had gone to the clothes chest to study its contents with loathing. Zanja went back to the table and picked up the ink brush. Perhaps if she wrote enough flags she would write herself beyond fear, into insight. But she did not know enough glyphs.

When Zanja had gone to the kitchen earlier, Garland had been feeding egg pie, fruitcake, hot bread, and a vat of tea to the weary but still exhilarated volunteer guard force. Seth had been there, discussing weaving, gardening, roofing, and a dozen other commonplace subjects with them. Zanja had made a short speech. Now the guests all had departed, leaving a mess of dishes to be washed. Zanja set to work drying a mountain of mismatched cups and saucers, and was nearly finished when Seth arrived, glancing bemusedly at Karis, who was putting a shine on a soot-black pan.

"You'll always find her doing the dirtiest job," Zanja explained. "Will you help me put away these teacups?"

Travesty was not a uniformly horrible house. Garland loved the kitchen. And one of the rooms in his domain, the crockery room, which was tucked behind the kitchen chimney, was a warm and secret place. On one wall a bank of windows looked out onto the frozen garden. The other walls were nothing but shelves on which were stacked an enormous quantity of dishes. The only furniture was a small table with two chairs, and a ladder with which to reach the highest shelves.

"Whoever built this house was not entirely stupid," said Seth, spinning slowly to view the cozy room.

"It's a good place to escape to."

They put teacups on shelves in companionable silence. Zanja went out to fetch another tray of cups. When she returned, Seth said, "The best watchdogs come from a farm to the east, on the south bank. So long as the river stays frozen, it's a short day's journey there and back. If the ice breaks it will take us two days at least."

Zanja thought about walking across the countryside, about being able to see across the land and not merely across the square. Her entire body came alive at the prospect of leaving Watfield for the first time in many long months. "I don't know anything about dogs, but I could probably convince the farmer to give one to the G'deon."

"I know dogs."

"We should go soon—the ice could break up any day. The day after tomorrow?"

"There's another storm coming, but I think we'll be able to travel."

"Oh, you have the talent for weather prediction."

Seth's head tilted as though she noticed a change in the noise in the kitchen. "Are they cooking already? I promised Garland I would peel turnips."

Soon after Seth went out, Karis came in. "You washed everything but yourself," Zanja said, and gave her a dishtowel.

Looking out the windows, Karis rubbed the grease from her face. Outside, the leafless vines that climbed the stone wall had trapped snow in an ornate pattern of white lines on gray. "Green," Karis said. It was the color of one of the outfits Zanja had commissioned for her, which she had until now refused to wear. Green was a good color for a funeral.

Zanja looked at her wife's preoccupied face, thinking how much younger she had looked once. She thought of how far they had come together—how surprising it had been that they had and could love each other—and how near they had come to abandoning each other. "Do you blame me?" she asked.

Karis looked at her. "For what? Oh, I'm worrying you, is that it? You're thinking I'm angry at having become what I am, and that I'm blaming you because you finally made it happen."

"That is what I'm asking you."

"I admit it was much easier when I was the G'deon no one wanted. Now that some want me and some don't, the complications are intolerably stupid and aggravating. What do people think, that there's another choice, a second G'deon hiding somewhere?" Karis sighed. "I guess some people do think that."

That's not today's problem, Emil would have said, had he been there. Zanja said, "You're not suited to the duties before you."

"I'm not. Not at all." Karis gazed out the window again, perhaps seeing what only she could: the waiting spring coiled beneath the ice, poised to break forth. "None of us are," she added. "You, for example: your great accomplishment of the day is that you've convinced your stubborn wife to wipe grease off her face and change her clothes."

Zanja laughed. "I've done other things. I told all those volunteers that you were grateful for them staying up all night, and that you'd tell them yourself except that you were still asleep. And I have arranged to get you some watchdogs. Or rather, I allowed Seth to arrange it."

"Watchdogs?" said Karis. "That seems too simple. But—" She didn't finish, but slowly began to smile.

"I like Seth," Zanja said.

"I like her, too—she's like me, only sane."

Zanja leaned lightly against Karis, which was like leaning against a tree that happened to be warm, if not particularly soft, and Karis put an arm around her. "I do blame you," Karis said.

"I know you do."

"Loving you is an incredibly complicated and dangerous business."

"You may be up to the task, though."

The visit to the imprisoned assassin gained nothing, as Emil had predicted. Karis healed his broken arm, and he cursed her, calling her a pretender and an impostor even as she used the power of Shaftal to snap his shattered bones back into place.

Karis said to him, "Without my permission Harald G'deon vested me with the power of Shaftal. Then I did not exercise that power for twenty years, until councilor Mabin accorded me the right to do so. So in what way am I a pretender? Or are you blaming me for the fact that my mother was an innocent who fell into harm, and my father was a Sainnite who lay on her without caring to learn her name? Is it possible you think I'm at fault for my parents' actions, though I never knew either one of them? Or do you think you blame me for having been forced to do sexual service to my father's people when I was just a child? Or that I somehow chose to become addicted when they insisted I take their drugs? I'm just trying to understand why you are cursing me like this."

The man offered no answers. Perhaps in his mind the foulness and contamination of the Sainnites was a real thing, like the murky mess below the hole of a privy, or the stinking putrefaction of a wound, which must be cut out before healing became possible. To convince the man that his belief was merely a metaphor, and a false one at that, was the work of the Truthken he had forbidden from his presence. Karis did not attempt it.

"You seem determined to die," she said. "What would you have us say at your funeral?"

"Say that the people of Shaftal are sheep," he said. "You have promised them healthy children and good harvests, and so they are following you. The destruction of Shaftal's heritage, the thousands of dead, the widowed husbands and wives, the parentless children—they're willing to forget these crimes. But we are not."

"What justice do you have in mind, imposed on whom? And what difference would it make in the end?"

"Shaftal would be cleansed!"

"By killing all of us? Those like me, begotten by indifference or rape? The Shaftali-born Sainnites who have done nothing but help the cause of Shaftal? The people raised to be soldiers who were never given a chance to learn another way? The children of half Sainnites? The babies in arms?" Karis paused. "It seems like a lot of killing. But when we are all dead, you'd still be unsatisfied with what is left, and because you would be so accustomed to killing anyone who displeases you, you'd start killing each other. What a hell you'd make for yourselves—I'm half-tempted to let you have it!"

After they left him, they walked back to their bedroom, as sound of the city's clocks tolling the hour sounded faintly and then were echoed loudly by the clock in Norina's law school. When they were alone and Karis was changing her clothes, Zanja said, "I was wrong: you *are* suited for your duties."

Karis did not reply, but she looked distinctly unhappy.

Chapter 9

Six years ago, when Clement was a garrison commander, she had not seen Gilly for a long time, for she had finally been promoted out from Cadmar's shadow. When the old general died, it had not even occurred to Clement that Cadmar might be chosen to replace him, but when the commanders gathered and she saw Gilly again, he had been certain Cadmar would be chosen. "And he'll ask you to be his lieutenant, and you'll refuse. Before you do that, think what will happen if that man gets all the power he wants, and doesn't have you to talk him out of his stupid decisions."

"If he has any hope of being general, it's because you and I made him look smarter than he is for all those years."

"What else could we have done?" Gilly asked. "And what will become of you, Clem, should you become subject to his idiotic commands?"

Cadmar was chosen general, and Clement had abandoned forever a position she was good at and accepted one she hated even more than she feared she would. Now she again offered herself for a position she did not want, and the garrison commanders did not want to give it to her, either. Wearisome day after wearisome day, she had explained her decisions to them, and they had rejected her justifications. They refused to be convinced—because they refused to forgive her.

In the death field outside the city, where hundreds of Watfielders had gathered to return the seven murdered people to the elements, the commanders clustered around Clement like gray fence posts in the snow. Some twenty garrison soldiers were also present, but they had dispersed into the crowd. Most of them were talking to Paladins now, expressing their condolences in phrases Gilly had drilled into them, or, if they knew enough Shaftalese, venturing into the unfamiliar terrain of conversation. Perhaps the soldiers would ask polite, bewildered questions, and would secretly conclude that these Paladins were simply crazy for examining so closely the natural, obvious, unquestionable fact that injury begets injury, and when one is hit, one hits back, harder. But later, soldiers and Paladins both might puzzle over their own incomprehension, and might take one more slow step towards understanding, just as Clement's many bafflements were slowly becoming comprehensions.

These visiting commanders, however, did not even realize there was something they did not understand. They stood silent, giving Clement only their obedience.

"It is not nearly enough," she muttered to herself.

Beside Clement stood Ellid, a wry, hard-working veteran, the only garrison commander whose friendship Clement could still rely upon. Misunderstanding Clement, Ellid said, "It seems like enough mourners to me. If the number of mourners determines the status in the afterlife..."

"Do the Shaftali even believe there's an afterlife?"

"Well, why so many people, when these seven dead were strangers to the city?"

Gilly seemed to be getting tired of explaining the Shaftali to Sainnites. Perhaps he found his task too absurd, given that most Sainnites had lived among the Shaftali for most of their lives. He said somewhat impatiently, "I'm sure it's out of sympathy for those who did know them."

"It's to shame the murderers," said Clement. "It's what Watfielders do with their anger."

"You're getting to understand them better than I do."

She glanced at him and as always was surprised to see her twisted, crippled friend straightened by the G'deon's hand. At least his ugly old face was the same.

For some time, people had been filing somberly past the seven biers, decorating them with flapping funeral flags. Gilly and Clement had made some flags that morning, and he had helped her to shape the Shaftalese words: *regret, senselessness, sorrow.* Now the afternoon bells rang, and nearby, people began whispering and craning their necks. Shaftal's new G'deon was making her visible way through the parting crowd, with her vivid red coat unbuttoned to reveal an embroidered green tunic. Mabin and Norina walked at her right, and at her left trod Zanja, like a preternaturally alert, indescribably exotic black hound. Beside Zanja walked a Basdown cow doctor.

"Gods of hell," Clement muttered.

"They're coming towards us," said Ellid.

Clement and Ellid stepped forward to clasp hands with these governors. Karis's cold, bare hand conveyed a burning sensation that made Clement catch her breath. Zanja said quietly, "Ellid can introduce us to the commanders, can't she?" She passed Clement to Seth.

Clement could hear Zanja talking to Ellid, in her clear, precise Sainnese, then greeting Gilly as they moved towards the gray posts of the commanders. Clement fumbled to take Seth's ungloved hand.

Seth said, "You're always walking away from me, it seems."

"I apologize. Gilly told me I should write you a note at least, but I don't know all the letters yet."

"So you thought of me once," said Seth.

Clement had thought of her—many more times than once—midsentence sometimes, or lying awake on her hard bed, or snatching a hasty moment with her son. But her armor was the only thing keeping her standing right now; she could not take it off. She said, "I hope for my son that when he is grown he can choose his lovers freely."

Seth gazed at her—and Clement couldn't guess what she was thinking. She excused herself and returned to the commanders, who like stringed puppets each in turn looked startled and astounded as Karis's palm pressed theirs. Norina, from behind the shelter of Karis's broad shoulders, seemed to be assessing the character of these strangers. Perhaps she would be able to tell Clement something useful about them. Zanja and Gilly were translating, though all of the commanders spoke some Shaftalese, and some were as fluent as Clement. Some commanders managed to utter stiff compliments on General Mabin's leadership, for which she was legendary, even among her enemies.

Seth had gone away. A cold line trickled down Clement's cheek. She wiped it away casually, as if her eyes were just watering in the cold wind.

Finished, Karis held out a hand to Clement, and when she approached put a hand on her shoulder and bent to say in her ear, "Will it hurt you if I make a show of my regard for you? Zanja says I should."

"Regard—but not affection."

"I actually do approve of you, but I hate performing. And I'm bad at it."

Norina, apparently close enough to hear, said quietly, "You've done enough, Karis."

Karis did not lower her hand, though. "You're looking rather harrowed, if you don't mind me saying so."

Clement said, "My commanders won't accept me as their general, though my G'deon commands it. Try to imagine what a position that puts me in."

Norina said, "Those officers are so angry with you, they can't think clearly about what's in their own best interests. But that Taram fellow is already more than half willing to change his alliances. You have a history with him? You can use that to win him back to your side. And he and Ellid could win over some three or four of the others, if there are no more disasters." Norina then named the potential supporters, a surprising list of unsuspected friends. "That would give you six, anyway, six out of fourteen. Where are the other five?"

"The western commanders haven't arrived yet."

Norina glanced at Karis. "Are they on their way?"

Karis's gaze became unfocused for a moment. Then she said, "They're nowhere on the Wilton-Hanishport Road."

They had entered the thick of the crowd. People slowly made way for Karis, until the first bier loomed. Shaftali words of pain flapped from the wooden frame and from the firewood piled beneath it. A funeral flag unfurled in Zanja's hand. It seemed incredible that the cloth could float so lightly on the breeze when it was so burdened by the heavy black strokes of glyph signs.

Clement took a flag from her own pocket, but without paying much attention. What had become of the western commanders?

Karis pressed forward to gaze at a gray-haired dead man whose forehead and cheeks were marked with squint lines as though he had been peering in the dark all his life. Karis reached up and touched him briefly, as though to confirm that he was indeed dead.

A bridge had collapsed, a road was impassable. The western commanders had turned back, unable to even send Clement a message. That was all.

Karis had begun to weep. Clement tied a flag to a bier. The Shaftali words she had written with such difficulty looked like a child's scrawl: *Regret. Senselessness. Sorrow.*

Waste. Regret. Sacrifice. Three nights ago, Clement had become confused about where her body ended and Seth's began. In the warm hollow of their breasts, their hearts beat on both the palm and back of Clement's hand. Seth had stroked her head, kissed her eyes, told her what she had been thinking since they last saw each other. Clement told Seth some small pieces of her history—important only because she had never before had anyone to tell them to. And there had crept over her a sense of rest and rightness that was deeper and more important than mere sleep.

Value. Suffering. Service. A Paladin lay on the bier, peaceful, black-dressed, with a gold ring in her earlobe.

Thirty-five years ago, Clement had been a terrified nine-year-old, who with the other few children on the ship had been left to fend for herself while the adults battled a violent storm. Clement had comforted and been comforted by a girl she scarcely knew as the boat twisted and plunged. They had warmed each other when sea water soaked them. Years later, she and the girl had served their first year as soldiers together in Cadmar's company, and had been devoted lovers until they became rivals. Their first disagreement had been over Gilly, whom Clement befriended when others were cruel to him. When Clement and Heras met again, both of them were commanders, and Heras had become notorious across the land when she razed the region of Reese. Now she commanded Wilton garrison in South Hill, a region that had proven impossible for even Heras to defeat.

Heras had not seen fit to obey her new general's command. She had convinced four other commanders to join her in what must be an insurrection.

"So that was the G'deon," said Taram, as they walked back from the death field. "She does look like Cadmar." Ellid and Gilly had managed to herd him so he ended up beside Clement, where he could no longer avoid speaking to her.

The smoke from the pyres lifted up in columns that must have been visible for miles around.

Clement said, "She also has his temper."

"Is it because she's like him that you were so willing to accept her rule?"

After two steps Taram added grudgingly, "—General."

Clement still did not speak. She was weary of trying to convince these rock-headed people both that there had been no choice but to accept peace, and that peace was a good choice. She was weary of such contradictions, sick of having to do what she did not want, tired of the whole bloody mess: *Loss. Betrayal. Hopelessness.*

"Why doesn't she fight us if she's so strong?" Taram asked.

"Bloody hell, have you entirely lost your imagination? Can't you see that a person who needs no weapons is invincible? Can't you see how fortunate we are that she doesn't want to fight?"

"*Fortunate!*"

Well, she had goaded him into overt anger, at least. "You think I'm a coward?" she asked.

"Anyone who's fought beside you knows how you hate to fight! But it was your lack of vainglory that made you a great commander. You took care of your people, and you didn't let their lives be wasted. But now you have commanded every soldier in my garrison—in the entire country—to lie helpless and exposed to our enemy!"

"I commanded you to disarm because the Shaftali proved their honor to me right here in Watfield, where not one soldier has been harmed. Now your garrison is just as vulnerable, and your soldiers, too, are unharmed. Tell me, Taram, what will it take to convince you of their determination to win our trust? Perhaps I've become stupid, but you have become even more stupid."

"I've become a commander," Taram said, sounding very stupid indeed.

She looked at him, but she could no longer remember their friendship. He was the most likely of all of them to turn, according to Norina, but Clement couldn't think of what it would take to change one man's mind, even a man who had been her friend, as Heras had once been.

"You know better than anyone how little I wanted my last promotion," she said. "So instead of standing in the road preventing all of us from going forward, why don't you offer to be general? I'd vote for you."

"Bloody hell, Clem—" Taram began. But she walked away from them all, not even bothering to signal Gilly or Ellid. She would never escape—eventually they would find her.

Chapter 5

The dawn bells rang. Clement had scarcely slept, and as she walked with the grim garrison commanders through the sleepy city to Travesty, only Gabian, chortling inside her coat, seemed happy. Earlier, when he suckled his bottle beside the fire, she had gazed into his eyes, but her baby's peacefulness and joy did not infect her. Surely child rearing made taking the long view more natural to Shaftali, but for her it required effort—an effort that seemed only more taxing with every passing day. Today, all across Shaftal, people would celebrate the first council meeting of this land's resurrected government. But for Clement it could only be another dreadful day.

Gilly walked at her elbow, sometimes missing a step, for he was still learning how to walk straight-backed. Ellid marched at her other side, also silent, having dutifully tried and failed to engage Clement in a practical conversation. Taram kept five commanders between himself and Clement, yet his silence pressed between her shoulder blades like a sword's point.

At Travesty, arriving councilors and departing night-watch volunteers so crowded the entry that Clement despaired of getting in the door. But the Paladin commander spotted them, and in a moment ten Paladins had politely but firmly cleared the crowd and then stood on either side of the path, greeting the arriving garrison commanders in Sainnese as they passed. "Good morning, General Clement," said Saleen, at the top of the stairs.

She took his hand. "Commander Saleen, I was just thinking that you people can't sensibly organize yourselves."

"Then you will be many times surprised today," he said. In Sainnese. Like Zanja, Saleen seemed to have the fire talent for languages. He had made it his mission to learn Sainnese and seemed to be constantly teaching whatever he learned to the Paladins in his command.

As Clement's party entered the door, children hurried forward with towels to dry their boots, then a line of young people divested them of their coats. Saleen led the way to the big parlor, where Emil stood casually, sipping tea by the hearth. Immediately, a crowd of people paraded in to serve breakfast, and Clement's companions, lured by the promise of sweet pastries and hot tea, abandoned her.

"Good morning, Emil," said Clement, and Gabian uttered a joyful yelp.

Emil picked up a tray of pastries from a nearby table and offered it to her. "Will you eat something, Clement? You'll be wanting to be fortified."

"I fight better on an empty stomach."

Emil set down the tray. "Do you think this day will be so—" He fell silent, riveted by something that appeared to have just come in the door.

Clement turned. The woman at the door was dressed in a surcoat of heavy embroidered silk, in a blue that exactly matched here eyes. The draping fabric parted when she moved, revealing trousers and undertunic of shimmering purple. She lifted an arm, corralling Garland, the cook, in the doorway. The fabric, drawn back, revealed her muscular forearm. "What's become of our humble G'deon?" murmured Emil.

"It's only pastries!" Clement heard Garland protest, and then he escaped. Karis turned, noticed their stares, and joined them, saying grumpily, "What?"

"You combed your hair," said Emil blandly.

"Give me that baby, will you, Clement? Maybe he'll spit up on me."

Emil hastily flung a napkin across Karis's shoulder. Karis glared at him, but then smiled sweetly at the baby as Clement put him in her arms. "Greetings, little brother. What nonsense all this is!"

"I understand your commanders are being difficult," said Emil to Clement.

"Five are missing entirely and haven't provided an explanation."

"I know. I should hear from Wilton soon—I have people watching the garrison, and they can get me a message by the ice road in a matter of days."

Clement felt an uprush of anger. "You're spying on my garrisons?"

"Now, General, don't bristle at me. I trust you—it's Heras I'm worried about."

Of course. The first year Heras commanded Wilton garrison, Emil had still been commander of South Hill company. Medric had served directly under Heras, and Zanja under Emil. The razing of South Hill had scarred and educated all three of them.

Gabian, apparently fascinated by the crisp, shimmering fabric of Karis's clothing, grasped a fold and endeavored to drool upon it. Emil intervened, then said to Clement, "Does Heras think she should be general? Is this an insurrection?"

"Of course she thinks she should be general. She's astute, decisive, uncompromising, and doesn't suffer from divided loyalties. She'd be a better general than I would be."

"She's manipulative, ruthless, and closed minded!"

"She has all sorts of admirable qualities."

"Oh, you're being sarcastic," said Emil with relief.

Fortunately, Norina and her law students were busy elsewhere, for surely it would have been obvious to an air witch that Clement's statements had been more truthful than Emil seemed to think.

"This baby of yours is not cooperating," said Karis, whose astonishing outfit remained unstained. "Clem, this Heras had better remember that it's not you she is opposing, but me. And I'm not much impressed by bullies now that I am one myself."

Emil choked on a swallow of tea.

"And am I just your puppet?" Clement said. "No, never mind—I know what I am."

Karis began to reply. "Tomorrow's problem," Emil said.

"Tomorrow's problems are accumulating," said Karis. "What is wrong with that seer?"

"Maybe Zanja can do something with him."

They exchanged serious glances, and Clement felt a moment's pity for them. Then Emil said, "If you won't eat, Clement, then perhaps you will introduce me to the commanders, as I missed my opportunity to meet them yesterday."

Emil exercised his geniality on the commanders, with great brilliance but little effect. Clement delivered Gabian to a parlor that now was a playroom, where Leeba officiously instructed several children in the rules they all must follow. Then she and her commanders followed Emil and Karis into what she remembered as a vast, echoing, very cold room at the back of the monstrous building. But now its floors had been muffled with carpets of many sizes and colors; it was filled with chairs of many styles and heights, and the fire that had probably been blazing in the fireplace since before dawn had made it somewhat less chilly. People milled nervously through the space, talking to each other and staring about as though they feared they'd miss something. Clement caught herself wondering when these soldiers' captains would get them to quiet down and line up.

But a hush fell as Karis made her way to the front and sat down. Norina, Medric, and J'han had already gathered there, and now Zanja arrived and said something to Emil while shaking her head slightly— bad news about Medric? Then Zanja approached the chairs, said something to Karis that made her glance down at her outfit with an expression of despair, and settled on her heels at Karis's feet. People were finding seats, and Clement led her rigid, silent contingent to the row of chairs behind Karis. Gilly had joined the officious clerks crowded around a big table. On a second, smaller table lay a very big book, which Clement recognized as the Law of Shaftal, and a plain box of beautiful wood within which was preserved the original handwritten manuscript of Mackapee's *Principles of Community*. Between them lay a handwritten, much-corrected, and overwritten stack of paper—Emil's speech, apparently finished so late that there had been no time to recopy it.

Emil stood at the table, facing the murmuring room. "Norina Truthken will open this assembly," he said.

Why would the least likable be the first one to speak? And Norina's topic could not have been less interesting. Standing by the Law of Shaftal, she asserted her own status as a Truthken, and made various declarations about the lawfulness of the assembly, the legitimacy of the oaths already taken, and the verity of Karis's claim to her position. She asserted that Emil was properly named and confirmed as head councilor, and that all decisions agreed to by this body would become law. *Norina is the law,* thought Clement in surprise, *and the law is what leads them. Not Emil—not even Karis!*

"Madam Truthken!" It was a voice from the midst of the councilors. Everyone turned, startled.

Norina said, "Please stand and state your name when you speak."

The man leapt to his feet and said he was Jerem, a Midlander. He planted himself with his feet apart, as if braced for a fight. "Madam Truthken, I disagree with your conclusion that this assembly is lawful. For the Law of Shaftal does not permit the presence and participation of alien interlopers in the governance of Shaftal!"

"There are no alien interlopers present."

Norina spoke so flatly that it took a moment for people to realize what she had said. Then a dozen outraged people leapt to their feet. They started shouting at the tops of their voices: The Sainnites were murderers, thieves, destroyers, and parasites; they were stupid, oblivious, crass, and oppressive. They were mindlessly, pointlessly, persistently violent; they were beyond redemption; and they were aliens. Emil remained impassively silent, and Norina gazed coolly, not quite contemptuously, at the shouting people.

The room quieted. Still, Norina gazed at the councilors. A restlessness took over the room, and people began to glance about anxiously.

Norina turned her gaze to Clement. *Bloody hell!* Clement thought.

"General Clement, please explain by what right you and your people are present."

But Karis was already standing. "The Sainnites of Shaftal are Shaftali." Her hoarse, smoke-shattered voice could not carry far in that vast space, but the garrison commanders certainly had heard her, for there was a rustle of surprised movement among them.

"The Sainnites of Shaftal are Shaftali," Norina said. "Therefore, the Sainnites are entitled to the rights and protection of the law."

The angry Midlander, still on his feet, cried, "By what principle?"

"The declarations of the G'deon will be accepted as fact, without debate, objection, or confirmation, as you well know, Jerem of the Midlands."

"The law must be changed, then." The man looked pugnaciously around himself at the openmouthed people who now stared at him. "We can do that," he said to them.

Norina said, "Yes, the councilors of Shaftal may eliminate the G'deon's right, if they are willing to forego her power and protection, as well."

Karis looked directly at Jerem. So she had looked at Cadmar, when she gave him the choice he was too stupid and arrogant to perceive as an ultimatum.

Jerem, glowering, sat down. Clement felt the shifting among her commanders again, and for the first time in days she could believe, if just for a moment, that there was hope for her people.

There were no more objections. Norina gestured to Emil, who seemed not merely unruffled, but serene as he touched his fingertips to the tabletop and began to speak. "On Long Night, Karis G'deon pierced me with Responsibility, and then asked me to head a new Council of Shaftal. I could neither have accepted the responsibility nor taken the oath if not for my confidence that I was not expected to do this task alone. From that first day, my companions included Sainnites, and I am grateful to them for teaching me to avoid heedless statements about who these Sainnites are, and what they are capable of."

Months ago, when Emil told Clement he wanted her commanders at the council meeting, she had argued vigorously with him: the presence of the hated enemy at this significant event would make them targets for anger, she had said. She did not think that even she should go.

"That anger is our country's largest problem," Emil had said. "Shall we not say so? Should we make decisions based on our anger, rather than decisions about our anger?"

He had been right, thought Clement, as Emil began to review the history of the last thirty tumultuous, bloody years. He did not excuse the Sainnites' stupidity, but he explained it fairly enough, and he did not excuse the Shaftali either, for their failure to offer hospitality to the invaders, allowing the land the time necessary for it to exercise its power upon them.

"Many people have talked to me in the last weeks about the reconstruction of Shaftal, as though we needed to just take up the stones of a fallen wall and mortar them back together again. It must be understood here, and across the land, what the Sainnites of Watfield Garrison already know: The walls cannot be rebuilt. What we seek, what we need, and what is right for Shaftal, is not merely reconstruction, but transformation."

When the Paladins learned that Emil and Medric had collected many thousands of supposedly lost books, it had been the dead of winter, the time of killing cold. But a Paladin party had set forth to

fetch the entire library. Ever since then, Clement had hardly ever seen a
Paladin without a book. It had been explained to her why Paladins must
be scholars, but only now, as Emil began the heart of his speech, did
she truly see what a philosopher could do. Emil did not tell these newly
promoted councilors what must be done, or how. He spoke, instead, of
what mattered. Several times, to emphasize points that seemed likely
to rouse people's ire, he opened the box, leafed cautiously through the
fragile pages within, and read directly from the Mackapee manuscript:

> Community begins in simple acts of kindness. To be
> ethical is simple. Power is given, but never taken and
> never possessed.

Emil finished. People stood up and cheered. Clement also stood, and
the commanders imitated her: Blank, bored, sullen. They looked at her
as if to ask what her next unreasonable demand would be. They would
never understand in time.

People were crowding towards Emil to shake his hand. In the
rising din, someone shouted something about tea. Karis broke away
from a fierce conference with the Truthken. A chair blocked her way.
She yanked it aside and grabbed Clement by the arm. "Let's go." She
dragged her irresistibly away, through angry and eager conversations,
into and out of apparently impenetrable tangles of people, directly to a
heavy, earnest, weathered farmer, around whom had gathered a number
of equally earnest people, all talking at the top of their voices about
how dangerous and unjust it would be to ignore the terrible crimes of
the past. Karis interrupted. "You're the second man in four days to say
I've got no right to speak for the land. Should I be grateful that you said
it with words and not with snake poison?"

He stared at her, shocked. "I am not—"

"You aren't? Well explain the difference, will you?"

The Midlander glared up at Karis as though he were facing down
an angry bull. "Maybe if people felt they had another recourse—"

"So you'd do away with me so you can do whatever you want to
the Sainnites?"

Clement attempted to dislodge Karis's grip from her elbow, but it
was hopeless. The Midlander—a brave man, if a foolish one—continued

obstinately, "What kind of land will this be if we reward the criminals? We must have justice if we are to have peace! Murderers must be convicted of their crimes!"

"And you think that calling it justice will change the fact that it's vengeance?"

Clement said, "Excuse me, Karis. Councilor, there's no need to convict us. My people *are* murderers—I admit it, though I wish it were not so. Yet if you treat us as criminals, you leave us no choice but to continue to be criminals."

"Not if we defeat you!" the earnest farmer cried.

Some people in the group uttered grunts of agreement, but others drew back in dismay.

"I've learned not to infuriate Karis, myself," Emil said.

Clement stepped aside for him, and Karis's clench on her arm abruptly relaxed. He carried a beautifully painted porcelain teacup in an equally beautiful, though mismatched saucer, from which rose a plume of exceptionally fragrant steam. This he handed to Clement. In Shaftal, apparently, the reinforcements always arrive with a teacup in hand. Emil looked around at the people, and Clement tried to see what he saw: Jerem's power did not lie in his anger, his loud voice, his insistence, or even in his logic.

"Karis speaks for the land," Emil said. "Therefore, she *should* be impossible to ignore." The people who had drawn away edged even further back. One was glancing about as if seeking a friend in the crowd. Perhaps he would join the cluster nearby, where occasionally could be heard the voice of a Basdown cow doctor. *Power is given but never taken, and never possessed,* Clement thought. *How in hell would soldiers be convinced of such crazy ideas?* She herself had been convinced—not because of that day, but because of all the days that had come before. But the time in which the commanders might also be convinced was quickly fleeing.

Chapter 6

On that significant morning, Zanja had found Medric in the frigid, many-windowed round room that he had cluttered with pens and papers but hardly ever used. He huddled in a deep chair, cushioned by pillows of clashing colors, wrapped in at least three woolen blankets, with a book too massive to hold in his lap lying open nearby on a sturdy stand. His spectacles, both pairs of them, rested upon the book. With his eyes closed, he seemed ridiculously young—a skinny boy, possibly unwell, at a hazardous age.

Zanja squatted with her back against the closed door. Her breath condensed before her eyes. "You'll freeze," said Medric eventually.

His eyes remained closed. Zanja wondered what he was looking at. "This feels like a balmy spring day to me," she said.

"Oh, but your people, with their frozen hearts pumping icy blood, crawled about in snow tunnels like moles all winter."

"Except there is light under the snow, blue light—incredibly beautiful."

"What would you do," Medric said, "If you could bring them all back from the dead?"

Well, he was at his most bewildering today. Still, Zanja considered his question, for even his most random-seeming comments could prove significant. The answer seemed too obvious. "At what cost?" she asked.

"No price. Just the logical result: All that happened because of that massacre would not have happened at all."

Now it was she who shut her eyes, from pain. But what she saw with her inner sight was terrible, and she opened her eyes again. Medric was looking at her now, but without seeing her. With his eyes open he looked older, much older—older than any of them.

He was bearing a terrible burden today.

"Why are you asking me this question, my brother? It isn't my time to be mad with guilt and grief. Can't you wait for midsummer?"

"If you were given the choice, what would you choose?" he asked.

"I can't answer you. Which one of me is doing the choosing? Is it the one who is here now, holding back her impulse to strangle you? Or is it the one who once loved only her tribe and didn't even know it was possible to love a person like you?"

"Oh, you wouldn't miss me," he said.

"Certainly not, you dotty little man."

He grinned, but without much humor.

"Surely such a choice should never be given, and never be made, except by the gods."

"Elemental witches are gods, then, for we do and must make such choices."

What awful choice was Medric making with his silence? An answer came to her, a dreadful one. "Medric—not Emil!"

Medric fumbled for his spectacles, put on a pair, took them off, and put on the other pair. His breath fogged the lenses, and he took them off again and tucked them into his shirt to warm up. He would not answer.

Sometimes it seemed as if Emil knew everyone in Shaftal. Perhaps it was true, as he claimed, that during his years of wandering he had not expected all the incidental friendships he made to prove essential. In his mind he may have been just a peddler of beautiful tools, a rescuer of books, and a retired Paladin commander. But fire bloods do little by accident, and so now people all over Shaftal knew Emil, and trusted him. If he were to die...

Zanja could not bear this silence. "What can or will you tell me, then? Can you say what boundary I am to cross? Can you say what choice I am to make?"

"Time," said Medric. "And insight."

Time and insight, water and fire.

Zanja had left her glyph cards in her room, carefully hidden from Leeba, who found them irresistible. Not today, probably not tomorrow, but the day after, she might seek out the peace and solitude in which to ask the cards the questions Medric wouldn't answer: How can the boundary of time be crossed? How can insight, which always chooses, be chosen?

She said to the young seer, "Do you know what today is?"

Medric had shut his eyes again. He said with no apparent interest, "It is the day we have labored for—for months, even years. It is the day my husband becomes a paragraph in future histories. But nothing important will happen today."

"Nothing in particular will go wrong, then? That's good. Still, I think Emil would want you to be there."

"Emil would want me to think of tomorrow, as always."

He would, and so would Karis, when Zanja told her that her seer was seeking the very vision she had been demanding of him. "Don't freeze to death or starve," she said.

She opened the door and stepped out, and only half heard his reply. "Be buoyant," he might have said. "Be carried."

"What?"

But Medric never repeated himself.

Now, Karis had returned to the front of the meeting room, and the councilors had ended their restless arguments and begun to return to their seats. Standing beside Karis, Zanja commented, "You have gone to war after all."

Karis was gazing into the crowd, in which Zanja could not distinguish the offending Midlander from the many other work-bowed and weathered farmers in the room. "I'm glad he made me so angry," she said.

"You surprise me!"

Karis looked down at her, and almost smiled. "I didn't think that was possible. I understand something, that words won't change people's minds."

"Oh, don't tell Emil that!"

"People are changed by circumstances. Those I can change."

"If you know what changes to make!"

"I suppose I have to pay better attention."

Norina and Emil were waiting at the table. Most of the people had sat down, and now Karis did, in a hissing crackle of silk. Zanja sat at her feet. As Emil began to speak, Zanja glanced behind herself at Clement, who now sat alone in a row of empty chairs—Ellid had taken the commanders back to the garrison for meetings of their own. Clement's boots, set in precise alignment with each other, reflected lamplight in their high polish. Her face had so little expression, her back was so erect, and her shoulders so square, she scarcely seemed made of resilient flesh at all.

Emil was calling on the councilors of Shaftal to identify issues of common concern around which committees might be formed.

Zanja looked down at the carpet upon which she was sitting, which by no accident was the same Ashawala'i carpet that had been on the floor by Emil's worktable. The carpet was woven of goatswool, dyed in various reds: the red made from the inner bark of an oak tree; the red from a root that did not grow in the woods but was farmed instead in the valley; the red from a particular beetle, collected during the summer, then dried and ground to powder. The pattern of interlocking shapes and lines was ancient, and the carpet itself had been woven either by Zanja's mother or by her grandmother. Upon it Zanja had sat, day after day, while Emil wrote and paused and wrote again, and Medric wandered among the books, appearing regularly with information Emil needed before he knew he needed it. They thought in parallels, and when they spoke with each other, it was to articulate fragmented statements from a conversation that seemed to continue in silence.

On the day before the assassinations, the three of them had worked together in this peculiar manner all morning. A librarian had interrupted Emil to ask his opinion of a book, *Gerunt's Decision*, which was in dreadful condition. Emil put it upon his pile of books to be restored, and then glanced at Zanja. "There you are, sitting in the pattern woven by your ancestors," he had said. "Do you suppose that, just as you were woven into the pattern of the past, the pattern of the future will be woven from you?"

That had been the sixty-third day since Zanja returned from the dead. Emil, too, had occasionally cheated death through fire logic. But he was not a crosser of boundaries, and when he did die he would not return.

"Now," Emil was saying, "Let's not waste time trying to resolve issues that have not been properly researched or discussed. I will establish two committees, one for peace with the Sainnites, and one for punishment of them. Mabin, please guide the committee for peace. Clement, yours is the committee for punishment."

Clement uttered a grunt of shock or pain. No doubt Mabin, on the other side of the room, had been equally dismayed. Zanja felt Karis's leg muscles tense—she was holding her breath, fighting to keep herself from laughing out loud. "The two committees will make identical proposals!" someone said.

"Of course," said Emil blandly.

Throughout the room, stifled snickers became laughter. "Now I am certain that our land has other problems besides the Sainnites," Emil said.

People began to suggest other, more benign committee topics: rebuilding roads, managing commerce, reestablishing the old orders and guilds, reopening the schools and the university, and starting up a broadsheet to report on all these activities. As Zanja half listened, a peculiar thing began to happen. She began to be angry.

It took some time for her to understand why.

Emil glanced at her in surprise. She had stood up, as others were doing when they had something to say, and waited for him to call on her. At last he said with a trace of puzzlement, "Zanja na'Tarwein?"

"I am Speaker for the Ashawala'i," she reminded him. And then, to forestall Norina, who was at her most legalistic today, she added, "I have no standing on this council, for although the dead sometimes do speak to me, I do not speak for them. Nor do I speak for the nineteen other border tribes that used to send representatives to the House of Lilterwess. Not one of those tribes has sent a representative to this meeting, though, which was not by choice—"

Norina interrupted, as only she was permitted to do. "Speaker, even if your people still existed you would have no right to be heard here. The border peoples are not subject to and have no privileges under the Law of Shaftal. Instead, they are under the direct protection of the G'deon."

"Does that not seem even slightly patronizing?" said Zanja. "Are the border tribes like children whose powerful parent solves their problems?"

Norina said firmly to Emil, "Zanja cannot speak here."

Emil, looking pained, said, "Zanja, we will find a way to notify the tribes. But for now—"

Zanja walked out of the room.

☙

She spent the rest of the day in the china room behind the kitchen.

The sun had gotten bright enough with the slow turning from winter to spring that the snow in the garden outside had begun to melt. Water streamed across the window panes and puddled in the garden. Water shimmered on the surface of the snow, and when the garden fell gradually into shadow, the water then fell still, shimmered like glass, and dulled as it turned to iron.

As the garden sank into darkness, so did the little room. The racket in the kitchen peaked. Dinner was being served.

Later, Garland came in with cheese melted on toast, decorated with crisp bacon, and a cup of cider so cold it was frosted with ice.

Garland had only produced this combination of her favorite foods one other time, the day after her return from the dead, when he was trying to assure himself or herself that there was room in the house for both of them. That he was serving it to her now seemed a bad sign. Zanja forced herself to take a bite and then was overmastered.

When he returned for the empty plates, she asked, "Has Emil reconvened the assembly?"

"Yes, a while ago."

He left her alone again.

Long past nightfall, she got up stiffly from her chair for a long-delayed trip to the outhouse. The watch volunteers were singing loudly, cheerfully out of tune and rhythm with each other, interrupting themselves with bursts of laughter. Within Travesty the halls were quiet, lit by carefully placed lamps, watched over by a couple of Paladins who talked together in serious voices. Zanja found the library empty and didn't want to disturb Emil if he had already gone to bed. She went to face Karis instead.

In their bedroom, Karis sat in the chair by the fireplace, where flames licked lazily around a half-burned log. Leeba, who probably had exhausted herself trying to be leader of a pack of strange children all day, lay limply asleep in her arms. Medric had come downstairs, and he and Emil had contrived to share the other chair; J'han and Norina sat together on the floor; and Garland sprawled on the bed, sound asleep.

Zanja shut the door behind herself and put her back against the doorjamb.

Emil said, "Zanja, it never once occurred to me, in all the years of our friendship, that you are not Shaftali."

Norina said, "Zanja is Shaftali—but the Speaker for the Ashawala'i is not."

Emil rubbed his weary face. "Land's sake, Norina, she's both."

Zanja said, "The Otter People are surrounded on all sides by Shaftal, and have lived in Shaftal longer than history remembers. But they are not Shaftali."

"They are protected from Shaftal," said Norina. "They cannot be what they are protected from."

Emil said, "I'm offended on your behalf, Zanja. But if you can think about the future rather than the past—"

"Oh, I know what you're going to say." Emil certainly had thought through what must happen, much faster than Zanja had.

There was a long silence. Zanja feared she had offended all of them, and she could not lose her family and her country on the same day. She said, "I wish I had not been so wounded on a day we've been looking to for so long."

Karis, her head bowed over the tousled, sleeping daughter, said quietly, "But it's an old wound, not a new one—much older than both of us. But it's one that we can repair, isn't it?" She looked up into Zanja's eyes. "Will you begin to visit the tribes? As soon as Emil can manage without you here?"

Zanja stared at her, speechless.

Karis had been somber but now began to look amused. "Did you think I hadn't learned to let go of you? Did you think you'd have to die every time you wanted to get away from me?"

"Yes, every time," said Zanja wryly.

"Then I guess we both can be stupid as rocks."

J'han stood up, saying, "I'll take Leeba tonight."

"No, we'll take her," said Medric.

Emil groaned. "Medric, I beg you—"

"We'll go skating in the morning. I'll sneak out with her, and you can sleep all day."

Medric extricated himself from the chair, lifted Leeba from Karis's embrace, and kissed her whiny complaints back into sleep again. J'han and Norina woke Garland, who was nearly as cranky as Leeba. Zanja, at the door, got a cool kiss from Norina, a warm embrace from J'han, and a shy handclasp from Garland, who promised to pack a traveling meal for her and Seth in the morning. Emil kissed her twice, and when she told him he had been magnificent that day, promptly agreed with her. "Oh, and have I mentioned to you how glad I am that you're alive?" he asked.

"Sixty-seven times," she said.

She kissed Leeba's head, and then she kissed Medric's, and he wagged a finger at her, like a teacher reminding her of an important lesson.

Early in the morning Zanja took the back hall to the kitchen to beg for some hot water. Garland seemed to find her pitiful, and made her sit and drink some tea while he lit the stove in the bathroom and hauled hot water to fill the tub. She had just eased herself into the bath when Seth tapped on the door and said, "I just want to let you know I'm ready. Don't hurry, though."

"You can come in if you want."

Seth came in, looked disapprovingly around the dark, crowded space, then overturned a water bucket to use for a stool.

"People insisted on discussing you with me all afternoon."

"They complained to you about my self-importance and temper, I suppose."

"No, of course they didn't! Mostly they were mystified that none of them had even thought about the border people, even with all the thinking we have done lately. It's because the border tribes live in protected lands, some said, and so a person might live seventy years without ever setting eyes on one. They're like a story to most of us."

"But why?" Zanja said. "What are we being protected from?"

"From us, maybe," said Seth.

Zanja had not left the city and in fact had scarcely been outside for most of the winter. To stretch her legs and make them do some work was good, but to stretch her vision across the sun-brilliant landscape and rolling hills made her mind feel opened up, as well. Seth was not the chattering type; they walked a long time in silence.

They left the road to follow the river and had reached a place where a much-used footpath pounded into the snow continued across the ice.

The river was wide and shallow here, which was believed to make the river ice more stable. But Seth looked distinctly uncomfortable. "Walk ahead of me to prove it's solid, will you? And walk quickly."

Zanja glanced up into the brilliant sky at the raven that followed them. Karis, who might be watching through the bird's eyes, would be terrified while they were crossing. But the ice was hard and solid.

They walked briskly but had to pause to give way to a couple of Paladins on ice skates, who flew past like falcons, leaving the walkers to tread through the wispy vapors of their hot breath. "Oh, we are so slow," Seth complained. "They'll reach Watfield before we reach the south bank!"

Zanja looked after them yearningly, for although she had never even used ice skates, she had always wanted to skate the ice road, for no good reason.

Storm clouds began to sweep in, which gave their eyes some relief from the sun glare but made the cold wind seem even colder. They asked their way at various farmsteads until they located the farmers who raised watch dogs. Zanja shamed them into giving up two young dogs to the G'deon. Seth picked them out and spent quite a while with them, and as they began their return journey, the dogs cheerfully and enthusiastically did exactly what Seth told them to do.

Soon Zanja began to envy the dogs for their fur coats. She and Seth kept a fast pace, but the raven landed on Zanja's shoulder, too weary to continue fighting the wind. When they reached the river and started across the ice, the bird abruptly said, "Emil thinks you are in danger."

Zanja stopped short. "What kind of danger?"

"He doesn't know."

"Well, I don't sense anything. Raven, will you fly ahead and check?"

As the raven lifted from her shoulder, Zanja looked back at Seth, who was several body-lengths behind her. "Did you hear that? Emil's having some kind of presentiment—"

The ice cracked open under her feet, and she fell in.

The shock of cold froze the breath in her chest.

She scrambled wildly to get hold of the edge, but the current dragged her away.

Seth lay on the edge, reaching for her, shouting at her to grab her hand. Their hands were inches, then feet, then yards apart.

The ice was more than thick enough for safety, Zanja noticed resentfully. It certainly should not have broken under her weight.

Then the current sucked her under the ice. It lay above her: translucent, beautiful, impenetrable.

Part Two: Mud Season

Chapter 7

The council meeting had lasted far into the night. As Saleen and a few other Paladins escorted Clement to the garrison, she had been able to hear the midnight bell ringing. Gabian awakened and yelped politely until she could provide him with fresh diapers and a meal of warm milk. She sat in the hard bed with him cradled against her shoulder, rearguing the day's arguments in her mind, first to correct her own mistakes, then to say the many impolitic statements she had avoided. She couldn't decide which would be better: to make no mistakes, or to say whatever she liked.

Finally, her son's peacefulness infected her, and she slept for a few hours until Ellid opened the door, bearing a pot of tea and a scorched lump of bread. That dawn meeting to review Ellid's progress with the visiting commanders had been both frigid and fruitless. After Ellid left and Gilly came in seeking to know his day's tasks, Clement went banging around the room, slamming chest lids and kicking her boots across the floor.

"You're losing your patience," Gilly observed.

"I'm the general! I shouldn't have to be patient! Bloody hell!" She sat down abruptly to cup her hands around a stubbed toe.

"Oh, you are much more than the general, little though that pleases you."

"I'd strangle you if I didn't need you so badly," she muttered.

"Cadmar did throttle me any number of times," he replied.

"Gods, I miss that stupid bastard."

Gabian, cradled in Gilly's unlikely but competent arms, broke free from sucking his bottle to gurgle contentedly at his ugly uncle. Gilly might be Gabian's tutor one day, if all of them survived that long.

Yesterday, the commanders had toured the garrison's damages, seen with their own eyes the mountain of weaponry that in one moment Karis had turned to trash: shattered crossbows, blunted sabers, broken axes. Unimpressed by a weaponer's demonstration of the impossibility of sharpening even a humble kitchen knife, they themselves had taken turns at the grinding wheel. The blades, picked randomly out of the pile, all had shattered into gravel.

These demonstrations seem to have convinced them that Clement had accepted a truce because she could not fight. Yet their opinions of her hadn't altered. They wanted to be led by a mythical figure, a forceful, decisive idiot who looked good on a horse. They did not want a soldier who accepted shameful peace, no matter how necessary and unavoidable; who only fought when she had to and then did it badly; who knew everyone's name; and, most of the time kept her feet on the ground.

She slid her foot into the abused boot, whose shine she had damaged as she kicked it across the grimy floor. "I've become a straw target between battle lines, the only object that anyone on either side dares to attack."

"Well, you are convenient," said Gilly. "And maybe it's better this way. No, listen before you start throwing things at me."

"Talk quickly, then!" Clement yanked her bootstraps.

"People will insist on seeing their conditions as choices, and will always embody those choices in whatever people are convenient. To the commanders you represent one choice, an unappealing, costly, and extremely unsettling choice. They will never accept you gladly. You cannot change that fact. But if you accept the blame, and suffer the consequences of our situation alongside or instead of them, you'll earn their gratitude and admiration."

"That might be true," said Clement, "if not for Heras."

She looked up and found him staring at her. Apparently it hadn't occurred to him that the absence of the western commanders was Heras's first foray in a campaign to be general.

"It's tactically brilliant," Gilly said finally. "So long as she remains absent, the commanders are able to invent her. They can believe she is your opposite. They can tell themselves that she represents the power, honor, and continuity you are prepared to surrender."

"And she looks good on a horse." Clement stood up, finished doing up her tunic buttons, put on her hat, and peered into the campaign mirror. It gave her a blurry view of exhaustion held upright by a stiff uniform.

"You look tired enough to be a general," Gilly said. "Do you even sleep anymore?"

With Seth, Clement thought, for a few hours I truly slept. She kissed her son and went out to meet with the garrison commanders one last time.

The nine commanders awaited her in the hall of the new building, under walls that had received only the first rough brown coat of plaster, by windows that were still smeared with the glazier's oily fingerprints, near a fireplace where a brisk fire painted the first stains of smoke on the new bricks. Nothing cushioned the harsh sound of chair legs scraping on the bare floor as the commanders rose to greet her, too slowly, with too little genuine respect.

Let them have Heras, thought Clement. And for a moment the prospect of freedom dizzied her: Seth, Gabian, a comfortable bed at night, a flower garden.

And yet, though these commanders persisted in thinking they had only to choose between one general and another, in fact it was a choice between changing or dying. If these particular soldiers were to die, it would make little difference to Clement, so weary she was of them. But thousands of soldiers who followed their commands would die with them, and for them she felt dreadfully responsible. For most of her life, she too, like these commanders, had substituted discipline for vision, had ignored her doubts and done her duty. Her commands had helped to deliver her people to this quandary, and she must deliver them from it, if only because no one else would.

The commanders were waiting for her to speak. Ellid gazed at her with concern, Taram with a suggestion of apprehension, Doley and some of the others with open hostility.

Clement cleared her throat. "Good day, Commanders. You have seen what you needed to see in Watfield, and I won't keep you away from your garrisons any longer." She added after a moment, "When you arrive, you'll find a missive from the western commanders awaiting you. That letter will urge you to join their mutiny."

She should have made them sit down, for most of them were taller than she. They gazed down at her, and it was impossible to know which of them were dismayed by her use of this dreaded word, and which were overjoyed to learn that so many had joined this mutiny. Their expressions had closed and now revealed nothing at all.

Clement said, "The western commanders will call it something else, no doubt, something more palatable. They'll explain themselves in words you find appealing, and they'll laud Heras: her bravery, her cleverness, her loyalty to tradition. No doubt they'll call her honorable, while claiming that I have dishonored all Sainnites because I permitted bitter reality to replace these heroic stories. Perhaps you'll agree with Heras and her cohort—some of you agree with her now, and some of you might have joined her insurrection had you known of it sooner. Perhaps you, too, will find it easy to pretend that you're doing something else. But it is mutiny, and the penalty for mutiny is death."

She regretted her words instantly, for she had said them in hope of finally gaining something from them, and still they gave her nothing. Now she could tell them to sit down. She could talk to them as she had already done many times during the five days they had attended her, like a friend rather than an enemy, like a fellow soldier suffering with them through a lousy campaign. But words had failed, and would continue to fail, and to persist in this tactic would only emphasize her poverty of options, which would make her seem even weaker when they demanded the illusion of strength.

The Shaftali talk; the Sainnites act. With every word Clement spoke, she proved to the commanders that she was not one of them at all.

"That is all," Clement said. "You are dismissed."

Late in the afternoon Emil arrived in Watfield Garrison. His hair, tied back in its usual tail, still was damp from a bath; his chin was pink from recent shaving. "I've slept most of the day," he admitted, as he unpacked his basket onto the battered table: meat pies, baked apples, sweet cakes, a wedge of cheese, bottles of ale. "The Paladins waited for me to start moving before they gave me your note."

Gilly came in bearing the duty rosters from the five western garrisons, and his eyes lit up. "Cake!"

Emil handed the cakes to Gilly. "Any problem seems unsolvable on an empty stomach."

"Is that Garland's philosophy?" Clement bit into a meat pie and remembered that except for a mouthful of scorched bread at dawn she had eaten nothing. Inedible food made it easy to go hungry. That seemed to be the philosophy of the garrison cooks.

Emil uncorked a bottle of ale and picked up a wedge of cheese. "Oh, Garland's more of a doctor than a philosopher."

"Whatever he is, he was ours first," said Gilly.

They had been arguing for months over who had the better claim to Garland, but Clement couldn't bring herself to play any games today. They ate, and talked about the kinds of things people like to discuss when they're eating. When Clement had eaten two turnovers and Emil seemed to have satisfied his appetite, she raised the topic of the note, which Gilly had transcribed shortly after her final meeting with the garrison commanders. She said, "Most of the commanders have already departed, even with a storm coming. I could have kept them here longer, but I didn't think it would serve any purpose."

He cocked an eyebrow at her. "Even should you become a Paladin, you won't have to justify yourself to me unless I ask you to. Or is it yourself you're trying to persuade?"

"Clem is browbeating herself," said Gilly, though he would never have said such a thing in the presence of a Sainnite.

"That's not my particular weakness, fortunately," said Emil.

Clement said, "I told the commanders that the western commanders are engaged in mutiny. Now that I've called them mutineers, I have to kill them. And I can't."

"There's a third choice," Emil said.

"Shall I unsay the words I've already said? Shall I contradict the rule on which all Sainnite discipline is based? Shall I demonstrate to my commanders that I'm as soft and indecisive as they think I am?"

"There's another choice. We just don't know what it is." But Emil's voice seemed flat and hollow. Perhaps it was an effect of the threatening storm.

Clement said, "For you, maybe. Why don't you just use fleas to assassinate the mutineers? Or all the commanders? That would give you the general you want with no further difficulty."

Gilly said, "Well, as far as I'm concerned it would be a pleasure to kill some of those commanders—I've even got an idea or two of my own about how to do it. But we mustn't lose the loyalty of the soldiers in their command by arbitrarily doing in their commanders. And as far as I know, there's only one way to gain a soldier's allegiance."

"Earn it, of course," said Emil distractedly.

"The penalty for mutiny is death," Clement said. "That's the way it is. And I can't start killing my own people. I could hardly bring myself to kill Shaftali, even when I believed it was necessary and right."

"Agh," said Gabian. She stood and took him up out of the cradle. He blinked at her somberly, as though he somehow knew her every pain; as though he understood better than she herself did what it was like to have the survival of seven thousand depending on her blind decisions. And one of those seven thousand was him, this sweet-tempered baby. For his sake, could she order some thirty Sainnite soldiers to be put to death?

The very idea revolted her. "I can't do it," she said to her son. "It's like Karis says, there's all kinds of dreadful things she can do, but what she can't do is be the kind of person who does such things."

Gilly, always pragmatic, began to explain that in any case they could only break into the barricaded garrisons by force at the cost of many lives, so whether Clement could execute her fellow Sainnites was irrelevant. But Emil, whose attention Clement had never before known to waver, started halfway to his feet, sat down, then abruptly rose again. "Excuse me," he said. "I must talk to a raven."

By the time he entered the hallway he was running.

"Erp!" exclaimed Gabian as Clement pushed him roughly into Gilly's arms. She ran after Emil.

She shouted for the surprised soldier in the hallway to follow her. She heard Emil bang out the front door. "Come with me!" she cried to the startled door guards, who had been warming themselves at the fireplace. She pushed out the door, and the bitter wind took the breath right out of her lungs.

Emil had stopped a few paces from the building and was shouting at the sky. Already, a raven was plummeting down from the eaves to land, flapping wildly for balance, on Emil's outstretched arm. "Tell Zanja she's in danger!" Emil cried.

"You get our coats," said Clement to one of the soldiers that crowded out the door behind her. "You find me a signalman," she said to the next. "You—go to the training field and muster any company that's already geared up."

The soldiers scattered. Clement could hear the raven saying, "Zanja senses no danger. She asks for Medric's opinion—Karis is finding him now—and she is seeking shelter. The raven is lifting to survey the—" the bird broke off its narration, then said in a tone oddly like Karis's racked voice, "Zanja has fallen through the ice!"

"Clement, I need some soldiers," Emil said.

"I already am mustering a company of fifty."

"Seth is trying to grab her," the raven said. "No! She has gone under! Under the ice!"

"What is Karis is doing?" Emil asked.

"Running down the street."

"Are Paladins following her?"

"Yes."

The soldier appeared bearing their coats, and Clement sent him to find Commander Ellid.

"What is Seth doing?" Emil asked the raven as Clement put his coat over his shoulders.

"Trying to track Zanja under the ice. The ice is opaque, but the dogs seem to know where she is. No—the dogs have lost her. Seth has dropped her scarf there. She's running towards the farmstead."

Clement said, "Emil, go. Leave the raven to guide us."

Emil's hair may have been gray, but he could still run like a boy. He had disappeared from sight when Captain Herme and his company appeared in one direction, a signalman in another, and Ellid in a third. All of them also were running, as they should do when urgently summoned by their general.

The Sainnites had learned the dangers of Shaftal's river ice, and Clement knew they were unlikely to even find Zanja's corpse. But if they did, it would change nothing, for Karis could only heal the living. And even as Clement buttoned her coat, put on her hat and gloves, and assessed her own readiness to travel in a snowstorm, Zanja was already dead. Nothing would be gained by hurrying. Nevertheless, they all did so.

The day was darkening and a few flakes of snow had begun to fall by the time Clement and fifty soldiers, guided by a raven, reached the place Zanja had fallen in. It was an insignificant place, a common crossing, where the break in the ice had already healed itself and become indistinguishable under fresh snow. Seth's rust-red muffler lay near a hole that had been chopped in the ice. A couple of farmers stood by the hole as though waiting for Zanja to pop up, but Emil and six Paladins, vague shapes obscured by falling snow, were searching the ice downriver. At the nearest bend, probably the likeliest place for Zanja's body to be lodged, Karis stood on shore, with Seth and two dogs beside her, flanked by unmoving trees. The snowfall had grown heavier, and it became dreadfully quiet.

Clement went downriver with Herme's company, carrying tools and lanterns. They scraped snow from the ice and peered down as if through a cloudy glass, seeking a shape or floating shadow. Occasionally, someone imagined something was there, and they chopped a hole in the ice, but everything they did was futile. Hours later, with snow falling thick in the lightless night, Clement sent Herme to collect his people. Alone, she sometimes lost her bearings and wandered into the center of the river, but the ice didn't even crack.

Lanterns hanging from a tree branch illuminated the spot where Karis still stood, ankle-deep in freshly fallen snow. Seth huddled at her feet, with the two dogs pressing her knees. Someone had recently brushed the snow from Karis, but snowflakes were quickly covering her again, as if she were a statue in a garden.

A vague figure extricated himself from the nearby knot of Paladins. "Clement, is that you?" Her lantern briefly illuminated Emil's harrowed face.

"Emil, I've told my people to stop searching."

He looked downriver, and Clement turned and saw the approaching lanterns of Herme's company. "Then bring them to shelter," he said.

"Is there room for us in that barn over there? They should have rations in their kits. And if they don't, they deserve to go hungry."

Emil nodded. He gazed blankly downriver.

"Your people are even colder than mine," Clement said.

"The Paladins must stay with Karis," he said. "And Karis will not leave this place."

Captain Herme was a stickler for regulations. Every last member of his company carried the required rations, even though they had only been engaged in routine drills when Clement summoned them. She told Herme she was glad it had been his company that happened to be out in the field. Herme, who was nursing frozen fingers, said glumly that it had been luck, but not good luck. The farmers arrived with buckets of drinking water and kettles of hot tea, and the shivering soldiers eagerly dug tin cups out of their kits. It was obvious that Clement must allow Herme and his company to warm up before she told them they'd be taking turns watching over Karis out in the snow all night.

She assessed the resources in the barn and went back out into the storm. The specks of distant light at the riverbank appeared and disappeared behind the dizzying veil of snowfall. She followed the lantern flames as well as she could, slithering on the hard ice that lurked beneath the soft, fresh snow. When she lost her footing entirely, she fell onto stones and realized only then that she had reached the rocky edge of the river. Limping, she finally joined the frozen cluster of people, the lanterns that dripped melting snow. The six Paladins were discussing how to build a shelter around Karis where she stood. Emil was nearly invisible at a distance, still staring downriver. Snow-covered Karis and her snow-covered attendants already seemed paralyzed by the cold that might well kill them by dawn.

Clement squatted beside Seth. The dogs lifted their heads, snorting snow out of their noses, and looked at her suspiciously. "Seth, you're going to freeze to death," Clement said. "You don't have these dogs' advantages."

Seth gave no reply. Clement brushed at the snow until she could see Seth's eyes and eyebrows—the rest of her face was covered by her hat and coat collar. Seth's eyes were squinted shut. With her breath, Clement melted the ice that froze her lashes. Seth's eyes opened. "I'll help you get up," Clement said.

"But—Karis—"

"She's got seven other people looking after her."

"—my fault."

"You did everything anyone could have done." Clement tried to lift Seth by the arm but found her immovably rooted in the snow, as some boulders are rooted in earth. The immobility of earth logic. Little wonder Karis, who had twice Seth's size and strength, could not be forced to abandon her vigil.

"Commander Saleen!" Clement yelled in exasperation.

The Paladins came over and helped haul Seth to her feet, and Clement wrapped her arms around the Basdown cow farmer to keep her from sitting down again. She said to Saleen, "Commander, I'll send my soldiers to you with the building materials and tools that are in the barn. After we've put Karis in some kind of shelter, we'll rotate people in and out every hour. At least we'll all suffer the same."

"I'm staying with her," Seth mumbled.

"You're not in your right mind," Clement said.

"What do you know?"

"You think I've never felt responsible for someone's death? Then you have no idea what my life has been like—no idea at all!"

Bloody hell! When had it become acceptable to indulge her hurt feelings, like a child? "You've been out in this weather all day, Councilor," she said. "Come indoors for a while, drink some hot tea, let your fingers thaw."

A clot of snow fell, and another. Clement realized Karis was moving, very slowly. Eventually the G'deon was looking at Seth, and her face was as pale as the snowflakes clotting the mad curls of her hair. "Go inside, Seth," she said.

"Not until you do."

Two earth bloods, equally intractable, might stand here all night glaring stubbornly at each other. Clement said, "Karis, don't you see that none of us has any choice but to freeze with you?"

Karis looked around herself at the cluster of Paladins, and then towards Emil, who was outside the reach of light. Her stiff shoulders slumped, and she turned and began walking.

In the barn, the soldiers who had finished eating were bedding down in pairs on the cold stone floor, using one coat as a mattress and the second as a blanket. The farmers had run out of straw, explained Herme, and he had refused to use the hay they offered instead, for he thought this family had too little hay for their animals as it was. He reported that the soldiers had all checked each other for frostbite and put on dry stockings. He told her where the latrine buckets were, and then gestured towards the women's side. "Your old bedmates asked me to say they'd be glad to sleep with you as they did on our last campaign."

"Thank them for me, Commander, but I doubt I'll even lie down tonight."

Saleen and the Paladins appeared in the passageway to the ell, bearing lanterns, bowls of soup, and lumps of bread. Clement, who had neither the standard rations nor dry socks, shared their supper and their silence. No one said the elegies one might expect to hear upon a person's death. Clement felt oppressed by that silence, but she didn't think it was her place to insist they acknowledge that Zanja was dead. Seth, Emil, and Karis all refused food and beds, and disappeared into the dark barn. The Paladins bedded down with each other, and then Clement sat alone beneath the only lantern with its flame turned low, and the darkness and silence took on a quality of unsettling permanence.

Like Gilly, Zanja had done her work invisibly, but to Emil as well as Karis she certainly seemed indispensable. Yet only a few months ago her family had thought she was dead, and they had managed without her. They would do so again.

But Zanja had become a friend who both understood Clement and was not subject to her. Now she had only Gilly once again. Could she weep for herself on this dreadful day? Was self-pity ever permissible?

A footstep scraped in the sawdust, and Seth stepped into the dim light of the lantern. Shivering, she put her coat on the floor, and Clement unbuttoned and removed hers for them to share as a blanket. With the dogs pressed against their feet, they sat huddled together with their backs against a dividing wall, on the other side of which someone uttered an occasional snore. Seth's shivering gradually eased. Time crept slowly forward.

In a while, Emil arrived and sat on Seth's other side. "Listen, Seth," he said in a low, rough voice. "This is not Zanja's final death."

Seth's head lifted. "How many times can a person die?"

"The first time, anger kept Zanja alive though she should have died from that crack in her skull. The second time, Karis made her heart continue beating while she healed her. The most recent time, I killed her spirit with my own hand, and I knew in my heart she was dead. This time I know she is alive."

Seth said, "I nearly grabbed her hand. But she slipped out of reach. She went under the ice. She did not come up again. She has drowned."

"I know what happened. But feel my heart."

Clement heard clothing rustle as Emil endeavored to lift Seth's hand to his chest. "This is not my logic," Seth protested.

Karis's distinctive voice spoke in the shadows. "But by earth logic Zanja isn't dead either. Not one hair of her head, not one flake of her skin, no part of her, however minuscule, has touched the river bottom." Karis came out of the darkness and, despite her massive size squatted easily among them. "She simply isn't here."

Emil said, "She has crossed another boundary."

"What boundary could she cross that would cause her to physically disappear?"

Suddenly, Clement could hear the quiet ticking of Emil's watch. She leaned forward, expecting to see him peering at it in the lantern's dim orange light. But he was merely holding it.

"Time?" said Clement. "Time is a barrier, I suppose. But how can it be crossed, except by remembering?"

Karis tilted her head back. "That dimwitted twit of a seer had better be awake," she said, apparently addressing the rafters.

A raven dropped down from the darkness. "Medric has just opened a window for a raven," it said. Then it added, "He agrees he's a twit. But don't call him dimwitted."

Chapter 8

Zanja was ice: lungs, blood, and bone. Her will was ice; the flame of insight was frozen; she floated in a mindless, timeless darkness, dead again.

"Not again!" she tried to say, but choked on ice. "I've died enough," she tried to protest, but the words froze into silence.

"Hush. Hush. There's naught to fear."

It was a singing voice, that sang so lovingly and soothingly that Zanja's rage and terror could not persist. "Hush. Hush. There's naught to fear," sang the voice.

> You hear the gale wind,
> The river flowing near,
> The reapers in the glen...

A lullaby. Karis sang it to Leeba as she rocked her by the kitchen fire. That was in their old house, soon after the seven of them became a family. A family, a tribe, an order, a confederacy, a circle formed around Karis as much as it was around Leeba.

This was not Karis's broken, raspy voice, though. And Leeba had become a willful, active little person with no patience for lullabies. And Karis was the G'deon now.

I must be alive, Zanja thought. For time has passed and is still passing.

"She's trying to speak," creaked a voice.

"She's terrified, I guess," the gentle voice said.

Each unexplained utterance was folded between leaves of silence. Zanja began to see a flickering light. The ice had turned to fire. Her body burned upon the pyre. She cried out with pain.

> Dearest, I am always near.
> Hush! Hush! There's naught to fear.

A fresh log flung sparks across a gray stone hearth. A baby uttered an impatient cry and then began to suckle noisily. Knitting needles clicked rhythmically.

A dark, knife-scarred hand lay half-open, the fingertips gray with frostbite.

"She'll kill us all," the grim voice said. "Her kind has no laws."

The hand flexed. The wool blanket burned. Zanja tried to lift her head, but the ice froze closed again.

The grim voice made a disgusted sound. "She's puking."

"Hold the baby."

A rough cloth wiped Zanja's face. The kind voice said, "You tried to swallow the river, but I guess it disagreed with you." Zanja saw a swirl of features: a plain, round face, a thick plait of hair, an opened shirt and milk-heavy breasts. The baby uttered a frustrated, demanding cry. "Can you lie still?" the woman asked Zanja. "Until this little one is satisfied? Then I will help you."

The other voice said impatiently. "She's not our kind. She will not understand us."

Zanja said, "Yes. I can." She coughed for breath. Black spots swirled. There was a far-away murmur of surprised conversation. Ice and fire filled Zanja's chest; her limbs burned with hot cold.

"Keep coughing," said the nursing woman. "That water in your chest, it could make you sick."

"I'm alive," Zanja rasped.

"Some people were down at the bend. A farm there is getting flooded—"

The other voice interrupted. "People warned that family they'd get washed out, didn't they? But they couldn't resist living right on that good soil, could they? And now their stupidity causes nothing but trouble for their neighbors."

"I doubt she cares about that," said the nursing woman. She continued to Zanja, "So someone spotted you half-drowned, hung up on some rocks, and you were pulled out and brought here."

"Another mouth to feed, too ignorant to work..." The voice faded to a grumble.

"I guess you fell in the river and got swept away somehow."

"I am Zanja na'Tarwein."

"You're what?"

"My name: Zanja na'Tarwein."

"Well why don't you have a name that can be pronounced!" exclaimed the crabby one.

Zanja turned her head quite cautiously. She lay on the floor of a small, windowless room walled with mortared stone. A brightly painted baby cradle swung gently from the roof beam. In a plain, narrow bed was propped a skeletally thin man with a wool cap on his hairless head. He knitted unceasingly without looking at his hands. In fact, he looked at nothing, for he was blind.

The nursing woman had begun chafing Zanja's hand. Her own hand was rough with work, and chapped with cold. "It must frighten you to be so far from home. But never mind him! He's always like this."

"Zanja na'Tarwein," Zanja said again. Perhaps they had not understood because her lips were stiff with cold.

"Well, my name's Mari."

"Karis will be frantic—"

"Oh, yes, I'm sure." The rough hand patted hers.

"If you'll go outside and tell a raven—"

The old man snorted. "Deranged!"

"Tell a raven? I will if I see one." The nursing woman patted her again. "You shut your eyes and rest, now."

The house was quiet when Zanja awoke. She hazily remembered the sound of the family coming home, stomping loudly in the adjacent kitchen to clean their boots. Now, it was much later, the middle of a very quiet night. Zanja disentangled herself from the heavy wool blankets that wrapped her and crawled across the stone floor to a latrine bucket. Then, following the faint glow of coals, she crawled into the kitchen and used a chair to lever herself to her feet. Among the coats and clothing that hung on pegs by the chimney, she found her shirt and trousers, stiff but dry. Her coat, belt, and shoes were still damp, though, and she turned them so they would dry evenly. She found her dagger in its sheath and the glyph cards in their pouch. She went to the door barefoot, lifted the latch, and stepped outside.

No starlight glimmered there. In the unrelieved darkness Zanja could not guess where she was, or which way lay the river. "Raven?" She called quietly. She felt her way down a stone path. When she stepped off it by accident she found herself standing in ice-cold mud. How could a thaw have happened so quickly? "Raven!" she cried. But no large bird flew out of darkness to dig its claws into her shoulder and speak reassuringly of how quickly people would arrive to bring Zanja home. Even if Karis had lost track of Zanja in the water, she would have found her again when she was dragged to dry land. But there was no raven.

She made her way back to the open door and scraped the mud from her feet before stepping inside. She built up the kitchen fire and spread the glyph cards on the hearth to dry. Many hand-drawn cards had been added to the pack over the years, and on these the ink had now run, so that on some cards only a ghost of the design remained, and on others the design had become a smear. However, the original cards of the pack had survived another misadventure intact. Zanja's knees were giving out; she sat on the hard floor. Her vision filled with glyphs flickering in firelight.

"Oh, are you awakened then?" said Mari cautiously from the shadows. The baby in her arms grunted fretfully. Even Mari's words were disorienting, for she pronounced them strangely and with a lilting rhythm that made her seem to be about to sing again.

"Thank you and your family for saving me."

"Oh, it's what anyone would do, I guess." The young woman approached. "Are you feeling much improved? Perhaps you'd like something to eat?"

"Yes, but let me serve myself."

Mari sat in a chair by the hearth and nursed the baby while under her direction Zanja lit a candle and found bread and butter. It seemed a poor household, without even a spice cupboard or tea tin, and Zanja cut herself only two slices of the coarse bread, though she could have consumed the entire loaf.

She returned to the hearth to find Mari looking curiously at the glyph cards. "This one would be you." Zanja touched a finger to a damp, blurry card. "You can't read it now because the ink was washed away but the glyph was 'Nurture' and it had a drawing of a nursing mother sitting by the fire, just like you. It's a very lucky card."

"Perhaps you'll tell my fortune when the cards are dry."

"I'm not a fortune-teller."

"What are you, then?"

Hadn't Zanja answered this question already? She said, "What is this place?"

"This is Vinal's Farm, and we fished you out of the River Corber, down by the bend. Long Bend, most folks call this place."

Zanja knew of no place known as Long Bend. "Is this the north bank, or the south?"

"The south, of course."

"How far away is Watfield?"

"Watfield?" The baby uttered a complaint. Mari switched the infant to her other breast, and there was peace again. "Oh, I guess you mean Waet's Field? Upriver, on the north bank? I'm not certain, though."

"Why not?"

Mari seemed puzzled. "We don't know them. And it's not easy to get across. In this flood—"

"Flood! The ice hasn't even broken up yet."

"It broke up fifteen days ago." Mari's shy glance was more than a little bewildered. "Have you forgotten the entire season?"

"No, I remember it clearly: a cold winter and a late spring."

"You're a bit addled from your accident, maybe. It was a warm winter and an early spring."

After a moment Zanja asked, "Is the bridge out at Lit Narrows?"

"Bridge?" said Mari. "There's no bridge. Just the one to the west, for the highway. I understand it's a long way from here."

Zanja gazed a long time at the glyph cards. They were warping as they dried, and she finally roused herself to turn them over. Perhaps her confusion and lethargy was from a head injury. She felt her skull but found no bleeding or swelling. Perhaps the cold and shock of nearly drowning had so confused her that she now remembered facts about Shaftal that were not true. But was her entire life not true?

She said, "You've never heard my name? Zanja na'Tarwein?"

"Oh, we don't hear much of the border people here in the Midlands. They stay in their own place, I guess, just like we do."

"I'm Karis G'deon's wife!"

"Karis G'deon?" said Mari. "Well, I'm sure he's worried about you." Her voice sharpened. "Tadwell G'deon died so young? This is dreadful news!"

No matter how remote the farmstead or how reclusive the farmers, any six-year-old could recite the names of the G'deons and the years of their service. Tadwell had died old, after thirty-eight years as G'deon. That had been some two hundred years ago.

As Zanja set forth from Vinal's Farm, the light was rising though the sun was hidden. The fields surrounding the farm were mud, churned up by frost, not yet dry enough to plow. The track Zanja followed, which Mari assured her would take her to the riverbank, did not go north at all, but due west. Yet the river did appear, though in the wrong direction, and it was not frozen, but sloppy with flooding on the near bank. Even though Zanja could see that its big bend folded it back on itself, so that the water lay to the west instead of to the north, and its east-flowing water turned northwestward, she persisted in feeling that she stood on the north shore with Watfield to the right of her. She walked to the left in a direction she kept telling herself was southwest, with the sprawling river usually in sight though she had to climb to high ground to avoid the flood.

All day the landscape remained unfamiliar. Zanja's disorientation persisted until midday, when the landscape began to seem less alien, and her reversed sense of direction abruptly righted itself. She must be near the farm where she and Seth had gotten the dogs. She believed they had crossed this brook, though it had been frozen then. Now she should see an orchard. But the slope that yesterday had been planted with apple trees today was uncleared woodland.

Finally, Zanja felt certain she had passed the place she had fallen in. Unable to cross the flood, she continued along the south bank, fighting her way through wild woods now, until at midafternoon she stood directly across from Watfield.

Watfield was a perfect site for a river port, with the flood plain on the south bank, and the north bank safe on higher ground. The sun had burned through the clouds, and Zanja should have been able to see the city's clutter of docks and peaked slate roofs even at this distance. But on the far shore the cleared land was scattered with farmsteads. Watfield wasn't there. Where Zanja looked for a city there lay only a field that belonged to a family named Waet.

Chapter 9

Living in uncertainty is what makes the marvelous possible, Emil had said to Clement more than once. That night, in the bitter cold of the barn, surrounded by sleeping soldiers, with the snowfall extinguishing all sound, for a little while Clement understood why Emil, a man of extraordinary rationality, could subscribe to such a mystical philosophy.

"We think the past is over," said the raven, speaking Medric's words. "To us that's fact. But by water logic, the past is present."

"You know as little of water logic as I do," Karis snapped. "You're reciting from a book."

"Reading, actually—the book is right here on my lap," said the seer. "And it's a good thing I know how to read."

Emil said, "Medric, please don't test Karis's temper tonight. Has Zanja been taken by water magic? Say yes, or say no."

"Yes," said the Medric-Raven.

"A water witch is meddling with my business, and you didn't see fit to tell me?" Karis said in outrage.

"No."

Medric seemed to have given his entire answer. By the dim lantern light Clement saw Emil lay a hand on Karis's forearm. "I assume you're unwilling to explain why, or you would have done so already. But will you tell us where, or what?"

"She lies not too far from here, in a cottage on the south shore, near a horseshoe bend of the river, where there's an old man who's blind and knits. She's been mostly drowned and nearly frozen, but to her that's not much worse than a hiccup."

"There's no such place," Karis said. "And she certainly isn't there."

The Medric-Raven said, "No, not now. But two hundred years ago there was. And she is."

Their dreary wait for daylight became an impatient one. Karis wanted to travel north to find a water witch she had met once in a border tribe, and she and Emil argued about the wisdom and practicality of this venture. With Zanja gone, he pointed out, no one in Shaftal could even speak the Otter Elder's language, even if the old man was still alive. And he reminded her, several times, that an air witch was trying to assassinate her. "Zanja will find her own way back to you," he said. "After six years with her, how is it possible you don't trust her to do so?"

At dawn, Herme rousted his company and set them to work at clearing snow. The farmers served pot after pot of porridge, as quickly as they could cook it. By the time the sixty of them began the march to Watfield, columns of sunlight supported a cracking ceiling of clouds. They walked from sunlight to shadow to sunlight, and weary people grumbled in two languages that they didn't know whether to sweat or shiver.

Clement found Seth with the dogs at the rear of the column, plodding wearily in the trampled snow. They walked together for half the morning without saying a word to each other. Once only, Seth glanced sideways at Clement, and her expression was so full of contradictions that Clement could make nothing of it.

Emil walked ahead with Saleen, and Karis spent most of the journey in the very front, doing the hard work of trampling a path in the fresh snow. Eventually both of them fell back. The dogs pushed up to be near Karis and she rested her big hands on their heads. The dogs grinned up at her, seeming very pleased by her approval.

"I like that captain of yours," Emil said to Clement. "His name is Herme? Can he read and write? Does he speak Shaftalese?"

"No, no, and no. And you can't recruit him to the Paladins. He's going west with me, to be a new garrison commander's lieutenant. It will break his company's heart to lose him, though."

Seth looked at Clement sharply. "You're going west?" she said.

"I must. I have a problem there that only I can resolve."

Emil said, "The Paladin irregulars have always avoided direct attacks on the garrisons because it would take too many people and too much heavy artillery. What will it take for you to break into a garrison by force?"

"You Paladins were wise with your resources," said Clement. "It would require a battalion, at least, and a great deal more time than I have."

"And I don't want armed battalions marching the countryside again."

"I'll bring only thirty people—a commander and five lieutenants for each garrison. And no weapons."

"But the mutineers won't open the gates and let you in," Emil said, "no more than our own rebels will open their own gates to Karis. To do so would be an admission they were wrong, and it's both too late and too early for that."

"You think you know Heras, Emil, but you only know her as an enemy. You don't realize Heras is my superior in every way: more subtle, more determined, more ruthless. My promotions were gained by patronage, while hers were gained by worth. So she has told me, more than once."

"She's a stupid woman, whoever she is," Seth muttered beside her.

"You don't have to convince me she's ruthless," Emil said quietly. When Emil became quiet, he was forcing people to put effort into listening, which meant he was angry. "But that woman's subtlety and determination were greatly reduced when a certain rogue Paladin tempted her dimwitted twit of a seer into turning traitor. When Medric abandoned her, so also did her greatness."

"Greatness by whose standards?" said Clement. "And is that a prediction or an opinion?"

"You can keep trying to throw me off track all the way to Watfield if you like, though it seems a pointless and exhausting way to spend a morning."

"What do you want me to say, Emil? That third choice you believe in? I have no idea what it might be."

"But I can think of an easy way for you to resolve this entire matter."

"If you let me have a weapon I can kill myself," Clement said. "That would be easy."

Seth said, "It would be easier to let that stupid person be general instead of you."

Clement stumbled over her own feet.

Seth glanced at Emil, as though she feared she had spoken out of turn. But Emil said, "And that's what you want to do, isn't it Clement? If Zanja were here, she'd tell you the story of the demon in the wild-wood, who terrified all passersby until one of them called it by name."

"The demon's name was 'Fear,'" Clement said. "I heard her tell that story in the garrison."

"Well, then," Emil said. Whatever target he had been aiming at, he seemed to think he had hit it.

Clement said, "I'll leave for the west as soon as my people can be ready. A few days."

Seth said, "You can't. The weather has changed. Don't you feel it?"

Clement raised her gaze to survey the landscape. There was snow and more snow as far as could be seen. Her feet and hands were numb, and even when walking in sunlight she felt disinclined to unbutton her coat. But surely the sun's climb into the sky was surprisingly steep. And where the patches of sunlight lingered long enough, water drops began to fall from the snow-covered tree limbs.

"Mud season," Karis said. "In just a few days it will start to rain."

"How long will the rain last?" Emil asked.

"Fifteen days," Karis said. "More or less."

"Thirteen," said Seth.

They conferred, but Clement, engaged in her own calculations, didn't care about the exact number. She said, "It's not so difficult, is it, to find someone to predict the weather?"

"Not at all," said Emil. "A person with a strong earth talent can predict a good twenty days ahead with certainty, and beyond that with less certainty."

"Are there people like that in South Hill?"

"Three or four of them, at least. Do you think Heras has become able to make weather her ally? Perhaps a prisoner, or a younger soldier has the gift of weather-wisdom? Still, if she did plan to use spring mud in her favor, it will just delay you, and what's the benefit of delay?"

"The delay could be as long as forty-five or fifty days if I were to send emissaries first. And then I couldn't travel to Wilton at all, because I'd have to stay here for the confirmation. With all that time, Heras could consolidate her support among the other commanders."

Neither angry nor desperate, but weighed down by the heaviness of what lay before her, Clement continued, "But the weather can work in my favor, also. We'll simply travel in the rain, and I'll arrive in Wilton while Heras is still assuming I'm too cautious and sensible to take her by surprise."

"I'll go with you," Karis said.

"You will not!" Clement cried. "Don't you think I have burdens enough?"

"Karis has somehow forgotten again that an air witch is trying to assassinate her," Emil said. "But now that I've reminded her, she will offer you a raven instead, while she remains where she can be protected by these noble dogs, these Paladins, and our Truthken. But I'll put Mabin, Saleen, and as many Paladins as I can spare under your command, Clement. With Mabin and the Paladins able to demand food and shelter in the G'deon's name, that'll mean you can travel light."

The river, which had veered away, came into sight again, its ice glittering white with new snow except where people and horses worked to plow and smooth the riverbed. Sunshine glared on the south shore. With her eyes shaded, Clement could barely make out the gray haze of a distant, leafless woodland. The docks of Watfield became visible on the north shore, hemmed in by tilting plateaus of river ice. A haze of smoke floated above the city's slate rooftops, and now a small crowd appeared at the city's edge: Paladin's black, soldier's gray, the patchwork of many colors worn by citizens. Gilly was not as easy to spot as he used to be, but still he was the only one among soldiers without a uniform. Clement heard Gabian's joyous cry and felt a clenching in her dry breasts. Some children came flying towards them, a red-coated girl at the lead, who rushed directly to Karis, who caught her and swung her into the air.

Leeba flapped her arms. "I'm flying!"

Karis swung her up into the sky again, a yodeling red bird swooping over the heads of the weary travelers. "Mama!" the red bird cried. "Is Zanja dead again?"

"No, my love, she's having an adventure while we stay home and do the dull work of putting this country together."

"If you consider it an adventure to eat bugs," said the squinting man in spectacles who had worked his way through the crowd to wedge himself under Emil's arm.

"Bugs?" cried the Leeba bird. "I want to eat bugs, too!"

Garland and his helpers had been busily distributing pastries. With his basket already empty, the cook drew near to be kissed in greeting by Emil. "Nobody eats bugs," he said disapprovingly. "There are no recipes." Behind him came Norina and J'han, while on the other side Gilly and Ellid approached, and at last Clement could embrace her little boy again, with his flailing limbs, grasping hands, and wide, wise eyes. "Eeee!" he shrilled.

Clement greeted Ellid Shaftali-style, with a handclasp and a kiss, which so astounded the Watfield commander that she neglected to offer a report.

They walked in an unmilitary straggle through the streets of Watfield. Emil was surrounded by Paladins now, and Mabin was arguing with him, as usual. Leeba, grown weary of flying, had run off with her friends. Seth walked alone, looking forlorn. Clement told Ellid and Gilly that the apparent loss of Zanja seemed to be something else entirely, and promised to explain more when she was able. Then, she jogged ahead to Karis, who plucked Gabian out of her arms and kissed him noisily.

It was possible that Cadmar had fathered Gabian in his old age, just as he had fathered Karis in his youth. Yet Clement had never asked if Karis knew whether Gabian was her half brother. She feared Karis's claim on the baby could be stronger than her own. But now she almost hoped her suspicions were correct, for it had begun to seem all too likely that Gabian would soon be motherless. "I meant to ask you this earlier, Karis, but we were never alone. Will you take Gabian into your care until I come home from the west?"

Karis gave her a concerned look. Clement continued hastily, "In the garrison only Gilly knows what to do with him, and Ellid will be needing Gilly while I'm gone. But you Shaftali can hand a baby from one person to the next and be confident that he'll be looked after. To not know what to do with a baby is unheard of."

"I'll take care of your son," Karis said. "Let that be one thing you need not worry about."

Chapter 10

In early spring even a land-wise person could starve. By luck or intuition Zanja might have found a squirrel cache or a bee tree, but both luck and intuition had abandoned her. She discovered in the spongy wood of a decaying tree stump some finger-long accuser bug larvae, which she speared on a willow wand and roasted over a little fire of dry twigs. On a sloping hillside, uprooted saplings suspended over a wedge of boulders gave her a rough shelter. There she built a nest of twigs in which she curled under her coat as the stars began to come out.

It was early spring, the stars told her. She had traveled generally westward all day. Despite these assurances, she dreamed she was lost in a wilderness.

Long before sunrise, cold made further sleep impossible. She walked through darkness, stumbling over invisible obstacles of stone and wood, until the rising light of dawn showed her the way up a knoll of bare stone. The snowmelt-flooded river began to glow a pale pink as the half-light brightened to sunrise. Her fingers were so cold she used her teeth to untie her card pack's leather binding.

"What has happened to me?" she asked.

She cast one of the four elements: a joyful, dancing woman who flung over her head an arc of water from a shell. The second card, the artisan, she lay over the first. The two cards together suggested elemental craft, or magic.

The river shone now like polished brass. The domains of the water element were music, mathematics, humor, weather, and time. Could time bend like a river, so that it might seem to flow backward, as the Corber had seemed to be flowing yesterday? Could Zanja have been captured in a backward-flowing current, so the Corber deposited her far in the past?

"Why?" she asked, a question so undirected she certainly deserved the vague reply the cards offered: the owl, the crosser of boundaries, which signified herself. Perhaps she had been brought into the past because of who or what she was. Perhaps she was required to cross the boundary between present and past for a purpose she did not yet know. Or perhaps the cards were as useless to her as all her other faculties seemed to have become. She rose stiffly up and continued her journey westward.

Two days later Zanja finally reached the bridge. Three days' hard travel, on an empty stomach, under the open sky, had wearied her so she could scarcely climb the slope to the highway. The sky had been threatening since dawn, and now rain began to fall. She crossed over the swollen river.

Early twilight arrived on the back of the storm clouds. She walked in shadows and then in darkness, feet aching in wet boots, head hanging to keep the cold rain from striking her face, glancing up from time to time to look for a farmstead's telltales: light, a side road, a fence. Yet she had been walking beside a stone wall for some time before she recognized it and realized that the trees beyond it were too orderly to be a woodland. She retraced her steps to a waterlogged wagon track and followed this muddy lane through the leafless apple orchard to the quagmire of a farmyard, around which houses and barns huddled in a dark mass. She was hard put to find a door on which to knock.

"Take shelter in the barn," said the man who finally responded, and he shut the door again.

A cow lowed as Zanja entered the barn, then a lamb bleated. She spotted chickens in the rafters, vague shapes that disappeared entirely in shadow as she wrestled the big door shut. No one arrived with a light to help her get settled, and she had to feel around for a good long time in the darkness before she located the traditional shelf and pauper's loaf, which was hard as stone and dry as sawdust. She found a tin cup also, hanging on a hook, so she made a cold porridge of bread soaked in rain water, and slept in a cold bed, in wet clothing, on damp straw. She awoke weary, ravenous, and aching with cold as the farmers arrived to feed the animals and milk the cow.

"Leave now," said a burly man. He glowered to intimidate her.

"I'd gladly work for breakfast," she said.

"Go back to your own kind."

She donned her sodden coat and went out into the rain. But she did not trudge back to the road, and instead slogged through the muck to the door on which she had knocked the night before. This time she let herself in, found the way to the warm kitchen, and sat at the table. The people who were kneading bread, stirring porridge, and dressing children, stopped work in startlement. Zanja drew her dagger and lay it in front of her. "I will leave quietly after breakfast," she said.

After the children had been hustled away and the burly man had been fetched from the barn, they eventually decided it would be easier to give her a bowl of porridge than it would be to fight her. A man who limped on a twisted leg wrapped some bread and ham in a rag with a couple of wizened apples and boiled turnips. The burly man kept his eyes on Zanja's dagger as she wolfed down the porridge, accepted the stingy packet of food, and left. "We worked hard for that food!" someone muttered behind her.

The burly man followed her to the door. Out in the rain again, with the packet of food in her shirt to keep it from getting too wet, Zanja wanted to say something angry and bitter, but instead asked, "Isn't Shaftal's first law to treat all strangers as friends?"

His hostile expression became blank. "You think the law applies to you?"

"You think it doesn't?" Getting no answer but the man's unreadable expression, she asked, "How far to the crossroad of Hanishport Road? I'm going to the House of Lilterwess."

"The House of Lilterwess!"

"The border tribes are under the G'deon's protection, are they not?"

"Such things are not my concern." He made as if to shut the door, but, possibly fearing she would not leave until her questions had been answered, added, "If you travel hard you'll reach the crossroads today. But it's another six days from there to the Shimasal Road."

And it would rain without ceasing, he might have added, if he had intended to change his mind and offer her shelter after all, for people died in cold rain as easily as they died in snow. However, the man shut the door.

During the entire journey from the River Corber to the crossroads, and eastward along the Hanishport highway toward the next crossroads,

Zanja was never invited to dry out by a fire, never offered a hot meal, and never given more than a sliver of meat. Sometimes there was not even a pauper's loaf to eat, or clean straw to sleep on.

Arguing only increased people's hostility, and Zanja could not bring herself to beg. She would have been more willing to steal, but these people kept as close an eye on their food stores as they did on their children. That some might never become comfortable with Zanja's alien appearance was a fact she had long ago accepted. But this general lack of common courtesy affronted her. Seething, she trudged doggedly from one unfriendly kitchen to the next, through showers, downpours, and occasional sleet storms. This alien Shaftal was a land of closed doors and shuttered windows, through which she could force her way only by intimidation.

The first crossroad had been marked by a piece of hewn granite. But the second had a square pillar intricately decorated with stone leaves and flowers. It was inscribed with glyphs Zanja could scarcely identify, so ornately were they carved. The road south would return her to the River Corber, where if she were more desperate she might fling herself in the water in hope of being returned home. On the northern side of the pillar were inscribed the glyphs of the three elements that also signify the three orders—the Truthkens, the seers, and the healers—along with a fourth glyph that signified the Order of Paladins. Above this collection of symbols was carved Death-and-Life, the G'deon's glyph.

It would soon be dark, and the air had turned chilly. Zanja had passed an inn not long ago. Possibly, the keepers of a highway inn would be better accustomed to strange-looking people than the farmers had been. But she felt an excitement as she ran her fingertips across the symbols carved in the pillar, an eagerness that was all the more intoxicating after ten days of anger, bewilderment, and misery. The House of Lilterwess had once been a gathering place for the powers of Shaftal, a place of excitement, ferment, and contention, to which the farm families proudly dispatched their most talented children to be raised by one of the orders. Zanja herself had been destined to serve there—but had never set eyes on the place.

She turned her steps to the north. Here the road was not made of the rough and uneven cobbles that for days had been bruising her feet and turning her ankles. Instead it was laid with finished stone, smooth as the floor of a fine house. Even the ditches were stone-lined, filled with water that flowed in silence. For a while Zanja walked swiftly, but as night fell and the clouds began to pelt her with tiny shards of ice, her pace slowed.

The wind picked up and dug cold fingers to her very bones.

"What shall I do?" she asked out loud, to force her sluggard mind to wakefulness. "Get out of the wind," she advised. She peered ahead, shielding her eyes from the sleet, but could see nothing. The wind uttered a roar. She ducked behind a dark shape that she took to be a rock, but as she huddled against it with the wind whipping around her, she recognized it to be a wall of dressed stone that was so tightly fitted she couldn't even feel the seams.

The House of Lilterwess had been renowned for its stonework. For the Sainnites to reduce it to rubble had required many months' labor.

Hunched, hands jammed in wet pockets, shuddering so violently from cold she could scarcely walk, Zanja followed the wall, which marked a lane. She was too cold to talk to herself any more, but her inner voice droned a distant commentary on her own condition: the pain of the cold, the racking shudders, the dullness of her thoughts. She was going to die from the cold after all. But when she spotted a yellow light she could not think why it was significant, and she stumbled directly into the door above which it hung.

Someone on the inside looked out and exclaimed, "Name of the land!"

The door was opened by a young Paladin who took Zanja by the arm and pulled her inside, into a cramped guard room with a small stove that radiated a palpable heat. Then somehow Zanja was sitting in a chair, dripping water. The young woman hung her waterlogged coat on a hook and brought a steaming cup Zanja could scarcely hold for shivering. "Just sit there and warm up for a bit," said the Paladin.

The young woman dried Zanja's head and face with a linen towel and said fretfully, "You'll never get warm in those wet clothes, but I have nothing for you to put on. Drink that tea—don't just hold it."

Zanja sipped from the heavy mug as the young doorkeeper mopped up the puddles. She had fresh, appealing features that were almost childish, though her hair was shorn and she wore undyed cloth-ing woven of variegated black wool. She wore not even one earring.

"You've saved my life," Zanja said, "but I'm even more grateful for your kindness. Are you a novice?"

The woman raised her face, surprised. "This is my fifth year. Most border people speak another language, don't they?"

"Yes, but I am a fire blood with a gift for languages."

"Oh! You must be a Speaker then."

"No, I speak for no tribe. But I do need to talk to the G'deon."

The young Paladin sat back on her heels, looking intrigued and discomforted. "But Tadwell—" she began.

She was interrupted by the entrance of another Paladin, an older woman with two earrings. "What's this?" she asked sharply.

"This traveler has just arrived, half-dead with cold."

"Could she communicate her business to you?"

"Yes, she is very well spoken. She is here to talk to Tadwell."

The commander's forehead creased. "What for?"

"It is my right, is it not?" said Zanja. "Is it necessary that I explain my reasons to you?"

Despite the novice's assertion that Zanja could speak, the com-mander started with surprise. She turned to Zanja with her jaw set. "It is your Speaker's business—"

"I am far from my tribe. I must speak for myself."

She realized belatedly that she had imitated the commander's tone, as if she were talking to a confused child. It took effort to erase the anger and sarcasm from her voice. "Pardon me, Madam Paladin. For many days I have been in dire straits, and except for this young woman, not one person has offered me kindness instead of insults."

The commander cast a chiding glance at the young Paladin, as though her impulse to offer help to a traveler nearly dead with cold somehow indicated a character flaw.

Zanja said, "Madam Paladin, I was attacked by a rogue elemental. The G'deon must be told about this."

"What?" exclaimed the commander. She turned to the novice. "Orna, fetch a Truthken."

"I will not be in the same room with a Truthken!"

The novice, halfway to her feet, stared wide-eyed at Zanja.

"If you will just ask Tadwell—" Zanja said.

"The G'deon is not here to make that decision." The commander turned away and said to the young Paladin, Orna, "This woman may stay one night only, in a room by the stable. Give her supper and breakfast and then expel her."

Looking unhappy, Orna said in a muted voice, "Is seems wrong that she suffer because Tadwell is gone."

"As she will not permit a Truthken to inquire into her virtue, we must assume that she has none. Sometimes the tribes exile their criminals."

No matter how tired, injured, or crazy she might be, Zanja had always known when it was time to surrender. She unbuckled her belt so as to remove from it her sheathed dagger, which she offered to Orna. "Please guard the blade for me—it is my only treasure."

The young Paladin might have never seen a weapon before, so surprised did she seem. Yet she said formally, "I accept this charge." She took the blade and knotted the tie-fasts so the dagger could not easily be unsheathed, and tucked it into her belt rather than leave it here, where the commander might touch it. "I'll show you to your room and fetch you some supper. Good evening, Commander."

The senior Paladin said nothing. Apparently, at least one thing in Shaftal was as it was supposed to be: a novice need not display abject obedience, not even to her immediate superior.

Zanja followed Orna through the door, into the House of Lilterwess.

She found herself not in a hall, but in a roofed boulevard as cold here as it had been outdoors, but much drier. Black squares high in a wall suggested openings to the night, a necessary ventilation, Zanja supposed, in a building the size of a small town.

"This is the perimeter way," said Orna. "It goes all the way to the stable, near the guest rooms."

To be housed near the stables certainly indicated low status. "Will I at least have a fire?"

"Of course you'll have a fire!"

They passed an occasional lamp hung over an ornate doorway, and by that faint light Zanja could glimpse the fine stonework, the soaring arches of the vaulted ceiling, the interior windows through which the breeze could blow. But most of the time they walked in near darkness, and she was so slow and limping that her guide had to stop and wait for her to catch up. "Should I fetch a healer for you?" she asked.

"I just need a few days of rest."

The young woman gave her a guilt-stricken look.

Zanja said wearily, "Where must I go to find the G'deon?"

"Oh, he's in Basdown again. I'm sure you've heard about the boundary disputes."

"Basdown? To get there I must go through the Barrens, where there's no shelter at all, not even a tree!"

"You could remain here and await him if you would talk to a Truthken."

Should Zanja ignore her inexplicable aversion, to save herself from dying of exposure? She sighed. "If I start ignoring my own convictions, I'll have nothing left. Even my self will be lost. It's better to die."

"If you've got nothing to hide—" the young Paladin began.

"There are other reasons than fear or shame for keeping something hidden."

"What other reason could there be?"

"To avoid doing harm."

Such a possibility seemed beyond Orna's imagination, and she lapsed into silence.

Zanja's nose told her they were drawing close to the stable, for even the best-maintained stable stinks in springtime. The Paladin showed her through a doorway, and they felt their way up a black, narrow flight of stairs. Standing in pitch darkness, Zanja could hear Orna's hands rasping on wood, then a latch lifted and they entered a small, chilly room. The sound of rain had been muffled by stonework, but here it was suddenly loud. Orna said, "Oh, it's turned to sleet. I love that sound. Ouch!" She had thumped into something. "I found the bed," she said. "Why don't you take off your wet clothes and get under the covers, while I fetch food and fuel for you?"

After she left, Zanja followed the sound of sleet on shutters to the window. She first had to remove a waxed cloth screen and then wrestle open latches that were stiff with rust, only to get a face full of sleet for her pains. She was looking out at a continuous wet rooftop, all angles, punctuated regularly by towers and dormers, rather like Watfield might look if all its rooftops were joined into one.

She could have climbed out and gone walking across the top of the city. Thoughtful, blinking ice from her eyelashes, Zanja gazed out into the rain.

Chapter 11

During spring thaw the snow melts to an icy slush, beneath which water flows along the hard surface of the frozen soil. As the soil slowly thaws it turns to mud as soft as batter, and the liquid that inevitably finds its way into the best-greased boots deposits a fine silt that must be removed several times a day. Walking in snowmelt, the feet become stone blocks that are dragged from step to step. The sun shines but is an unreliable friend, warming the shoulders while leaving the legs and feet in winter. A traveler's most precious belonging becomes a pair of dry socks, tucked inside the shirt, protected by the rain cape until day's end.

Her feet warm and dry for the first time since dawn, Clement lay on the floor of a farmhouse parlor near a collection of boots that steamed on the hearth. The farmers had put an iron kettle of wet socks into the kitchen oven to dry, and the entire building smelled of wet wool. It was kind of the farmers to make this effort, though the soldiers' and Paladins' feet would be wet again almost as soon as the day's march began. Tomorrow was the day Karis had predicted that the rain would begin. The sun's friendship, halfhearted though it had been, would be much missed.

Clement was trying to read the little book Emil had given her before she left Watfield. One of his clerks had hand-copied a portion of *Ethics and Attentiveness* by a long-dead philosopher named Zhiva, and Emil had bound these pages in waxed leather. Clement kept the book tucked in her tunic alongside her dry socks, and in the evenings she was reading it—so slowly that she lost the sense of the sentences and had to reread, over and over, until she unintentionally memorized entire paragraphs.

She would not have wasted a moment on Zhiva's drivel, except that Saleen appeared to have been assigned her tutelage, and, much like Emil, he could be inexorable. Their company of thirty-seven was usually quartered in three or four households, but Saleen always contrived to share Clement's roof so he could be nearby to help her read the bloody book. He violated the Sainnite tradition of separating the sexes at night, for Paladins had no such tradition, and he even refused several offers to share farmers' beds, though the other Paladins quartered in other households were taking full advantage of that hospitality. Being a Paladin, one of Clement's officers had enviously noted, was not all work.

Now Saleen and one of the officers, Mereth, who was destined to be a lieutenant commander, sat in nearby armchairs while several other women officers already slept on the floor. The Paladin and soldier were exchanging polite, often nonsensical statements in alternating languages.

"I want eating the bread," said Saleen in Sainnese, though the farmers had been very generous with their food.

"Is this road for bakery?" asked Mereth solemnly in Shaftalese.

"Walk left at the—the big—"

"Fountain," suggested Mereth in Sainnese. But it was a word Saleen did not recognize, and Clement drowsily translated it for him.

"Oh, yes," said Saleen in Sainnese. "The fountain."

"Are you hunger for butter?"

"I hunger for all things," said Saleen. "Head-hunger."

"Curiosity," Mereth suggested. Her clipped hair looked as black and soft as cat's fur, and she had a rather square, strong-jawed face. Like Saleen, she was young to be an officer, yet she kept the balance between authority and flexibility far more naturally than some of the more experienced people.

"Curiosity," said Saleen. "That is head-hunger?"

Since the truce's beginning, the Paladins had been making steady progress in understanding their enemy's language, and now that Clement traveled with them, she saw how that progress was made. They constantly practiced with the Sainnites, and taught every new word to each other. By tomorrow all the Paladins would be using "fountain" and "curiosity" at every opportunity.

"What is this?" Clement grumbled. "A military mission? Or a training exercise?"

"We trade curiosity," said Saleen in Sainnese.

"It is school!" said Mereth triumphantly in Shaftalese.

"Lie down and go to sleep," Clement commanded twice, once in each language.

The next day, they plodded through a downpour. Once, the main roads in Shaftal had been passable from early spring to early winter, but during the years of occupation road repair had been neglected. Large sections of this road were now obscured by mud, and everywhere the cobblestones had been uprooted and overturned by frost. Clement found Mabin plodding beside her and said to her, "We could repair the roads."

Mabin's rain hood obscured all her features but the cold glitter of her gaze. She said, clipping each word as though she were trying to conceal her anger—which was how she always sounded, angry or not, "Your comment lacks a context."

"A disciplined force of people," Clement said, perversely deciding not to give Mabin what she requested. "Accustomed to cooperative tasks. The bigger and more visible the project, the better."

Mabin said sarcastically, "And not one soldier would feel demeaned by such brutal labor."

"They need work that's worth doing. And they'll do as they're told."

"They need to learn to work from obligation," said Mabin. "And they need to do it proudly. How will you engineer that, General?"

"How do you engineer it?"

Mabin said nothing for a few slogging steps. "We Shaftali used to worship the land, and still we treat it with reverence and humility. But you Sainnites are parasites—scavengers—and what is necessary to your survival is not that humble acceptance of the land's power. Instead, you have an arrogant belief in your own power. Why should you fear, or even take into consideration, the winds and weather, the fertility and resources, the shape and the moods of this land? These things are irrelevant to you. You take what you think you need, and you let others worry about how to replenish what you have consumed."

Clement said stiffly, "You may be right. But our history makes us what we are, just as yours does."

"So a new history is what you need."

Though Mabin had spoken sarcastically, Clement mulled over her statement long after they had parted. Since events of the future inevitably became events of the past, to engineer a new history actually was possible. One merely need to choose one's actions carefully, and allow enough time to pass.

Another Paladin, who in his rain cape looked much like everyone else, now walked beside her, picking his way across the tumbled cobblestones. "Saleen?" Clement asked.

"Yes, Clement." In the Shaftali style, he did not use formal address except in formal situations. "Are your feet wet yet?"

"My boots are soaked through. I believe the leather is dissolving."

"We'll need many new boots by the time we reach Wilton. I hope they have good cobblers."

"We'll all need new feet, I think."

"Yes, but there's not much a cobbler can do about that," said Saleen cheerfully. "The raven tells us to go cross-country here, to avoid high water. Towards that lopsided hill." He pointed. Clement shouted at the people strung out ahead of her, and they stepped off the road into the sucking mud.

She had thought it might be a relief to walk among trees, but the leafless branches did nothing to ease the downpour. The leaf mold was soft and springy underfoot, though, and she enjoyed that until the seepage of cold water numbed her toes.

"This philosopher, when did he live?" she asked Saleen.

"Zhiva was a woman, I believe. She lived during the years of Sperlin and Tadwell. It was near the end of her life that it first became possible to print books, and before that, the books were all hand-copied, like that one you carry. Most people had never set eyes on a book at all unless they were scholars at Kisha. All knowledge was spoken. It's strange to think of Shaftal without books!"

Clement said, "It's not so strange to me. I doubt one in ten of my people can read, and we have no books except records that nobody cares about."

"Imagine that your people suddenly made an effort to write and publish everything you know—everything that is usually taught the young by the old. Zhiva devoted the end of her life to putting this spoken philosophy into writing. Many people objected to her project, arguing that philosophy would be misrepresented by being written down. People said that writing ideas down obscured the fact that a person must come to these ideas, must work with them and make them real. If people merely read ideas, they might think that understanding comes only through the eyes."

"That explains why Zhiva insists so many times that words alone are without significance or value. But that business about the reader writing the book, what does that mean?"

Saleen responded by asking for her interpretation. They had walked all the way to the base of the lopsided hill before they finished discussing the four sentences of *Ethics and Attentiveness* that Clement had managed to decode the night before. After they left the scrubby trees, they crossed an open, barren, rocky countryside that ran with water. In the hollows water lay ankle-deep; elsewhere it flowed across stones in sheets and rivulets. The land looked flat to Clement, but still the water flowed southward, towards the Corber River. How did the water know which way to go?

They splashed through the puddles. Clement's people began singing a marching song to help them keep the pace up. The Paladins picked up the tune and some of the words, and for the rest of the song they practiced a babble of Sainnese words, including "curiosity" and "fountain." Where trees began to grow again, the road came back into sight, and there at a cluster of farmhouses people had come out on their porches to watch the group's approach. Clement caught a whiff of wood smoke and the mouthwatering scent of baking. She hoped desperately that these farmers could spare enough tea for them all to have a mouthful before they stepped out into the rain again.

Zhiva had finally finished instructing her reader how to read the book and had begun to explain the basic principles of ethical decision making, principles that struck Clement as both simpleminded and incomprehensible:

> Were all people just and upright, evil would never be done. Or, were it done (by failure of insight or misapprehension of the situation) it would be quickly halted and the damage repaired. But this is not the case: we surely need not waste our time arguing that all people are not just and upright; the evidence of our experience should be sufficient.

Like Clement, Saleen could repeat this passage word for word, and did so, several times. "Are you certain this book was written two hundred years ago?" asked Clement, for it had begun to seem that every encounter with Paladin philosophy would constitute a further condemnation of herself and her people. But Saleen gave her a puzzled look, and not for the first time, Clement wished he were a soldier like herself. With Saleen she could not help but feel defensive as she explained, "What's evil to one person may be just and upright to someone else." She remembered suddenly that she and Zanja had discussed something similar while climbing a staircase in Travesty.

"Oh, yes," said Saleen. "Always."

"But Zhiva says that one is right and one is wrong. Aren't they each wrong to the other?"

"Oh, yes. People kill each other over such disagreements."

"People like you and I."

Saleen smiled, showing his teeth a little. "Not yet, Clement."

Her fingers, jammed in wet gloves into wet coat pockets, gave an involuntary twitch.

"I hope not ever," Saleen added. "It would be very difficult for me to think of you, Mereth, Herme, and all these other companions as people I must kill. The goodness that is in you is easy to see! Your loyalty to each other, your devotion to duty, your amazing ability to act in concert—"

"The very qualities that have made us your bitter enemies for all these years," said Clement.

"Of course," said Saleen. "They are your strengths. And yet you must sacrifice them."

"Not yet," said Clement.

Clement expected that a book about making ethical decisions would at some point tell how to actually do it. But, through page after page of difficult text that Saleen insisted was easy, Zhiva drew close to such straightforward instruction, and each time pulled away again. In hand-to-hand combat, some people might fight like this: feint after feint, never actually striking a blow. Clement hated such fighters: hated them because she herself, not particularly talented with edged weapons, had herself won most often by dodging and trickery. She fought, Gilly was fond of saying, by clever avoidance, which seemed very similar to the philosopher's argument.

One very wet morning, she said, "Why doesn't she just tell me what to do?"

Saleen, nearly invisible in his rain cape, into which he had huddled like a cow into a shed, said in a muffled voice, "Oh, but she is, Clement. She is very clear."

"Where? How?"

"To make ethical decisions, be an ethical person. That is what she says."

"But it's nonsense!"

"How so?"

If Clement had a warm coat for every time Saleen asked her, "Why?" or "How?" she could outfit five battalions for the winter. She said, "Each half of Zhiva's argument is defined by the other half. How do I make ethical decisions? By being an ethical person. How can I be an ethical person? By making ethical decisions."

"Yes," said Saleen. "That is exactly what her opponents have said. You are doing very well, Clement!"

"What happens," she said through clenched teeth, "when two different people, each ethical by their own estimate, make ethical decisions that are diametrically opposed to each other?"

"You know what happens," said Saleen.

"It's decided who is right by who is the best fighter? That's not philosophy."

Saleen said, "I don't think Zhiva imagined the possibility of war. So I will tell you, not what Zhiva wrote, but what the Paladins have been saying among ourselves for many years: War is a failure of philosophy."

"Do you mean that philosophy can't account for war? Or that war occurred because of people failing to think properly?"

"Oh, we are still arguing about that," said Saleen. "Which do you think?"

"I think you people waste your lives in argument. War occurred because the Shaftali people refused to give the Sainnites anything to eat."

Saleen shook his head. "War occurred because Sainnites believe every problem can be resolved by force."

Sometimes, because Clement and Saleen conducted their discussions in Shaftalese, the nearby Paladins would join in, or would start their own arguments with each other. Lately, the Paladins would politely switch languages and limp along in Sainnese, and the soldiers were bored enough to actually participate. It seemed a bad idea to embroil their entire column in an argument about the cause of the war, but the rain had saved them from this outcome. People huddled in their oilskins, isolated from each other by their desire to avoid getting any wetter. The noise of the downpour had kept anyone from overhearing.

Clement said, "My people should have accepted starvation."

"Do you mean that? Is that a choice your people could have made?" asked Saleen, with a curiosity that seemed genuine.

"I doubt it. When people are faced with death, they never wonder whether it's better to die than to survive."

There was a silence. Then Saleen said, "Paladins do. Or we try to."

"Because you're all insane."

"Because sometimes it truly is better to die than to kill. And sometimes death is necessary to achieve the first principle of ethics."

"Ethical people might have to die in order to prevent evil from entering the world through them?"

"Yes, that is the case."

As Clement became friends with Saleen, she had come to appreciate the blend of sincerity and playfulness that constituted his character. Now he was somber.

She said, "Well, to my people a dead soldier is just a dead soldier."

"Is there nothing you would refuse to do on principle?"

Clement made herself consider this question seriously—Saleen's sturdy patience made her feel obligated to devote as much effort to this peculiar venture as he did. She finally said, "I do what works. If I do something that doesn't work, I have not done evil; I have merely made a mistake. I try not to repeat it."

"You would break your promise to the Shaftali people, if that is what would work? You would betray your friendships with Karis, Emil, and myself?"

"Not if I had a choice."

"What would you consider to be a choice? Would you betray a promise to keep from going hungry?"

"No, of course not."

"Would you do it to save your own life?"

"No."

"Would you do it to save your people from destruction?"

"Yes. And so would you."

"I would find another way," said Saleen.

"Bloody hell! Did Emil give you this task so you could instruct me in making third choices?"

Saleen's oilcloth crackled; he was either shaking his head or laughing. "It would be a failure of philosophy," he said, "To accept that there are only two choices."

"Sometimes there are only two choices, Saleen!"

She could see his teeth as he grinned in the shadow of his hood. "If I refuse to allow others to define my choices for me, then all doors remain open."

"In your mind, at least," she said. "But when you're in the middle of a sloppy, bloody, hand-to-hand fight, there is no philosophy."

"Exactly so," he said agreeably. "Therefore, we must aspire to avoid such fights."

"On this one thing," Clement said, "we can agree."

The rain eased occasionally, for as long as half a day at a time, almost as though the sky had kindly decided to give the saturated earth a chance to breathe. The raven detoured them up out of the Corber Valley—a hard climb on aching legs, followed by several long days on a rocky trail through rough country. Sometimes they traveled along a ridge, where the trees dropped away and they could see the flooded river. The streams that fed it were torrents, and the farmsteads that scattered the valley were islands of high ground surrounded by a sheen of water.

"Are you learning anything?" Mabin asked Clement one day, when the vagaries of weather and travel had once again thrown them together on the trail.

"I'm learning that I'm old," gasped Clement, "and not as smart as I should be." The trail was steep and slippery with mud, and her legs wobbled like warped wagon wheels.

"It's always possible to get older and stupider," said Mabin, who did not appear to even be out of breath.

"I appreciate the encouragement," said Clement. She scrabbled for footing and got herself to flat ground, with soldiers and Paladins grimly scrambling up behind her. It was not exactly raining, but a cold mist filled the air. Clement was muddy to the thigh and soaked to the skin in spite of her rain cape. A breathless Paladin set the raven on a gnarled tree branch, where the bird stretched his wings and then let fall a great gob of crap.

"Oh, the soul-stirring glamour of a Paladin's joyful life," the Paladin commented in Sainnese.

"The glory of soldier courage!" exclaimed Mareth in Shaftalese.

"Fidelity! Solidarity!"

"Philosophy," Clement muttered.

They crowded the rocky ridge, gasping with breathless laughter, holding onto each other to keep from sliding back down the hillside. Soon after they had started walking again, the mist congealed into rain, and the soldiers launched into a complaint song that the Paladins had taught them:

> Sky, why must you rain on me?
> I've got such a distance to go—
> Across the Midlands all the way to the sea
> And south to Keneso.
>
> The rain it keeps on falling, falling
> It isn't going to end
> The river is rising—I'm drowning in mud—
> What misery this weather portends!

One morning, Clement was seeking the outhouse in the privy yard of the farmhouse in which she had slept, when in the corner of her eye she spotted a furtive movement. It was a dark dawn. Black storm clouds still clotted the sky, shutting out the sun and dooming the sodden land below to twilight. All colors looked gray, so it might not have been a gray uniform she had spotted, drawing back into the shelter of a massive, leafless vine. Surely it was one of the farmers, shyly pulling back at the sight of a sleep-groggy Sainnite slogging through the mud.

After Clement had finished in the outhouse, she reentered the house and then went quietly out the front door, stepping softly around the house and pausing at a distance where she could see and not be seen.

At first, though, she saw nothing. And then she saw a sudden movement that her mind interpreted as violent, except that afterwards all was motionless again. She sorted shapes out in the gloaming, and gradually her eye began to perceive something that she wanted to call both wonderful and impossible: Paladin black and Sainnite gray, entangling, disentangling, stumbling apart, inexorably drawing together again. The water-burdened air swallowed sound, and yet Clement could hear a panting, laughing murmur.

Later, when her composite company was reconstituted and walking forward again, Clement said quietly to Saleen, "I have an ethical problem. What am I to do, when I discover a woman soldier has seduced or been seduced by a man, who is a Paladin?"

After a silence, Saleen said, "I have recently learned that such an alliance is doubly forbidden for a woman soldier, so I imagine that she would be secretive and he would find her hesitation difficult to understand. I imagine that the problems of language might prevent him at first from understanding that it is wrong for her to come to him. And once he understands, they would agree to keep apart from each other."

All this hypothetical speech tried Clement's patience. "In the meantime, has Mereth gotten pregnant?"

"Of course not!" He seemed quite shocked.

"See that it stays that way, Commander."

"Yes, General Clement. But I must ask, how do you justify your position on this matter? Since you have a child, and have taken Shaftali lovers?"

Clement was not in the mood to explain how a soldier's potential lovers are radically reduced by every promotion, or how and why her people had always increased their numbers through adoption. She said, "I outrank Mereth."

"That is your entire justification? And that is acceptable to your followers?" Saleen shook his head in disbelief. "I will never understand you Sainnites!"

Chapter 12

Zanja dreamed that Karis walked down a long road carrying a starving infant in her arms. The river rose, flooding the land with water as far as the eye could see. Karis paced up and down the water's edge, and the infant began to wail. "The road is still there," Zanja said. But Karis did not hear.

"Wake up, madam. My apologies for walking in, but you didn't hear me knock."

"Orna?" Zanja said blearily.

A shadow in the dim room, Orna fingered the thick woolen clothing that Zanja had hung haphazardly on the pegs. "Your clothing has hardly dried at all!"

"I was too tired to keep the fire alive." Resigned, Zanja sat up, rubbing her face to get the blood moving. "It doesn't matter—I'm just going out into the rain again."

Orna gestured at a bundle on the floor. "That's a tallow-cloth cape, and some travel rations for the Barrens."

"Well!" said Zanja with sleepy surprise. "That won't have been your commander's idea."

"She says I'll understand her harshness when I have her responsibilities. But I'd rather not ever understand such a thing."

Zanja ate the porridge and bread that the young Paladin had brought for her. Putting on her sodden clothing was about as pleasant as rolling naked in snow. "Thank you," she said as Orna helped her fasten the stiff cape. "You've made the remainder of my journey seem almost possible."

"But you can hardly walk! I hope you can find somewhere to rest."

"The people of Shaftal have been surprisingly hostile. But I never expected to be denied shelter in this house, where border people are supposedly welcome."

"I think you're being unjust—" began Orna.

"If you met with a disaster and arrived at a strange farmstead seeking help, would you expect to be treated like a stray dog?"

"Of course not. But I'd explain to the farmers why I was in such straits."

"Yes, but before anyone even asked for an explanation, you would have been wrapped in blankets by a roaring fire, your hurts would have been tended, and you would have been given as much as you wanted to eat. 'What the land gives to one is given to all,' the farmers would say."

"You're quoting Mackapee?" said the novice in astonishment.

"I beg your pardon. I persist in forgetting that I'm an uneducated tribal woman."

The young woman did not speak again until they had descended the stairs and once again were following the Perimeter Way. The rain had stopped, and cloud-muffled sunlight coming in through the windows seemed dazzling after so many dark days. The young Paladin's face was flushed with anger, or embarrassment, or both.

Cold in her wet clothing, limping in her waterlogged boots, cranky with sleeplessness, Zanja made no attempt to mend Orna's feelings. They walked in silence, passing through areas of muffled sound: children reciting, a man singing, a dog barking, people conversing. Yet the Perimeter Way remained vacant but for the two of them.

Zanja said in a low voice, "I am not in the House of Lilterwess at all, am I? I am still outside."

"I did all I could for you," the young woman said.

"And now you expect me to assuage your guilt by acting more grateful."

Orna set her mouth in a line. When they reached the guard room, where the commander impatiently awaited them, Orna said, "Here is your blade. I can't imagine what you need it for."

If Zanja told the young woman how many people she had killed in combat using that dagger or other weapons, she would have been appalled. In this Shaftal, where the doors had neither locks nor bars, where Paladins were unarmed doorkeepers and farmers were ignorant of what lay beyond their farm boundaries, Zanja may well have been considered a murderer even though she had never killed except by necessity. Musing on this unpleasant thought, she took her leave with cold courtesy and turned her back on the legendary House of Lilterwess.

Overhead the clouds had thinned enough to admit a diffused glare of light from the hidden sun. But from the northeast, where spring storms march hard on each other's heels, black clouds crept ominously southward, extinguishing the landscape behind them. The tallow-cloth cape crackled in the cold wind as Zanja limped down the walled lane. When she reached the main road, she finally could view the spectacular pile of the House of Lilterwess. Perched on a hilltop, escorted by squadrons of leafless orchards, dressed in the ragged remains of summer's blooming vines, the massive building seemed both grandiose and accidental: a mountainous, random configuration of towers and peaked rooftops wrapped in a package of tightly fitted stone. A thick haze of smoke trailed away from its multitude of chimneys, and here and there people were standing on balconies and rooftops, enjoying a few moments outside before the new storm arrived. The hillside was busy with activity: horses let out to exercise wheeled around a muddy field; carts hauling manure or big pots of night earth rolled away toward distant middens; laundry flapped in the cold breeze. Even the gardeners stood out in their walled plots, perhaps inspecting winter damage or arguing about where to plant the peas.

These people are all dead, thought Zanja—or I am not yet born. This Shaftal is just a memory—or my Shaftal is just a possibility.

She walked until the rain again began to fall. Then she turned around and retraced her steps.

The House of Lilterwess came into sight again: the laundry brought in, the horses stabled, the manure carts sheltered, the windows shuttered. Zanja could scarcely see the building through the driving rain. Certainly she, a small speck, shapeless in a cape the color of earth, was invisible to anyone who might be looking her way. She climbed the wall that edged the lane, circled the hill, and approached the pile through a park in which shapely pine trees overlooked straw-blanketed flower beds. The rope that she had stolen from the stable during the night still hung undisturbed from the chimney where she had secured it. She had chosen that spot carefully, and there were two window ledges and a balcony to support her vertical ascent up the outside wall. But even with the knots she had tied in the rope giving purchase, it was not an easy climb. When at last she hauled herself with trembling muscles over the roof's edge, she sprawled there gasping, with rainwater run-nelling past her down the gray slate. She had climbed sheer rock faces for the thrill of it when she was young and fearless, and this looming building was not much different from a mountain precipice. But she was neither young nor fearless anymore.

Barefoot, with the rope gathered up and wrapped around her waist, she crept across slippery, creaking slate. Sometimes she heard muffled voices behind the walls and shutters. Mostly she heard only the din of rain on stone. The rooftop was a mysterious, dangerous landscape, and the previous night's landmarks looked unfamiliar now. Twice she fumbled her footing and fell, but no one seemed to notice the racket even when a slate broke and cut open her knee with its jagged edge.

The shutters, left unlatched, had blown open. In the room within, the blankets had been folded away in a cabinet and the ashes emptied from the stove. She stripped off her sodden clothing and wrapped it in the tallow-cloth cape to keep from dribbling telltale puddles down the hall. These remote rooms were unlikely to be used again until comfort-able travel became possible. She picked the most inconvenient room, hung up her wet clothes, took the blankets from the cabinet, and lay down, groaning with exhaustion on the bed. She would sleep. When everyone else slept, she would go scavenging for food. If she was to be treated as a stray animal, she would act like one.

Weariness had replaced her anger and bewilderment. Loneliness echoed in a hollow behind her breastbone. She yearned for the sensa-tion of Karis's solid bulk pressed against her back. But Karis did not exist. Nothing Zanja loved existed, not even the Land of Shaftal itself.

Perhaps Zanja dwelt among a thousand people, but she shared the shadows only with the cats that patrolled the dark labyrinth. She did occasionally spot a distant Paladin on night duty, but otherwise, people kept out of the hallways after the lamps had been put out. She found the courtyard in the building's center: a garden, overhung with balco-nies, where trees and fountains and blooming flowers would soon lure the long-confined residents out of doors. For now, though, it lay bar-ren and under water. She learned that people generally lived on the second floor and worked on the first. She found three separate dining rooms: one ornate, one comfortable, and one plain—and three separate kitchens, all with locked larders—the only locks in that entire building. However, in the kitchen that went with the comfortable dining room, Zanja discovered that a kind cook set aside some food in a cupboard every evening for the people who could not sleep. It was usually bread and cheese; occasionally an apple or some butter; rarely a bit of meat. She drew all the water she wanted from cisterns, enough to bathe herself and wash her undergarments with stolen soap. She found firewood and kindling and even a candle. She had little need for light, though: she had nothing to read, and when she was not skulking through the hallways, she slept. She was so tired that several days passed before she even became aware of the tedium of those solitary days and nights.

During Zanja's imprisonment after the massacre of her people, she had also been alone all the time, within yet isolated from the world. Then the time had passed strangely, sometimes in swift flashes of awareness with long black stretches between them, and sometimes creeping. Now she felt a similar displacement.

She had become accustomed to relying on the wit and intelligence of her friends. Now, with no one to talk to, she felt stupid as well as lonely. She imagined Emil: gray hair tied back with a thong at the nape of his neck, furrowed face and lively brown eyes, laugh lines deepening as he turned from his lamplit worktable to face her where she sat on the Ashawala'i rug by the fireplace. "Haven't you bound that book yet?" Zanja asked him.

Emil glanced ruefully at the battered old book that still awaited his attention. "Poor Gerunt," he said. "What arguments he and Zhiva must have had! I'll get around to rebinding the book soon. I've had a number of distractions."

He seemed to perceive the whole of her in that unique way of his, and continued, "My dear, you are in a pickle. Before you can resolve anything you must accept the reality of the place you are in."

"But I don't belong here!"

"How can you be so certain of that?" Emil asked. "And what choice do you have?"

The daydream ended abruptly. She sat up in bed, listening, but she heard only silence. The rain began a muted patter on the slates.

Her glyph cards, like her dagger and her rope, lay ready for her to snatch up should she need to flee out the window onto the rooftops.

She took the cards out of their water-stiffened pouch, but she did not attempt to undo the bindings. She had tried to make herself both invisible and insignificant to the seers, intuitives, and sensitives that certainly lived here. A deliberate exercise of her fire talent, even in private, would make the presence of the silent stranger living in the vacancies of that great house much more noticeable. She did not dare ask the cards whether she was in danger, or what that danger was.

Later in the night she padded down cavernous hallways, yearning to see these passages by daylight, to push through a crowd of air children or young philosophers, to see the councilors consulting gravely with each other, to be part of the bustle she distantly sensed during the day. The cook of the comfortable kitchen had actually put a small meat pie in the cupboard. She wished blessings on her benefactor and ate right there in the kitchen. Perhaps the cook imagined that a pregnant woman overtaken by unpredictable appetites was consuming so much food.

She lit her candle and made her way to the school rooms. In one, the students seemed to be engaged in the enormous, tedious project of hand-copying the Law of Shaftal. On each desk lay a similar sheaf of papers, filled on both sides with carefully numbered paragraphs of script. In this law school, apparently, the teacher stood at this lectern, reading out loud while the students wrote the teacher's exact words, day after day. Air witches forget nothing, so this dreary method certainly guaranteed that the students knew their material. What tedium, though! Zanja sat at a desk and borrowed a student's pen and ink to redraw the washed-out images on her glyph cards. She drew Nurture first, thinking of Mari, the rarity of whose kindness Zanja had not known to appreciate. Her version of the nursing mother was a cartoon compared to the original.

Now, Death-and-Life. She dipped the pen and drew the glyph, which was a plain pattern of overlapping lines. The ghostly shape of the half-burned woman's skeleton had survived the water, and she could follow the pattern with the pen tip, remembering with a jolt of fondness the winter day J'han had drawn this card for her.

There was a sound, the slightest sigh of door hinges. Zanja's hand jerked with startlement, spattering the stiff, warped paper with ink. She blew out the candle, scooped up her cards, and dropped to the floor.

"There is no other way out," a man's voice said reasonably to her. "You might as well step forward."

So her night vision might be restored, she avoided looking at the light he carried—a bowl lamp with a sputtering wick. The little flame cast long shadows, and she slipped swiftly from one into the next. Rain pounded on the closed shutters, obscuring the small sound of her movements.

"You are in the front corner near the lectern," said the man patiently.

Zanja drew herself into a squat. "I just wanted pen and ink," she said.

"Most people need not steal supplies from hard-working students."

Zanja did not reply. She did not move, either, as the man walked toward her. He moved like a blade fighter. He was armed. If Zanja clashed directly with him she might win, but not quietly. And any violence in this peaceful place would not be forgotten or forgiven. She must surrender again.

He paused at a distance. "Four nights you have been lurking in this house. I feel your restless, aimless presence in my sleep, and I awaken feeling that something important lies just out of reach."

"My presence is not worth noticing, sir. And I am doing nothing wrong: The Law of Shaftal permits the starving to steal bread and the homeless to demand shelter when hospitality is denied them."

"You were denied hospitality in the House of Lilterwess?"

"I was. But I plan to leave as soon as the sky clears. So I ask that you let me be; let me keep my secret, until the end of mud season."

She heard a sound, but the man had merely set down his lamp on one of the desks. He walked away from the light. It was now possible to escape past him, but instead Zanja looked directly at him. The diffused glow made him a sculpture of light and shadow: cheeks and eyes were dark hollows; chin, cheekbone, nose and forehead were sharp with illumination. His black hair cascaded down his back in a hundred slim braids.

She felt that she could not breathe. She stood up.

He said with bland courtesy, "I would be honored if you would share tea with me."

"It would be my pleasure to accept." Zanja spoke as he did, executing the ritual of friendship that was only necessary between strangers. But through this simple exchange they had each implied a promise: I will not harm you. I will not betray you.

She picked up her candle, neatened the desk, and followed him.

Chapter 13

Zanja's host's lamp flame dimly revealed a room filled with the warm, soft colors of northern dyed wool: the brownish green that comes from the bark of a sturdy shrub that blooms with its roots still in snow; the reddish brown from the skin of wild onions; the black from the under-ripe nuts of a high-altitude tree; the bright green of a certain clay that in Zanja's time had become difficult to find. Rugs, each of a different pattern, covered the walls and floor; the new piled on top of the old so that the floor was as soft and springy as the ground in a pine forest. The space was as like an Ashawala'i clan house as art could make it.

The man's nest of blankets also were of Ashawala'i make, as was his tunic, the intricate red border of which told Zanja he was a na'Morlen, which was a fire clan like the na'Tarweins. From his belt, which was woven of deerskin strips in the same pattern, his dagger, tied in its sheath, hung at an angle across the small of his back. He had not taken the time to knot his braids, which hung loose to his waist. He knelt at the hearth to build up the fire. Noticing that Zanja still stood in the doorway, he said formally, "Enter and be welcome. Share my fire."

There were tears in Zanja's throat. She said hoarsely in the language of her people, "The blessings of the nine gods be upon this dwelling." For seven years she had only spoken that language in her dreams, when she visited the land of the dead to be chided and accused by her murdered kinsmen. The first time she had visited there after her hair was shorn, the retribution-hungry ghosts had told her it was proper that she had short hair like an outcast, for she should be ashamed of her refusal to seek revenge.

She tugged her one surviving braid out of her shirt collar where she had tucked it so it would not drag in the ink.

The katrim looked at the braid, then at her face. Then he somewhat belatedly replied to her ritual greeting: "The nine gods bless your dwelling, also."

Zanja took a seat beside the hearth. It was not proper for a guest to initiate conversation, but her host said nothing. As he certainly was the Speaker of the Ashawala'i, he also was a fire blood like herself, likely to accurately guess the answer to a puzzle, but unlikely to ask questions and demand explanations. So, as he certainly puzzled over the oddity—impossibility—of an Ashawala'i who was a stranger to him, she considered the question of why the Speaker of the Ashawala'i was here in the House of Lilterwess rather than where he should have been at this time of year, at home in the Asha Valley. Something must have delayed him in the autumn until snow closed the door of the pass.

Her presence would not be easy for him to account for. He gazed into the fireplace. Zanja shut her eyes and took a deep breath of the vegetable-dyed goatswool. It was the smell of home.

She did not want to lie to a katrim. But only to the G'deon did she dare tell the truth. How could she answer this man's questions—the questions he wouldn't even ask—without lying and without engaging his imagination? It was impossible. She should have allowed him to assume she was from another tribe; but, like many of her insights, this one came too late.

She took another breath of the familiar scent. When she had last stood in the Asha Valley she had smelled only blood and smoke. But this was the smell of a strong, proud, ancient people, a people whose skilled spinning and weaving allowed them to survive the harsh mountain climate. Fourteen days Zanja had wandered this alien Shaftal, but only now did it occur to her that in this Shaftal, her people were not yet lost beyond retrieval. She had not yet failed to protect them from the Sainnites—and she might finally lay down her dreadful burden of culpability.

Medric spoke in her memory: All that happened because of that massacre would not have happened at all. Karis would be a smoke-addicted metalsmith. Emil would be killed fighting Heras in South Hill, and Medric's visions would be what killed him. And Leeba would not have been conceived.

The Speaker had turned his gaze to her. She felt his attention but did not open her eyes. The teakettle began hissing and humming. She heard the man rise to pour the water into a stone pitcher so the ambient chill would cool it to the correct temperature. She heard him measure tea into a teapot and pour a small amount of water over it. He swirled the water and tea leaves. Zanja sniffed loudly to let him know the grassy aroma had reached her. He poured and swirled, again and again. She opened her eyes as he filled two tiny cups and set them on a tray between the two of them.

She matched her movements to his, taking up her cup at the same moment he did, holding it to her nose, then slurping noisily. The tea was perfect: hot but not scalding, strong but not bitter. Their empty cups touched the wooden tray at the same moment, with the same nearly inaudible ringing of rare porcelain.

He said, "I am Arel na'Morlen, the Speaker for the Ashawala'i."

"I am Zanja na'Tarwein. Once I also was the Speaker for the Ashawala'i, but now I am a ghost."

He did not blink; nor did he object or seem surprised. What a gift it was, that fire blood's talent for absorbing and accepting the incredible!

She said, "My hair was cut in ritual, to separate me from all that bound me, so I could cross more easily between worlds. I am a wanderer but not an exile. However, it has been seven years since I saw or spoke to a kinsman."

"Seven years!" Arel paused. "You must miss dancing the katra."

This is a clever man, Zanja thought. A knife-dancer's skill was impossible to feign. She stood up and waited for him to untie the holdfasts on his dagger sheath, then they drew their blades, struck a traditional opening pose, and began to dance.

Shortly after the hostile beginning of her difficult relationship with Norina, the Truthken had commented sarcastically, "You fight as though it were a courtship." Zanja, though appalled by Norina's efficient violence, also had learned that beauty and artfulness had no place in war. Yet she had continued to practice her solitary katra, the one that kept evolving with the changes of her body and character. And she had taught many of the traditional katra sequences to Emil during the five years they lived as a family. Thus she was not nearly as out of practice as she could have been, and she and Arel were closely matched. When she was able to cease worrying that she might cut him with her supernaturally sharp dagger, she began to enjoy herself.

They danced. The rhythmic ringing of their blades was the music they danced to.

And then the dance began to change. Arel improvised, challenging her to improvise in return. Zanja's reactions became reflexive—and unavoidably self-revealing. And then she tripped on the edge of a carpet and fell, and Arel's blade pressed lightly against her throat.

He was breathing heavily. His sculptured face glittered with droplets of sweat. His predator's eyes were in shadow. She laughed out loud. "I protest! I was not defeated by you, but by the carpet!"

He grinned and sat back on his heels. They clasped left hands to left wrists and so counterbalanced each other as they rose up from the floor and slid their blades back into their sheaths.

"You're recovering from an illness," Zanja commented.

"You're under an alien influence," he replied.

"I doubt my own relatives would recognize me," she said.

"I had an ailment of the lungs in the autumn. Would you like more tea?"

They returned to the fireplace and knelt again on either side of the tea tray, but now formality had become unnecessary. "I cannot account for you at all," said Arel. "You call yourself a ghost, but you're alive enough to make me bleed." He gestured at his slashed sleeve, where some drops of blood now glowed.

"I'm afraid my blade is very sharp," Zanja said. "I am a living ghost, alive but out of time. Half a month ago, I crossed a boundary of water into this world. I have been cold, wet, hungry, angry, and bewildered nearly every moment, and I understand no more about why I am here than I did when I first arrived."

Arel grunted. "You are very good at replying without answering. You are indeed a Speaker." He offered his hand—his right hand this time—and Zanja clasped it. "My sister, whatever world you are from, and whatever world you are going to, you are here now, and I am glad to welcome you. Stay with me—not as an outcast or ghost but as my guest. Perhaps I can help resolve your mystery."

Zanja had to take a deep breath before she could reply, her heart was swelling so. "I wish I could give you an assurance that I will cause no trouble, but trouble seems to always follow me—"

"Trouble is good!" Arel's face had come alive. "Your presence is wonderful!"

"It is?" Zanja gazed at this man, her forbear, her twin. His statement was like the sun breaking through the gray misery of rain. "It is wonderful," she breathed. "Yes, it truly is."

Zanja shared Arel's bed, as she would have shared the bed of any katrim. In the morning, with her clothing sponged and pressed, her hair combed and her boots oiled, she walked beside him through the lively hallways, where young people rushed to their classrooms or duties, Paladins passed in energetically talking groups, and a wonderful mix of vague, intent, hurried, or aimless people made their way to and from the dining rooms. Arel assured Zanja that Truthkens, being jealous of their every privilege, did not eat in the less ornate dining rooms. So she went in with him, to take a bowl of hot porridge from a harassed cook, and to sit shoulder to shoulder with people who were the stuff of legends. Those to her left were loudly discussing the relative merits of two breeds of sheep. Those across the table seemed sullen over the continuing bad weather. At her right, Arel looked over the crowd with an interest as lively as her own, until he abruptly lowered his head and muttered, "Unfortunately, the house commander is approaching."

Zanja nonchalantly ate her apple-studded porridge with genuine enjoyment until the commander's hand closed painfully on her shoulder.

"Good morning, Commander," said Arel.

"How did this woman get in?"

"She climbed to the roof and entered through a window, as any mountain person could have done. Not everyone walks only on flat ground like cows and horses."

"This time she will leave under escort."

"She will not leave at all, Commander."

"No one enters this house without my permission, no matter who it is!"

"My sister regrets that she was forced to violate this custom. May I ask why she was not given shelter at this deadly time of year?"

In the crowded room all conversations had ceased as people listened with undisguised curiosity to this fiercely polite conversation. The Paladin commander glared around herself, and some of the people began to make a pretense of eating, but many did not.

A Speaker's status was ambiguous: protected rather than elevated, under no one's command other than the G'deon's but expected to practice exemplary behavior. That flexible combination of expectations and independence, Zanja's old master had said, was beneficial to everyone. Right now it was beneficial to Zanja.

Arel laid a hand on Zanja's arm and said in their own language, "Don't do anything that will cause me to laugh." He looked up at the commander and said in Shaftalese, "I am explaining to my sister why I must promise you that she will behave properly." Then he said to Zanja, "Pretend to be offended."

"But I am a katrim!" Zanja said in Shaftalese.

"Still, you must accept my guidance in this matter," said Arel.

Zanja made a rude gesture, which Arel pretended was a gesture of assent. He said, "Commander, I give you my word of honor that Zanja na'Tarwein will conduct herself honorably." His expression was utterly serious, except for his eyes. The house commander abruptly lifted her hand from Zanja's shoulder and stalked away, leaving Arel and Zanja to struggle to finish their breakfast without choking on their own laughter. And now, at last, she was free to walk in the House of Lilterwess by daylight.

Despite the malaise that commonly beset people at this time of year—a gloom, lethargy, or outright surliness of temperament—the House of Lilterwess bustled with energetic activity. Zanja felt as if she had gone from being a ghostly haunt in a nearly vacant city to being a holidaymaker caught up in a lively crowd. Everyone's business seemed urgent, and most of it also seemed joyful. The purposeful activity was punctuated by unexpected entertainments: the intentional ones of musical performances and bits of staged dramas, and the unintentional ones of inexplicable behavior, intriguing conversation, and angry shouting behind closed doors.

Zanja and Arel were rare indeed, not just because they were the only border people in that wonderful place, but also because they had no burden of responsibilities. Arel showed Zanja his favorite places: a fountain, a gallery, a covered walkway where they could view the hills rolling away like ripples towards the distant sea.

"I have never seen the ocean," Zanja said.

"You haven't? Oh, it is a marvel. And it is intoxicating, also. Anyone who lingers beside that vast water becomes either peaceful or silly. Yet it is very dangerous."

Later they walked among the classrooms, where children of similar age, demeanor, and dress were variously learning their letters, reciting history, debating each other, practicing musical instruments and more useful tools, naming the bones of a wired-together human skeleton, and working sums on slates. Zanja was so drawn to more than one class that Arel had to pull her away.

"I myself have taken up several subjects over the years," he admitted. "Currently I'm interested in history and mathematics."

"Mathematics!"

"It is a mysterious and frustrating subject. But mathematicians can predict eclipses and the movements of the stars!"

Zanja could not see any use in that ability but didn't say so. "Do they hold classes on interpreting glyphs?"

"Glyphs? Now there's a peculiar subject."

"I suppose so. But it has long interested me."

"Well, every Speaker is an eccentric, they say. Most glyph masters teach at the university, of course. But we do have a Paladin here who teaches a kind of class."

Soon, Arel went away to attend his mathematics class, leaving Zanja seated in a plain wooden chair in a group much smaller and less uniform than the classes she had observed. Many wore Paladin's black but were of every age and rank. All were fire bloods. Zanja wondered if she had been foolhardy for letting Arel introduce her into so curious and insightful a group, but her arrival was scarcely noticed.

On an easel, illuminated by lamps, stood a large, stunningly beautiful glyph illustration. It showed a scene of mountains framed by fantastic vines and stylized clouds, with a sunset that seemed to glow with its own light, a light that was in turn reflected in the water of a lake that stood in the middle distance. In the foreground a weary traveler reclined against a tree, with his walking stick and knapsack beside him. Though the traveler was at the end of his life, he looked forward rather than backward, wondering what he would discover beyond the setting sun. Zanja was familiar with that glyph illustration, for it was included in her card pack, one of a group called the Four Directions that each illustrated a person in one of the borderlands of Shaftal. This glyph, the one titled West, was often also called A Traveler in the Land of Endings.

The group had already been discussing the illustration for some time when Zanja joined them. Soon the glyph master, who was younger than many of the students, removed the painting from the easel to carefully wrap it in a cover of soft leather. Its gilding flashed and glittered as it was turned before the lamp flame. She saw its unpainted side and realized it was a piece of copper, green with age.

The teacher unwrapped a new illustration and lifted it to the easel. He spoke briefly, giving information about the glyph's relationship to other glyphs and the particular glyph group it belonged to, but Zanja lacked the knowledge to appreciate this learned commentary. It did not matter—even the name of the glyph was irrelevant. She gazed at the painting, stunned.

It was the glyph she had imagined: Clement's name sign. A woman on her knees cupped a flower bulb in her hand. Its roots clasped and intertwined her fingers instead of earth, and its brilliant flower bloomed in the light that radiated like sun from her face. All around her a fantastic array of people and creatures intertwined, struggled with, and destroyed each other. But she heeded only the flower.

When the class ended, Zanja felt as though she were awakening from a lengthy and not particularly restful meditation. She stood up stiffly as the others also yawned and stretched and spoke a few muted words to each other. They left the room and paced dazedly away in various directions. For a few moments Zanja could not remember where she was, or where she should go. She felt drained of energy and ravenously hungry. She doubted that Arel's mathematics class would leave him feeling this way.

"The class was odd—and marvelous," she told him when they met in the fountain courtyard, where now a cluster of young flute players hooted and wailed on their instruments.

"Let us flee this racket," said Arel. He added, as they turned down the hall toward the dining room, "Everything odd is marvelous."

"Of course it is. But I have discovered that I accurately imagined a glyph, both its name and its meaning, though I had never seen or heard of it before. That is even more odd and marvelous than usual, don't you think?"

She told him about Blooming, about its emphasis on the importance of the patient attention necessary to bring a dormant possibility into being, and of the danger posed by the constant distraction of more immediate demands that are more easily and less effortfully fulfilled.

"Ah, my sister, these glyphs are like the gods to you," he said, as they joined the line of people waiting to enter the dining room.

"I do see the gods in the glyphs," Zanja admitted. "To think that there are a thousand of these paintings, carefully stored somewhere nearby... I could almost remain here the rest of my life so I could study them all."

Arel shook his head at her, benignly indulgent in the face of an enthusiasm he did not share. "But you cannot remain here, can you? For it is your doom to cross again to yet another world."

After a midday meal of bean soup with bread, which was exactly what Zanja would expect to be served on an ordinary day in her own Shaftal, Arel took Zanja visiting. She sat quietly in one room while he discussed poetry with several friends, and in another room while he discussed vegetable gardening with some more. A gardener gave Arel a packet of seeds, a variety of green pea that would not drown even in exceptionally wet weather. "The seeds are for the farmers of the Asha Valley," explained Arel to Zanja. "If the weather allows me to go home before the spring planting season is over!"

They had walked to the Perimeter Way, so Arel could take the daily brisk walk that a healer had advised. They were not alone in this activity, for as farmers exercise their plow horses to condition them for the hard work ahead, so also many people were conditioning themselves for the journeys and labors of the coming warm season. Paladins loped around and around in organized groups, and despite the fast pace still managed to converse with each other. Others made the circuit less swiftly, in pairs or alone. Zanja watched for the shorn heads and white robes of Truthkens, but saw none. Perhaps they were carried everywhere they went, and so did not need to harden themselves to travel. She found it difficult to imagine Norina requiring or accepting such treatment.

The setting sun seemed to have hammered a hole through the clouds, for on the western side of the building red sunlight was cast in slanted squares on the walls opposite the high windows. The light made the people who passed here seem ruddy with good health. Arel and

Zanja had been discussing her situation as well as they could, considering that she felt reluctant to reveal any details. "I have never seen or even heard of a living water witch," said Arel.

"I actually did meet one once—I didn't spend much time with him, though."

Up ahead, on the southern side of the perimeter near the front door, a confusion of people had clustered. Paladins who had loped past Zanja and Arel several times had come to a halt there, as had many others, who peered curiously around those in front of them.

"Oh!" exclaimed Arel. "But why has he returned so soon? That cannot bode well."

Zanja's faculties drew taut, like a bow being strung. She said regretfully, "This leisure has been so pleasant!"

The collected people began to move back as if in response to an invisible pressure from within the crowd. Then a hole broke open, and out squeezed a number of filthy Paladins in dripping rain capes, whose faces even at this distance appeared gaunt with tiredness. They pressed the people back to create a wider passage for more of their travel-weary fellows, who in turn added their bodies to the human wall. Finally a short, stocky man walked swiftly down the passage they had built. Behind him, in a neat choreography, the Paladins reshaped themselves into an escort. Others, perhaps out of curiosity or just out of habit, trailed behind the escort so that it was a group of twenty or thirty people that bore down on Zanja and Arel.

They stepped back to make room for this crowd. But the short man headed directly towards them. He was as muddy as his companions, but unlike them did not appear tired. His wide girth, Zanja realized, was an illusion created by muscle, not by fat. Even his hands looked powerful, with thick fingers, coarse skin, big wrists, and veins that popped out when he clenched his hands into fists. His momentum did not slow at all, so it seemed he were going to crush them up against the wall like a falling boulder. Then, within arm's reach, he suddenly halted: a pugnacious figure with his feet apart, his chin jutting forward, his nostrils flaring and narrowing with each breath.

His glare carried the momentum forward, so that Zanja felt its impact like a blow. She had distantly heard Arel murmur a warning in their shared tongue, but already she stood frozen, with her hands well away from her dagger even though like Arel she had knotted the holdfasts.

The man uttered a growl of words: "What are you?"

She said, "Tadwell G'deon, I must talk to you in private."

Then she cried sharply, as his hand reached as if to grasp her wrist, "Do not touch me!"

Chapter 14

Seth was not the only person seeking refuge in Garland's kitchen. Though his operation was vast, complex, and highly organized, it still remained a place where farmers like Seth could find familiar, soothing work at any hour. She peeled a lot of vegetables: carrots, turnips, potatoes, and onions. The peels went into the broth pot and the rest would be chopped, fried, boiled, and used in one or another recipe, eventually winding up being fed to an unending, unpredictable, appreciative, and always hungry crowd. Karis came in every day to sharpen the knives and scour the pots, and Garland often cooked a meal only for her. The G'deon's appetite seemed a measure of her state of mind, and she wasn't eating well for a person so large and hard working.

If Seth noticed that the pots were less than pristine or the knives were becoming somewhat dull, she went looking for Karis, often bearing something from Garland's oven—something simple, like a small loaf, trailing the toasty, rich scent of fresh-baked bread. She almost always found Karis in her bedroom in a big chair by the window, watching the rain fall, cuddling the always-cheerful Gabian, with the dogs asleep nearby. She might not eat, but she never wanted Seth to leave. So Seth learned that the G'deon of Shaftal was no less haunted than her wife, though by a different set of ghosts.

The Truthken intercepted Seth one day and took her to one of Travesty's cold little windowless rooms that had no possible use except as places to collect things that any sane person would give away. This particular room was crammed with horrible furniture, and Seth found herself backed up against the snout of an ugly carved pig that poked out of a headboard someone had understandably not wanted to sleep under. Perhaps the Travesty's crazed builder had taken pleasure in giving his houseguests nightmares.

"That's supposed to be the Black Pig of the Walkaround," said Norina. She shut the door and the light was gone, all but a faint, watery crack at the bottom of the door. In darkness, Seth discovered, she felt able to shift forward so the pig's carved tusk wasn't jabbing her in the shoulder blade.

"I have this effect on people," said Norina, just a voice in darkness now. "It seems to help if they can't see me."

"Have I done something wrong, Madam Truthken?"

"Not at all, Madam Councilor, though I understand why you might think so. My public acts all involve identifying errors and false-hood, and people assume that's all I do."

"You teach young air bloods to do the same."

"It must be done. But I also make people sane; I protect them from themselves. I even managed to keep Karis alive for fifteen years, with only one near failure, until people finally came who could do a better job of that than I could."

"The suicide scars on her wrists," Seth said.

"I was scarcely more than a child myself at the time, and Karis has a will that—well, I wasn't adequate to the task, and Mabin wouldn't permit me to seek help. That's all past now, fortunately."

"But everyone is worried about her. I am."

"She has her dark days, but self-loathing is no longer her greatest weakness. Madam Councilor—"

"Call me Seth."

"No, not yet. Madam Councilor, there are plenty of things you could fix in this house, but you're the sort of earth blood who would have become a healer if not for the chaos of our time. It's broken people you are most drawn to. And though you have neither a proper education nor any particular power, you've become quite skilled at using the reality under your hands to influence the reality beyond your reach. Another earth blood with your propensities might drive herself to distraction by the enormousness and inconclusiveness of such projects, but you appear to have a strategy for determining and delimiting your commit-ments. Whatever you're doing is quite effective. Is it a rubric of some sort?"

"Rubric? That's red clay, isn't it?"

"Red ink is made with that red clay, and in the Law of Shaftal the headings and subheadings are printed in red. By scanning these rubrics, the appropriate section can quickly be found. But a rubric might work in the other direction also, to screen the mess of the everyday to determine what is irrelevant and what is significant. An air blood must engage in such sorting all the time."

"I would call it judgment, or a sense of proportion."

"Yes, of course you would call it that."

Seth realized that the Truthken's neutral tone was even worse than hostility. Its blankness must be one source of her unpleasant effect on people. All people have had their shameful failures, and Norina's absence of warmth could inspire a bout of self-recrimination in anyone. For a Truthken to distinguish genuine guiltiness in a room full of desperately self-conscious people must require a screen of great sophistication. A rubric.

"I suppose I do have one," Seth said, "Though I never thought about it. Some things are fixable and some are not; some things are important and some are not. It's not difficult to sort it out."

"Don't examine whatever you're doing; it works well in its natural form but might stop working if you try to do it deliberately."

"Why point it out to me, then?"

"You need to be told that your careful friendship with Karis is appreciated."

"You approve of it, you mean."

"There is nothing fragile about her. She can only be harmed by certain kinds of people, and she identifies them as well as I do. So you are correct that it is not my business to approve of her friendships."

There were words beneath words, unspoken meanings that echoed in the meanings that were spoken. Seth knew this, but to converse with a person who could address both levels of meaning at once was unsettling.

Norina spoke again, a voice in darkness, a voice as blank and flat as a whitewashed wall, "It is appreciated. When Zanja died last time, Karis removed herself. This time she remains with us."

"I lost a wife and two babies all at the same time. I fell out of that family and could never join another one."

"It is apparent to me that you can learn from pain, so I'm not surprised by this history. Of course, the situation with Karis is different, but not that different. Karis has married herself to a crosser of boundaries, a hinge of history, and from the first moment of that affair I thought it was the worst possible match.

"In all of Shaftal, children are precious, but the children in Lalali are thought of as vermin, and if they survive they grow up to be slaves. There Karis was monstrously betrayed, from her first breath. By the time we found her she was damaged, distorted, stunted, subverted, addicted—and that is what Harald filled with the power of Shaftal. No one thought Karis could ever be worthy of that power. I never thought so—the Fall of the House of Lilterwess ended my training, and I hadn't yet been taught how to compensate for the great weakness of all air bloods, that we easily become only able to see flaws. But Zanja—she sees possibility, and when it can't be seen, she feels it, and when she can't feel it, she can act in blind ignorance, for any movement at all in any direction can become a way to enlightenment for her."

"I don't understand what you're trying to tell me," Seth said. "And it's the same problem I'm having everywhere I go and in everything I do. I'd conclude that I'm incapable of being a councilor except that everyone on my committee is as confused and overwhelmed as I am."

"I'll say it in one sentence, then: Zanja is Karis's trailbreaker—and without her, Karis can't trust the unfolding moments of her extraordinary life—but Zanja cannot be what she is without abandoning Karis, and Karis cannot hold onto her except by letting her go."

"So what?" said Seth, for she was beginning to feel very crabby. She didn't like being trapped in this dark clutter of a room, and the Truthken's arrogance in confining her here and lecturing her like this was more than aggravating. "Karis has an awareness of the world that makes my own seem childish. How could she understand so much, and have so little faith?"

Seth then felt the full power of a Truthken's silence. That, too, gave an absence of information in which a person's anxieties might begin running wildly about, squeaking with terror, like mice who suddenly become convinced that a cat is in the room.

"What did you hear," Seth asked her, "in what I just said?"

"That there is nothing feigned about you."

"Of course not. I'm as dull and honest as any earth blood."

"So you don't realize how much you're influenced by air. You have an unusual elemental balance, with almost as much air as earth, informed by fire—that would make you highly adaptable, able to see all sides of things, while the fire saves you from indecisiveness."

"Air?" said Seth, having hardly even heard the rest of it.

"Yes."

The silence again, and Seth said, "Well, I guess I'm doomed to learn all kinds of things about myself that I'd rather not know. What else did you hear?"

"In Basdown you have been protected from the worst that people can do to each other. I suppose it's a result of that unshakeable Basdowner decency. You are aware that you've been protected, yet you don't realize the extent to which it limits you."

"I had to ask," Seth muttered. The pig's snout banged on her back, and she was tempted to give the headboard a good kick.

Silence can work in two ways, she realized after a while. Norina, by holding this conversation in darkness, had deprived herself of information she might have gained by merely watching Seth's face. So Seth said, "I'm trying to figure out how anyone could come to know what they lack."

"We stumble across it, of course, and some of us recognize it and some do not. It's a problem of perception; a problem of how one sees, and how able one is to accurately see what is there."

"You learned all this about me from—what was it, two sentences?"

"One sentence followed by one question, actually. Yes, Seth, I did. And in our conversation since then I have learned how quickly you change. Observe."

Norina opened the door. Now Seth could see her again, the scar that slashed across her inexpressive face; the hair that was shorn even closer than Clement's, so close that her scalp looked very much like the chin of a man who has gone two days without shaving; the eyes, the coldest and sharpest thing about that extraordinarily cold and sharp woman.

A moment passed. Seth realized the pig wasn't poking her in the back. Norina, able to see her face now, said, "I am not so frightening as you thought."

She walked away, leaving Seth feeling quite dazed.

Later that same day, Karis clasped Seth's hand, and it was like being licked by a tongue of lightning. Seth yanked her hand away.

Karis said, "I'm sorry—I wasn't thinking. I intrude on people in my family all the time without asking permission first."

"And that's why they're all so healthy, I suppose."

"That's why Emil grew some new teeth, and Norina got pregnant—just the one time, though."

They were in the bedroom, and when Karis retreated there she had always lost her sense of humor. Seth laughed, though she was laughing alone. "I'm not offended, Karis—I was just startled. I wouldn't mind a new tooth or two."

Seth offered her hand and Karis clasped it again, but it was just a handclasp. Karis said, "I feared there was something wrong with you. But no, you've just been talking with Norina."

Later, Seth peeled turnips with Tam, a member of the Peace Committee who was an apple farmer from the north, near Kisha. At first he had been living with a distant cousin who was a clerk in a business that Tam didn't understand well enough to describe. But he had moved to Travesty when he realized that the backache that had nagged him for years disappeared entirely when he was in that building. He had moved into one of the chilly rooms in Seth's wing, which no doubt would be sweltering by summer. He had an easy way about him and was a good neighbor. They frequently wandered into each other's rooms, asking each other for definitions of words or help with understanding a particularly unreadable sentence.

That morning's meeting of the Peace Committee had aggravated him as much as it had aggravated her. He said, "Emil writes us those notes, which I'm sure he intends to be helpful, and we try to answer him, but no matter what question he asks we keep saying the same thing: We must change the Sainnites into Shaftali. As if saying it would make it happen somehow."

"I constantly feel like I don't know enough," Seth said.

"But how much more can we possibly know? My eyes hurt from those mountains of books we're reading. My ears hurt from all that talking people are aiming in our direction. Yet the more I learn, the stupider I feel."

"It's odd," said Seth, "that we have a good four hundred years of knowledge between the ten of us, and yet that doesn't seem to be enough."

He glanced sideways at her, and it occurred to her that turnip-peeling might be quite clarifying. Maybe the entire committee should start meeting in the kitchen. "All this knowledge," Seth said, "maybe it's just a lot of clutter. When I was learning what to do when a calf is coming out backwards—"

"I'm getting tired of your cow stories."

Tam could peel a turnip without hardly looking at his hands, and the peel came spiraling off in a uniform piece, which was all the more remarkable considering how difficult turnips were.

"Like peeling a turnip without knowing what a turnip is, without having ever seen one, without having seen anyone else try to peel one. You could tell someone how to do it—you could waste a whole year on it, probably. But that person still wouldn't be able to peel a turnip."

Tam said, "It's closer to five hundred than four hundred years, I should think. You're a bit younger than most of us." The peel spiraled away and then he glanced at his hands and said, "If I even think about it, I can't do it."

"You've peeled a few thousand turnips, I expect."

"And we've seen plenty of Sainnites, all of us have."

Seth thought for a while about how they all thought they knew what a Sainnite was. Then she considered how all this might be a failure to perceive. She had thought Clement was a farmer in soldier's clothing; she had been surprised by Damon's friendliness and good humor; she had been affronted by the blood spilled in the hallway, as though the assassination attempt had been a failure of etiquette. People had seen their families butchered by a friendly and good-humored soldier just like Damon, who was acting on the orders of an intelligent, lonely, contradictory commander just like Clement. That was the sort of thing Seth thought it was important to understand.

"We have to know all sides," Seth said, "but especially the inside."

"What?" said Tam, who thanks to Seth appeared to have lost the knack of turnip-peeling.

"We're trying to put it inside of us, but we need to put ourselves inside of it."

"What?"

"I don't know," Seth said. "I don't know what I just said. But still, we should consider that we might be doing this thing the wrong way."

☙

Two days later, she went back to Watfield Garrison. This time she had a letter from Emil, written to Commander Ellid, which Gilly had to translate. Ellid didn't speak Shaftalese at all.

Seth feared she wouldn't be able to learn their language, either. But neither would most Shaftali, so that was a problem they needed to find a way around.

Ellid said something in a tone that certainly sounded doubtful, if not disbelieving. She had an extraordinarily neat office, unlike Clement's. Gilly said, "The commander finds it difficult to understand why you wish to do this."

"It's because I don't know the right things, in the right way. I thought this might help. If it does, all the Peace Committee members might do something like this—in different garrisons, of course."

Gilly translated, Ellid responded, and Seth could tell that she was even more skeptical now. "There are practical problems," Gilly said.

"I'm sure there are, but I'm a practical person."

"But a soldier's life—!" Gilly paused, as Ellid was speaking again. Before he could translate, though, Seth said, "For just one day and one night, then."

He seemed surprised. Seth said, "I'll come back to Commander Ellid, of course, and ask her to allow me another day—I guess you should tell her that's what I intend to do. But after one day, she'll know I'm not going to die of whatever she thinks I'll die of, and she'll let me stay another day. And if I'm still alive then…"

Gilly gave her a cool look, and it occurred to her that he might actually be angry with her—angry for Clement's sake. How long had he worked with Clement, his hand in her glove? How had a Shaftali man become a general's secretary, and what was it like for him, to be in-between? Was Clement his family, and was she hers?

Seth had a great deal to learn, that was certain. But she could feel herself sorting things out, by that method Norina had urged her not to pay any attention to, because it worked without thinking, like turnip-peeling did. Right now, she thought, I just need to go into a solder's barracks, and put my satchel onto an empty bed—or whatever they sleep on—and look around to see who's next to me, and tell her my name. That's all I need to do.

She ended up in Prista's company, which of ten possible companies was the best she could have hoped for, though she didn't even realize it until various soldiers began yelling for Damon. The young, good-natured soldier eventually appeared in the barracks mud room, though he didn't step into the sleeping part proper, due to some kind of rule, Seth supposed, about men going into the women's barracks, which she assumed would also apply the other way around.

"Councilor?" he said, clearly astonished to see her there.

"Just Seth. I'm spending the night here. Ellid's orders."

His eyebrows rose comically, and he spoke to the confused women, then said, "But there are bugs in the beds."

Seth began laughing so hard she finally had to sit down on the bed, lest she fall over. The women liked her much better then, and even more when she went out into the city and convinced the greengrocer to talk to the herbalist down the street, who was as mystified as everyone else, but let her have a big bag of strewing herbs, which took care of all the bugs in all the beds. So her life as a soldier began.

Chapter 15

In Clement's childhood, her mother's company had scarcely left the coastal region of Hanishport. Here, in Shaftal's only safe port, many of the first influx of refugee soldiers had landed, and here they had built their first garrison. As a youthful foot soldier she had fought on the leading edge of the occupation, into the Midlands and southward to Han, but not until the death of Harald G'deon and the attack on the House of Lilterwess did the Sainnites, reinforced by a new influx of refugee soldiers, move north and west. But Clement had never been far enough west to see the mountains, and although Saleen told her they could be seen anywhere beyond the Reestown crossroad, the clouds never lifted to let her see the view.

The Corber Valley had narrowed, the river ceased its meandering, and the flood finally lay behind them, to the east. They could follow the road again, and the road even was in reasonable condition, but still their progress was slow. They had taken a day's respite in a settlement near Haprin, but that rest had done little good. Day after day they hobbled westward, with the brown river on their left and the brown hills on their right, so hemmed in by the weather's gray horizon that Clement felt dislocated for days. Still, though her companions certainly were more than eager for the tedious journey to be over, she was not.

One evening they spotted some travelers at a distance, coming towards them through the drizzle. "Paladins," said Saleen. "Who else would travel in this weather?" He trotted forward to greet them.

He returned with a man Clement's age, whose lively face lost all expression every time he looked at Clement. Two gold earrings marked him as a true Paladin, Saleen's equal in rank, whatever rank meant to the Paladins. However, like his irregular followers he wore plain homespun the brownish gray color of very dirty sheep, the preferred color of the irregulars, whose strategies depended so much on their ability to melt into the landscape.

"General Clement, this is Ronal, Commander of Paladins in South Hill," said Saleen.

Clement offered her hand, but Ronal kept his own hands tucked under his rain cape. Saleen hastily continued, "Even though the ice broke up, Ronal did receive Emil's message several days ago. The letter was relayed from one settlement to the next and arrived in good time despite the weather."

"You understand, then, that your people are to be subject to my authority," said Clement. "But your direct orders will come from Mabin, just as my people's will come from me. However, my people also understand that under some circumstances they could be subject to your command."

Ronal said, "Yes."

He greeted Mabin with warmth, exchanged wry comments on the foul weather, and gave her a casual report as they slogged through a particularly muddy patch of the road. He had learned that all five rebel garrisons were shut tight, with the siege gates closed and the walls guarded as though in expectation of an imminent attack. In some regions the Paladin commanders had mustered their companies out of caution, and some had not. The fighters of South Hill company, some fifty total, had been mustered to Wilton, where they resided in scattered households but could quickly be summoned to the garrison. "But surely we won't attempt a direct attack on the garrison," he said to Mabin.

"No attack is planned," Mabin said. "According to General Clement, we have here a simple discipline problem, which she will personally resolve without conflict."

Ronal glanced at Clement with an expression of surprise that swiftly settled into hostile blankness again. "Does the general know Heras?"

"I know her very well, Commander. Our mothers were in the same company, we arrived in Shaftal on the same boat, we learned to fight together, and we lived together for ten years."

Ronal turned his gaze back to Mabin and told her that a nearby cluster of farmsteads was prepared to receive them, and that they would reach Wilton by midday tomorrow.

Saleen, at Clement's side, muttered, "My brother Paladin seems unready to give up his anger."

"He's been fighting Heras since he succeeded Emil as the commander of South Hill company—that's been five years, at least. Five years of fighting Heras would make me detest all Sainnites, and I am one."

"But the more bitter the enemy, the more important is detachment."

"Saleen, I beg you—give me a respite from philosophy."

He grinned. "Have I made myself unendurable? Then I have succeeded."

The city of Wilton had developed around a port on the Corber, but even in the lowland section of the city the buildings were not on stilts, and neither were there any derricks. Apparently, the river never flooded here. In the vast valley around the city the old farmstead boundaries could still be distinguished, but these fields were choked with dead weeds, the orchards were hewn down, and the farm buildings were nothing but black bones open to the weather. Heras had laid waste to the valley's rich farmlands, with the result that no one—beast, farmer, or soldier—had grain to eat. After two years of famine the highland farmers had recovered. Oxen to replace the plow horses arrived from all over Shaftal, pulling wagons of seed rye driven by experienced rye farmers, who remained to watch over the fields until the first harvest had successfully been brought in. All this had happened so stealthily that it wasn't until the next year's harvest that Heras noticed that her plan to depopulate South Hill had failed. "The Great Bread War," that fiasco was called in a mocking ballad sung all over Shaftal.

Clement heard many fragments of that story during the morning's journey. With each cluster of destroyed buildings they passed, the local Paladins recounted another piece of history; and their memories seemed to reach all the way back to the first spade full of dirt and the first seed dropped into the soil. Clement had escaped some of her tribulations when she left Watfield, and though a closed gate awaited her in Wilton she had taken hope in the journey—as Paladin and Sainnite endured common miseries rather than inflicting miseries on each other. Now Clement entered the darkness of spirit once again.

The five new garrison commanders—Mayer, Denit, Sarney, Efrat, and Sevan—walked with her on this last stretch of the grueling journey. She did not translate the Paladins' farmstead elegies, but her people understood enough, and it was not good for morale.

"General, I'd be failing in my duty if I didn't tell you my concerns," said Efrat. "If you permit."

"Continue, Commander."

"These South Hill Paladins—I don't trust them. And how do we know that Saleen and his few people would be able to protect us from Ronal's many, if they turn against us? As for Commander Heras, her people are known to be loyal to her. Practically an entire battalion followed her from Rees to South Hill! And General Cadmar always let her do as she liked, so she is accustomed to independence. Isn't it possible the people under her command are more loyal to her, and she more trigger-quick, than we expect?"

"Than I expect, do you mean?" said Clement. "Efrat, I'm not Cadmar. You can say what you're thinking without getting your face smashed in."

The commanders snickered, for the most recent face to be smashed in by Cadmar's heavy fist had been Clement's. "It's taken you long enough to tell me these concerns," Clement said. "I've been waiting for you to mention them since before we left Watfield."

"General, you are a great strategist. But we have begun to wonder if—" Efrat had to pause here, ill-accustomed as he was to frank speaking to a general. "—if your confidence might be somewhat feigned."

Mayer spoke, and it was a relief to see that the commanders weren't going to silently allow Efrat to make himself a target on their behalf. They were learning. "Yesterday, after you told us what to do should you be killed, we discussed these matters with each other. The moment you've appeared at Wilton garrison in person, Heras will know she has lost her gamble. Whether you kill Heras, or she kills you, she will not win what she wants. Her success depended on your not making this journey at all."

"So we think she will kill you," said Sevan in a low voice. "She'll have no reason not to."

Clement said, "I agree with your thinking. But what happens at the gate depends on the gate captains more than on Heras. She can hardly have given them orders to shoot me on sight—not if she wants them to believe in her honor. And she can't shoot me with her own hand, for she hasn't got the eyesight for distance weapons."

"I told you the general had thought it through," said Denit with relief.

"Still, it's a risk, General," said Sevan doggedly. "And you shouldn't put yourself in such a position. Send one of us forward instead. I'll go."

"No," said Clement. "I have to do this."

"Bloody hell," muttered Efrat. "What are we to do if you get yourself killed, eh?"

"You'll bring the written orders to your assigned garrisons and replace the chief officers as commanded. And then you'll vote for Ellid to be general."

"Ellid is a good commander," said Sevan. "But none of us think she can be a good general."

"I agree—but no one can be a good general. Cadmar managed because of me and Gilly; I manage because of Gilly, Ellid, and Emil; Emil manages because of a whole host of people. If Ellid becomes general, all of you become general."

As they entered the outskirts of the city, people looked out doorways and windows and gathered on the edges of the street to watch them pass. With South Hill company quartered in the city, the citizens seemed to have been forewarned to expect something to happen, and they watched the passage of this strange company in somber silence. Clement dropped back to speak with Mabin. "My officers' lives are in these Paladins' hands. Think of what it is like for us to have to listen to these endless grievances."

She expected an argument, preferably one vigorous and angry enough to distract her during this long walk to the garrison gate. But Mabin said, "Yes, General." She immediately went to Ronal, who soon was talking to his officers, and though they argued vigorously and walked with sullen faces afterwards, they also disciplined their tongues.

The rectangle of the book in Clement's tunic felt like a piece of armor pressing her breastbone. But for thirty-five years philosophy had failed, and so with neither shield nor weapon she walked forward.

When Clement's mother first adopted her and brought her home with her, Heras was already ensconced as a leader among the garrison children. The child gangs played soldier, of course, and fought each other with all the glee and desperation that they imagined their parents fought with, though their weapons were nothing more than pieces of wood and balls of mud. Heras had not wanted Clement because she was small, but another gang leader had liked her intelligence and sharp tongue. Clement, though a sudden growth spurt made her taller, was still blundering along at the bottom of that gang's ranking when, in the world outside their garrison, politics and firepower forced their company into the sea.

On the boat, Clement and Heras were exiled to the lower deck, forbidden to go above lest they get in the way of a sailor or get themselves blown overboard. Their flotilla sailed into a storm during which a number of the ships disappeared entirely. Clement, Heras, and ten other children clung to each other in the gloom, desperately seasick, frightened, abandoned, making up information because they could tolerate fantasies better than facts. They had seen their parents beaten and cowed; they had seen them take flight. They explained to each other how it was possible to simultaneously take to one's heels and be brave, and each explanation was more unlikely than the last. But they succeeded in making themselves believe in their parents again.

Seasickness leveled them; their old gang affiliations dissolved. They puked into buckets, and the buckets slopped over, and they had to clean up their own awful mess. Day after day, the narrow room plunged and ducked and swung, and they could not rest because they had to hold onto the bunks to keep from falling off, so they held onto each other, some holding and some sleeping in turns. By the time the sea calmed and their parents managed to check on them, a new hierarchy of age and responsibility had been established, a hierarchy that endured long after they finally shipwrecked on the coast of Shaftal. Clement's status had risen precipitously.

By the time Clement was sixteen, and a soldier, her people had been pariahs in Shaftal for seven years. The first wave of refugees had been followed by others, and by the time the Shaftali realized they were slowly being invaded, some ten thousand Sainnites were ensconced along the coastline. The dozen children who had survived that awful journey with Clement continued to be loyal to each other as, one by one, they took up the weapons of the fallen and became soldiers themselves. And one summer night, Heras pulled Clement into bed with her, and taught her lovemaking. They swore to be loyal to each other forever. Then they became rivals, and remained rivals for the rest of their lives.

Clement's hair was stiff and sticky, her uniform limp and grimy, her boots rotting off her feet, and her feet rotting as well. Her weather-battered appearance could not be repaired. However, with spit and salt and a dirty kerchief, Herme had polished the tarnish from her insignia—the badge taken from Cadmar's hat and pinned on hers before they lit his pyre, a badge that had in turn been plucked from the old general's hat when his body was burned, and ceremonially pinned onto Cadmar. And before the old general, someone in Sainna had worn the badge. Clement had worn it for less than three months, and Heras thought *she* should be wearing it. It was an old, familiar problem.

Wilton was not half as impressive as Watfield, and probably not half as old. Shaftali civilization seemed to have moved slowly westward, following a path similar to that of the Sainnite occupation. Wilton was the last city; further west the villages and settlements gave way to temporary camps, to tribal land, to wilderness, and finally to the mountains. This brick and sandstone city had a roughness that the granite and slate city of Watfield lacked. Its windows were smaller, and patches of unmelted snow revealed that it must be even cooler here.

"The raven asked to talk to you," said a Paladin. The bird hopped from his shoulder to Clement's, and the man discreetly moved away.

"Emil?" said Clement. "I must do this alone—I'm only more certain of that now. I can't be surrounded by Paladins like a prisoner. I can't be shielded by my officers like a coward. And I must make it obvious to all watchers that Heras only wants to be general because she can't endure that it be me."

"We trust your judgment," said the raven. The bird must be speaking not only for Emil, but for a group of people, probably all sitting together in a Travesty parlor. "Medric says there will be a heroic ballad about you and this day. A ballad sung by Shaftali."

"Bloody hell. Can't that man say something useful?"

"He's laughing," reported the raven. "Go forward alone, as you say you must. You are not alone, though."

The bird took off. Weighed down by wet feathers, it flew in heavily climbing circles until it reached a rooftop and walked to its peak. From there it flew in short bursts along the rooftops, keeping pace with the people below, until the local Paladins said they were nearly at the garrison. Clement's officers saluted; the Paladins stood in solemn silence; and Clement went forward, to turn herself into a heroic ballad.

Every time Clement did something like this, she could do it only because she had survived something almost as frightening in the past. At midwinter, when she walked unarmed across the open snow field towards a giant who with a single hammer blow had destroyed the garrison wall, that had been hard, even with the soldiers cheering her forward. Everyone watching her must have suspected she was walking quickly so as to stay ahead of her terror. And they certainly had known that she was making that walk in their stead, so that they would be spared. This time, without their cheers, it was much harder. Every time Clement walked ahead of her people it was harder to do, and the risk was greater. But she had led a lucky life. Someday her luck would fail, and maybe today would be the day. Still, she would do what she had to, as quickly as possible, so that it could be finished, and she could get on with the easier parts.

That was the true stuff of soldier's courage. It was not so impressive, really, stripped of its ritual and romance. What the Shaftali would find to sing about she really could not imagine.

She walked briskly up to the garrison gate. The siege gates were closed, and she could not see in. She shouted in her commanding voice, "Gate captain! I am your general! Open the gate!"

The raven could probably see what was happening, but she could only imagine the consternation that these nine words caused. The members of the guard peered at her through the balustrade overhead, then turned to each other, agitatedly confirming that she wore the general's badge. Eventually one person looked over the barrier and said, "I am Megert, captain of the day watch. Please pardon the delay, but no one in my company knows your face."

The bloody duty rosters, for years the most onerous of Clement's duties, would prove to have some value after all. "I know you, Captain. You've been captain of the day watch in three different garrisons, and six times you've been commended for swift action that spared the garrison from infiltration. I know that you have never been promoted above captain because you let it be known you didn't want it. You've followed Heras for over twenty years, though, since you were assigned to her company just after the Battle of Lilterwess, when she and I both made captain. I can recite every battle you've fought in, every injury. Shall I do it?"

"General Clement, I—How did you come here?"

"On my own two feet, Captain. What did you expect would happen when I learned that five entire garrisons were in mutiny?"

"Mutiny? But Commander Heras—"

"I am your commander's superior officer, Captain. Open the gate!"

"Yes, General. Lift the siege gate!"

My luck has held again, thought Clement.

And then she heard the crossbow twang, and the bolt's blow knocked her backwards to the ground. Sitting on the road, vaguely surprised, Clement looked at the bolt's fletched end sticking out of her belly. "Oh, hell," she muttered. She must move—get out of the way—for they'd use guns now...a crossbow requires too much skill...any bloody fool can shoot a gun...and even hit something...something fairly near, not moving...assuming they'd managed to keep the powder dry. Clement felt very tired.

Someone grabbed her arms. Saleen. Mabin lifted one leg. They carried her.

Bloody Paladins can't follow orders.

Mabin grinned like a tiger. She fell, still showing her teeth. So failed anger.

Saleen had been laughing. But now he sighed, and knelt, and bowed over a scarlet puddle that steamed in the chill air. So failed philosophy.

Roadstones slammed into Clement's back. Pain, now. Only pain.

They lay, the three of them, on the cobblestones.

Part Three: Transported

Chapter 16

The raven in Wilton stands on the rooftop, his wings half-raised. The Paladins, those in black and those in dun, are frozen in the alley. The three bodies in the courtyard have a different kind of stillness. Scarlet stains fill the gaps between the coarse granite cobbles.

A voice shouts something in Sainnese. The thirty soldiers in the alley jerk into motion and within two steps they are running—a mass of sodden gray, their water-rotten boots nearly silent on the stone, their fighting hands feeling for weapons they do not have. They splash into the street, into the line of fire.

The raven can see over the tower barricades. A few of the garrison soldiers are rushing to reload their guns and wind their crossbows. The gate captain is shouting at them. The raven does not understand Sainnese.

The thirty soldiers lift the fallen by the arms and legs, and run back to the alley. No one shoots at them. The raven leaps up and catches hold of the sodden air with his rain-wet wings.

The garrison gate drops away behind him. He swoops into the alley and lands on a Paladin's shoulder. She jumps with startlement. "Are they alive?" the raven asks.

The Paladin begins pushing into the huddle of shocked people, shouting, "Let the G'deon through!"

The fallen Paladins lie side by side. People kneel beside them, pressing on wounds with bare hands, feeling for heartbeats, holding a little mirror to Mabin's mouth.

"Mabin is dead," says Karis, in Watfield. The people sitting with her are silent. Emil covers his face with his hands.

Saleen is taking his last breath. The raven knows this but cannot change it: he lacks the G'deon's powers. In Watfield, Karis clenches her hands in her hair. The Paladin relaxes into death.

"Saleen is dead," says Karis. Emil flinches.

The Watfield Paladins reach blindly for each other, weeping. The

Wilton Paladins, who stand further away so they can watch the garrison, utter cries of anger. "A hero of Shaftal!" bellows one at the blank face of the garrison.

"Bring me to Clement," the raven says.

But the Sainnites have barricaded their general with their bodies, and even though the Paladin shouts at and pounds on them, they remain resolute, impermeable.

The raven jumps across them, from shoulder to shoulder, then soars to the ground beside Clement. Rifle balls have burned two black holes where they entered her flesh. The fletched end of the quarrel juts out of her belly. The soldiers roll her onto her side, revealing the blood-soaked back of her tunic, the smear of blood upon stones. The Paladin must have passed her knife across the barrier of bodies, for it is handed to Herme, who is on his knees and slices open the wool tunic to reveal the gaping wounds where the balls exited. She is still bleeding, therefore is still alive.

"Herme!" says the raven. "Mereth!"

Herme ignores the raven, but Mereth looks up at the raven and speaks a few words in Sainnese, then switches languages. "General lives," she says. "Need house now."

Karis has ceased to narrate events to the people in the room. She rises to her feet and reaches blindly for the baby in the basket at her feet.

"Take these Sainnites to shelter!" says the raven, who has traveled again to the Paladin's shoulder. "Clement is alive!"

The Paladin turns, notices the Paladin irregulars behind her, and utters an exclamation of dismay. The Wilton Paladins have weapons in their hands, and they are facing the Sainnites. But now the Watfield Paladins have put themselves between the armed irregulars and the unarmed Sainnites.

Ronal steps forward, holding his people back with his open hands. He and one of the black-dressed Paladins begin a shouted argument.

In Watfield, Karis has blundered out the door and down a hallway. Emil lunges after her, saying something, but she does not heed him.

In the garrison they were still on winter rations, which meant they were hungry all the time. Seth dropped her entire roll of rock-hard bread into her stew to soften, then with her fingers fished out a piece of meat. Beef? She put it in her mouth and began to chew. It was like trying to eat a wet piece of cheesecloth. Day watch had finally ended. Prista's company, except for a handful of people on guard duty, had spent most of the watch indoors, oiling the floors in a nearly finished barracks. Then a freight wagon of furniture had arrived, and they had hauled beds on their backs from the gate to the building, for the passage across the restless remains of the wall was too cluttered for a wagon to pass. Now every last one of them was soaked to the skin, and the refectory smelled more of wet wool than it did of food.

Koura and Stel were arguing again. Prista came over and bellowed at them. Both women stood up and moved to either end of the refectory but continued to glare at each other. Stel had given Koura a black eye two days ago, but three days ago they had been lovers—and had been wildly noisy about it, also.

Seth swallowed the hard lump of meat and tried to pick up a piece of carrot, but it dissolved. By the time the bread had soaked up most of the broth, the bowl would contain a pap of carrot mush. The potatoes, however, held their shape well enough to be picked up.

After dinner, they would go to their barracks and entertain each other for a few dull hours, while Seth studied a book by lamplight—she brought her own lamp oil from Travesty, for that, also, was rationed here.

Her stomach growled, and she ate to quiet it.

She thought she heard someone shout her name outside. The people sitting near the door picked up the cry: "Seth!" She left her half-eaten dinner—someone else would finish it—and went outside into the rain.

A soldier—Damon, whose shift at the gate often ended late—and a Paladin, both breathing heavily and wearing rain capes, awaited her. Her heart sank. "What has happened?"

"Please come with me," said the Paladin.

She started away with him, then remembered she was supposed to be a soldier, and turned back. "Damon, will you explain to Captain Prista—"

Damon gave her an ironic salute. "Yes, Councilor!"

The Paladin said in a low voice, "Emil asks that we keep this matter private. Clement has just been gravely wounded by her own people in Wilton."

After a moment the Paladin took her arm. "Shall we sit down somewhere?"

"No—no, I must go to Travesty."

She began walking, though her legs worked like the stiffly jointed legs of a puppet. "What happened?"

"I have told you all I know, Seth. Emil was in a hurry."

"I see." In Travesty, she could put on dry clothes and eat a decent meal, she thought stupidly. But Emil probably wanted her to do something. To help bring the news to Ellid and Gilly? They would be—the entire garrison would be—Clement is dying, Seth thought, with a jolt of dreadful clarity. Her stiff legs stumbled her feet awkwardly over the cobblestones. She focused her attention on them, in order to make them move faster.

In Travesty, the Paladins directed Seth to Karis's bedroom. There Gabian lay on the unmade bed, gabbling happily as clothing was flung over him. Emil stood nearby, talking loudly to Karis, who seemed oblivious to him, to the happy baby she was burying in shirts, and to Seth. "Wagah!" said the baby, as Seth plucked him out of the clothing. He showed her his pink gums.

Karis pulled a heavy wool shirt over her head without unbuttoning it. She reached for her belt, from which dangled a pencil, a ruler, a small knife in its sheath, and a pouch of the sort that usually contained flint and tinder.

"If we lose you, we lose everything!" Emil cried. "Have you forgotten about the assassins?"

She turned to him: plain face, hard eyes, square chin. "Do you really think I can't protect myself?"

"But when you sleep—"

"I won't sleep." Karis sat on the bed and jammed her feet into heavy boots. Emil sat in the big chair by the fireplace and put his head in his hands.

"What's happened?" asked Seth.

"Clement went to the garrison, and it seemed they were going to admit her, exactly as she said would happen. But then a member of the guard shot her."

Karis, buckling her boot straps, said angrily, "Clement lied!"

"Oh, I don't think—" said Emil.

At the same time, Seth found herself blurting, "Of course she lied—she had to lie—you made her lie!"

They both looked at her in surprise.

"The third choice, remember, Emil? You kept insisting—" Seth tried to stop herself, but the words kept coming out. "She told you there wasn't a third choice; but you wouldn't accept that. So what did you think she was going to do?"

Emil put his hands over his face again. "I thought she'd argue with me," he said. "Like a Paladin."

Karis said in her harsh voice, "Put that baby in a sling."

"You're taking him with you? In mud season?" Seth cried.

"She is his mother," Karis said. She came around the bed and took the baby. "He is a child of Shaftal."

Something in Karis's voice stunned Seth into silence: a coherence, a resolution. She lined a silk shawl with diapers and used it to secure Gabian against the broad chest of the plain-faced, wild-haired woman who had the power of Shaftal in her forge-blackened hands.

Karis went out. Seth and Emil chased after but could not keep up. The dogs barked anxiously. Paladins appeared from all directions—and then Medric was there, clutching his spectacles with one hand to keep them from falling off, grabbing Emil's arm and crying, "Let her go!" And Norina, arrow-swift, strode beside Karis for a few steps, saying a few precise words. A woman rushed in the front door with Leeba in hand. Everyone came to an abrupt halt. Karis scooped Leeba up onto a hip so they could talk eye to eye. As always happens when children are urged to be brave, Leeba began to cry.

And then Karis handed Leeba away to J'han, who also had arrived suddenly from somewhere, and he dazedly answered the sharp questions she asked him as she was going down the front steps, past the Paladins, while the people who hovered around the building stared after her in dismay. "Is that Karis?" someone asked. "Has another person fallen under the ice?" said another.

Karis strode into the pouring rain. Medric held Emil steady at the top of the stairs. Karis was gone.

Seth said to Emil, "I'm so sorry—I was—"

"You were right." Emil sounded calm now, terribly calm. "Come inside, Seth."

Leeba's cries echoed in Travesty's huge hallway. Emil said to the Paladins, "General Mabin and Commander Saleen have died. They died trying to save General Clement, who is alive, but with the kinds of injuries no one survives. Karis is going to Wilton, alone because companions would only hamper her now." He fell silent.

Norina said, "For now, keep these matters to yourselves. Emil will come and talk to you later."

The shocked Paladins managed small nods. Seth, her thoughts again in tumult—Mabin dead!—followed Emil, with Norina and Medric, scarcely aware of her own existence until Emil closed the parlor door behind them. "Seth, I'm sorry to have to say this so bluntly—Clement is going to die, and it's better for her if it's soon."

Seth sat—dropped—into a chair. Medric sat next to her and patted her knee in an awkward, ineffective way. Emil said, "We need to discuss what to do. What to tell Ellid."

Norina said, "Well, it isn't finished, yet."

Seth looked at her in dull puzzlement.

"I can't imagine what Karis—" Emil began.

"The G'deon," said Medric.

They all looked at him. He closed his lips, like a child keeping a secret.

The raven seeks a healer who J'han thought might be in the region of Wilton, flying from one farmstead to another, following the healer's route from illness to birth to injury to more illness. By the time the bird finds the healer, it is full dark, and the bird is exhausted by the effort required to fly all day in the rain.

Karis has walked all day, and now she walks all night in the unrelenting rain. The baby tied to her breast is warm and does not seem to mind being wet. Every few hours Karis stops at a farmstead and finds a woman to give suck to the general's son.

At late morning, Karis is still walking.

The raven and the healer arrive in Wilton in a borrowed, horse-drawn cart. At the building where the Sainnites have found shelter, a mob of people shout their hatred for the Sainnites. Their angry grief at the death of Mabin unites them. Three black-dressed Paladins block the door, armed only with their moral argument.

Shaftal's rage has collected here in South Hill as water gathers in a vernal pond. Yet the angry people cannot bring themselves to attack a Paladin, or to disregard a Paladin's conscience.

The healer cannot push through the crowd. When he shouts that he is a healer, the people shout back at him. "Let her die as she deserves!" The healer stands up in his cart, and the raven flies to his shoulder. "This is a G'deon's raven!" the healer shouts. "In the name of Karis G'deon, give me passage!"

Glowering, sullen people begin moving in one direction or the other to let the healer's cart get through. The healer mutters to his bird companion, "I see why mobs are always called 'ugly.'"

The horse leans in the traces, and the wagon goes the last few feet to the door.

"Raven, we've been looking anxiously for your return," says a Paladin whose eyes are red with sleeplessness and weeping.

The raven says, "Is the general still alive?"

"Yes. But in terrible pain."

The grim healer begins to unload his pack and supplies from the wagon, with help from the Paladins. He says to them, "I've told the raven that even a minor gut wound makes survival doubtful. But the bird—the G'deon—insists I try to keep her alive."

"It is the Sainnites' custom to spare each other the pain of a lingering death," said the Paladin. "Her people are demanding—"

The raven says, "Keep them away from her."

Both men look at the bird in anguish. "You haven't heard her screams," the Paladin says.

"A merciful death may be all I can give her," says the healer.

"But she must live."

Far away, Karis is climbing to high ground, for the Corber has burst its banks. She pauses. Rain drips from the tips of her hair, from her eyebrows, nose, and chin. The baby sleeps in her arms, in utter peace. Karis gazes sternly westward as though she can see across the vast distance that separates her from Wilton. Her lips move.

"Kill me," the raven says. "And feed me to her."

Chapter 19

In a small, barren room with a newly built fire crackling on the hearth, Zanja stood in the presence of the angry G'deon, surrounded by Paladins. Arel, evicted from that crowded room despite his vigorous protests, waited outside the door—or at least Zanja hoped so.

The G'deon had shed his muddy rain cape but ignored the fire's inviting warmth. He paced restlessly back and forth down a narrow avenue lined with armed guards.

The house captain burst in the door, out of breath and already in a rage. "What has this woman done now?"

"Good evening, Commander," said the G'deon, "What do you know about her?"

The house captain willingly launched into an account of Zanja's history and crimes. She was not half finished when Tadwell interrupted. "Nothing you are saying is relevant."

"I beg your pardon, Tadwell. I am telling you what I know."

A silence fell. It was so quiet Zanja could hear water dripping from clothing to splash on the stone floor. The G'deon's sodden boots squished audibly as he paced to the stone wall and turned back. He came to within a step of Zanja, and his square hands lifted as if of their own will.

"Don't touch me, sir—not before witnesses," she murmured. Whatever Tadwell had sensed, it had been strange enough to cause him to abandon the Basdowners, to lead his Paladins on a precipitant race in miserable weather, directly to Zanja. When he touched her, Zanja feared, it would be a shock impossible to conceal.

Tadwell lowered his hands. "Why do you refuse to speak to a Truthken? What are you keeping secret?"

"I will answer your questions, sir—but only in private."

"Tadwell, you should not be alone with her—she is a violent woman, possibly a murderer!"

Zanja dropped to her knees on the cold, damp stone. She unbuckled her belt and tossed it out of reach, and followed it with the knife from her boot sheath. She sat back on her heels to make herself even less dangerous, and rested her hands on her thighs.

Many of the Paladins now eyed her appreciatively. But was this drama overt enough for even an earth witch to understand?

Tadwell's gaze lingered on Zanja's discarded weaponry: the dagger, the knife, also unique in Zanja's time, forged by the hand of a smith who had at least twice Tadwell's power.

"All of you, wait outside. Silence!" Tadwell added, as the house captain began to protest. "Leave her weapons where they lie."

The room emptied; the door was shut, and the silence began to itch and ring in Zanja's ears. Tadwell stood over Zanja's belt and blades.

Zanja said, "You will be startled, I fear."

Tadwell picked up the bootknife and dropped it with a grunt of surprise. It rang on stone with a piercing purity of sound.

Zanja said, "My blades were shaped by the hand of my wife, who will be the G'deon two hundred years from now."

Faint voices could be heard outside the door where the Paladins, as always, had begun to pass the time in vigorous conversation.

Zanja said, "On an errand for her, while I was crossing a frozen river, the ice gave way under me and I fell in and drowned. When I came to consciousness I had been removed from my own time. By logic—fire logic—I know I fell into a trap of water magic that was designed to capture me and carry me here."

Tadwell continued to stare at her, dumbfounded.

"I am a katrim, like Arel," Zanja said. "I am considered a hero of Shaftal."

At least Tadwell didn't declare in outrage that no border woman could achieve such a status.

In a strained voice, he said, "Why were you brought here?"

"Only the water witch knows that."

"But if you have a fire talent, you have suspicions, at least."

"Survival has required all my attention and energy. But a seer from my time did predict that I would cross the boundary of time, and choose insight."

"I have no time for riddles! Someone must explain!" The G'deon began pacing agitatedly again, this time in a circuit of the room. "The Basdowners are feuding over trivial issues, actually killing each other—and won't acknowledge their true problems of too many children and too many cows. For three seasons in a row the lambs in the western sheeplands have been decimated by illness, and no one can determine what to do about it. The people of the midland cities are requiring farmers to pay for the privilege of selling in their markets, and the farmers are banding together and refusing to go to the cities at all—"

It occurred to Zanja that Tadwell was young, both in age and in experience. She said more acerbically than she had intended, "Certainly, every crisis should wait on your convenience."

He stopped, and glared. "I see you are accustomed to taking a familiar tone with the G'deon."

"Is that a reprimand? Is it considered correct behavior in this Shaftal for everyone to avoid speaking plainly to you? Or do I just seem arrogant to you because I don't accord with your expectations of a border person?"

Tadwell loomed over her—belligerent, pugnacious.

"Do you leave everyone kneeling before you like this?" Zanja said.

"Stand up, then." He offered his hand.

She put her hand in his, and he staggered. She stood up without his help. He took many rapid, harsh breaths. "Give me your hand again," he said. This time he clasped her hand in both of his. In time, his breathing slowed. "You have had a terrible life," he said. "Or at least you have been both terribly unlucky and astonishingly lucky: You should have died from your injuries. You should be too crippled to walk."

"Everything you say is true."

He dropped Zanja's hand and paced away, paused, and turned back. "Shaftal will become so dangerous? Her heroes will be survivors of repeated violence? What will be her enemies and how will they appear?"

"Tadwell, I don't know how to judge what I should and should not tell you. This is why I dare not be in a Truthken's presence, also."

"Such judgments are not yours to make!"

"I agree with you—but whose judgments are they? Would you have me satisfy your curiosity with no concern for the effect? If our positions were reversed, would you do such a thing?"

"I would do anything to prevent future ills."

"How could you possibly do so? Sir, it is arrogant and naive to think you know what is best for a people not yet born, in a land that will be much changed."

"By that logic, no one has any right to do anything at all under any circumstances!"

"Then I'm wrong," said Zanja. "I will begin by telling you when and how you will die."

"No!"

She gazed at him. Finally he looked away, muttering, "I suppose your caution is sensible."

"Arel knows I am journeying in time, but he doesn't know what direction I have traveled in. I've told nothing to anyone else."

"Good," he said. "But if you are dangerous—"

"The seer would have intervened!"

"Seers!" he said in disgust. "Why would a water witch choose you? What is it that you alone are capable of doing? And how can anything you do be right when you have been forced into doing it?"

"I don't know. But I must face this quandary alone."

"And you expect me to simply trust you to do what is right?"

"Yes, Tadwell. Just as Karis would trust me."

He looked at her, and looked away. "I cannot argue. The value she places on you is unmistakably present in your flesh. It is more convincing than any letter of introduction."

He walked away from her and stood in silence, gazing into the fire, as many people do when they are thinking. But he would not see any inspirational visions there; like any earth blood he was thinking about the problems of cause and effect, of risk and result. As he considered the situation she had presented him with, she considered the one he had presented to her: What am I alone capable of? It seemed a fearsome question, for she had done some awful things—however justifiable. She understood why Tadwell might be reluctant to set her loose upon this peaceful land.

Eventually she raised her eyes to find he had turned to her again. She saw a man beset and troubled, empowered but not particularly wise, a man like Karis and like herself, whose responsibilities usually seemed impossible to fulfill.

"You may continue to reside with Arel," said Tadwell. "But you may not leave his quarters."

"Yes, Tadwell."

That seemed to be all he had to say to her. She did not ask when he would decide what to do with her, for, like Karis, he would act as he felt compelled at whatever time his action seemed necessary. Zanja could only wait, an art at which she had little natural talent but much unfortunate practice.

Tadwell was heading for the door, and soon the room would again be crowded with anxious Paladins. "Sir," said Zanja. He turned sharply as if he anticipated he would have to assert his will over her some more. She strove to make her tone more humble. "May I study some glyph paintings during my isolation? For they are beautiful, and I would consider it a great kindness to be so allowed."

"Glyph paintings!" he exclaimed. "What use are they?" Then shaking his head, he added, "On the other hand, what harm are they?"

"This is a very peculiar imprisonment," commented Arel as Zanja ate the meat pie he had brought for her supper. When he first arrived, the door to his rooms had stood wide open, as the glyph master took his leave after reluctantly delivering to her a precious painting.

Arel said, "Where is the lock for the door? The armed guard? The shackles?"

"I think the G'deon is testing my obedience."

"At least you seem resigned."

"Then I am a finer actor than I thought."

The meat pie was delicious. Its flavorful gravy covered the deficiencies of long-stored vegetables and reconstituted meat. Living under the influence of an obsessive cook for just two months had taught Zanja to notice and appreciate kitchen skill. She paid attention to her meal. Arel was uncharacteristically restless. Perhaps he was feeling his own confinement, for Tadwell certainly would have forbidden him to ask Zanja any questions. Or perhaps he felt the tedium of mud season.

Zanja licked her plate and her fingers. She said, "Surely Tadwell will decide my fate before he returns to Basdown. But you'll be able to leave before he does—there's rarely a flood in the north, and the mountain ways will probably be passable by the time you reach them."

"Come with me," he said.

Zanja found herself unable to reply. Return to the Asha Valley? How could that possibility have not occurred to her? To travel into the mountains! To traverse those bright, dark, dangerous places with easy confidence! To go home!

She took a breath. "But it is not my home, my brother."

"You are Ashawala'i, a person-from-the-valley-of-stones!"

"It is not my valley—not my people—not even my stones."

Arel squatted before her. His braids swept the woven carpet. "My sister, do you think I cannot see your loneliness? Six years you have wandered! It is time to cease being a ghost. Your family, your lovers—they will not be there. But your tribe is your tribe, always."

She turned her face away from him. She heard him rise, giving her the distance and privacy that her gesture had requested. His movement across the room was nearly soundless. He stepped into the water closet and shut the door. He didn't come out until she was no longer weeping.

"I will sleep somewhere else tonight," he said.

"No, my brother—not for my sake. I enjoy your company."

He squatted again—at a distance. "I will tell you something: I have a lover here, among the Shaftali, and he has asked me to come to him."

"I am shocked," she said.

"Of course you have managed without a lover all your years of wandering."

Zanja met his gaze, and they both began to laugh.

Only after he had left did it occur to her that his lover was probably Tadwell.

The rain stopped falling two days later. News arrived that the Corber River had flooded. Tadwell would not attempt to return to the south until he could cross the Corber by bridge, and that would not be until the flood waters subsided.

As soon as the rains ended, a gentle wind began to blow almost constantly through the rooms and hallways of the House of Lilterwess, for every door and window was left open by day, and often by night as well. There began a cleaning revelry, a scrubbing and airing and washing that included every stone and even the skin, for people and even animals were bathed and combed. Laundry lines were strung in the open courtyard below Arel's one window, and there began an amazing beating of carpets that lasted from dawn to nightfall for several days. All of Arel's carpets were hauled out, and while he was taking his turn with the carpet-beaters, Zanja wore out a scrub brush and used up an entire cake of soap.

Then Arel left for the Asha Valley, without her. She had told him she must consider whether it would be wrong for her to bring into the valley those alien influences he had noticed when they first met. "We all carry our histories with us," she said. "But I am a Speaker—and like you, I am to be changed without causing change." She might go home with him in the autumn, she added. But she regretted even that modest promise when she said it, for such a wound of yearning opened up that she feared it might cause her intuition and judgment to become unreliable.

Choose insight, Medric had said: absurd advice, when insight pierces like arrows of light from the stars, or drops down out of an empty sky like an owl upon its prey. Yet a person does choose to climb the hillside towards the stars, or make oneself available to the owl. In this Shaftal, Zanja must live each moment like a casting of glyph cards, be able to ask any question and to accept any answer. By no other method would it be possible for her to slip through without destroying or undoing the Shaftal in which she did belong. She must desire only to return there—nothing else.

She began to be glad of her solitude, then. The days passed, and she danced her katra alone. She did not try to converse with the glyph master when he visited every day with a new painting, nor with the Paladin novices, Orna among them, who brought meals and carried away the waste. She did not even look out the window anymore. She meditated on the glyph paintings, and, gradually, all else ceased to matter.

At last, Tadwell came into the room and closed the door. Zanja had been meditating on a particularly difficult glyph painting, and her flesh felt like it had woven itself into the carpet. "Greetings, Tadwell. Please excuse me—I am somewhat befuddled." She hung the leather cover over the painting so it could not distract her.

As she turned back to Tadwell, he said abruptly, "Can you pretend to be a Paladin?"

Zanja made a long study of her bare feet, which she had absent-mindedly placed so they were harmonious with the carpet's pattern. "Lately I wish I had a Paladin's ethical training," she said. "And I doubt I can pretend to love speech as they do. But the greatest obstacle would be my appearance."

"I asked the Paladins if there's a reason a border person can't join them, and they say there isn't."

The answer would have been different, Zanja suspected, had she been a genuine aspirant. But she said neutrally, "I will pretend to be a Paladin. But I will not be one."

"Is there a difference between acting and being?"

"To a fire blood there's almost no difference at all, which is why I must defend the distinction so carefully."

Tadwell uttered a disgusted snort. "And in the meantime, the Paladins are convinced that permitting an impostor will denigrate the value of the reality. They did consent—but the integrity of the order must be defended. I promised them that if you violate their principles, I will personally hunt you down and…punish you."

"Would you kill me?"

There was a silence.

"I would expect you to," Zanja added.

"I have never killed anyone. But I would have to, I suppose. For if you prove to be unable to keep a simple promise, then I certainly can't trust you to guard yourself in the manner necessary to avoid an even greater harm. I have tried to imagine what could happen if you set some small event in motion…but all I feel certain of is that it must not happen. Therefore, I will kill you with my own hands if I must. You cannot hide from me, Zanja na'Tarwein—you are too singular for that. If you flee, I will chase you across the nearest border and let the desert do my killing for me—or the mountains—or the sea."

"I choose the mountains, then—and I will go willingly."

He said after a moment, "It would be your own life you'd be destroying if you were to fail. So you feel the importance of this more keenly than I do, don't you?"

"I am trying not to," she said. "Fear is no better than desire in my situation."

He turned away from her and opened the door. The house

commander and the novice, Orna, who had been waiting outside, came in. Orna hauled an impressive load of clothing and gear, and appeared to be stifling a delicious amusement. The house commander avoided even looking at Zanja. She laid a gold earring in the G'deon's hand.

Zanja knelt so Tadwell could pierce her left ear with a needle, and rose with the gold depending heavily and distractingly from her stinging earlobe. Orna helped Zanja to change into a Paladin's rough wool clothing—she was allowed to keep her underclothing, her boots, and her belt—and then stood back to look critically at her. Her forehead creased. She opened her mouth, but said nothing.

"Do I look so strange?" asked Zanja.

The young woman said rather helplessly, "Commander, it's just a piece of jewelry, a few articles of clothing. It should not make such a difference!"

The commander finally looked at Zanja. She made a study of her. Then she said to the novice, "Everything is framed: everything we know, everything we see. What has no frame cannot be seen at all. Yet the frame also shapes what we see, and even determines what we can see. To change the frame changes the thing itself. So now we have here a Paladin where there used to be a vagabond."

The girl protested, "I cannot believe that! I think she was—is—a Paladin in her heart. The clothing just makes her heart's truth visible."

Zanja said, "You are both wrong. I have been a katrim since I was twelve years old, and I am a katrim now. But a katrim is similar to a Paladin, and it is easier for you to see me as familiar than as strange."

"Apparently none of you realize how weary I am of philosophy," said Tadwell grumpily.

The two Paladins walked ahead, showing the way to the front door. A few people began to trail behind them—perhaps curious, or wishing to speak to Tadwell should there be an opportunity. They kept a polite distance, and Tadwell and Zanja managed one last private conversation. He said, " If there are any water witches in Shaftal, they are very secretive and they are invisible to me."

"There's a lake northwest of Kisha that I know as Otter Lake. I once met a water witch there, in an entire tribe of water people. It was an excellent place to live, so perhaps that tribe is also there now. I speak their language somewhat, so I'll go there first."

"You won't find any farms in that region," said Tadwell. "It's rough country."

"I'll live off the land, then."

"Only if you have the right gear!"

Tadwell called Orna back and quizzed her on the contents of Zanja's pack. Soon she ran off to find fish hooks, rabbit snares, and a light bow for fowling. When they reached the exit Tadwell gave Zanja some coins, irregular blobs of silver or copper stamped with the assayer's mark. In Zanja's time some of these ancient coins would still be in circulation, for, primitive though they looked, their weight would still be accurate. She stood with Tadwell in the balmy sunshine, waiting for Orna. By the time the young Paladin arrived, out of breath, her arms loaded with gear, Tadwell's face had softened with pleasure in the glorious day.

And why not be glad? Zanja was being set loose in a marvelous land that history had turned its back on during her lifetime. The earring meant that she would no longer suffer from hostility and suspicion. The foul weather was over and would not return until autumn. This adventure might well have a terrible ending, but why should she not enjoy it while she could?

"Farewell, Orna. Farewell, Tadwell."

"Safe journey," they both replied.

Suffused by eager curiosity, Zanja started down the road.

Chapter 18

When Clement isn't screaming, and isn't unconscious, she demands that her officers be brought to her, for she knows they will give her the last mercy. But the stranger who looks after her refuses.

"Endure," he says. "Endure for the G'deon, and for Shaftal."

"Shaftal's arse!" Her voice has broken like the frayed rope of a catapult.

Sound: horrific, monotonous, unrelenting. It tortures her, reminding her she has not managed to die.

A lukewarm broth is dribbled into her mouth. She closes her throat against it.

"Swallow."

She spits it out.

"It will help the pain," he says. "Swallow, Clement. I beg you."

How strange that her torturer has been weeping.

A warmth is rising in the back of her throat. Her jaw goes slack. He spoons more broth into her mouth. The warmth spreads from neck to shoulder to arm to fingertip. But the rhythmic, humble, horrid sound continues.

She wakes up, screaming. As in a nightmare, her torturers hold her down. The stranger's hands are bloody. "Give her more," he says.

The broth. The warmth.

The ordinary factuality of the horrific, rhythmic sound.

"Clement, endure. You're stronger than you know."

"How long?" she cries. "How long?" But she makes no sound.

Thud-thud. Thud-thud. The clockwork jerks mindlessly on. Each second lasts an hour.

Her guts are rotting. Her heart spreads the poison throughout her body.

The clock ticks on.

Clement heard someone breathing. She heard a wagon rolling past on a cobbled street. The faint, far-away carol of a rooster. The sturdy, rhythmic ticking of a distant clock. A baby yelping joyfully in her ear.

She opened her eyes in startlement. Scarcely a hand-span away, her son gave her a toothless, helpless, utterly joyful grin.

"You smiled!" Her voice sounded like tearing paper. "Gabie!"

She raised her hand with great difficulty, but then it seemed to float away, gaunt and bloodless, tethered to her heavy body by a wasted arm. She dragged her floating hand downward. It flopped nervelessly onto Gabian. He grabbed her finger, brought it to his mouth, and began sucking it happily.

A weight shifted. A sweat-sticky body, she realized, was pressed against her—the entire length of her. The hand that had been a weight on Clement's belly moved to her throat. Clement coughed, and coughed again.

A voice only somewhat less hoarse than hers said, "That son of yours will suck anything."

"Karis," Clement said. Her voice had become clear.

The hand moved down again to Clement's belly. "No more pain," Karis said. "Go back to sleep."

Clement's boy sucked her finger ecstatically, drooling, kicking his splayed legs. His tongue was soft as melted butter, but his suckling had amazing strength. Clement shut her eyes, and milk flowed from her fingertips in her dreams.

When Clement awoke next, the distant clock was still ticking, and muffled voices were shouting at each other. Gabian and Karis both were asleep. With much trouble Clement extricated herself from between the giant and the helpless infant. Then she fell off the bed. Her legs were so weak she could scarcely sit upon the chamber pot. She dragged herself into a cushioned chair and sat there, panting from effort.

She occupied a plain room with unpainted plank walls that were orange with age. Its one window was shuttered, though the air smelled quite foul. On the floor lay gray wool, shredded, black with old blood: her uniform. Beside it was a pile of blood-rusty bedsheets and bandages, and a quarrel with its iron head removed.

She looked down at her flat belly. A few flakes of dried blood were there, but no wounds and no scars.

She breathed deeply. Her heart beat. She felt the horror that crouched in the shadows.

The door opened. The stranger from her nightmares entered silently. He tucked the baby under Karis's arm and pulled the sheet to cover her. Clement noticed the soggy pile of Karis's discarded clothing. The bottoms of her cast-off boots had so little leather left that they hardly looked like boots at all.

The stranger asked, "Would you like to wash, General Clement?" His voice was quiet, respectful, gentle: not the voice of a torturer.

"Master healer," she said, "I must talk to my people."

"They will be glad of it, I think. But I'll take you to another room so the G'deon can rest."

He lifted her skillfully and walked her out the door, into a hall, where the shouting became very loud, and through another door into a room as plain as the last, but where the air smelled of rose petals and mold, not of death. He sat her in a chair and brought a bedsheet for her to wrap herself in. The sheet had been scented by wind.

"The rain has stopped?" asked Clement.

"The sun has been shining for two days now." The healer left.

The shouting ceased, and Clement heard booted feet hurrying down the hall. Soldiers filled the doorway and froze there, staring as though she'd risen from a bier with her rotting flesh sliding off her bones. Then Herme flung himself forward, clasping her hand in both of his and crying, "General! General!"

They crowded in after him, taking turns touching her, grinning crazily, furtively rubbing their eyes.

"Report—anyone," Clement said. "I was shot—that's all I know."

Herme said, "After the Wilton soldiers shot you with the cross-bow, they shot you with guns—and all the while, the gate captain was shouting at them to hold their fire. We carried you out of range, and the Paladins took us to this house. That Shaftali medic arrived the next morning and put his hands right into your belly to sew your bowels together with needle and thread. He forced a draught into you, but if it was for pain it didn't do much good, or not for long."

The horror stepped out of the shadows. She willed it back, but it lay down and watched her.

"What happened then?"

"The Paladins wouldn't allow us to give you mercy," said Efrat. "And they kept apologizing to us, the bastards!"

"The Paladins killed the raven," Herme said. "They made a broth from its carcass and fed it to you. The bird told them to do it."

"Gods of my mother!" cried Clement, appalled.

Mereth said, "With wounds like that, you shouldn't have survived one day. But you survived six. And last night the G'deon came."

"From Watfield? In six days?"

"In the middle of the night she slammed right through the door. The latch and lock broke into a dozen pieces."

Another said, "Day and night she must have walked without rest. Her feet were bleeding—she was pale as death."

"The local Paladins didn't know who she was. They thought it was an attack."

Sevan said, "Well, she's better than a whole battalion, eh? Whose side is she fighting on, though?"

Clement said, "Why does it matter? We just have to make bloody certain we're beside her, whichever way she happens to face."

Thirty officers laughed, saying, "That's right, general. It doesn't matter. Not a bit." Mereth fell silent first.

Clement remembered Saleen's laughter, and his sigh as he collapsed so neatly to the wet cobblestones. "Commander Saleen was killed."

Mereth nodded, quite expressionless. "And General Mabin." Clement remembered the old woman's feral grin. A poor governor, maybe—but a great leader, justly revered.

Efrat said, "We could have been killed in retribution. But the Paladins we'd traveled with put themselves between us and the irregulars, and they've been protecting us ever since, I guess, keeping the Wilton Paladins away from us and standing up to the shouting mobs that have gathered outside the door."

"And apologizing?"

Efrat grinned wryly. Sevan said, "They've been good friends to us, and that's the truth of it. And after all this, Watfield Garrison's gates are still closed."

The horror gazed steadily at her. "What were you shouting about?" she asked.

"Oh, that was them, the Paladins," said Denit.

"Bloody hell! Paladins never shout." But with Mabin and Saleen both dead, the bitter Commander Ronal was the senior Paladin officer.

"That would be the Watfield Paladins, arguing with Ronal," she said. "Have they been shouting at each other for six days?"

"Not all the time," said Denit dryly.

"Someone bring Ronal and his officers to me," Clement said. "In fact, bring all the Paladins you can find."

Two of them went out, chuckling with anticipation, and returned with Ronal, some of his officers, and three exhausted Watfield Paladins.

"What were you people arguing about?" Clement asked Ronal.

"I will not answer to you," Ronal said.

"I am the officer in charge of this operation!"

One of the Watfield Paladins said, "Clement, Ronal has mustered all the companies in the west—nearly two hundred Paladin irregulars and their commanders—and many have already arrived, with more arriving all the time."

"Do you intend to violate the truce, Ronal?" asked Clement.

"Mabin has been killed by Sainnite guns! The truce has already been violated!"

"Mabin and Saleen defied my direct command and put themselves in the way of the bullets my people were shooting at me. At me!"

"The Watfield Sainnites concealed from us that they had not given up all their weapons—"

"The decision to renew the war is not yours!"

"The war is over," said Karis.

She filled the doorway, red-eyed, dirty, dressed only in her limp longshirt. She held Gabian in one arm, and with the other supported herself against the alarmingly creaking door frame. The Wilton Paladins gaped at her. A Watfield Paladin said, "Ronal, this is Karis G'deon." Ronal began to say one or another of those bloody Paladin courtesies, but Karis said impatiently, "Why am I hemmed in by sharpened edges? Does everyone in this city have a weapon?"

Ronal let his breath out. "Paladins are arriving from afar to defend Shaftal."

"Oh, for land's sake! Send them home!"

Ronal's mouth opened. One of the black-dressed Paladins lay a hand on his shoulder and murmured to him in a tone that was urgent but kind. Ronal studied his feet. "Would you speak directly to the commanders, Karis?"

Karis sighed. "Yes."

Ronal's jaw muscles were working. "I'll bring them to you." He quit the room, and moments later the front door slammed shut.

"Give Karis a place to sit," said Clement to her people.

A path was opened to a chair beside the bed. Karis glanced at the chair, handed Gabian to the nearest soldier, and sat on the floor. Her shirt was buttoned crookedly, and the hair on one side of her head was squashed. Rubbing her eyes, with her long legs folded beneath her, she looked like a gigantic child awakened from a nap.

As Gabian was passed from soldier to soldier, each of them in turn had to figure out how to hold the baby. At last Efrat handed Gabian to Clement. He blinked at her, clutched a bit of the wind-scented sheet, and fell back asleep.

"Well, General," said Karis. "What now?"

Bloody hell, thought Clement. How could Karis have come this far and have no plan?

"Emil wonders if there are people in Wilton garrison whose hearts, at least, are in mutiny against Heras."

"I'm certain there are—but it's the officers that matter. Now it seems Heras may have people in every company whose orders come directly from her, and the officers know it now. And they know she tricked them into mutiny." Clement felt something—a bit of hope— and then realized what it meant. The horror grinned at her.

Karis said wearily, "You're not lying to me, are you?" At least she seemed too tired to be furious.

"Karis, if Heras had killed me, that would have ended her ambitions also. The commanders won't accept as general anyone who kills her rival. Strategically, it was worth the risk."

Karis said nothing. It occurred to Clement that Karis's ability to lead had never been tested. She was a woman of strength—strength in many forms—but not of subtlety. Her decisions were made by aversion and instinct; people did as she asked because of devotion rather than persuasion. But to think through options, to make unappealing choices, that was unnatural to her. She was intelligent—intelligent enough to carefully deploy or inhibit her own impulses, intelligent enough to surround herself with and heed advisors who could make certain she never acted in ignorance, or on impulse.

Karis may have been thinking something similar, for she said, "I'm unable to consult with Emil. These Paladins—" She glanced at them, and they blinked owlishly at her, practically asleep on their feet.

Clement spoke hastily, fearful that the horror would leap out and grab her by the throat. "I must go back to the garrison."

Efrat, apparently understanding Clement, cried in their own language, "They'll shoot you again, General!"

Clement kept her gaze only on Karis, who gazed steadily back at her.

"Right now," Karis said finally, "I couldn't save you if they shoot you again."

"Right now I can't even walk by myself."

"You just need to eat," Karis said. "Tomorrow, then."

It took three people to get the G'deon to her feet. The Paladins took her away.

As two of the women officers helped Clement to bathe and eat, she frequently heard the front door open and close, and there were voices and noisy footsteps in the hall. The women lay Clement down to rest in the room that smelled of roses, with Gabian in an improvised nest of blankets on the floor. Karis seemed to have brought nothing with her but the baby. When the more urgent business had been taken care of, Clement would ask a Paladin to fetch a bottle and diapers.

She started awake at the sound of the door latch. Karis, ducking her head, filled up the doorway as Mereth, on guard in the hall, saluted smartly.

Karis sat heavily by Clement on the groaning bed. "Norina can strangle people with their own opinions in just a few words. It takes me most of the afternoon."

"Karis—my people told me about the raven."

The lamp's flame had become a dim red glow, and the light that filtered through the shutters was a dim haze. Karis dug her fingers into the tangled mess of her hair, and her features were lost in shadow. "My raven's death hurt me," she said. "But it condemned you."

The horror smelled like rotting flesh. It dug its long teeth into her viscera and ate a leisurely meal. For six days it had eaten her. Six days.

Clement was shuddering too violently to speak.

"Clement—stop."

Karis's callused hand lay heavy on her forehead. The G'deon's eyes were red and swollen; her hand was rough and cold. And the horror was gone. Clement took a deep breath.

Karis said, "In Lalali I awoke every morning knowing I would be raped that day. They gave me smoke to make me pliable, and I soon came to love the drug. Under smoke, being raped was quite ordinary and painless. So I ask you, was the drug a gift or a curse?"

"If there is no escape—"

"I would have escaped when I was old enough—if not for the drug."

"I understand," Clement said. "I am very, very clear."

Karis's hand still rested upon Clement's forehead. And when she lifted it, the horror would return.

"My courage is gone," Clement said.

"I know."

"I can't go to the garrison—not tomorrow, not any day."

"I know," Karis said.

She did not lift her hand, not even when the healer looked in. "Can you make a sleeping potion for the general?" she asked him.

"Yes, Karis. And for you also."

Clement saw her gaze shift to something on the floor. The baby.

The healer said, "We've found a couple who are able to look after him. They have a son of their own, a few months older than he is. And she has plenty of milk."

"Have someone bring Gabian to them," Clement said. It should have been agony to say, but it wasn't.

"I'll drink your potion," Karis said to the healer.

The healer left, taking Gabian with him.

"They'll shoot you again," Karis said.

"More than likely."

"How many times will it take, to convince them you cannot be killed? More than two? More than three?"

"I don't know."

Karis lifted her hand, without warning.

Clement said, "You were making a joke."

"A grim joke."

The horror was there. Clement must talk quickly, for it soon would take her by the throat again. "What you did makes me clear—clear but stupid. The longer you did it, the stupider I became." She must talk faster, faster, faster. "Can you change me, make me like that, so I continue like that, even without your touch?"

Karis said nothing.

"Answer quickly," Clement said.

"I can do it. But down the road—"

"To hell with the bloody road! Do you want a hero tomorrow? Or a spineless coward? Bloody hell!"

It had her again. And then it was gone, for Karis laid a hand upon her forehead. Karis said, "Listen, while you are clear, before you get stupid. You will pay a price, a terrible price. Every day you're without pain will give you a legacy of worse pain. This fear may be intolerable now—but later it will drive you insane."

"I understand, Karis," said Clement. "But only tomorrow matters. I'll pay whatever price must be paid."

Karis did not speak again. She stayed with her. Until the healer returned with a potion, until the potion began to take effect, Karis remained beside Clement, with her hand upon her, granting her that costly mercy.

Chapter 19

The roads were firm, the sky clear, the air cool but not cold, the inclines gradual. Zanja's winter fat had sloughed off like the skin from a snake. Though her load of gear was not light, she jogged easily past other early-season travelers. Even a rich man on horseback with nothing better to do could not keep up as he attempted to engage Zanja in conversation. She ran most of the distance to Shimasal, where she left the highway and trotted along eastbound wagon tracks, waving to farmers in orchards and in fields, where the spring plowing and planting had begun. After she reached the Kisha highway her pace slowed somewhat as she climbed into the highlands, down into the Aerin River Valley, across the river and up into highlands again. She had outrun spring: Some few flowers had begun to bloom behind her, but here in apple and nut country the trees had scarcely awakened, and nearly the entire populace had turned out to repair the highway.

When Zanja told a friendly innkeeper that she intended to leave the road to go west, the innkeeper protested, "There's nothing west of here. Nothing but rocks." He was wrong, for there were more cultivated lands, but after one last night in a bed and one final generous breakfast, Zanja trotted right past the edge of Shaftali civilization. Now, far ahead of her, she could sometimes spot the hazy jumble of foothills that marked the meeting of western and northern mountains. Trees became sparse and stunted, and she had to slow to a walk so she could hunt for meat and collect firewood as she traveled. The pathless last leg of her journey was by far the slowest. Yet by the time Zanja was wading through the heather that in her time still would cover the rockscape of the northwestern borderlands, only fourteen days had passed.

Alone in the desolate landscape, she was the only thing moving between the horizons. Shaftal's walls had been built to make the world smaller, she supposed, so that within those narrow horizons people could feel like gods. Now, especially at night when she lay in the open without even the symbolic comfort of a fire, there was no escaping her own unimportance. She could believe it was possible to literally die of loneliness.

At last she reached the edge of the canyon, that vast earthwork with which the Otter River guarded Shaftal's northern border. She had not been to this place since she and Emil and Medric had brought Karis here, after rescuing her from Mabin.

There Karis had been helped by water magic as she fought her way out of addiction. There Karis had begun to remake all her old decisions. There she and Zanja, on the verge of clasping hold of each other, had nearly lost each other. And then it had begun.

The wind made a hollow cry as it moved through the canyon. The sun lay low on the horizon, and to the east and the west the canyon seemed a black wound in the ruddy flesh of the earth. But at Zanja's feet the canyon was so wide that the beautiful lake that lay cupped in its vast hands still glowed with light. She could not possibly have failed to find Otter River, but she had not expected she could aim herself so accurately at the lake itself. Now, to find herself unexpectedly so close to her destination made her impatient—too impatient to even look for a path. She stashed most of her gear, took off her boots, and climbed down the escarpment by twilight.

The sky was still red, but in the canyon it was full dark when Zanja reached the loose boulders and rubble that cluttered the canyon bottom. Here she was at greater risk of injury from uncertain footing than when climbing the perpendicular walls. She had to scramble over boulders taller than she, and the moonless night grew ever darker. When she reached the lakeshore, she was scraped, bruised, and limping. There she could faintly hear frog song and the echoing cry of a waterbird.

The island in the middle of the lake lay silent: no distant fires glowed, no voices or laughter carried sweetly across the water. The possibility that she might not find the people she sought had scarcely occurred to Zanja. Yet this canyon was no more inhabited than the rocky heath above. The Otter People were not here.

She sat on a stone, stunned. The sky filled with stars, and suddenly she could no longer bear to be under the open sky. When she and her friends had taken shelter in this canyon, there had been a pebble beach and a cave. She certainly would go to bed hungry this night, but if she could find the cave, at least she might have a roof over her head. She began to follow the water's edge, feeling her way across unsteady stones.

A big boulder blocked her way. With sore hands she hauled herself up to the top. There she knelt on bruised knees, gazing with astonishment at the pebble beach she sought, and at the campfire that burned near the water's edge.

As she drew closer, she could see a little boat scarcely bigger than a washtub that was drawn up on shore. She could see the small, withered man who squatted on his heels by the fire, dressed only in a simple skirt. And then she could see him clearly enough that she could realize she knew him. It was the Otter Elder who would befriend Karis some two hundred years in the future.

Zanja stood for a moment on the water-smoothed stones. *As far as my intelligence casts its light, I think that is all that exists. But in fact I only see a small part.* She walked up to the campfire and bowed with her hand over her heart. "I greet thee, Otter Elder," she said in his tongue.

"I greet thee, Zanja na'Tarwein. Wilt thou eat with me?"

She set down her boots and bedroll, and sat beside the Otter Elder's fire. The air was clear and still, and the smoke flowed directly upward. She smelled the crisp, mineral scent of the lake. Her heartbeat thrummed in her ears.

The Otter Elder skewered fish that he took from a basket, and suspended them over the fire to cook. "Thy journey hath been long," he commented, grinning so wrinkles spread like ripples across his leathery face: the face of a man who had been laughing for hundreds of years.

"Yes, Elder—a very long journey. And a very surprising one."

"Thy way is always uncommon," he said, or something similar. Zanja's command of the water tongue was tentative, and she relied heavily on intuition to understand him.

She said, "Yes, Elder. Will you explain to me something? Water/ time flows downhill, but now it also flows up—back." She made her hand into a wave and showed it climbing upward. "How can that be?"

The Otter Elder made a clearing gesture as if to remove the invisible picture Zanja had drawn. "Time/water does not flow. It is a still lake. We swim, we float, we fish in it."

Zanja tried to imagine herself swimming steadily in one direction through the vast lake of time. Someone intercepted her, dragged her under, and pulled her backwards, so she came up in a different place. For a moment this little story almost made sense to her.

But if time were a still lake, then why could she and most people only experience it as if it were moving? Why could she not stop, or even go backwards, whenever she liked?

And how was it possible to be human under such circumstances? To be shaped and burdened by the past, to have desire or determination for the future, without these qualities a person would come to a standstill, would exist in each moment without pain or purpose. Should that happen, wouldn't Zanja's passions and griefs, accomplishments and disasters, all prove to be mere delusions?

To water logic such a prospect might seem a funny joke. But to Zanja it was dreadful. Polite only with effort she said, "I fear thou art thought-broken, elder."

He laughed out loud with such delight that Zanja found herself smiling in reply despite herself. "Zanja na'Tarwein, thy thoughts are small!" His hands shaped a vessel the size of a person's head. Then he threw out his arms in a gesture that seemed to encompass the whole of the lake, the canyon, the sky. "Thou canst not hold this…."

He used a word that Zanja could only guess at. Perhaps he meant wholeness or completeness. Perhaps he meant that moment of time.

She said, "If I am swimming in time/water, then how can I swim home?"

"Thou canst not swim at all!" declared the old man.

"I can swim," she grumbled.

The Otter Elder grinned. "The one who fetched thee here must return thee to thy place."

"Must?" she asked sharply.

"Yes. Or drown with thee."

"Truly?"

He nodded, smiling benignly, as a parent smiles upon a stumbling toddler.

"Was it thee who did this to me? Or dost thou know who? Or why?"

"Thy life is a dance, Zanja na'Tarwein. Thou danceth the steps that suit thee best, and to observe thy dance is to know thy heart." He rose up, grinning, and danced a few steps to illustrate.

It was the beginning of the katra—Zanja's katra, graceless, but recognizable.

Hooting with laughter, he capered to his boat and lifted out a basket filled with the bread the Otter People made of wild grain that they cooked in thin cakes on flat stones. The old man did not interrupt Zanja's offended silence until the cooked fishes became loose on their skewers and he neatly caught the flesh with pieces of bread as it fell.

They ate. Zanja instructed herself to observe, heed the impulse of curiosity, formulate a question. "Dost thou know who else has been observing my dance?" she finally asked.

"Thou art interesting," he said. "The way thou floatest on the flood. The way thou continually turnest to face the rising water. The subtlety of thy movements as thou drowneth and reclaimeth thy world. There is no one else like thee!"

"I am only living as I must. That I am interesting does not seem a thing to be punished!"

"Ah, thou seekest fairness," said the Otter Elder mockingly.

Zanja understood his words but not his explanations. She tried again: "Who has brought me here?"

"The other one."

"Another water witch? Another Otter Elder?"

"She is a woman of the tides, as I am a man of the floods; she is a woman of salt water, not sweet."

"Is she of a coastal tribe, then? Or is she not a tribal woman at all?"

The Otter Elder shrugged as though such details were of no importance. "I know her; I do not know her." He abruptly took a bone flute out of its fish skin sack and began to play.

At first, the hollow, melancholy, sweet music of the flute did nothing to ease Zanja's frustration. Like the conversation, it seemed without pattern: one note led to the next, but without sense, phrasing, or predictability. The music was sweet without being pleasing. Yet Zanja could only listen, for to interrupt would have been unimaginably rude.

She remembered she was tired. Her feet and muscles ached from the hard, fast journey. Slowly, sharp-edged stars blurred; their edges melted together and the old beauty of their separate lights became a glorious new beauty: vast sweeps of light, shimmering and strange. They swirled—no, Zanja herself spun below them even though she sat still—no, it was the bands of light that were moving, after all. The light was the music, the music was the light. The turning of the sky was the turning of the land. Zanja was dancing her katra, the dance of her people. Her dancing met the music; the music met the stars; the stars turned with the earth; the earth supported her dance.

When the music ended, it seemed Zanja still could hear it. Slowly, the dance left her. She was sitting by the fire. She noted incuriously that the fire had not died down although no wood had been added in all the time she had been there. She did not know how long that had been, whether hours or days.

When she awakened in the morning, the Otter Elder was gone, along with his boat, his flute, his baskets, the ashes of the fire, and even the smoke stains on the rocks. She ate the oatcakes she had carried with her into the canyon, as the sun rose over the glimmering, wind-ruffled lake. The island was alive with birds but not with people; the only swimmers were the fish that marked their presence with radiating ripples. Zanja had no boat, and she did not know how to row or sail one, anyway. The river offered a way to the sea, but if she went that way, intending to scour Shaftal's contorted coastline for a single individual, she must accept that it might take years to accomplish her task.

She rose stiffly up from her stony bed. She could still hear, or feel, the music of the Otter Elder's flute, but the sound was as distant as a dream. The passing moments of her life had caught her up in their current again, and unlike the Otter Elder she could not swim backwards, except by remembering. What she remembered now was the university at Kisha, which she had seen once before the Sainnites destroyed it. But an old saying had survived the university's destruction: "There are no mysteries in Kisha." She would go to Kisha, with its vast library and revered scholars, and there seek someone who could tell her where to look for an ocean tribe.

Kisha lay where Zanja had already gone: she could return along her own trail, camp in the same sites, build new campfires in the remains of the old. This repeat journey might prove valuable or might prove useless. She felt she had gained something here at Otter Lake, and perhaps she might gain something more at the university. But she feared that her journey had scarcely begun. In the meanwhile Karis struggled alone along a path she could not see, with the future of Shaftal in her arms. Karis needed Zanja, and Zanja was not there. Lonely, joyless, and troubled, she once more set her aching feet on the trail.

Chapter 20

The Paladins give Clement Saleen's dagger. This was not in the plan.

She holds the weapon, and it is cold and heavy. No rust, no rust pits, carefully and properly sharpened, well balanced. "A good blade," Clement says.

The Watfield Paladins nod, and one says, "A good man." Their eyes are shining.

"You will remember him in the blade," Karis murmurs. The G'deon is standing with all the others in the alley. Her face is pale. Her feet are so painful she can hardly walk. But she has come, so she can save Clement again.

"In the blade," Clement says, "I will remember Saleen."

The Paladins brush at tears. Two step forward to remove Clement's belt, attach the sheath, and put the belt back on her. She does know how to do this herself, though. The belt is necessary to keep the blood-stiff, shredded remains of her tunic from flapping open, for she wears no undershirt. She is glad the Paladins put the belt back on her.

Earlier, one of the officers had taken off her own tunic for Clement to wear. Clement was doing the fastenings, then the plan came to her. She had taken the tunic off and given it back. "I'll wear my ruined tunic. Find Karis for me."

Karis had come in, and Clement had told her the plan. Clement had acted very calm. But her breathing, that had been wrong. Karis had said, "Shall I do it now?"

Now Clement is clear. She sheaths Saleen's knife. She steps from the shadowed alley into hazy sunshine.

She wades in mist. Her blood-stiff trousers chafe her crotch. The thick sunlight casts a damp warmth onto exposed skin. Her steps disturb the mist. A haze of light rises up around her.

She has reached the gate. The quarrel that had pierced her is in her hand. "Soldiers of Watfield Garrison!" she cries. "Tell Heras her general has returned her quarrel!"

She flings the bolt up into the light, over the wall, over the barricade.

Up on the rampart she hears exclamations, and the creaks and thuds of hurried movement. Now scuffling, grunting, the whack of a fist. A gun blast. A ball of lead smacks into a building's stone wall. These soldiers need target practice, Clement thinks.

The plan: Clement pulls back the rags from her unscarred belly. "Shoot me!"

She waits. She observes the spyholes and glimpses movement. The soldiers are peering at her. She reviews again what she had told herself before, before Karis made her so clear. A new captain, for Megert had not been loyal enough. New orders. Heras thought Clement was dead. Heras realizes that Clement has won. She might kill her again, but then Clement will win again.

Heras has always been clear.

Clement waits. A shutter slams down the street. A dog barks. A vendor sings. The sun has risen a little more.

"A long wait is good," she had told Karis before dawn. "It means someone is fetching Heras, which means the gate captain doesn't know what to do. And that means Heras is beginning to lose her people."

From the other side of the gate there comes a clangor. The bars that secure the siege gate are being removed and dropped. The gate begins to vibrate and utter a squawk as a dozen soldiers grab handholds and endeavor to break loose the rust-frozen rollers. An officer shouts a cadence. In short jerks, with many an ear-splitting squeal, the gate opens. A palm's width, an arm's length. The breadth of a single soldier. Clement sees, through the bars of the primary gate, the new captain squirting oil into the massive lock. He begins wrestling with the key.

Clement waits.

The lock opens with a squawk. Two soldiers step out to swing the gate upon its shrieking hinges. The narrow opening in the siege gate frames a person on the other side. She is waiting. It is Heras.

"The soldiers will think I'm a ghost," Clement had told Karis.

The two soldiers stare, wide-eyed. Clement steps forward. She had once thought of Heras as a predator. She had realized she herself was the prey. To be with her had become terrifying. Yet Clement had never ceased to want her.

Speak so the captain can hear. No one else will matter.

"I am your general," Clement says. "I am taking command of this garrison." She makes her voice loud. She speaks clearly.

"Welcome, my general," Heras says.

Clement steps forward. Heras looks at her closely. But Heras is not important. Clement steps into the garrison. The primary gate clangs shut behind her.

"Heras will lock me in," she had said to Karis, "to prevent me from being dragged to safety again."

Loudly and clearly, Clement says, "The G'deon is here."

"Is she?" Heras says. "Will she rescue her puppet general? Will she knock down our walls? I'd like to see that—but this G'deon is an impostor, isn't she?"

Clement says, "Captain, take Heras into custody for mutiny."

The captain doesn't move. Heras draws her saber. Saleen's dagger is a weight on Clement's belt. To draw it is not in the plan.

"I will not spill Sainnite blood," Clement says. She is speaking to the captain. "But if my blood is spilled, this garrison's walls will fall down."

Clement drops to one knee. The saber slashes in air where her throat had been.

"Draw!" Heras cries. "Draw, damn you!"

"I would rather die," Clement says.

Heras lifts her arm. Clement has seen many a dummy decapitated by the blow. "I can't put your head back on your body," Karis had said that morning. Clement is looking into Heras's eyes. Heras does not blink. The saber begins to sing.

There is a dissonant clang of steel on steel. Heras's saber flings itself upward over her head. She snatches it out of the air. The blade that blocked the blow rings on stones. It will have to be resharpened.

"Guard your general!" someone cries.

Soldiers fling themselves between Clement and Heras. Clement stands up. The gate captain is now beside her. He has no weapon. He shouts up at the rampart. Soldiers grab at each other. Weapons are drawn. The captain shouts. The resisting soldiers are overwhelmed.

The gate captain says, "General, please pardon that I didn't act sooner, but they had to see that she would kill you with her own hand. Shall I have myself placed under arrest?"

This was not in the plan. Clement does not know the answer to the captain's question. She ignores it. "Heras and all the lieutenant commanders are to be arrested. Open the gate. Your new commander is waiting outside."

"Yes, General." The captain pushes through to Heras and tells her to surrender her weapon.

Heras places her saber point over her heart, and falls. The blade plunges through. The soldiers cry out.

Heras has missed her own heart. She is silent, grappling with the saber. She puts a leg out, but cannot rise. She pulls the saber. She slashes her hands upon its edge.

Clement draws Saleen's dagger and cuts her old friend's throat.

Chapter 21

At a settlement in the north, a woman is standing outdoors under the vast awning of an ancient oak tree. The tree is bare, not even budding yet, and the raven normally would not come so close to the woman. However, several other ravens have gathered here to dispute possession of the tree, and the raven is able to hide in this small crowd of black-dressed hoodlums.

The assassin is painting a portrait on a piece of wood that has been cut and planed as thin and smooth as human hand can manage. The central figures are complete: the two youngest children of the family, dressed in their best clothing and holding favorite toys. It is odd to see them remain so neat and still, for in life they are neither. Now that the rain has ended, the assassin has begun to paint the background. Having sketched in the shapes of the hills and trees, the fields and buildings and orchards, with her brush she now lays down layers of color. But her colors are not the grays and browns of the muddy landscape before her: she dresses the hills with grass, the trees with flowers, the sky with birds. She paints the spring that has not yet begun.

In the Barrens north of Basdown, not even a raven can find sustenance at this time of year. The fast-moving voles survive on the grass hay they gathered in autumn. The crickets have not emerged yet, nor have the lizards and snakes. Little else can live in this wasteland. Every evening the raven flies the long distance to the nearest farm in Basdown, where the cow dogs permit him to share their supper, and then flies back in darkness to continue his surveillance of the assassin.

Now that the rain has ended, the assassin cooks outdoors, and as he nurses his small fire he whittles sticks into snakes, or deer, or birds. He throws the shavings into the fire, and then the finished carvings as well. He has very little wood.

One night, the raven arrives from his usual scavenging journey to find the camp as usual, the man in shelter, probably already sleeping. Not until morning does the raven realize his quarry has slipped away. He flies to a great height and surveys the empty landscape but sees no movement in any direction.

The door of sunset creaked each day to a close, and the dawn bells marked the opening of the next door. Ten times this happened. After Seth's duties with Prista's company ended each day, she sought out Gilly, whom she usually found in Ellid's work room. He would look up from whatever he happened to be reading or writing and say briefly, "No news."

Only three people in the garrison knew that Clement was probably dead.

Several times, Seth visited Travesty to meet with the Peace Committee, and changed clothes before she went, folding her handed-down uniform into the nearly empty chest, putting on her wrinkled breeches and longshirt. This changing of clothing helped her to move from one culture to the other, but it became increasingly difficult, and then nearly impossible, to change back to being a soldier again. Yet she was merely pretending to do the thing they hoped to ask these soldiers to do in earnest.

When the rain finally ended, some things improved and some things grew worse. Prista's company went for long, brisk marches through the countryside, and Damon often was removed from interminable guard duty to join them. During off-hours, many soldiers fussed over the flower garden, and Seth took over the care of Clement's bit of garden. She lifted the mulch to reveal hundreds of green fingers poking through the heavy brown soil in which they had wintered. Damon told her to look in Clement's quarters for more bulbs, bulbs that were too tender for Shaftal's hard winter. She found baskets of them, clean, dry, packed in straw as if they were precious glassware. Damon taught her how to plant them, and she managed to not weep until he had left to pursue his own tasks in his precious bit of earth.

They opened up the barracks to the breeze and scrubbed everything, including their uniforms and themselves, and Seth no longer felt ill from the stink of twenty-two women living shoulder to shoulder all winter. She no longer had to wake up in dead of night to watch over the stove for an hour; its fire had been allowed to burn out. But now there was battle practice, which Seth loathed; the seething angers of barracks-weary soldiers became an aimless bewilderment that no one knew how to manage; and the food became even worse.

One day a note, grimy after having been passed from hand to hand all over the garrison, was handed to her. On a small square of paper was written a single word, followed by Emil's glyph. "Healed," it said. On her knees in wet earth, with a basket of stable muck beside her and a cultivating tool in her hand, she stared at that note for a good quarter hour. She had expected Emil to confirm that Clement was dead. She didn't know what to do with the fact she was alive.

When she visited Gilly as usual that day, she found him alone in Ellid's work room, with tears on his face. She sat with him, and he talked about Clement: how when they were young she had protected him from Heras; how after battle she always was ill; how she had detested Cadmar; how haunted she had been by her crimes against Shaftal.

"She told me this mission was going to kill her," he said, "and I'm the only one she told. But she's alive. She killed Heras with her own hand. Four more times, she must do something similar, or worse." He rocked with pain upon his clerk's stool, still holding his pen upon which the ink had long since dried. "It will destroy her," he said.

Emil sent for her. At Travesty, Seth greeted the off-duty dogs and noticed that the floor was clean. The walls also had been scrubbed, the lamp hooks were polished, and the furniture was dusted. In the big foyer, where random people had always hung about, the furniture was turned topsy-turvy. Three people hoisted a rolled carpet to their shoulders. Several others carried armloads of cushions and draperies. A half dozen people with buckets and scrub brushes worked their way across the dingy stone floor.

"Keep those dirty dogs away!" A man approached, armed with two feather dusters and a basket of cleaning rags.

Seth grabbed the dogs by the collars.

"There's a mountain of laundry to be done," the man said. "Fireplaces, ash cans, windows,…" He listed tasks, his gaze flicking about the room as though he trusted no one to do the work properly.

Seth said, "I'm Mariseth of Basdown. I'm a councilor."

He put his hands on his hips and subjected Seth to a minute examination. "Apparently, you can sew. So why does everything want mending?"

Astonished, Seth said, "I'm learning how to govern the country!"

"How can you govern when this place is so filthy?" He stalked off.

"Goodness!" said Seth to no one. "He needn't be so brusque about it."

One of Norina's young students admitted her into the restricted part of the house. Here the dark corners still housed dust kittens, and the walls were gray with old soot. The dirt from Karis's demolition work lay thick on the ornate furniture. The dining room, though, was pristine as always, and unusually empty. Seth looked into the kitchen, where a crowd of cooks were chopping, frying, kneading, trimming, mixing, and talking loudly and cheerfully as Garland moved briskly from table to stove to storeroom, murmuring commands and compliments. He spotted Seth and came over to give her a kiss, with his floury hands clasped behind his back so he could not use her as a hand towel.

"Did you know you've got an army of housecleaners in the front half?" she asked.

"No, but blessings on them, I say."

"I'm sure they'd do the rest of the building also, if the Truthkens let them in."

"I'll have to feed them too," Garland said happily. "And are you hungry?"

He gave her a generous plate full of food, which she brought to the library with her. There, Emil sat at his worktable with his back to her, and she could tell by the stink of glue that he was repairing a book. Deep within the bookshelves, she heard a shuffling, a sigh, and then silence. Emil turned his head, though she had not spoken. "I'm almost done, Seth. How have you been?"

"Living with the Sainnites is a misery. Why must they eat such swill? And why must they sleep in such uncomfortable beds?" She sat in one of the armchairs, which was not as cozy as it looked. "Why must they be informed of my position and authority before they'll talk with me? Why must they always stand as though they have beanpoles rammed up their butts?"

"Because they do have beanpoles rammed up their butts," said a muffled tenor voice from within the maze of books—Medric.

"It's a good idea, though," said Emil. Medric laughed sharply. Emil clarified, "To live with them. Don't let a librarian see that you've brought food in here."

After dealing with angry and listless soldiers, Seth thought she could manage a librarian. She sat in an armchair by the fireplace, where a low fire burned day and night to protect the precious books from damp. She ate a piece of meat pie, vegetable patties, stewed dried peaches, and a fat slice of butter cake. Emil finished his gluing and wiped his hands on a rag. "Medric, have you got a map yet?"

Medric, who must have been the source of the shuffling among the books, didn't answer.

Emil sat in the chair opposite Seth, glanced at her empty plate, and said, "No crumbs. You even eat like a soldier."

"Or like a starving animal."

"We must get those people better food."

"And worthwhile work. By now they would normally be running around the countryside, collecting taxes and fighting Paladins. The captains keep us busy, but everyone knows it's just empty activity. That's not good for people. We have to believe we're doing something worth doing. And since soldiers only value fighting—" She sighed.

That hollow in her belly had not been helped by food. Perhaps it wasn't hunger at all. "They're teaching me to kill people," she said.

"That can't be an easy job for them."

She glanced up at his face. Yes, it had been a wry joke. "Gilly thinks that Clement won't recover from what she has to do."

"Why don't people tell me things when I can do something about them?" Emil seemed more weary than angry. He shut his eyes for a moment.

"Can Norina help her, do you think?"

"I don't know. Norina had to settle for half measures with Zanja."

Medric spoke, startlingly close. "What a couple of gloomy people you are. Your map, General Emil." He delivered a Sainnite's salute, mockingly exaggerated, and handed Emil a rolled piece of parchment.

Emil glanced at the notations on the outside of the document. "It's two hundred and thirty years old. A Truthken's map—Norina might be interested in it. It'll work, I suppose."

He carefully unrolled the crackling, ancient parchment and held it open across his legs. "Where is our missing assassin, Master Seer?"

"Don't call me that," Medric said.

"But you called me 'general.'"

"Oh, revenge is it?"

Medric pointed at the map. Emil turned it so Seth could see what Medric was pointing at: Basdown.

Seth felt the gorge rise in her throat. Medric promptly handed her a cup half-full of cold tea, which may have been sitting on Emil's table. She swallowed a mouthful. It may have been old, but it settled her stomach. "This work is too hard. I think I'll go back to cow doctoring."

"Will you? I'll be a librarian, then." Emil gestured at Medric. "And my husband here—"

"I can shoot. It's my only useful skill."

"Useful in war. Too bad we're at peace."

"I'll starve, then," said Medric cheerfully.

The two men smiled at each other. This silly banter made Seth impatient. "So there's an assassin in Basdown," she said.

"Karis finds us tiresome, also." Medric wandered back into the books.

"I've been terrified for Karis," said Emil. "I'm sure you think I've been parsimonious with information, but I would have told you more had I known anything. The ravens stopped talking a day after she left for Watfield. I only knew Karis was unharmed because of that one note a couple of days ago, and it was chary with detail—she doesn't much like writing. But I guess it occurred to her that I might be worried by the ravens' silence, and she sent another note. She had the Paladins kill a raven to save Clement, and now she can't make the ravens talk. She can't be in them, though she still knows what they know. So she told me that a raven had lost track of one of the assassins, and that it had looked for him in Basdown but had been unable to find him. So I need you to go to Basdown to locate our man and tell the raven where he is."

"You want me to make a ten-day journey to help a bird?"

Emil gazed at Seth. Her face began to feel warm. He finally said, "A broken thing is nagging at you, something you can't fix."

"Plenty of those."

"But you're making good progress. It's a slow project, but that shouldn't trouble you."

"Seth should go to Basdown." Medric's voice, muffled by books, seemed very far away.

Emil's eyebrow lifted. "Well, you may ignore me with impunity, but ignore Medric at your peril."

"Bloody hell," Seth muttered.

Far away in the books, Medric burst out laughing. "She's cursing in Sainnese!"

Seth had grudgingly learned to appreciate the importance of the garrison's protocols. Every cow farm in Basdown raised its bull calves with great care so the animal would be accustomed to obedience and placidity. Even so, young bulls sometimes became unmanageable and had to be killed. The garrison was much like a cow farm that raised only bulls, people who from childhood were taught to be killers. Such people must be strictly controlled lest their violence become unmanageable. This much Seth had learned from observing the company captains, who ruled their soldiers with a mix of affection and loathing that matched exactly how Seth felt about bulls.

When she returned to the garrison carrying a basket of butter cakes from Garland's kitchen, she went first to Gilly, who accompanied her to the commander's quarters where Ellid was eating a meal. Ellid accepted a cake, approved Emil's request, and wrote the order to be delivered to a lieutenant who would tell it to Captain Prista, who would tell it to Damon. No one would ask Damon what he thought of these orders, nor would the young soldier expect to be asked his opinion. Seth gave a cake to Gilly when they parted and brought the remaining cakes to Prista's company.

The next morning, as Seth was packing her books to return them to Travesty, Damon knocked on the door frame of the mudroom. "I report to you, Captain Seth!"

"Emil asked me to make this journey and wanted me to have a companion. Then I realized I could bring a soldier with me. You can tell me what it's like to live with Shaftali people."

"I am to spy on farmers, eh? Like you spy on soldiers."

Damon seemed cheerful at the prospect, but Seth said, "If you don't want to do it, please tell me so."

Damon gave an exaggerated salute, much like Medric's from the day before. "I am willing. An adventure, eh?"

"Not a battle."

"Very good. For I do not fight well." He displayed his left hand, which had only a finger and thumb.

"You fight better than I do."

"It is true," he declared. "You are the worst soldier in the army."

Seth had bid her bunkmates farewell before breakfast, and Damon's bunkmates had wished him well, and apparently subjected him to unmerciful teasing, when he received his orders. At the mudroom door, Damon took the heavy satchel and slung it over his own shoulder. "These books are good to eat?"

"We'll get some traveling food at Travesty and return the books to the library. But first we are going shopping."

"Shopping?" Damon seemed nonplussed.

"You need some clothes."

Damon frowned down at his clean but many-times patched and repaired uniform. "But this wool has grown into my skin."

"Then changing your clothes will be an adventure," Seth said, "The first of many."

Chapter 22

"Cider? There's been no cider since summer!" The tavern keeper, a burly woman of small patience, added sarcastically, "I'd think you were a scholar who can hardly bother to look out the window to see if the world is still there. But with half the road on your clothes and the other half on your face, you're no scholar, that's for certain."

Zanja could hardly tell the woman that last summer she had been two hundred years in the future. She dropped her heavy pack to the floor with a sigh. "Beer, then." She hated the stuff.

"You're no apple farmer, either, or you'd be waking every morning with fear in your heart that a late frost has blighted the fruit-set again."

"Not a farmer," Zanja said. "Under all this dirt I'm a Paladin. What have you got to eat?"

"Just bean soup."

"No meat?"

"This is a student's tavern, Madam Paladin. You can get finer stuff at a finer place!"

The tavern keeper stalked off, pausing to rap a young patron's head and declare that it was hollow.

Seven days had passed since Zanja climbed out of the canyon and began retracing her own footsteps. She had reached the Kisha highway the previous afternoon and, driven by vague urgency, loped down its rough cobbles half the night before lying down to rest just off the roadbed. When she was awakened at dawn by a passing wagon, the first thing the sunlight revealed was the clock towers of Kisha rising up over the hilltops in the near distance.

The same urgency that had driven her to the town in such haste had compelled her past a Paladin domicile where she would have been entitled to every comfort. Here in this poor tavern she would soon have to surrender some of her limited coins in payment for the rough and reluctant service. It was still morning, but young people had crowded at the tables nearest the windows, raising such a din that it took Zanja some time to realize they were studying. They recited and reiterated lessons out loud, frequently interrupted and corrected by their fellow students—corrections that often deteriorated into loud arguments. Every last one of them had a beer mug at the elbow, but rarely did anyone take a sip. A young woman came in—her hair a tangle and her clothing threadbare—and shamelessly went around begging her fellows to contribute a mouthful of beer to her mug so she could stay here and study. The tavern keeper caught her at it and chased her out.

"Can I have a light?" Zanja asked when the woman arrived with her soup and beer. It was gloomy away from the windows.

"For another penny."

Zanja opened her purse again and was given a cheap candle, which she stood in the accumulated wax of other candles that made a fluid sculpture in the small table's center. After one sip of beer she set the awful stuff aside, but she was so hungry she didn't care that the soup was a tasteless mush.

Only one other candle burned in that dim place, and it was guttering at the table of a young man who scowled at a paper, moving occasionally to dip his pen in an inkwell, only to return again to thinking without writing at all.

Zanja felt a familiar itchiness in her fingertips. She hastily untied the pouch from her belt and took out the glyph cards. Like the student at the other candlelit table, she lapsed into abstraction. To turn an intuition into words—especially into a question of the answerable sort, as Emil would say—could be excruciating. Finally she managed to compose a question and whispered, "Who or what in this room can help me learn what I need to know in Kisha?"

She plucked a card. Its simple illustration revived her longing for the glorious complexity of the glyph paintings. But the card did give her an answer, one so unambiguous and direct that she uttered a grunt of surprise. The glyph might signify expertise and knowledge, or it might suggest the seeking of information. The illustration was of a man at a candlelit table, who frowned at a paper that seemed to be rolling itself up in order to avoid being read.

The young man at the other table uttered a curse. His candle had burned to the end of its wick and gone out. He glared at his curling paper in the darkness. Zanja said, "Here, take my candle." She broke it loose from its wax footing and went over to set it in the melted puddle that remained of the young scholar's candle.

Without a word the young man began to write—or draw, rather, for his much abused pen was scrawling a rapid string of glyphs. He seemed oblivious to Zanja standing at his shoulder.

He paused at last, studied his work, and then put down the pen and sat back, waving a hand vaguely to blow air across the drying ink. He glanced at Zanja and said without surprise, "You can't be a Paladin."

"Why not?"

"Because you're eating and drinking swill."

"Your proof seems inadequate. Perhaps I'm too hungry to care what I eat. And I've hardly tasted the beer."

"One taste is enough," he said. "It's cheap, though."

"I thought no one was drinking because the beer's so bad. But then I realized that the tavern keeper won't let anyone stay who has an empty cup."

"But everyone is penniless at the end of term."

"May I see what you've written?"

He gave her a narrow look. The candle flame revealed a rather dissipated face: eyes red, skin blemished and puffy, mouth dry and cracked. His hair had not been combed since summer, she thought—nor washed. "Oh, you're a fire blood," he said, and handed over his page. Zanja sat down and studied it, somewhat distracted by the young man's sharp and rather anxious gaze. She had seen this composition of glyphs before, or something similar. "Take root in youth, or fail," she said finally. "I suppose you mean to be ironic?"

The young man uttered a surprised but humorless laugh.

"But I'm afraid I only know a hundred or so glyphs."

He gave her a shocked look.

"I've never been a student," she explained. "And this is my first visit to Kisha. I'm an oddity, as you surely can see."

"I thought all Paladins were scholars."

"Some of us just long to be scholars."

The young man took his poem back and made no offer to transliterate it for her.

Zanja said, "Your poetry will be renowned some day."

"Oh, are you a seer?" he said sarcastically. "And will you tell me how I'll get bread to eat, or a roof to sleep under?"

"No, Coles, I am not a seer, and I can't say how you will manage. But I can tell you what you're going to say next."

He looked at her, chewing his lip.

"You're going to ask how I know your name."

"How—" He stopped himself, and laughed sharply. "No, I'm not." He picked up his mug and nearly drowned himself with a swallow of beer. Choking and sputtering, he managed to say, "So you know I'll be a poet?"

"You know intuitions can be inaccurate. But yes."

He threw his head back and laughed so loudly that several students bellowed at him to shut up. "Come up to my room!" he gasped. "I beg you—my friends will never believe me."

At the building next door, where a dingy tailor's shop and an even dingier pie shop occupied the first floor, Coles showed Zanja down a narrow alley and up a rickety set of stairs to a dark hallway. He opened a sagging door, saying, "Careful—you might trip on someone."

The room, as dark as the hallway, smelled of dirty clothing, rotten food, and stale piss. Coles felt his way to the window and opened the shutters. Now a faint light managed to fight its way through the tallow-cloth screen, and Zanja could see three bodies sprawled upon the floor, snoring away on thin mattresses amid a debris of occupation: wooden crates served as furniture, and an overflowing chamber pot suggested they all had recently drunk too much beer.

"We're late to lecture!" Coles shouted cruelly.

"Ha, ha," a sleeper mumbled.

"Jackass," declared a second.

The third, having noticed Zanja's presence, sat up in alarm.

"She's not a prefect," said Coles. "But she does act like one. Wake up, will you? It's nearly midday!"

Zanja took a pile of dirty plates off a crate and sat on it cautiously. The three disarrayed young men blinked at her blearily.

"Allow me to present my friends—who are closer to me than brothers—and from whom I must soon part—forever!" Coles's excess of feeling was greeted by groans. "This is Speck." He gestured at a very slight, very pale man whose face was covered with freckles. "This is Briefly." The alarmed man retired beneath his blankets without uttering a word. "And this is Legs."

The third man rolled onto his back and cheerfully kicked his long legs in the air, like a colt having its first roll in the grass. "Aren't exams over yet?" he asked.

"Not for six days," said Speck gloomily.

"Then what were we celebrating last night?"

"Ourselves," said Briefly, his voice muffled by blankets.

"We were celebrating having the wherewithal to celebrate," said Coles. "And now we're poor again: the same old tragedy. Oh, by the way, this woman—this oddity—this Paladin—"

Briefly emerged from under the blanket, freshly startled, apparently not having recognized Zanja's Paladin habiliments in the gloom.

"—whose name I don't even know—"

"Zanja."

"This woman, Zanja Paladin, has declared I will be a poet of renown."

"He will."

The roommates gazed at Zanja for a moment, then began hooting with laughter.

"His stuff is unreadable!"

"He'll starve!"

"Gibberish!" declared Briefly, and pelted Coles with the stockings he had been about to put on.

Coles said complacently, "She knows the future."

They leapt out of bed and gathered around her then, demanding that she tell them all their futures. Although the exams they had been prematurely celebrating would mark the end of their last term at the university, not one of the four young men had any idea what he would do next. Zanja took out her glyph cards and made a show of shuffling them.

"Tell me I'm not going to be an accountant," pleaded Legs.

"No," said Zanja, drawing a card at random. "Or at least, not for very long."

"Will I marry?" asked Speck rather anxiously.

Zanja could not determine if this were an appealing prospect or not, so she said, "Not until you can be a good husband."

Briefly stood silent, scratching a flea bite on his ankle. Fleas were not yet dangerous plague carriers, but still Zanja's skin crawled. She selected a glyph card for Briefly and silently showed it to him.

"The Secret!" cried Coles. "Tell, tell, tell!"

But Briefly shook his head and retrieved his socks.

Zanja said, "Incidentally, my predictions aren't very reliable."

"What good are you, then?" asked Speck in disgust. "If we can't make a living we'll all have to go back to farming."

"You'll manage the same way everyone does," she said, much to their dismay.

"Does Briefly actually have a secret, though?" asked Coles.

Zanja glanced at Briefly, who was now strapping his shoes. "That's for him to tell, I guess. Listen, before you go wherever you are going, I want some advice."

All four of them sat happily on the floor, apparently glad for any excuse to delay going to class. Emil, whose only opportunity to be a student at Kisha had been stolen from him, would have been disgusted.

"I need to know something about the water tribes—those that live on the coast. I need the information quickly. What should I do?"

In the long silence that followed, Zanja began to regret attending to her impulses. At last Coles said, "I doubt anyone knows anything about the tribes. I've never heard them mentioned in a single lecture. And I do listen."

Speck uttered a snort.

"Analytics, Anatomy, Botany,..." muttered Legs, apparently listing the fields of study in alphabetical order.

"Ale-itics, Animosity, Beerography,..." echoed Speck mockingly.

"History," said Briefly.

"A historian might know something," said Coles. "It depends on what you need to know."

"I'm looking for a specific person, a water witch, who is with one of the coastal tribes."

"Elementology," suggested Legs.

"But Professor Sperling drowned himself," said Coles. "And Esher is on leave. Who's going to give the exams, do you suppose?"

"Geography, Glyphology…" continued Legs.

"Geography," said Zanja.

"The geographers are all away on an excursion," said Speck. "And all those who love them are so very lonely."

"My mathematics tutor used to study geography," said Legs. "He said it was nothing but wandering around the countryside looking at maps."

"Why don't you just look at a map?" Coles asked Zanja.

"Will a map might show where the settlements are?"

Two young men shrugged. Briefly said, "Librarian."

"Madam Paladin hasn't got a letter," said Speck. "Or she'd not be wasting her time with us. And without a letter a librarian won't even talk to her."

Zanja didn't bother to inquire about what kind of letter, or from whom, or even whether such a letter could be forged. She supposed she could go to the Paladins for an official document, but not without being recognized as an impostor. She said, "Will one or all of you go to the library with me and help me look for a map?"

"You think they'll let mere students walk those hallowed halls? We can't even get in the door! And neither can you, without a letter."

Surely books exist to be read! Zanja thought. But in her own time few people could go in and take a book from Emil and Medric's ever-growing library, and probably for much the same reasons: preservation and protection. In both past and future, librarians were guardians, and books existed not to be read, but to be copied.

The young men appeared to have reached the end of their suggestions. Yet they also seemed unsettled, as though each was wondering whether one of the others would say something he himself was determined not to say.

"So I can't get in the door," Zanja said.

"You want us to help you break into the library?"

"We would never attempt such a thing!"

"Such fragile and irreplaceable treasures as are housed in that monolith are not for reckless, shortsighted youths such as ourselves," declaimed Coles solemnly. "It is instead our duty to save them in pristine splendor for those youths who will come after us, who in turn will be forbidden to step over the threshold—"

Briefly attempted to suffocate him with a bag of laundry. Soon dirty clothing was flying through the air, accompanied by many shouts and yelps, and a fellow boarder began thumping angrily on the wall.

"You've broken into the library before," asserted Zanja, taking a very smelly undershirt off her head.

"Never!" Legs protested.

"Once or twice," admitted Speck.

"Frequently," Briefly corrected him.

"Well, we are curious fellows!" said Coles. "But we always leave everything as we found it."

"Show me how to get in. I'll take only what can be carried in my head."

"You're no Paladin," said Coles. "At least not a very good one."

"You're right about that," she said.

Chapter 23

Where the road to Hanishport, the road to Keneso, and the old road intersected, the ancient crossing-stone was still rooted in the earth. Damon paused to scrutinize its chisel-chipped surface. "What did the stones once say?"

Seth's original journey to Watfield had followed the low road that parallels the Corber, a road that was now impassable due to the heavy rains. The Waystone at this crossroads was famous. The glyphs had been obliterated, but the memories had survived. "It used to say that Haprin lies to the east, Basdown and Keneso to the south, and the House of Lilterwess to the north."

Damon glanced northward with a frown.

"People say the soldiers tried to destroy the road like they destroyed the House, but it couldn't be done."

"Very good. It is a beautiful road."

Seth went with Damon to take a closer look at the road. Its stones were smooth and flat, its ditches clear of mud. Seth was abruptly reminded of the restless fallen stones that now ringed Watfield Garrison. She said, "I think this road will never fail. Just as the G'deon's power can tear stones apart, so also it can hold them together."

"I wish I had seen the House of Lilterwess."

"It must have been like the Travesty, but a lot bigger. As big as a small town, the old people say."

"You never went there?"

"No. This is my first time north of the Corber. I was a farmer, you know. Farmers don't travel, as they can't bring the farm with them. You were a boy when the House of Lilterwess was destroyed—you don't remember it?"

"My father was there, at the battle." Looking embarrassed, Damon rubbed a foot across the unworn surface of an enchanted road stone.

Seth pointed southward. "That's our road."

Damon scarcely said another word all morning.

They passed through Genton that day, where the nearest garrison to Wilton sat with its gates ajar but watched by armed Paladin irregulars. The next day, and most of the day after that, they were in the Barrens, where rock frequently broke through thin soil and the plants were all sturdy miniatures: tiny trees, tinier shrubs, and a scattering of early flowers that looked like blue-dyed dust. The rock fields were of solid black stone that appeared to ripple like water. Some people found the Barrens disquieting, but Seth liked the spare landscape and the mournful wind. Damon was restless beneath the open sky and kept looking anxiously towards the horizon as though to spy an enemy before he himself was spotted. "What's that?" he asked sharply, pointing to the west.

"Oh, those are the Three Sisters. They're hills, though they are oddly shaped. The man we're trying to find was camped over near their base, but he's gone now."

"This is a strange place," he said, in his simple, blunt way.

"Yes—but listen to the wind singing on the stones. You won't hear that anywhere else."

She pointed west. "We're two days from the coast, where the rocks flow right into the sea, like a stone river. I have walked that way to the coast almost every year. In the spring, you can see huge fish swimming northward, and in the autumn you can see them swimming southward. Once, one of those fish washed on shore. It was seven times my length! Now its bones are still there. I have spread my rain cape over the ribs and camped inside the skeleton."

The land dropped gradually towards Basdown; the gray haze became a leafless forest that stretched from east to west as far as could be seen, frequently interrupted by long stretches of rich grassland, where the cows of Basdown grazed. Seth could have named each of these pastures or hay fields but did not subject Damon to that recital. Soon, their vista was delimited by trees. The road began to meander this way and that, though generally it went southeast. The Threeflowers were blooming: three-leaved plants with three-petaled white blossoms. Damon asked her to name the plants for him, and Seth explained, "They spread by roots, but it's impossible to dig one up and move it. They shrivel up and die; they won't accept any unfamiliar dirt."

As they drew near a farmstead a couple of cow dogs appeared to keep an eye on them, and then a raven flew down from his hidden perch in a tall tree, to land nearly at Seth's feet.

"You must be the G'deon's raven," Seth said to the bird. "You've been watching the road for us, I guess."

The raven eyed her steadily, not at all like a wild bird. "Now you just have to follow us, and when I find the assassin I'll tell you. I'll put food out for you, also."

The raven lifted off and disappeared into the overhead branches as abruptly as it had appeared.

It was late afternoon, and Seth's bones ached from last night's rocky bed in the Barrens. Her feet also hurt, and she was actually looking forward to a bowl of the salt-beef stew she was usually so tired of by late spring. But if she and Damon walked until dark, they could reach High Meadow Farm tomorrow. She gave the distant cow dogs a wave and continued down the highway.

Damon, who never questioned or complained, walked steadily beside her, and she named more flowers for him. He asked, "How does Karis-the-G'deon make the ravens?"

"I haven't thought to ask her."

"But since you are like her—you have the same center—"

"Element," she corrected him.

"Element, yes. It is the same, so you think the same."

"Somewhat," said Seth, remembering Norina's assessment of her elemental makeup.

Damon considered for a few paces. "How would you make a raven?"

"The ravens would make one for me. I guess I'd take and raise the hatching—maybe that's what Karis did. But some physical part of her must be incorporated into the bird somehow. I know that one G'deon was able to halt a famine by scattering his blood in the fields, so maybe it's Karis's blood that the ravens have." And that, also, Seth realized, explained how Clement had been kept alive until Karis could reach her.

"Once I thought I understood everything," said Damon. He made a soldier's gesture of helplessness. "Now—nothing. Nothing at all."

☙

They stayed the night at Hundred Farm. ("A hundred what?" asked Damon, and couldn't believe that no one remembered anymore.) There the farmers treated them with minimal courtesy. Even when Seth directly chided them, it made no difference. Damon made several light remarks that earned only blank stares. Seth reported the doings in Watfield, and not even when she stressed the importance of Karis's declaration making the Sainnites into Shaftali did they become friendly. "We heard that from another traveler," said one without enthusiasm. Another made a caustic remark that it was not a surprising declaration from a half-Sainnite.

Seth was so consternated that she could not trust herself to make a reasonable reply. But Damon said, "You have many travelers here? We see only ourselves."

No one responded to him, as though they had agreed to pretend he did not even exist. Then, one of the older children spoke, for like Seth he seemed to find that silence inexplicable and unbearable. "So far there's been just one. He taught me how to carve."

"Will you show me?" said Damon.

For a man who had never had contact with children, he was managing well. Despite the ill-disguised objections of the boy's parents, Damon and he soon went into a nearby parlor. The boy launched an enthusiastic explanation of how he had carved a stick into a bird.

Seth said to the remaining people, "Do you know that Basdowners' decency is renowned all over Shaftal?"

The Hundred Farm people applied themselves to their stew as though they had not eaten for weeks.

"When I visited you last, on my way to Watfield, you all said you wanted peace. Therefore I'm on the Peace Committee, and I've brought Damon to Basdown to see whether a Sainnite soldier can be comfortable on a Shaftali farm. He's here because of you."

One of the people at the table had been Seth's brother. They had grown up together at High Meadow, and it was possible they might share a parent, though no one paid attention to such things here. He muttered at his soup plate, "Well, we were wrong. And so are you."

"How do you know?" Seth looked around the table. "How am I to speak for Basdown, if Basdown won't speak to me?"

A few of the farmers brought themselves to talk. They said things

Seth had heard many times already, unarguable facts and arguable judgments. Seth's experience as a councilor, tiresome though it could be,
proved itself useful. She restrained her impulse to disagree, and merely
asked questions and listened. She began to hear a name, Jareth, that
didn't belong to anyone in Basdown.

She and Damon slept in the cow barn that night. She didn't want
to leave Damon alone, and the farmers didn't want him in their guest
room. They made their beds in a hayrick where it still smelled like last
summer. "I guess the assassin has another kind of poison," Seth said,
as they lay in the soft darkness. The cows were left in the field at night,
now it was spring, watched over by cow dogs. Seth and Damon were the
barn's only occupants.

"They don't know he's an assassin," said he.

"Well, I'll tell them as soon as I can. I hope that makes them
reconsider what they're thinking."

Hay rustled under Damon. He yawned noisily. "They should just
think what you tell them to think."

"What? They're not soldiers!"

"They are stupid as soldiers."

Now Seth wanted to disagree. But she lay thinking, and Damon's
breathing told her he had fallen asleep. The boy had mentioned to
Damon that the wood carver, Jareth the assassin, had guested at Hundred Farm for ten days, the longest any stranger could reasonably stay
anywhere, and then moved on to another farm farther to the south.
He was behaving more like a suitor than a traveler, remaining in each
household long enough to demonstrate his personality and skills. He
was in no hurry to leave Basdown's comforts, and it was not difficult
to imagine why, as he had camped in the Barrens through the end of
winter and most of the mud season.

She wanted him away from Basdown. She wanted to cull him out,
like an unhealthy cow from the herd. Just find him, Emil had said. But
Emil had not thought about the damage one man could do.

And why could he do that damage, Seth wondered? In ten days this
Jareth had managed to change opinions that Seth would have assumed
were unchangeable, as they were built on a foundation of ideals: hospitality, respecting boundaries. "A farm is a farm," Basdowners often said.
They would say it about people who expressed odd ideas, or did things

in a peculiar manner, or fell in love with an unlikely person. It surely had been said often about her.

The journey to High Meadow the next day proceeded slowly, for Seth and Damon stopped at several of the farms that abutted the road. They did not find the assassin, but Seth could easily tell which households Jareth had guested in. They had to cease looking for him finally, because Seth had become so furious she feared she might rush up and hit him. She would ask Mama where he was, for Mama was so gregarious she could hardly bring herself to stay at High Meadow for more than three days at a stretch. Only Seth, whose fame as a cow doctor had kept her moving from farm to farm, had been less likely than Mama to be found at home.

High Meadow Farm bordered the highway near the southern edge of Basdown, and Seth's family had done a lot of business with the Sainnites who managed the children's garrison located in the wilderness further south. Seth and Damon had scarcely come abreast of the farm boundary when she heard the High Meadow dogs signaling each other, and soon a half dozen had gathered, a panting, grinning, enthusiastic escort that kept pace with the travelers but did not set one foot into the road. Damon seemed nervous, so Seth taught him how to determine that they were friendly.

"The cow dogs of Basdown are famous," she told him.

"Because they look funny?"

"They are funny. They even play jokes on farmers and each other. But they're more famous for what they won't do. They will not cross any farm boundary, they observe a strict daily schedule, and they berate anyone who does something they disapprove of. It's impossible to move cow dogs from one farm to another, even as puppies. If they're prevented from returning to their home farm, they become melancholy and die."

"Like Threeflowers," said Damon.

"And don't tell Basdowners that their dogs look funny."

"But their legs are too short."

"So the cows will kick over their heads."

"They have no tails."

"So the cows can't step on them."

"Their ears are huge."

"So they can hear everything that happens on the farmstead."

"They are so hairy!"

"So they are impervious to wet and cold."

"They are perfect dogs?"

"Exactly. Now, this is important: cow dogs believe there are only two creatures in the world: dogs and cows. And you don't want to be a cow, believe me."

"No!" said Damon earnestly.

"So learn to be a dog. Here's the track to the farmstead—I'll take your arm so the dogs can see that you're with me." She tucked her hand in Damon's elbow, and as they stepped off the highway they were surrounded by milling dogs whose noses Seth had to kiss in proper order before she and Damon could go one step further. Soon Damon, laughing breathlessly, had a young dog pulling on his shirt sleeve to try to convince him to wrestle.

"Councilor Seth, this dog is eating my shirt."

As Seth turned to help Damon, she noticed a figure hurrying toward them down the track. "Oh, there's Mama!"

"Is that Seth?" Mama cried, when she was close enough to see. "Well, no wonder the dogs are so excited."

They embraced, and Mama kept talking. "We never expected to see you so soon. Is something wrong? We have heard about the terrible attack, and how the G'deon's wife got drowned."

"I'm fine, Mama. I'm just home for a visit."

The young dog, apparently having determined that Damon didn't know how to play, was now demonstrating and encouraging him with sharp barks. Damon knew how to take orders; he was already mastering the elementary chase and retreat.

"This is Damon, a Watfield Sainnite who's here to learn how farmers live."

Mama examined Damon with an expression Seth couldn't interpret. The soldier left off his playing and came over to make a formal greeting, with his eyes still crinkled with delight. "Your dogs are perfect!" he declared.

"We could not farm without them," said Mama. "Well, come to the house. You must be ready for a sit-down."

Soon they were settled on the porch with the other stay-at-homes, sipping tea and eating cheese biscuits. Two babies crowded Seth's lap; children asked Damon awkward questions; the old dogs whose job it was to herd the toddlers away from the fire and the stairs, or to show ancient Sarmon the way home when he got confused, all lay yawning in the sunshine. "You can sleep in your old room," said one of the elders to Seth. "But Damon will have to share with someone."

"He can't have the room in the attic?" That room, though crammed with boxes and chests of stored goods, had a spare bed for visitors.

"Another visitor's using it, a man named Jareth who seems to be looking for a family."

"Oh," Seth managed to say. "Damon will share my room, then."

The setting sun painted the rolling hills of High Meadow in vivid splashes of color and shadow. On the far side of the farmstead the heavy-uddered cows trod the path to the barn in stately indifference, while their calves bounded madly up and down the dignified procession. The dogs self-importantly guarded the rear, uttering occasional instructional barks to the lightsome calves. The milkers also had begun to parade down the cobbled paths from the dairy and the main house to the barn, shadowed by cats, who wanted their evening dish of milk.

The laborers were walking down the path to Seth's right in twos and threes, with their hoes on their shoulders, raggedly singing a question-and-answer song:

What will you do when the water flows
When the earth falls apart and the cold wind blows?
I'll stay by the hearth when the water flows
When the earth falls apart and the cold wind blows.
For I'm no fool and I'll never leave home.

Beyond them, beyond the southern edge of the farmstead, a distant patch of water glimmered, marking a low wetland where people sometimes went to gather rushes or try their luck at fishing. There were no more cow farms in that direction, nor any farms at all, as far south as Seth had ever traveled—just wilderness.

"By the land! Is that Seth?" someone cried.

She waved to the laborers. Among the familiar, dirt-stained, wind-furrowed faces she saw a young man with a bounce in his step and a guileless smile on his face. Seth gave him a nod, as she would greet any stranger, and looked away to answer someone's query about why she had returned so soon. "I missed the cows," she said.

"You didn't!"

They were upon her now, jostling each other as they kissed and embraced her. Their hands were rough; their hats and headcloths sweat-stained. They smelled of honest work in the warm sunshine.

"This is Jareth," someone said.

Seth forced herself to clasp the young man's hand. "Greetings. I'm Seth."

"Seth is the Basdown Councilor!" someone said importantly. "She has been at the big meeting in Watfield!"

"You must have stories to tell," said the young man.

"Why have you come home so soon?" asked Liralin, Seth's favorite niece.

Seth gladly turned away to greet her. "Well, what are you doing here? Aren't you married?"

Lira gestured as if waving flies from her face. "I didn't like that farm after all. They couldn't cook!" She tucked her hand into Seth's elbow. "They had some strange ideas about cheese. And no one wanted to sleep with me."

"You scared them, probably."

"Oh, I guess."

Even at High Meadow people found Lira difficult and irritating. She was a knowledgeable cheese-maker, but so inflexible that no one wanted to work with her. Seth had taken over the job of planning her future when Lira's mother died of a fever three winters ago, but this was the second time a marriage Seth arranged had failed. Seth said, "Maybe you'll spend your entire life at High Meadow, like I did."

"What a horrible possibility," said Lira.

In the company of these people Seth returned to the main house, with the assassin behind her and the skin of her back crawling in anticipation of a deadly pinprick. Damon stood alone on the porch. In his canvas breeches and travel-stained longshirt he looked like any other farmer.

"Who's that?" asked Lira.

"My travel companion, Damon."

"He hurt his back, did he?"

"No, all soldiers stand that way."

"Oh, you've taken up with another Sainnite? How am I to keep up with you?"

"I like him, but he's not my lover."

Lira continued to tease her and could hear Jareth's voice behind them, but not what he was saying. Silence followed. "You've brought a Sainnite to guest with us, Seth?" one of the young men asked.

Seth gritted her teeth, for after her day's visits even that tone of voice could make her angry. "There's a law against it?" she said over her shoulder.

"There should be," said someone, possibly Jareth.

"Maybe we should return to how we used to be, turning away and even killing every stranger."

No one answered, and Lira gave Seth's arm a tug. "Now, Seth, it's my job to be the most disagreeable person in Basdown."

"I'm not sure of that any more."

"You're crabby with hunger, I guess. Of course the food will hardly be worth eating."

"Come visit me in Watfield sometime. I know the perfect husband for you, except that he's married to his kitchen already."

On the porch, Seth left Lira and went to Damon to tell him which of the people was Jareth. "Shall I kill him?" asked Damon.

"You're not serious!"

"No, no," Damon said. "No, no, no."

"It would not make you more popular, not at all."

Damon shrugged. "It will not make me less."

He had remained so cheerful all day that Seth had begun to think he was impervious to hostility. But now she felt a fresh fury. "What is wrong with these people!"

"What's wrong with you?" someone said.

She turned around, and it was Jareth. She grabbed Damon's arm, but the soldier seemed entirely relaxed. "Greetings! I am Damon," he said.

Jareth made a sour face. Seth said, "I'm not going to explain to a stranger why I've brought a friend to meet my family. And I won't apologize for being rude, since you're being rude also."

"Oh, I am sorry," the assassin said. "Greetings, Damon. I'm Jareth. I think all soldiers should be treated as the criminals they are."

"I will not always be a soldier."

Jareth seemed dumbfounded. Even Seth was startled by Damon's simple, perfect response to the other man's belligerence. She managed to say something, making her voice loud so that everyone on the porch could hear her. "Maybe you haven't seen that book, *A History of My Father's People,* by Medric the seer. He writes that we should marry the Sainnites. The G'deon printed that book, every single page of it. Did you read it, Jareth?"

She wanted to make it impossible for him to argue with her, but he became even more angry. "It was written and printed by Sainnites! I would not go near that cursed book!"

"Goodness," said Seth. "Did you mean to call the G'deon a Sainnite?"

"Of course she's a Sainnite! Only a fool would think otherwise!"

"She was rescued by Dinal, Harald G'deon's Paladin wife, and was raised by General Mabin and Norina Truthken. Are the three of them Sainnites also?"

Now people crowded forward to lay hold of Jareth. He yanked his arms out of their grasp without seeming to notice how his words had shocked them. They began crowding him away from Seth, and then he turned and went into the house. Soon Seth and Damon were alone on the porch.

Damon raised his eyebrows at her. "No killing, but wounding is good, eh?"

"Maybe he'll bleed to death." Seth leaned over the porch rail. "Are you there, raven? Did you see him?"

The raven flew out of the tree in which it had been hiding and landed a distance from the porch. "Ha! Ha! Ha!" the bird cried. It lifted off and disappeared again.

"I guess our mission is finished," said Seth. "And I'm glad, because I don't want to stay here at all."

"Yes, Captain." Rarely did Damon sound so unenthusiastic. And Seth wasn't eager to make the return journey to Watfield without resting first.

"You haven't been able to spy on any farmers yet," she said.

"No, Seth. They don't like me."

"Jareth hasn't been to every farm in Basdown."

"You bring me to another farm, eh? But your family…" Damon seemed to run out of Shaftalese words, as happened sometimes.

"Oh, nobody expects me to do anything in the usual way. We can come back to High Meadow before we begin our journey back to Watfield, and hope that Jareth has left by then. Let's go to Ten-Furlong Farm tomorrow."

"Ten furlongs from what? Nobody remembers?"

"Ten furlongs from the highway. You might meet some people there who love flowers."

They went in, and Seth told Mama they would only stay one night. Mama had already heard about the altercation on the porch, and halfheartedly tried to convince Seth that their houseguest's hostility to Damon wasn't significant. "Oh, Damon's not the one I'm worried about. I'm the one who can't endure the man. I don't understand why you don't give him some food and send him on his way."

Seth wanted to tell her everything, but Mama would never be able to keep such an important and frightening secret. Jareth must not think to look for the raven that he though he had evaded. Nor should he be taken into custody by outraged Basdowners, and thus be prevented from going wherever he was going.

But what if he were traveling with a supply of that deadly snake poison? If a person could kill the G'deon, wouldn't he be able to kill anyone?"

"We need to steal his poison," Seth said to Damon that night in her bedroom, "If I can think of how to steal it without him realizing it."

From his pallet on the floor, Damon murmured sleepily, "Whatever you say, Captain Seth."

Chapter 24

Young men were gullible, but Zanja had never before taken advantage of that fact. Had she gotten out of the habit of virtue, she wondered?

She wandered like a pleasure seeker through the crowded streets of Kisha. Like all northern towns, Kisha was built of stone. Its sturdy buildings, though they already seemed ancient, were familiar to Zanja. But the massive stone library, from whose wide steps spread the city square, would become in Zanja's youth a roofless stone shell filled with the ashes of its books. Standing before that building, where she would first hear a herald reveal the disasters of Harald G'deon's death and the fall of the House of Lilterwess, a vertigo came over her. None of those events had happened yet, but she was scarred, burdened, and changed by them. Her life might lie far in the future, but she had already lived a great deal of it, including the massacre of her tribe.

If she did decide to try to rescue them from their fate, how could it even be done? By contrast to the Shaftali people, who recorded and studied their past and worried or wondered about the future, the Ashawala'i had hardly thought about events from before their lifetimes, nor did they look beyond the next season. How could anyone, no matter how clever, send a message ten generations into their future?

She sat on a stone bench and turned her back to the doomed library. Now she looked across the city square, where several food stalls did a brisk business. Students moved, settled, rose, paced, left, arrived, and left again with seeming randomness. Yet there was a pattern to their movements: a dance, a massive, chaotic, and yet harmonious katra. The dancers, oblivious to the grand pattern, thought they were preparing to make a living or to take their exams. But the actual outcome of their energetic activity lay beyond comprehension, just as Zanja's lay beyond hers.

Zanja found herself muttering the ancient axiom on which was based the ideology of the Paladins: "Evil may enter the world, but it will not enter through me." To Zanja this goal now seemed not only simpleminded, but unachievable. No person could ever know the ultimate result of his or her actions, and no person could know whether that result might be good or evil or something else entirely.

She could not bear to sit still. She stood up and again wandered the narrow stone streets. Students seemed everywhere: scrawling equations, practicing recitations, rehearsing debates. They sat anywhere sunshine could be found: on rooftops, in windows, on stairways. Some paced with anxiety, and others lay peacefully asleep.

In Kisha, perhaps ideas were floating in the air like seed pods for anyone to capture and plant. Walking past a paper shop, Zanja realized that an idea had taken root in her own agitated mind. She stepped into the shop and bought a very expensive sheet of paper that the paper seller assured her would last a century under the right conditions. She took over a table in a crowded outdoor cafe and, using the reed pen, dry ink, and ink stone that were part of her Paladin disguise, wrote a letter to Emil.

After visits to the pie shop, the chandlery, and the rope shop, Zanja's purse was nearly empty. She would soon regret her poverty, she supposed, but now it seemed of no importance. Night fell; students fled the chill. Zanja's four conspirators traipsed rather noisily past the shuttered windows, shouting an occasional hilarious greeting to friends they suspected to be within. Sometimes a window opened in their wake and they went back to exchange trivial pleasantries. Zanja made herself invisible and wished she could have managed without their exuberant help.

The young men eventually quieted and occasionally seemed almost somber as they made their way to one side of the grand, looming library. At the building's corners the fancy stonework included numerous carved projections whose regularity must have been aesthetically pleasing. But they also offered a stone ladder to the roof, albeit a dangerous one, and there the heads of bare-toothed creatures might offer sturdy handholds. The young men began to bicker over who would get the glory of climbing up first and hanging the rope for the others. Zanja pulled off her boots and climbed up. The screaming eagle and snarling bear that gave her handholds became belaying pins for the rope as, one by one the young men secured themselves and climbed up. Eventually, the five of them crept across the rooftop past numerous gables with windows of actual glass. Coles said that those windows could not be opened, and the ceiling was famously high. "But there's an easy way," he added.

This way proved to be a trapdoor for workmen, where a sturdy ladder dropped down into a dark pit, at the bottom of which was a door that opened into a lightless room that smelled of glue, paper, leather dressing, and lamp oil. Zanja lit a candle and saw what she had expected: worktables on which massive deconstructed books lay in various stages of repair. Legs managed to trip on a stool, and Speck accused him of being clumsy as an ox.

"Quiet!" said Coles, busy at the next door. It was locked, but the lock was not particular. Coles poked in it with a stiff piece of metal, and soon the door swung open. Beyond the door, the vast space of the library opened up like all possibility.

Zanja stood there, holding up her little flame so she could see the crowded bookshelves, row upon row, disappearing into the gloom, and seeming to continue forever. Medric or Emil would set up housekeeping in such a place and never set foot outdoors again. Still, they would be unable to learn everything, even if they remained here until the Sainnites set the building afire.

The boys also stood quietly, giddy no longer, seeming overpowered by the significance of that place. They stood in the presence of all knowledge, more than they could have learned if they studied here at Kisha for two hundred years.

Zanja surrendered the candle to Coles and mutely followed him down the narrow aisles. The linen-wrapped books on these shelves were very large, and in the unsteady light seemed poised to drop on her head in an avalanche.

"We do not belong here," she whispered.

"No, of course not," muttered Coles. "We presumptuous boys, who for the price of a pie are giving up the secrets of all history to a complete stranger."

"I only need one fact, Master Student, not the secrets of all history. But where do we seek it?"

"I don't know yet," he said cheerfully. "How is your prescience?"

"It's kept me alive a few times, but not always."

"What is it like to die?"

"Lonely."

"You warn us of skulking librarians, the suspicious bastards! And I will both seek and find, for I am a glyphologist, and I am never intimidated by Mystery!"

The three young men behind Zanja snorted sarcastically. But they all followed Coles's light. From time to time he paused to shine his fluttering flame on the dark, carved side of a shelf upright, where one or two ornate glyphs were painted and illuminated with gold leaf so their shapes shimmered in the faint light. Their forms were fantastically decorated and to Zanja were unrecognizable, yet Coles needed only to examine them for a moment, and not only did he understand them but he also perceived a logic in the overall arrangement. First one way and then another he turned, paused, backtracked, and turned again, finding a way through the invisible labyrinth.

"Ah!" he gestured so extravagantly with the candle that he nearly blew it out. "Did I not promise you?"

His light revealed a map rack, which stretched into the gloom like the wall of a dark and not entirely unhazardous alley. In each of its pigeonholes resided a rolled up, linen-wrapped map: at least a hundred in total, though it was not easy to estimate in the uncertain light. Coles, trying to read a label pasted to the shelf's edge, held the candle flame too close to the linen, and Zanja felt a sharp panic. "Do you want to become notorious for burning down the library?"

Coles made an exasperated sound but moved the candle. "If you had gotten a lamp—" He studied a paper label pasted on the edge of the shelf. "Lilter 45," he read. "At least the labels are in letter form."

Zanja handed out candles to the three others, admonishing each of them against carelessness. "Find me the most recent map of Shaftal."

The young men lit their candles and moved to push back the darkness that filled the narrow space between the cases. Zanja could scarcely bear to watch their flames so near that dry paper.

The young men began reading labels out loud to each other. Legs drew out a map, at great hazard. Zanja said, "I'm going to go away on my own for a short while...I want to see what I can, as I doubt I'll ever be here again. I think we're safe enough from the librarians."

Coles gestured vaguely.

He would write a glyphic poem about this night, a poem that Zanja would one day transliterate. And she would quote it to Emil as they climbed some stairs to discover a huge store of books that one brave librarian would rescue from the fire. She felt the vertigo again.

She couldn't find the way by reason and began to take her direction from intuition alone. Her candle showed only the next step, but that was enough. The students' lights disappeared. She made her way past the dim, unrelenting secrecy of the shelves, the ambiguous, glittering glyphs, the heavy darkness that only grew heavier. The boys behind her became memories; she only knew that what she wanted became more achievable with every step.

She looked up. The books were not so grand here: small but fat volumes bundled up in bleached linen like so many packets of flour.

She stopped with her hand on a bundle, neatly tied up with cloth ribbons. She undid the bows and opened the cloth, and there lay *Gerunt's Decision*. She had last seen this book on Emil's worktable: not this exact book, of course, but a later edition from the time that printing presses came into general use and any plowman or barber or blacksmith could afford a book. But Emil's copy, which had needed much repair, had been saved from this very library. This handwritten book was as direct an ancestor of his printed copy as Zanja could hope to find.

This book was beautifully, ornately bound in dyed leather, with gold leafing and painted decorations. Zanja folded the letter to Emil into a slim packet and slid it carefully into the spine. Then, she wrapped up the book again and tied the ribbons, and, with a feeling like one gets when shooting into darkness, left the book as she had found it. To send a letter in this manner was ridiculous.

She followed her feet again, and gradually the murmur of voices and the light of four candle flames emerged from the heavy silence and darkness. All four students knelt at the corners of a map they had unrolled onto the floor, with their hands cupped to catch the dripping wax as they illuminated the contorted coast of Shaftal. Even at this distance Zanja could see the extraordinary detail of a Truthken's map. But she felt indifferent to whatever they had discovered.

During her entire time in this Shaftal, she had engaged in wrong-doing when she had to, while striving to avoid doing any real harm. In order to sustain this contradictory balance she must now leave, promptly and quietly, with the library and its contents undisturbed. She had achieved what she needed to achieve. But she was not finished.

"Hist!" Coles had noticed her standing there. "Are they coming?" he whispered.

Zanja could not recall who he referred to. "No one is coming," she said.

"Well, come see the map."

His nervous impatience brought her back to the world, and suddenly she did care what the map revealed. For she needed to return to where she belonged; she needed to be part of the land and not merely a visitor. And she needed to escape this constant disorientation, this unrelenting sensation that nothing anyone did was trivial. She knelt beside the young men, added her candlelight to theirs, and examined the coast of Shaftal. Where might she find a water witch? Among the water people. Where were the water people?

Briefly pointed. "Here."

"And here."

"And here."

They were pointing at places that major rivers met the sea. Those regions were bordered red and labeled with the G'deon's glyph: protected lands, lands where no one may plant, gather, hunt, build, cut, or dig.

"But not at Hanish Harbor," Speck commented.

Zanja thought she might safely skip visiting the tribe that supposedly lived at the mouth of the Otter River. The mouth of the Aerin River lay due west of Shimasal, farther away from Kisha than Otter Lake. And the third place, where the coastline looked like shattered piece of pottery on a blue tablecloth, was far in the south, between Basdown and the Juras grasslands. That place had a name printed in the same careful hand that had added information to the map over many years of travel: Secret.

"No matter where you go, you'll wish you had a horse," Legs commented.

Zanja sighed, for her feet were sore and her legs aching already. "Well, little though the information pleases me..."

"Why aren't there any border people at Hanish Harbor?" Speck asked. "It's a good place, with good farmlands, good weather, access to the sea. Of course we would have no seaport or water road if Hanish were inhabited by..."

"Oh, stop your mumbling," said Legs. "You sound like a professor."

"Briefly, what is the history of that region?" asked Speck.

"Long gone," Briefly said.

"Were border people living there once, but a long time ago?" asked Zanja.

Briefly nodded.

"But why——" began Speck.

Legs and Coles forced him to his feet and put away the map. Zanja herded them out: back to the workshop, where Coles relocked the door; up the ladder, through the trapdoor, across the roof, and down the stone ladder, where they seemed more than willing for Zanja to be the one who climbed down last, without a rope. As she hauled up the rope, their faces as they looked up at her seemed like children's—so far below her, so mischievous, tired, and naive.

She lay the coiled rope beside her on the rooftop. "I'm going to stay here a while."

They continued to stare at her.

"It's peaceful up here," she said. "I need to do some thinking."

"Surely you won't sleep up there," said Legs.

"When I come to get my gear from your house, maybe I'll see you. If not—well, thank you, and farewell. This has been a fine adventure."

They wandered rather reluctantly away. Zanja, squatting at the edge of the roof, knew that when Coles looked back he would see that she was keeping watch alongside the building's stone guardians, as solemnly, fiercely, and determinedly as they. But Coles did not look back. She had reminded them that tomorrow the exams would begin, and they needed to get some sleep.

Zanja had slipped Coles's lockpick out of his pocket. She returned to the library. The lock was not as easy to open as Coles had made it seem, and Zanja struggled interminably before she finally got the trick of it. Intuitions often lose their intensity over time, but this intuition—or impulse—returned with renewed vigor as Zanja again entered among the books. She followed insight through the library like a string through a maze: across the second floor, down the stairway to the first, and among even more crowded shelves to an archway guarded by stone beasts that reared up to grasp her in their claws. The massive door was strapped with iron, and the keyhole in its middle was as big as two fingertips. Coles's bit of metal rattled uselessly inside the works of the lock.

Might this be the rarely opened vault that housed the Mackapee manuscript? The Sainnites, probably expecting to find something wonderful behind such a door, would break it down with great effort and then vent their frustration on the ancient, to them valueless, documents. Of the vault's contents only the Mackapee manuscript would survive the destruction.

But something locked behind that door cried out to Zanja, piercingly and insistently. She was locked out, and it was a fact she could not accept.

The librarian who kept the night watch was young and vigorous and equipped with an alarm bell should she need to summon help. But she succumbed to force, it seemed, from astonishment alone. Zanja cut the bell rope and used it to bind the woman to a chair. Then a belated fit of bravery sealed the librarian's lips, but the keys were not difficult to find, in a cabinet with a latch Zanja could break with a twist of her dagger point. The vault key, a monstrous, heavy thing decorated with an ornate silk tassel, was impossible to mistake. Zanja took it, along with a vial of oil and a feather. With a last threat to enforce the librarian's silence she returned to the vault and oiled and unlocked the door.

Her flickering candle revealed what the Sainnites would also see: A polished mosaic floor of astonishing beauty, its radiating geometric pattern centered on the carved stone pedestal on which lay the Mackapee manuscript in its plain wooden box. The candlelight picked out elements of the fresco with which the high walls were painted: A person riding the back of a great fish; all the fruits of the land ripening on a single tree; a grinning, catlike creature with a snake in its jaws. Waist-high cabinets ringed the room. Zanja broke another latch with her dagger. Within she found mute packages: some of linen and some of wood, precisely placed upon dust-free shelves. She put her hand upon the largest and sighed with exasperation.

It was a book—she could feel its end boards through the cloth—and it was massive, one of the biggest she had seen in the library. When she got her hands around it to lift it, she found it heavy as a hod of bricks. She staggered to her feet with the book braced against her hipbones, tilting herself backward to counterweight it. She could walk like this, but not while carrying a candle, which didn't matter because the book blocked her vision anyway. With her snuffed candle in her pocket she shuffled across the vault and bumped her way out the door. Partly by the instinct with which all creatures can retrace their steps, and partly by bumping blindly around obstacles, Zanja made her way to the foot of the stairway. Climbing it was nearly impossible; three times she lost her footing.

When she reached the roof ladder she had to abandon her prize to get the rope. The tome came through the trap door diagonally, scraping and catching on the frame. Had the opening been only slightly smaller, her escapade would have ended with the book stuck there. Then, with the help of the snarling guardians, she crossed cracking slates, bowed over by the weight of the book that was now slung onto her back. As she lowered the book to the ground, she thought she could hear the librarian calling for help now, but it was a muffled, distant sound swallowed up by the vast, paper-filled spaces of the library.

Finally Zanja climbed down the convenient stone ladder. At the bottom, Coles was waiting for her.

"I brought your gear," Coles said. "I wish I hadn't."

Zanja stood with her back against the stone building. The massive book lay on the ground beside her. "Coles, I do respect and like you—in a way much different from those silly friends of yours, who just think of you as a good playfellow. I hate to harm or humiliate you. But I will escape Kisha with this book."

"I wish I had never met you."

"And I wish you had done as you were told, for once, and gone to bed."

"I never do what I'm told to do."

The young man's agitation quieted. Now he would bargain with her, Zanja feared, and thus waste what remained of the night, costing her what chance she had of escaping Kisha while the theft was still undiscovered. She could not take him hostage, for she could not manage both him and the book. And if she trussed him and left him helpless, as she had the librarian, he would just become a compass to point her pursuers towards her. And there would be pursuers, lots of them, for she was not merely a thief, but a rogue Paladin.

She said, "Well, you've carried my gear this far—keep carrying it, will you?"

To her surprise he shouldered her pack and bedroll, muttering, "What do you need all this stuff for, anyway?"

Zanja heaved the book across her back. They wound through Kisha, Zanja going northward by the signs of the stars and the direction of the shadows. The book burdened her with more than just its weight.

At the northern edge of Kisha, the warrens of crowded lodgings and dingy shops gave way to finer habitations that had gated yards, stables, and turrets from which the residents could view the picturesque countryside. Here the town abruptly gave way to the rough landscape of the northern borderlands, where in Zanja's time far-scattered hamlets marked the few fertile areas, separated by wide stretches of rocky heath. But the farmers of this time probably hadn't ventured far to the north. She would only find shepherds' shelters and flocks of sheep.

"You're not going to haul that wretched book into the wilderness!" said Coles. "You don't expect me to go with you!"

"I'll hardly be able to feed myself in this season. Go back, Coles. Go to bed, or alert the librarians and Paladins, or write a poem—or whatever else suits you."

He dropped her gear with a noisy thump and stood scraping a foot unhappily in the gravelly soil. "How can I know what suits me, when you have not allowed me to understand you?" He added, self-pityingly, "This night is no longer amusing."

"Names of the gods! It is past time for you to grow up!"

Zanja could scarcely bear to contemplate the physical effort that lay ahead of her. Even Karis, who could easily carry a burden of four stone or more, would hesitate to haul both book and gear. Zanja would somehow do what she must. First she must do something about this young man, who had helped her and deserved some courtesy.

She said, "I would explain myself to you, but I don't know how to do it. I don't know when I will understand why I've done this, if I ever do understand it. I don't even know what book I have stolen."

The young man sat where he was on the stony ground. "Let's take a look at it, then. Too bad there is no moonlight."

Zanja took the candle and matchbox out of her pocket. She had not thought to buy more matches and she lit her last one reluctantly.

But if she were about to be forced to strip her gear down to a few tools and a blanket, the inconvenience of a flintstone would be the least of her problems.

Coles unwrapped the book, careful to keep it out of the dirt. "Oh, it's very old. It's not made of paper at all, but sheepskin, and the boards are wooden."

"No wonder it's so cursed heavy." Zanja held the candle carefully over the book as Coles opened and delicately turned a gigantic page.

"By the land!" Zanja breathed. She was looking at a glyph illustration as ornate and complicated as those she had studied at the House of Lilterwess. It showed a woman on her knees, with a tree growing in her cupped hands. She was framed by climbing plants and attended by birds and beasts, and under her knees were the various soils and minerals of the land.

"Earth," said Coles unnecessarily. "And the next page will be fire."

"Then water and air," said Zanja, still breathless with surprise.

"Then the four directions, the four implements, the four passions,..." Coles turned the pages as he spoke, giving Zanja glimpses of gorgeous, overpowering pictures, and of the facing pages that were crammed with glyphic text in the same ornate style as had been used in the library.

"It's a lexicon? I've stolen a lexicon?"

"Yes, an incredibly old one. I wonder why the explanations are written in glyphs rather than in letter form. What is the sense of that? A person who can read glyphs doesn't need a lexicon!" He paused in his page turning to examine an illustration unfamiliar to Zanja. "What are those creatures who are contending with each other? It's supposed to be two men fighting. And why is that wagon axle broken? It changes the entire meaning—perhaps even reverses it..."

Zanja firmly but carefully shut the book and lay it in its wrappings. Coles, gasping like a landed trout, cried, "The illustrations have changed over time? I've studied them for years, and yet my masters never even mentioned that fact?"

"What does it matter?" Zanja's hands burned as she folded the linen carefully over the book. Unlike Coles, she felt abruptly, relievedly at peace.

"What does it—?" Coles began to repeat, in outrage.

"Your people will have no more opportunity to make sense of it."

"That lexicon belongs to the scholars!"

"No, it belongs to the future." Zanja had to calm his passion or he would certainly send pursuers after her. "Coles, I am not stealing this book. I am rescuing it."

"The difference between one verb and another is a matter of merest opinion."

"Master Poet—"

His head jerked sharply, as if he were a hooked fish.

"Master Poet, take my hand. Just take it! Stop thinking like those scholars you have so little respect for!"

She felt his fingers touch her palm, and, as Tadwell had done, he flinched away with a gasp. Zanja knew that Coles had not felt in her the solid traces of earth power, but the fierce heat of fire: his own element. "You don't have to trust me," she said. "Trust the elemental fire. People will think you're mad, just as you think of me. But if you can't trust that fire, what are you? A boy who likes glyphs."

He sat back on his heels. Zanja struggled into her gear and heaved the mighty book over her shoulders. He observed her thoughtfully. "You are correct," he finally said.

"Farewell, Coles."

He stood up then and clasped both her hands in his. For a few moments he held onto them as grimly and stolidly as a warrior enduring a rite of initiation. Then he let go.

Chapter 25

The workers left early for the fields, Jareth among them, while Seth and Damon were still eating their porridge. "Oh, I meant to bring a hat," Seth said to Damon and to anyone else who might not be entirely preoccupied with feeding children or kneading bread dough.

Upstairs the big house seemed deserted, for no matter how early the sun rose or how late it set, the days were never long enough during the warm season, and no one ever lounged late in bed unless they were sick. Seth took a straw hat from its hook in her bedroom and continued down the hall and up the attic stairs, to the room where Jareth's narrow bed was crammed among the clothes chests and broken pieces of furniture. The High Meadow farmers were as unwilling as anyone to get rid of things that might later prove useful, and these attic rooms were crammed with the junk of generations. All Jareth's belongings seemed to be in the knapsack tucked under the bed. Seth pulled it out and went through it but found only clothing and commonplace travel gear: a tin porringer, a match case, a sewing kit, a spare shirt. There was nothing in the bedding or tucked under the mattress, nothing secreted above the door frame or underneath a loose floorboard. But it looked as if the dust under the bed had recently been disturbed, and Seth began pulling things out.

In various crates she found an unlikely assortment of oddments: a broken spindle, a very bad poem, a sock, a curling lock of hair, several pewter spoons, a mouse nest. Having crawled entirely under the bed now, she found a last box, so heavy she could scarcely drag it out. By the light of the one unwashed window, she saw the dirt-stained wood and brass strapping that were nearly black with age. But there were handprints in the dust and bright new scratches in the escutcheon. Jareth had tried to force the lock, but he had failed. The snake poison would not be there.

Seth's hand, the one with which she had grasped the box's brass handle, was feeling peculiar, as though it had brushed across nettles. But the sensation was fading, and she fought back a rush of panic. She was not poisoned. But what was that sensation, and why did it seem so familiar? Was it earth magic? She ran her hand across the band of brass that reinforced the box's hinged lid and felt the indentations of stamp marks. She blew away the dust and peered at the marks in the dim light. They looked like glyphs.

She had spent too much time here already. When she came back, if Jareth was gone by then, she would investigate this box further. She shoved everything back under the bed. The room looked no different than it had before. If Jareth had hidden poison somewhere else in this junk, it would take hours to find.

She heard voices in the distance and hastily left the room. As she crept down the stairs, the loud conversation turned to shouts, then a crash.

Seth ran the last few steps to the kitchen. There two chairs had been overturned, and Jareth, breeches smoking, was being hauled out of the big fireplace. Someone had apparently tossed a bucket of water onto the fire, and ashes floated everywhere. Damon was pinned into a corner by two mothers with shrieking babies in the crooks of their elbows. Old Sarna threatened the soldier with a gigantic porridge spoon. Mama had picked up a knife.

Seth said, "Damon, you promised you wouldn't get into any arguments."

"He called my mother a whore," said Damon, sullen as a rebellious child.

Seth said to Jareth, "You did? Well you deserved it, then."

Two people were brushing away cinders and tutting over the holes burnt in Jareth's clothing. "I'm fine," he said. "Leave me alone."

Mama put down the knife on the table. "Seth, aren't you ready to leave yet?"

Seth picked up Damon's satchel and shouldered her own. Damon edged past the squalling babies and the upraised porridge spoon. He took the satchel from Seth, and she pulled him out the door into the sunshine. The ruckus had drawn people out of the vegetable garden to stand uncertainly near the house, rubbing dirt from their hands. Several dogs had also appeared. "It's nothing," Seth told this audience. She dragged Damon away by the arm before anyone could notice he was holding his breath to keep from laughing.

"Twisted his ankle, he said," said Damon when they were well down the cart track. "I stopped him."

"Did you have to push him into the fireplace? You should have cracked his skull with an iron pot instead."

"Oh, Seth! I thought you were angry at me!"

"I couldn't find his poison," she said glumly.

"Maybe it is burned now."

"I doubt that. I guess he came back so he could see us leave with his own eyes."

Grinning, Damon tucked his hand into the crook of her elbow. "Now we retreat, eh, Captain?"

Their retreat ended at Ten-Furlong Farm, where Damon stopped short at his first sight of the cultivated fields. "But this is no cow farm!"

The furrows curved gently, following the undulations of the sloped hillsides. A line of bowed figures bearing baskets of seedlings to be planted stepped and stooped in cadence with each other—they certainly were singing, though they were too far away to hear. Closer by, a field of scarlet flowers was in full bloom. Damon gazed at this field in astonished silence, eyes wide open as though to see better. "But what do these farmers eat?" he finally asked.

"Flowers," Seth said, laughing. "For that's all they grow."

"Why no cows?"

"They have no cow dogs, so they have no cows."

"How have they no cow dogs?"

"It's said that long ago the Ten-Furlong farmers killed their own dogs."

"And no remembering why."

"I'm afraid not."

The Ten-Furlong family always found it difficult to gather new family members and were happy for the extra help in this busy season. They didn't care that Damon was a soldier, and one of the farm wives even took a quick liking to him and kept him company in the room above Seth's, where she could hear the bed scraping and thumping at all hours of the night. Damon, at first merely surprised, became confused, then dazed, and then happy. Seth had thought he was already happy, but this was a different thing entirely.

"That young man likes his flowers," an elder commented to Seth over breakfast. "He knows many, also: Nasturtium, Red-Seal, Flowering Pea, Strawberry Up-Tuck…"

He named each flower with relish, and his list continued like a love ballad, through porridge and toast and a fresh pot of tea. Through the open window Seth could hear the remote cry of a falcon, the cackle of chickens, and the soft sigh of a breeze. Then she heard laughter as Damon and his new lover distracted each other from the work of turning soil in the vegetable garden. Seth said, "All soldiers seem to love flowers."

"I keep forgetting he's a soldier. Must he return to Watfield with you?"

Seth had been wondering about that herself. Could she leave Damon here? He surely would want to stay. Had she inadvertently brought him to the exact place he belonged, or would he eventually start longing for his bunkmates? Did he even realize he was being tested as a possible husband?

She finally said, "When I go back to High Meadow in a couple of days, I'll leave Damon here to see how he manages without me. When I come back, I'll ask him what he wants to do. I think I could let him stay for the summer. In Watfield he's just one of five hundred soldiers, and no one needs him."

The day before she was to leave, Seth carried the midday meal to a flower field where Damon, with several others, was hoeing weeds and even tying young vines to trellises, for he was deft with his maimed hand. His shirt was sweat-stained, his face dirt-smeared, and his shorn hair covered by a white head-cloth. His back was even starting to bend.

They all sat on the rough stone wall that edged the field and started sharing out the food. "You are quiet," Damon commented.

"I was thinking how I'd miss your company. Then I though what a marvel it would be, to come back for your wedding."

She had thought Damon would be startled by this possibility, but it seemed his lover had already mentioned it. "I am not a good soldier," he said with a grin.

"Well, I hope that you're only the first. Maybe the Peace Committee will become matchmakers."

Damon began telling Seth about the flowering peas, which were a unique variety grown only on this farm, that was much sought after for the vividly colored flowers. "But when people on other farms save their seed, the colors fade from year to year, until they are only pale pink. Why do they do that?"

Everyone within hearing engaged in a lengthy discussion of the importance of keeping a unique variety pure, which led to Damon's exclamation, "And that is why Ten-Furlong Farm grows no common peas in the vegetable garden!"

"We'll make a flower farmer of you, sure enough," someone said.

Seth began to say something but stopped short with surprise at the sound of a dog's bark.

The flower farmers were so astonished that some jumped to their feet to peer southwestward, where the sound had come from. It had been a peddler's dog, some said. Others said it could have been a fox.

Seth said, "I'd swear that was a High Meadow cow dog."

"But it's impossible!"

Damon was standing beside her, tensely alert, a soldier again.

At the sound of another imperative, impatient bark, Seth shouted, "Come!" In a few moments, a group of four panting cow dogs came into sight, and the flower farmers cried out with surprise. But Seth could not utter another sound. The chief dog, leading the group, carried a limp black corpse in his mouth. He raced up to Seth and dropped the dead raven at her feet.

"I must go home at once!" Seth cried.

"I will fetch our gear." Damon started for the house at a run. His lover followed, breathlessly asking plaintive questions.

The dogs all fell to the ground, scarlet tongues lolling, chests working like bellows. Seth picked up the water jug and went from one dog to the next, dribbling water onto their lapping tongues. Cow dogs were sturdy and agile, but their bodies were not shaped for running. Still, the chief dog had chosen young, vigorous dogs as his companions, and Seth's quick examination revealed that they were tired and hot, but not injured. The farmers gave the dogs the meals they had been about to eat.

Seth examined the raven, then cut it open with her work knife. The bird had died of a broken neck. She sat back on her heels and looked around at the befuddled flower farmers. "Someone has killed a G'deon's raven."

"On purpose?" asked one stupidly, while others gasped.

"Of course it was on purpose," said another. "Everyone knows not to kill or harm any raven!"

"Even the dogs know."

The farmers' confusion turned to sober astonishment, and then to outrage. "That's the same as murder!"

"Or assassination," said Seth. She wrapped the raven's body in a sweat-stained head-cloth and the farmers buried it under a tree. Damon returned with the knapsacks and kissed his miserable lover farewell. The woman had managed to tie a small love-knot in his short-cropped hair.

"I hope you told her you would return," said Seth, after the two of them had been walking for a while, with the tired dogs trailing behind them.

"A risky promise, Seth. I did not say it."

It was evening when they reached the boundary of High Meadow Farm and were greeted there by the rest of the dog pack. Seth found the dogs' ordinary enthusiasm reassuring. The farmstead seemed as always. The cows were being milked in the barn; shirtless people were washing off the mud and dousing each other with water by the well. Homely kitchen sounds and smells came from the propped-open kitchen windows. In the bright parlor, many of the adults had gathered as usual to wait for supper. But as Seth stepped in and was greeted with surprise, she sensed an unusual tension. "The chief dog came to Ten-Furlong Farm to fetch me here," she said.

Then, of course, people must exclaim at and discuss the extraordinary behavior of the dogs. Everyone thought the dogs were not even capable of crossing farm boundaries. But when Sarna began to tell a rambling dog story, Seth could not restrain herself. "I am in a hurry! Where is that visitor, Jareth?"

Mama, approaching Seth and Damon with cups of tea, said, "Oh, he's gone. He left in the dark of night, apparently. So put down your things and have a cup."

"In dark of night?" said Seth.

"What did he steal?" asked Damon.

They gave Damon a startled look, then one said in a disgusted tone, "We just noticed the donkey is gone."

"But Jareth had no reason to take the donkey," declared another. He was one of Jareth's friends, Seth supposed. "The donkey just wandered off, probably."

"He could sell it."

"A tired old animal like that?"

"The donkey just wandered off, I tell you."

This must have been the argument Seth and Damon had interrupted, an argument fueled as much by hurt feelings and embarrassment as it was by desire to understand the event or to make a decision. Seth touched Damon's arm and murmured in his ear, "I'm afraid this is my family at its worst. Everyone trying to be right for wrong reasons."

"They need a senior officer, Captain Seth."

"How did you know Jareth had stolen the donkey?"

"Because he sneaked away." Damon paused. "Donkeys carry things. He took something else, something heavy."

"Shit!"

The room fell silent at the sound of this barn curse, which was never to be uttered indoors. "Seth!" Mama hissed.

"Jareth stole a box that was under his bed. I'm sure of it. It was a locked wooden box, marked with glyphs."

A couple of people went upstairs to check. Mama, who was still holding the mugs of tea, thrust one rather violently into Seth's hand. "If you won't set down your burdens—"

"Mama, we have to leave almost immediately. Do you know anything about that box? It must have been there forever."

Mama, having also given Damon his cup, stood back with her fists on her hips. "What haven't you told your own family, Mariseth?"

For a moment Seth felt like a little girl being chastised. But it would not do. Damon was right: an officer was needed here, and, like it or not, that person was her. She raised her voice so it would carry over the bickering. "Didn't the dogs tell you which way Jareth went?"

"They were barking down by the southern boundary in the middle of the night," admitted one.

"I heard it, too. I thought it was that fox again."

The two people came back downstairs to announce that there was no locked wooden box under the guest bed.

Mama said, "I do remember a box like that. A long time ago, before you were even born, Seth, we had a bad leak in the roof and had to empty the entire attic. All of us puzzled over that box. We tried all the keys in the basket but couldn't unlock it. Some people were all for knocking apart the hinges. But in the end we just put it back where we found it."

The farm itself was hundreds of years old. The box could be that old, also. "I should have taken the box when I realized Jareth had been interested in it. But I was looking for his snake poison, the same poison that his friends used to attack the G'deon."

The room fell silent. Mama abruptly sat down. "Jareth was one of those people? And you didn't tell us?"

"I couldn't. But now he has killed the G'deon's raven that was following him, and we're going to lose him again. Now do you understand?"

They looked as if they could continue to demand explanations all night. Seth gave Damon's sleeve a tug. "Let's go."

A number of dogs went with Damon and Seth into the marshland and were soon leading the way, their white hindquarters easily visibly in the starlight. Seth, though still unsettled by the dogs' secret ability to cross farm boundaries, appreciated that escort. The marshland was not easy to negotiate even in full daylight, but the dogs never took them off the dry path. Then, at dawn, the dogs barked to draw Seth's attention and snuffled in the hoofprints that were quite visible in the sideways sunlight.

The dogs went home, and Seth and Damon followed the tracks directly into the tangled wilderness.

The next day, they caught their first glimpse of the sea.

Chapter 26

Zanja spread a blanket on the dry remains of last year's heather and sat on this crackling, lumpy mattress under the open sky. The blasted landscape of the Barrens seemed ablaze, but it was just the light from a brilliant sunset. Among stones of unrelenting black, Zanja felt that she had wandered into a vast coal fire. From dawn to dusk a heat shimmer had blurred the horizon, and she could see neither her back trail nor her destination. She had been lucky to find a pool of sweet water, but her last meal, provided by a friendly ferryman who had carried her to the south bank of the Corber, had been eaten two days ago. She would have to endure yet another comfortless night.

Her involuntary travel companion, a donkey she had stolen from a poor farmstead outside Kisha, was scavenging for greenery in the fading light. He had borne the monstrous book with reluctance as she fled through pathless wilderness, first north, hoping to mislead her pursuers into concluding she had taken refuge in the northern borderlands, then east, then south. When she finally reached Shimasal, a bland market town, she half expected that a company of Paladins would be looking for her there. But she aroused no more interest than usual.

In Shimasal she asked the glyph cards a direct question: should she go east, to the water tribe that lived near the mouth of the Aerin River? Or should she continue south, towards the shattered coastline and the place called Secret? She wanted to go west, for it would be a much shorter journey and she could avoid passing the House of Lilterwess. The glyph cards told her to go south, though. Now she had nearly reached Basdown without seeing any pursuit and could only hope that Tadwell was no longer there. Once news of the theft and the rogue Paladin reached him, she might as well surrender.

The stolen lexicon, the cause of her trouble, lay on the blanket beside her. She opened it carefully and lost herself in examining an illustration. The foreground and the background of the picture were so entangled it was difficult to distinguish the dog leaping across its center. Around it were intertwined images of other animals, wild and domestic, among trees, grasses, ponds, grasslands, and townhouses with upcurved rooflines like those in a garrison. The animals were as odd and fantastic as those Zanja had glimpsed in the fresco of the library vault. The cows were spotted, the lion was striped, the birds were blue; even the plants and trees looked like nothing she had seen. The chaotic illustration had too much vitality: Zanja could not take in the whole, could not think of how it made any sense. She struggled with it until dark, and then shut the book. The donkey had already lain down to sleep. So did she—but her stomach ached, the inexplicable illustration haunted her, and the twigs of her mattress dug into her back. She turned restlessly, exhausted and frustrated.

While eating supper with the four students in the Kisha pie shop, Zanja had asked Coles how long it had taken him to master all the glyphs. "It took more than four years," he had told her. "We learned the glyphs in groups, of course, so we could understand them by similarity and difference. And we learned them in sequence, so we could see how the meanings build upon each other. I'd say we learned one a day."

I'd learn much faster than that, Zanja had thought. But with neither a teacher nor an interpretive text—at least not one she could read—she was making no progress.

For a few days after she took the lexicon, she had been able to trick herself into thinking she had a personal mission here in ancient Shaftal—a mission to recover not just knowledge but wisdom. Then she reminded herself it would be impossible to bring the actual lexicon home with her. If she did find the witch, and if the witch was in fact required by the logic of her magic to return Zanja to her place, Zanja would make the journey in water, and the lexicon, even if it didn't drown her with its weight, would be destroyed. The book would travel only in her memory.

Surely the library contained many other lexicons, with plainer illustrations and readable text—why had she not seen fit to steal one of those, which she might be able to learn more quickly? Why had she burdened herself with a book that required many years of study? Her situation had not been clarified by the theft of the book; rather it had been made impossible.

She lay in discomfort, glaring at the distant, bright stars.

ℰ

Some hours later, the donkey scrambled up and uttered an ear-shattering bray. Zanja found herself on her feet, kicking away the entangling blankets and snatching up her dagger. As the donkey brayed his alarm again, she peered across the rocky, treeless landscape, seeking the flowing shape of a great cat, or the precise formation of a wolf pack. But what she spotted was a man walking towards her through the shadows.

At the same moment the lone traveler seemed to spot her. "Zanja na'Tarwein, can you not silence that awful racket?"

"Is it Arel?" she cried. "How can that be?" She hurried to meet him and they clasped hands, laughing at each other's amazement. "You are in the Asha Valley," she insisted. "You could not possibly have traveled there and back again so quickly."

"Then you are not here, either," Arel declared.

"I wish I could make you welcome, but I have neither food nor drink."

"Let's eat the donkey."

"I've got no fuel to cook him with."

He waved an arm extravagantly at the sky. "Star-fire!"

"That's too much trouble, considering that our shoes would be tastier to eat. But at least I have blankets we could sit on. Come and explain yourself to me."

"I believe I have some Basdown cheese in this satchel of mine," he said as they walked back to Zanja's campsite. "And possibly even some bread and dried fruit."

Zanja did not say much more until after she had satisfied her first mad rush of hunger. By then, having had time to consider, she said, "You must be attending the G'deon in Basdown. He has realized he cannot repair whatever is wrong there, and he sent for you because he thought a traveler-between-worlds could have insights that a mender-of-broken-things cannot."

"Yes, of course."

"But why did you return to the House of Lilterwess with your journey not completed?"

"Halfway to the Asha Valley I encountered some katrim who had set forth as soon as the pass was clear, to find out what had become of me. They took the ponies and goods to bring to the valley, and I turned back."

After a moment Zanja said, "The elders will disapprove."

Arel shrugged, as Zanja had often done in response to such concerns. "I was miserable with unsatisfied curiosity—too miserable to do anything but turn back. I had to find out what had become of you."

"Ah, a reason I understand. Well, I haven't found the water witch yet, but I think I know where she is."

So they sat talking, in a land so empty and quiet that they could hear wind whistling in the fissures of the bare black stones. Zanja did not tell Arel everything. In the morning, when in daylight he noticed the donkey's peculiar burden, he certainly realized she was keeping a secret from him. But the Ashawala'i were circumspect. Arel did not demand an explanation.

That day the sun rose over a bank of clouds that lay on the flat horizon to the east. The distant winds that normally move the clouds across the sky did not affect these vapors, and Zanja found their immobility disconcerting.

"It is strange," Arel agreed. "Tadwell told me it's water weather—a fog that through spring lies over the coastline at dawn and burns off by midday." He added, "Like me you have not been here before?"

As the bank of clouds faded away Zanja kept glancing to the east, but the ocean itself was too distant to see. She would view the ocean soon enough, for she was just a few days' journey from Secret. She couldn't avoid Tadwell now, so she continued as she had done since reaching Shimasal: she walked boldly down the highway as though she truly were a Paladin. Arel, who seemed to have become fascinated by the problems in Basdown, recounted with horror the most recent clash between two families in which one person had been so badly clubbed that he died, and another had been crippled.

"That is the worst of the feuds right now," said Arel. "But nearly every family has at least one long-standing grudge against another. The Truthkens say that the entire region has a madness, and even the children are afflicted with it. This madness has gone unnoticed for many generations. And even they do not know how to cure such a thing."

That the problem would be resolved Zanja knew, and she listened to Arel with a disinterested indulgence. "Tadwell must be furious with them."

"He would like to force them all to leave Basdown entirely and start new elsewhere. But the Truthkens say the Basdowners would bring the madness with them and thus infect the entire country with it."

"Have you thought of any solutions?"

Arel laughed. "I have been here three days, and the only person here who is more stubborn than these Basdowners is Tadwell. I don't know of a solution for stubbornness."

"How many Truthkens are with him?"

"Three now, and it is dreadful to converse with all of them at once. Tadwell is considering whether to send for all the Truthkens in Shaftal, over a dozen of them. If I were a Basdowner I'd flee."

Entering Basdown was like stepping over a threshold from the dry, sparse expanse of the Barrens into a sodden, lush land of dense woods and rolling hills. Soon the Barrens had passed completely out of sight, and here was a land of sunny meadows, shining brooks, numerous small ponds, and narrow, twisting woodlands that dug roots into the waterways that marked the lowlands between cow-scattered hilltops. Zanja soon noticed that live trees had been clear-cut wherever it was possible to enlarge the meadows; every farmstead was surrounded by stacked logs—much more firewood and timber than any family would need in a year. Zanja muttered, "Something is wrong with these people. They're laying waste to their own woodlands!"

"And they have too many children and keep too many cattle. They are greedy."

Late in the day, they reached a small inn. Here Tadwell's Paladins and Truthkens had more than filled the stable and the guest beds. Several temporary sleeping shelters had been built in the inn yard, and a number of riding horses ran loose in a meadow. By the time Zanja had set her donkey loose with them and dumped her gear in one of the shelters, a Paladin had come out to escort them to Tadwell. The Paladin looked sharply at Zanja's disguise but asked no questions. Zanja beat the dust out of her clothing and left her dirt-caked boots at the door.

"Tadwell says you are to keep from being noticed," the Paladin said. "Almost everyone is in the public room right now. Perhaps the Speaker will assist me in shielding you from being seen."

So Zanja entered the inn with the two men crowding between her and the open doorway of the public room. She caught only glimpses of sullen cow farmers and did not spot the Truthkens at all, although her skin crawled with awareness of their presence. Once they had passed the doorway, she realized she was holding her breath.

When they reached a guarded door, Arel stood back and she went in alone. Tadwell, unattended, sat at a table by the open window, eating beef stew. "Sit down," he said. "You must be hungry."

She sat opposite him and forced herself to take a spoonful from the bowl that awaited her, hoping that her appetite might overcome her tension so she could eat with proper enthusiasm. At any moment, a messenger from Kisha might arrive.

"Are you in Basdown to see me?" asked Tadwell. "Or are you simply making a tour of the borderlands?"

"I am traveling south. I found a water witch at Otter Lake, and he pointed me towards the sea people. At Kisha I determined where the ocean tribes live, and then my glyph cards pointed me southward..."

She didn't feel hungry but used the stew as an excuse to avoid meeting his sharp stare. When she couldn't avoid looking up he was still looking at her without any particular friendliness. "Have I done something wrong?"

"You're a charlatan!"

She let the spoon drop back in the stew. He had tricked her into believing he had not discovered her. Her prescience had failed to warn her. And she could not even explain why she had done what she had done.

"You seem to think I'm a rustic at a fair," said Tadwell. "Are you going to offer to tell my fortune now?"

Zanja could only hope that her face had not betrayed her terror. "No, Tadwell, people who let others choose their way for them are fools. I only use glyph cards to enhance my little insight, and sometimes they make my decisions clearer—especially when it is a direct question such as what direction to take." She took out her card pack and hunted through the pile until she found the one that had determined her direction: South, the Herder; with its grassland goatherd singing ecstatically to the stars. "It was a simple answer."

"But is it good?"

"If not, I'll ask again." Wanting to discuss the glyphs and her pre-occupation with them as little as possible, she continued her account, pretending that Tadwell's accusation had not practically stopped her heart in her chest. "The people who live on the coast south of here are the farthest south of the ocean tribes."

Tadwell's spoon scraped the bottom of the clay bowl. "Those people are great sailors and boat builders, and they often trade with passing ships. But they don't wander far, and the don't appreciate visitors. They send a Speaker to the House of Lilterwess only when there's something to complain of, and they've had nothing to complain of in my lifetime. Why is their witch meddling in Shaftali history?"

"I'll tell you when I know."

"Aren't you hungry?"

"Ravenous," said Zanja. She discovered that she was.

"I wonder," said Tadwell as she attacked the rich stew, "If I were to ask how to resolve this Basdown problem, would the cards give you insight?"

Zanja lay her hand on the card pack. It lay passive under her touch. "Not at all," she said. But then there popped into her head the glyph illustration that had so frustrated her the night before. "A dog. It is completely integrated into the landscape, part of a complex interrela-tionship of interdependent elements."

"What?"

She was already wishing she had silenced her impulse to speak. "It's a glyph I've seen but that isn't in my pack. It just came to me, but you must ask a glyphologist what it means, for I don't know."

"One of the Paladins will be familiar with it."

Zanja was not merely dismissed to continue her hunt for the water witch, but was even given a fresh supply of food. Arel walked down the highway with her, well into the afternoon, until they reached a big, busy farm within sight of the road, where a couple of short-legged, self-important dogs came out to keep an eye on them. Arel said, "That's High Meadow Farm. Tadwell was here two days ago. That family killed a neighbor shortly after snowmelt."

"I know someone from High Meadow."

"Is your friend temperamental, unforgiving, and shortsighted?"

"The exact opposite." Zanja's gaze lingered on the dogs, who had lain in a patch of sunlight, grinning cheerfully at the visitors, bright tongues lolling. "I wonder what Tadwell will do."

"Stay and find out. Why are you in such a hurry?"

"I dare not linger."

Arel gave her a hard look, and she sighed. "I wish I could tell you everything. But I will say that I'm trying to outrun trouble—trouble I brought upon myself."

"To run from that kind of trouble is always a mistake."

"It's honorable to face consequences and dishonorable to run from them. Yet I am running. The thing that's driving me is more important than honor."

She clasped his hand. "Farewell, my brother."

She left him, and did not look back.

Three days later, she reached the abrupt eastern edge of Shaftal and for the first time set eyes on the sea.

Part Four: Sea Change

Chapter 29

Emil yanks open a sticking window sash and calls, "Raven!" Emil's raven, never out of hearing, dives down from the gable in a vertiginous, curving swoop.

Karis is far away, and yet she staggers and falls to her knees. The Paladins whose onerous duty it is to watch over her leap out of the wagon where they have been eating a midday meal of bread and cheese. She gestures at them: keep away. Now that the raven has settled on the windowsill, Karis is able to stand up and go to the nearby stones that lie like giant broken teeth at the base of a steep hillside.

The raven—Karis—watches Emil pace from window to worktable, where an old book lies in carefully dissected pieces: boards, spine, and page signatures. "Emil," she says to him. "I need your counsel. I need your resolve."

But the raven says nothing. When the Paladins killed her raven to save Clement, that injury had been terrible. And when the assassin in Basdown managed to kill another, it had been worse. Now the surviving ravens cannot speak.

Emil says, "Karis, I know something that I shouldn't withhold from you. But I'm worried about how you'll react."

"Oh, for land's sake!" Karis mutters.

"I don't know if you can even hear through your ravens anymore. Perhaps I'm just a dotty old man talking to a bird."

Medric utters a muffled laugh amid the bookshelves. "Oh, she can hear you."

"That's something, anyway." Emil sits at his table. He leaps up. "Should I tell her?"

"How dreadful for you," Medric says, "to have to trust our G'deon's judgment!"

"And how dreadful for her, to have to trust herself!" He sits again. "How ever did I manage, Medric, before you arrived to transform every dark moment into absurdity?"

Karis notes the easing of the worry lines in his face. "It's a good thing I can't talk to you," Karis says. "For nothing I would say could make you happy."

Emil says, "Karis, your very clever wife has managed to send me a letter, by putting it in the spine of *Gerunt's Decision*. She must have remembered that book was on my table for me to mend. The letter is no longer in her handwriting—the librarians discovered it several times in the last two hundred years. Then one moved it to a new printing of the same book, because the original was beyond repair. The letter's entire history is carefully noted here—every librarian who found and read the letter has made a record of it."

He opens a protective folder, and Karis endures vertigo again as the raven flies to the back of Emil's chair. The many-times-recopied letter had cracked on its fold lines as Emil opened it, and now it has been pasted onto a fresh page. Karis gazes at it through raven's eyes, her hands covering her own.

Emil reads out loud:

> Emil, my dear friend: I have been abducted by a water witch. For over a month I have been trying to discover how to get home again, and I am writing this letter in Kisha, where the students—most of them—are preparing for examinations. I have met some people Medric will yearn to hear about: Tadwell G'deon, the current Speaker for the Ashawala'i, and a student in Kisha named Coles. But I dare not write of them.

Medric utters a theatrical groan. Emil says, "She doesn't even say why!"

Medric replies, "Oh, it's because I warned her to be careful." He adds, as if talking to himself, "She's met the Speaker? That's a worry..." His voice becomes a distracted mumble.

Emil continues to read:

> I have journeyed again to Otter Lake, where I found the Otter Elder waiting for me. His tribe didn't

even live there yet, but he looked exactly as he looked
when he helped us save Karis. He told me to find the
water witch who brought me here in the first place, and
do whatever she wants me to do. She must then send
me home to you, to *preserve the pattern.*

"She underlined those three words," says Emil. "I am not certain
why."

He continues:

The witch I seek may be found by you also. I believe
that she lives with a tribe, as the Otter Elder does—a
water tribe of the coast. Maybe Karis can seek her.

My dear brother, tell Karis this—if it proves
impossible for me to come home, I have promised
Tadwell that I will leave Shaftal. He fears what I might
accidentally do, though I have been careful, as Medric
warned me to be. If I must, I will travel over the western mountains, for I have always wondered what lies
beyond them. So tell her to seek in the mountains, or
beyond them, for my blades. And say to her, to everyone, that if I am dead, I will die yearning for our accidental, marvelous family—my beloved wife, my dear
brother, my impatient daughter, and all my daughter's
very peculiar parents.

Emil rubs his eyes. "That's all—except for the librarians' notations: 'Who wrote this letter?' 'Who are these people?' 'Why do we continue to replace this letter in the book?' Karis, if you discover Zanja's
blades, if you become certain she's dead, come home, I beg you."

Karis raises her heavy head from her hands and looks westward,
where the mountains rise, too far away to see. Deep below her blistered
feet the bones of the earth are gripped by fists of stone. She can follow
the line of those bones as far west as she likes—but not now. She looks
eastward to where the ocean tears away at the edges of the land. There
the hold of stone to bone is weak, as though it has been wrenched loose
before and might be so again. That ragged coastline keeps its secrets, even

from her. And she, who fears so little, fears to even think of that unstable edge of Shaftal and the vast, dangerous, unknowable ocean beyond it.

If Karis goes east despite her fear, she might be able to bring Zanja back. If Karis goes west, she might find sorrow, and with it might find peace. But she can do neither, for although she has saved Clement, she also may have destroyed her.

"I'm trapped," she says to Emil, though the raven is once again up in the gable, and Emil has closed the window to protect the books from damp. "I was too merciless and then I was too merciful. Now I'm not even Clement's nursemaid, as those aggravating Paladins insist on being to me. Instead, I am her puppeteer."

Zanja dreamed of Emil sitting at his desk, writing a letter by the murky light of an oil lamp with a dirty chimney. She observed him as if from far away, yet she saw every detail: a dissected book, the ink stains on Emil's fingers. She could read the letter as he wrote it.

> My dearest Zanja,
>
> You were much in my thoughts today as I dismantled *Gerunt's Decision*. I remembered the day the librarians put that book on my table to be rebound, when you and I were working in a peaceful harmony that I now miss dreadfully. You sat upon that rug that had been woven by either your mother or grandmother. Do you know that you always positioned yourself on that rug as though you were a component of the pattern?
>
> I glanced at you as you were thinking about something I had said, and it occurred to me that you were exactly as you should be. I remember that I said that I saw you in the pattern woven by your ancestors, and I wondered what the people of the future would have to say about you. Would they say that you were woven into the pattern of the past just as the pattern of the future was woven from you? I realize now that when I said those words, I was using water logic. I should have paid more attention.
>
> That was the sixty-third day after your return from

the dead. The ice has melted, the rains have fallen, and the flood has receded. Yet Medric commented wryly only yesterday, "We're all drowning in water logic." And then I cut open the spine of the book, and your letter fell into my hand.

Tonight I can't sleep for thinking of you and wondering whether or when you will return, or whether, as your letter suggested, we'll know your fate when Karis finds your weapons.

I want to think of you writing me a letter, or walking among the preoccupied students of Kisha, in that way you have of heeding everything while seeming completely uninvolved. I want to know how you met Coles, and whether he was in fact a poet, or just a man of too much talent and not enough sense, like Medric. I want to be with you when you finally view the sea— not in Hanishport, where most people see it, but from the wild southern coastline, where those broken battlements and crashing waves give sailors the horrors. Yet some clever coastal peoples manage to do it, and surely that requires more than skill and luck—they must have water magic.

Karis has gone to the west, and her ravens have stopped talking. I read your letter to my raven, though, and Medric says she heard it. Now I have sat up half the night writing to and thinking of you. The Travesty is a big, echoing building. Its heart is gone. Come home, my dear, I beg you.

Zanja awoke from sleep and found herself in the place Emil had written about. The night before, when she'd first stood reeling on the cliff's edge, she saw the starry sky sweep down to join the glowing surface of a restless horizon, and then flow towards her, almost to her very feet. Even in the treeless grasslands of the south, Zanja had not encountered the terrible, vast emptiness that yawned before her here, where it seemed she could take a single step and fall into the watery sky.

By daylight, she could distinguish water from sky, though the water continued forever. In the middle distance the glare of light from the surface dazzled her, but closer to shore she could glimpse the sea bottom, where was rooted a ropy forest of underwater trees. At the surface, their bronze leaves floated in the intersection of water and air. Though the water was churned to froth by the battle between ocean and shore, here the struggle became graceful: the dense stems swayed like lithe dancers with their hands spread to capture the sun. Back and forth they swayed with the rhythm of the swells.

In the tops of those sea trees she saw a splash, and then she saw the face of a creature that seemed to gaze at her with the same curiosity and wonder with which she looked down at it. An otter—many times larger than those she had seen in rivers. They dove and swam among the stems of their underwater forest, then emerged to loll upon their backs, wrapped in seaweed. Zanja felt like she could leap into the water and live with them in their exquisitely beautiful world. Surely such friendly and joyful creatures would welcome all strangers.

But when she lay on her belly to look cautiously over the cliff's edge, she saw what separated her from them. Shrieking white birds had found nooks in the vertical cliffs in which to lay their eggs, and they fought viciously to protect these perilous nests. Lower down, the sea spray began, and the wet rocks looked like black glass. Lower still, waves smashed against black boulders. These waves and rocks would destroy most of the Sainnites' flotilla, leaving them with enough people to survive, but not enough to decisively conquer this new land.

A large ship with a huge, square sail appeared—it had been sheltering behind one of the small offshore islands. Zanja watched with fresh astonishment as it sailed directly towards the inhospitable coast, followed by a soaring retinue of long-winged white birds. At a distance the ship seemed to move by its own mysterious will, but as it drew closer, Zanja could see figures working frantically upon its deck and crawling up and down its rigging. Then the ship seemed amazing in a different way, in the precise coordination of those many sailors, in lovely harmony, effort, and effrontery.

They sailed directly into the cliff. The sailors seemed too busy to notice their peril. The spray and froth seemed to consume their ship. It disappeared. It had slipped impossibly into an invisible gap in the cliff face—the harbor entrance.

Zanja's route along the ragged cliff soon came to seem nearly as precarious as the ship's—and frustrating, for she repeatedly encountered impassible ravines and rock falls from which she could only retreat, with the baleful donkey dragging behind. She expended many steps but made little progress, and it was well past midday when she could finally see Secret Harbor. To the east, at the narrow harbor mouth, the booming ocean muscled through the cliff's narrow doorway. To the west a waterfall poured over the cliff, a floating gauze scarf that seemed an unlikely source for the distant, ominous roar. Yet, despite all this agitation, the waters pocketed between the cliffs lay smooth and still. Here in that protected harbor, the water people had built their floating town.

In some folk stories Zanja had heard and told, there was a city of boats, where a person might live from birth to death without setting foot on solid ground. Now she saw it, not a city, but a tiny village of floating houses. Down narrow avenues between clusters of houses, boats were rowed briskly to the anchored sailing ship, where laden baskets were lowered to them by rope. The rowers returned to the town to deliver the goods to the houses. People worked busily on the decks as wheeling birds dove after the offal tossed into the water. Smoke trailed cozily from stovepipes. There would be fresh-caught fish for dinner tonight.

But unless Zanja could discover how to reach the floating town, she would eat hard bread and salted beef again. "There must be a path," she muttered to her reluctant companion, the donkey, who was unable to find any grass in the rocky soil and uttered a hopeless snuffle. "They might get drinking water from that waterfall somehow—but they also need wood for burning and building. They must be able to climb up to where the trees grow."

The day had ended by the time she found the pathway she knew must be there. The twilight sky's blue was turning to black, and lantern light from the village lay across the water in restless, fractured reflections. She had traveled nearly to the waterfall, and its roar filled her ears and mind, silencing her worries and impatience, filling her with a giddy exhilaration. She recognized it now: water magic.

A string of rowboats and a flat barge were tethered below at the base of the path. Above, near the cliff's edge, was a curing yard for messy piles of firewood and neat stacks of stickered lumber. Zanja led the donkey to the river for a drink and learned that the path followed its rocky bank, beside the plunging water. She followed the path, away from the water roaring into that harbor deep in its cliff pocket. In the dusk she spotted a shadow of forest and a faint prick of firelight. Hauling the weary donkey behind her, she walked towards the light.

She passed more boats moored on the rocky shore of the river. She heard distant laughter at the campsite and took a side path that was soft with leaf mold. She walked among knee-high saplings, until the young trees began to dance in the firelight. She called out to announce herself. People leapt up to greet her. "Sit with us, traveler! Share our meal!"

Even without the expansive gestures, Zanja would have understood them, for they spoke the same language as the Otter People. She stepped forward, saying her name.

Amid stripped logs, sawpits, and woodpiles the ocean people had built a canopy of woven lath, under which a thick stew simmered in an iron pot on the fire. People drew Zanja into shelter and put a pottery bowl of cooked fish in her hands. Others unloaded the donkey and took him to grass. They all ate until the food was gone, then smacked their lips and patted their stomachs to show gratitude to the cook. Zanja dazedly thanked them for their hospitality.

"Traveler, we saw your traveling," said one.

"On the cliff's edge you walked, seeing," said another.

"You were yearning for a shelter."

"You are most welcome here."

This cooperative, musical way of speaking made it difficult for Zanja to know who to address, what to say, or how to say it. Their ages and sexes were various, but in the balmy night all of them wore similar coarse skirts and shell necklaces. She said, trying to make her voice lilt as theirs did, "I have been seeking the people of the—the large water—for many days."

"This is true," they all said, but in various ways, using various words.

"Do the people of the large water know why I seek them?"

"The wind carried you," said a soloist. "For here you can rest."

"The current lifted you," said another. "For here thirsts are quenched."

"A voice spoke to you," said a third. "For here you may listen."

The others turned in startlement to this speaker. The eldest among these water people, her white hair glowed in the shadows. She had not been there before, and she had arrived without arriving.

Zanja said, "Grandmother, what shall I hear?"

The old woman said a word Zanja had never heard before. Its meanings were like light on the never-still surface of wind-ruffled water. Depth, and mystery and richness, and terrible power.

Zanja feared to look at the woman but dared not look away. "That word is your name. You are Ocean."

"She is," confirmed some, while others said, "She is not," and still others equivocated, apparently not caring what they said, so long as the words sounded beautiful.

The water witch laughed. And then she was not there.

Chapter 28

A packet has arrived.

The soldier who carried it is unknown to Clement. When he calls her "general," his tone is unusual, not like the others, who mention her rank on the way to saying something else. He pauses before and after the word.

It might mean something, but Clement can't imagine what.

"He is from Appletown, General," says Sevan.

Her tone is not as usual either, Clement notes. "Oh, Appletown, a small but well-fortified garrison. There was never a town at all, just a place for teamsters to load up their freight wagons. The farmers did grow apples. But it wasn't apples the teamsters came for, it was brandy, and cured pork. The farmers fed their pigs on apples, and smoked the meat with apple wood, and made apple brandy in the winter."

"Yes, General," says Sevan.

"Cadmar liked brandy. Euphan sent him a great deal of it."

The soldier says, "Commander Euphan sent the brandy because he admired Cadmar. General Clement. He mourns his loss. General Clement. And yet he is glad to see an experienced leader rise to his rank. General Clement."

"How peculiar," Clement says. "Cadmar thought the brandy was a bribe."

The soldier laughs in a manner that must strain his throat, then stops abruptly.

"We are going to Appletown garrison next," Clement says.

There is more to recount: that Appletown is the only one of the five rebel garrisons that lies south of the Corber, that crossing the river will be difficult since Karis refuses to get in a ferry, that marching to Haprin and crossing the river on the bridge there will take at best thirteen extra days, and that they will not then be able to quell the rebellion before they must return to Watfield for the gathering of the commanders. It is a difficult problem.

All this and more, Clement might have said, but Sevan speaks before she can begin, louder than is usual for her. "Will you read the letter from Commander Euphan?"

Clement unties the knotted bindings, unfolds the waxed, water-proofed leather envelope, and then breaks the seal on the folded sheet of paper within. All these are things she has done many times before. As Cadmar's lieutenant, she had read everything, and all routine matters she had dispatched without even mentioning them to Cadmar. (Cadmar could not read, and could not learn.) How had she decided which was routine and which was not? It had always been an obvious decision, but she can't remember now what factors had made it obvious. She begins to ask Sevan.

"Shall I read it, General?" asks Sevan and takes the letter from her. She glances it over, and then says to the soldier, "Go to the refectory and tell the cooks the general wishes you to be fed."

It does not seem normal for Sevan to give orders in Clement's name. Sevan is not even a commander yet—she will take over the command of Appletown garrison, after Euphan kills himself. But there will not be enough time for that, unless Karis agrees to get in a boat. Clement will ask Karis again, at the next opportunity, for it is abnormal to refuse to cross a river. She has never known anyone to be so adamant about so commonplace a thing.

Sevan says, "I will read the letter to you, General."

Clement notices that the soldier has left. He has gone to the refectory, though it is long past midday, and the evening bells have not rung. No one should expect to eat a meal at this hour.

Sevan reads the letter. Euphan expresses shock at the conspiracy of Heras and the other three commanders, who are all dead now.

If Euphan is shocked to learn of the conspiracy, then he did not know about it. Therefore, he must not be guilty of mutiny. Clement is surprised, for she remembers being certain that Euphan was part of the plan. She also remembers that she called him a corrupt criminal who lived like the lords of Sainna. It is wrong to live like that, but she isn't certain why.

Sevan, continuing to read the letter, says that Euphan has not contacted Clement and was unable to attend her in Watfield as commanded, because Appletown garrison has been under siege. How astonishing this is! For Clement had been certain there are no Paladin irregulars in that region. Now Sevan reads that bands of brigands had attacked the garrison. The brigands had always been Euphan's friends, for he permitted them to collect and sell the farmers' brandy so long as most of the money went to him. Or at least Clement had thought this was the case, but apparently had been mistaken. For her errors to be corrected was good— she had told her subordinates this many times. But why was it good?

Sevan reads, "The thugs seem to have hoped to mollify the new G'deon's anger at their criminality by attacking and massacring us. But they have recently abandoned the attack, because they learned that the G'deon is actually a friend to the Sainnites. My patrols cannot find them now, and I believe they have scattered."

Sevan snorts, which is odd behavior. "I see why you always declared Euphan to be a dishonest, lying thief," she says. "Does he think you won't guess that he has been rounding up and killing the brigands, so they won't be there to give him the lie?"

"Of course," Clement says. "Of course not." One of these answers will certainly prove to be correct.

Sevan says, in that tone Clement does not recall having heard until recently, "Euphan certainly has learned the fate of the other four commanders. He knows you are too wise to believe this fiction, for you even predicted that he would try to lie his way out of trouble—do you remember?"

"I do remember that I told you he would lie. But how did I know that?"

"You didn't explain that to me at the time, General. But I assume it's because you know he is without honor and is loyal only to himself. And Euphan knows you know this, and he knows you are not stupid."

That peculiar tone again. "I am not stupid," Clement says. She often repeats what other people say, for she frequently is expected to speak, but when she tells them all she knows, they behave in ways she finds perplexing.

Sevan says, "No, General, Euphan knows he can't trick you. In this letter he is telling you what he wants you to pretend that you believe. If you pretend, then he in turn will act like he supports you as general. He will give you his vote."

Clement is amazed. "Why did I think that winning their votes would be difficult? A great deal of what I thought was true is not true at all."

"General, that is not correct. Before Wilton, you knew what was true and what was not. Now you believe everything anyone tells you."

"That is extraordinary, is it not?"

"Karis took away your fear, so you could go to the gate and challenge Heras again."

"Yes, she did. I am glad of that, for fear has no use. I could not endure to suffer any more, and it is much easier to do my duty without suffering."

"I'm certain it is easier, General. But what is your duty?

"You know the answer to that question," Clement says. Yes, that is why Sevan's question seems absurd. "A general's duty is to do a general's duties."

"Of course, General. Why would accepting Euphan's bargain be a bad decision?"

"A bad decision," Clement says.

"Yes."

Now Sevan says nothing, and Clement waits for her to give the answer, but she doesn't. "To accept his bargain would be a bad decision," Clement says.

"Yes, general." Sevan's tone is unusual.

At the gate, which stands ajar, guarded by a mix of armed Paladins and unarmed soldiers, the bugler sounds a brassy call: Honored Guests Arriving.

"Karis is returning, I suppose," Sevan says.

"I suppose."

"Let us greet her."

Clement remembers that Karis said she would be gone until nightfall. But now it is only afternoon. Why do people persist in ignoring these schedules? She asks Sevan this question as they walk to the gate. "Unexpected events happen all the time," says Sevan.

"But that is unreasonable."

"Yes, General."

Karis arrives, riding in the wagon, as healer and Paladins require of her, for the soles of her feet have not healed since she marched without rest across the breadth of Shaftal. Clement's feet had also been sore after her own journey, and some members of her company continued to limp. But Karis's feet had been raw and bleeding, and now the healer is not pleased by how slowly she heals. A Paladin hops off the rolling wagon and approaches Clement and Sevan, greeting them in Sainnese though Sevan is as fluent in Shaftalese as Clement.

Clement recalls that she has never known Sevan particularly well. She had spent no time with her until the last few days, but now Sevan remains at her side from dawn bell to night bell.

The Paladin is telling them that Karis learned something through her raven in Watfield and wishes to speak with both of them in her quarters. "Which quarters are hers today?" asks Sevan, and Clement is baffled by this question until she remembers the Paladins are moving Karis to a new room every night. It is quite inconvenient.

The Paladin asks if they want to ride in the wagon. Sevan and the Paladin run after the wagon, so Clement does also. It is not unpleasant to run. They jump onto the running board as the wagon jolts along the road through the garrison. The thaw is past, and now the roads are being repaired as they are every year. In large sections the cobbles have been removed and the dirt dug out. Every time the wheels hit one of these, Clement is nearly bounced off her perch, and the Paladins say "Ha!" which is a soldier's tradition they have begun to imitate. Finally, the wagon halts and Karis follows a Paladin to her new quarters. Tonight Karis is in the same building as Clement, and they encounter the nurse, who is pacing the hall with two babies in her arms. The larger is howling, and the smaller is yelping. Karis can always make a baby stop crying, but she does not pause, and where a Paladin holds the door open, she goes in and glances around the small space.

She sits on the bunk, and Clement sits in the chair, and Sevan stands. The door is closed; the Paladin now stands guard in the hall.

Karis says, "I expected to hate being the G'deon, but I never thought the Paladins would be the most intolerable part of it. Any moment now, one will walk in with tea and a plate of those flat cakes they are always torturing me with."

Sevan says, "Karis, we have received a report from Euphan, the commander of Appletown."

Clement remembers the task she had earlier set herself. "Karis, it is not reasonable for you to refuse to take the ferry," she begins.

"No one expects an earth blood to be reasonable about water," says Karis. "And I will not take the ferry. Now be quiet, Clement."

Clement feels certain that, though Karis is always blunt and direct, she has lately become less polite. But now Sevan speaks at some length, and Karis listens without interrupting. Clement recognizes what Sevan is doing: after recounting the contents of the letter, she is assessing how the new information affects their strategy, and soon will discuss tactics. Clement used to engage in such conversations all the time, but now she has been told to be quiet. It is not right that a person of lower rank be allowed to speak when the person of higher rank is not, but everyone must do as Karis says, as she outranks everyone.

The door opens and a Paladin enters with a teapot and cup and a plate of little cakes. "Karis, you ate no dinner," he says, "And I—"

"I will eat something," she says. "Leave us alone, please."

Sevan pours tea and offers the plate to Karis, who says, "Would you eat them?"

"May I refuse?" says Sevan.

Karis sighs. "I told you to treat me like an equal, didn't I?" She takes a cake and bites it, then lays it on her knee. Her bite has removed a crescent from one edge, and the rest is quite round. "What will happen if we allow this Euphan to believe Clement has accepted his bribe?

"Euphan will have more time to plan and consolidate, or at least he will think he does."

They discuss positive and negative aspects of various options. Clement drinks a cup of tea and eats the little cakes, for Karis is not hungry and Clement is, as has been the case ever since Wilton. Karis says Clement's name but is not talking to her.

"—couldn't think what else to do."

Sevan is shaking her head. "She is obviously not herself. With every passing day—"

"Her old passion and determination was so strong—it took her through what had to be done in Wilton—but since then she has been gradually rolling to a stop."

Karis has said similar words to Clement many times, but never to another person. This alteration of custom may be difficult to explain. Clement decides not to attempt it.

"You can't undo what you did to her?" says Sevan.

"I can. I want to."

Clement says, even though she had been told not to speak, "I could not endure to suffer any more."

"Do you mean in the future?" Sevan asks, looking at Clement.

"The future? No I mean when Karis took the fear away."

Sevan turns to Karis. "I don't think she can imagine a future that's different from the past. By luck, her tactics in Wilton worked three more times, in three more garrisons. But Euphan's garrison is hardly a garrison at all, and Euphan—he is a wily commander—wilier than I am, I fear. We must have Clement back, Clement entire, for we will have to outthink the man if we are to overtake his garrison without violence.

"Without violence! What do you call what she's done to all those officers?"

Karis has been shouting, and now Sevan is gazing at Karis without expression, a tactic Clement knows soldiers use sometimes, when—when—when bellowed angrily at? Is that right?

Karis breathes. She breathes. She breathes. Her eyes are red. Her eyes are wet. She breathes.

"Karis," says Sevan. "The general certainly has been harsh—more harsh than anyone would expect of her. But the penalty for mutiny is death, as every soldier knows."

"If I put her pieces back together," says Karis, "She will still remember everything she has done. And she will feel it, also."

Karis breathes. She breathes again. "Norina—our Truthken—you know what Truthkens do? Our realms sometimes seem to overlap—both of us can cure madness, for example. But I do it by healing a broken brain, and she does it by healing a broken mind. You don't understand me at all."

"I'm afraid not, Karis."

"I can't explain air logic, and earth logic is so obvious ..." Karis breathes. "My wife," she says. "When her brain was injured, years ago, I healed her. But her mind was also injured, and at midsummer, she becomes mad. It's horrible what she endures—and yet Norina will not cure her, and I can't cure her. I can do something—I can break her brain in a way that makes her sane again. Norina forbids it, though. For as long as Zanja is broken, she'll feel no pain, but that's because she'll feel nothing at all, and her genius lies in her passion! Should I restore her feelings, she would go mad again, but it would be worse. And the longer she is without feeling, the worse her madness would be."

She is looking at Clement now, and she is breathing. "Do you understand," she says. "I forced Clement to endure that torture when she was shot. Now she has killed a lot of people—people for whom she was willing to endure any misery. She has felt nothing. Now do you understand?"

Clement is puzzled by Karis's words. "I could not endure to suffer anymore," she says.

"I do understand," says Sevan. Her face, Clement notes, has an unusual pallor.

Karis says, "I dare not fix what I have broken in Clement. I fell into the error of mercy, as Norina calls it—the error I am most prone to." Karis breathes. "I should have made her endure it."

"I could not—" begins Clement.

"Be quiet," says Karis.

Karis's cake still balances on her knee, with that single bite taken out of it. Clement picks up another cake and begins to eat it.

Sevan says, "You cannot undo what you did, because she'll go mad. But the longer you leaver her as she is, the worse the effect will be."

"She must be accepted as general," says Karis. She rubs her face. "Which Clement will the commanders like more, Sevan? Will they like her as she is? Or—"

"I suspect they won't like her either way," says Sevan. She glances at Clement and glances at Karis. "When we study tactics, we are told there are never only two choices. If two options seem equally unacceptable, we must reject them both, so we can imagine a third choice, and a fourth."

Karis utters a small grunt. "Norina," she says.

"Excuse me?"

"The Truthken is the third choice. I have to send for her." She breathes.

"But this option also dissatisfies you?"

How does Sevan know Karis is dissatisfied? Clement is puzzled. She eats the last cake.

Karis says, "She'll be angry—that's all. And it will take too long. Still, I need to write a note to be carried to her."

Sevan opens the door and speaks to the Paladin, who comes into the small room and removes from his waistcoat a rolled packet. He unties and unrolls it, and it becomes an ink-smeared, leather blotter that contains in pockets a wooden pen, dry ink, a small ink dish, and several sheets of paper. He apologizes that the paper is wrinkled, since it got wet during their long journey in the rain. He steps out. Karis stands up, and the cake falls from her knee to the floor. She dips her finger in her teacup and shakes a few drops of tea into the ink dish. She adds some ink powder and begins to mix it with the blunt end of the pen. That end of the pen was black already—it has been used for this purpose before.

"What did you want to discuss with…us?" asks Sevan. "The Paladin said a raven—"

"Something has happened that wants my attention," says Karis. Her head is bowed over the dish. The black powder floats on top of the drops of tea. She mixes, but the powder doesn't mix in. "Zanja," she says.

She drops the pen. Grainy drops of tea and specks of ink powder spatter across the Paladin's wrinkled paper. Her head has come up in a peculiar manner, not in her usual slow way. Her eyes are not right.

"Karis?" says Sevan.

Karis steps in the wrong direction, into the table. The table breaks. It cracks into pieces, and the pieces clatter to the stone floor. It is noisy.

"Karis!" says Sevan. She is clasping, is trying to clasp, Karis's arm. The Paladin has slammed open the door. "Karis!" says the Paladin. His voice is loud.

She has ruined his paper. His pen is rolling across the floor.

He is trying to clasp her arm. Karis does not breathe. Her eyes are not right. She looks at the wall. She steps into the pieces of the table, and they shatter. The Paladin tries to clasp her. "Karis! What is wrong?

She breathes. "Zanja," she says. "Her knives."

She turns. The door is there. She steps through it. Now she is gone. The Paladin is gone. The baby is crying in the hallway. Clement remembers that one of the babies is hers. She remembers that she loves him, but can't remember what that means.

"Bloody hell!" says Sevan.

"I never saw her break a table before," Clement says. "She spilled ink on my trousers."

Sevan breathes. "We must follow them, General, to find out what is happening."

Once again, Karis has failed to follow a plan. It is not reasonable.

Chapter 29

Seth had always avoided looking directly at the ocean—it made her queasy. When she had taken her occasional holidays by the sea, what drew her was the mystery of that unknown land, so close by yet so beyond her reach, where monstrous, beautiful, alien creatures lived in ways she wanted to understand. She would wander the beach, seeking the clues the water scattered there: a shell, a carapace, a scuttling creature, a peculiar corpse. She cut dead creatures apart to see how they worked: various fish, mollusks, once even a sea dog. And if she could force herself to glance at the sickening waters, misery might be rewarded by a glimpse of a great fish like the one within whose skeleton she lived, with her oilcloth roof spread on the rib cage and her cooking fire tucked in the jawbone.

Atop the cliff's edge south of Basdown, Seth and Damon ate breakfast together, him looking out towards the fog-shrouded sea, her looking towards the scraggly undergrowth. They had been walking since dawn and were more than ready for their oatcakes and cheese.

As long as the two of them had traveled together, Seth had been seeking in Damon a useful way to understand his people. But instead, he had ceased to be a Sainnite and had become a flower farmer loved by a Ten-Furlong woman who eagerly awaited his return. Even now, with Basdown behind them, and with Damon as eager as a hunting dog to catch their prey, Seth saw him as a flower farmer, not a soldier.

"What are you looking for?" she asked him.

"Sainna."

"It isn't there."

"Which way is it, then?"

"It's so far away it isn't there at all."

"Huh!" He continued to peer in the fog, though.

Karis had said the Sainnites were Shaftali. Perhaps she had not been talking of their status at all. Perhaps Karis, too, would only see that Damon was, or should be, a flower farmer. Perhaps the truth Seth longed for was a truth Karis had already told all of them. But what could be done with this understanding? How could it be made into a plan?

"Do you want to go to Sainna?" Seth asked.

"I have heard that the entire land is a garden," said Damon. "I have heard it is always in bloom. To see that—what an adventure, eh?"

"An adventure? A sea voyage?" Seth shuddered.

"Then I come back home, with many flower seeds!"

"That would be a fine dowry!"

Seth had to explain what a dowry was, and then Damon replied in wonderment, "You think my farmer wants me for a lifetime? She wants a child of me?"

"Of course she does. Even without flower seeds from Sainna."

Damon seemed too amazed to respond.

They had been trailing Jareth for several days. Although the assassin had previously lived for many weeks in the Barrens, he was an incompetent traveler—not only did he frequently wander into dead ends or stretches of rough ground and dense brush, but he had only once found drinking water. Twice, Damon and Seth had come upon cold camps, where Jareth had collected abundant firewood but had not managed to light it. Damon declared that they were tracking an imbecile.

"Or a city man," Seth had replied. "He knows how to lay a fire— just not a fire in the open, with damp wood. And he doesn't seem to be carrying dry tinder."

"Because imbeciles think that tinderboxes grow in the woods!"

Seth, preoccupied with deciding what to do, what to think, which way to go, and how long they could travel before dark, had hardly noticed the jest. Then it jumped her, and she had burst out laughing.

When the chase began, Jareth had been nearly a day and a night ahead of them, but they gained ground quickly. Once Seth realized he was inept, she could use her own aptitudes to take shortcuts past Jareth's wrong turns, for, like most earth bloods, Seth was never lost. By now, they had made three camps to his four, and when the landscape prevented them from seeing far ahead, they had begun to walk with caution, lest they encounter him as he doubled back on his trail, having gotten himself lost or tangled up again.

"What is our plan when we find him?" Damon had asked.

"Our plan?" Seth grinned. "I'll demand he give back my family's belongings."

"And I will punch him." Damon slapped his fist into his palm.

"I'd like to do that, too. But Emil just wants to know where Jareth is going, so it would be better not to find him at all—just to follow him."

"To Han? We'll be hungry."

"Not as hungry as him."

Damon, whose fascination with the ocean had caused him to eat slowly, finally reached for the water skin, to sling it over his shoulder. "Let us chase our lost man," he said.

They continued along the broken twigs and crushed seedlings that marked the donkey's trail. The fog burned off, and they shed their outer shirts.

"Maybe Jareth's company camps nearby," suggested Damon.

"I doubt it. No one is supposed to hunt here or even cut wood. We're in protected lands."

"Protected by what?"

"Just by tradition, and now by the G'deon."

"Then no one will try to hide from her here." Damon glanced skyward. "There is no raven guard."

Every time Seth thought of what Jareth had done to Karis when he killed the raven, her skin crawled. Awful though the night of assassinations had been, this felt worse—deliberate, intimate—and not merely wrong, but depraved.

"What's wrong?" asked Damon.

"Nothing. Be quiet and listen."

A squirrel rustled in a dry thicket. A bird called, waited, and called again. Seth could even hear the ocean, though it was calm today. Her feet felt the earth's shape, and how it pushed into sea, and the sea into earth, in an unending test of strength.

Damon said, "No sound of people. Jareth is here, lost. And we are here, not lost. Nobody else."

Seth found the mark of the donkey's hoof. "Look, he's figured out he's lost and has finally turned west. Maybe he's trying to get to Han."

Their westward journey took them into a drier landscape where the sunny, wide spaces between the trees were choked with twiggy bushes. Even though the donkey had trampled a path, they had to fight their way through, until the trees disappeared entirely and they entered a place where broken boulders lay in crazy, disarrayed piles. Seth disliked the place. It felt unstable, as if the peninsula were not properly attached to its foundation, as if the whole thing might break loose here and sink into the sea.

The boulders had herded the stolen donkey along only one possible route, and by early afternoon Seth and Damon once again walked through lush woodland. "We're near the sea," said Seth in surprise, for she felt a vast water ahead of her—even though the coastline should have been at their backs.

"Which way are we walking, eh?" Grinning, Damon held out his arms and spun in a circle, like a confused weather vane. "South! East! West!"

"We're walking west—but the ocean must have wrapped around the land." Seth scratched a picture in the dirt to show him how it was possible to walk away from the ocean while also walking towards it. She straightened up, but Damon continued to puzzle over her map. She said, "You see, we have to go far enough west to—"

Something crashed out of nowhere and bowled her over. She found herself on her back in a thicket. Once she had been knocked flat by a cow, and it had been like this: a great surprise, almost funny. She tried to get up, but the springy branches gripped the heavy pack and would not let go.

She heard bodies smash through undergrowth. A thud, a grunt. The slap of fist to flesh. A cry of pain or rage. More crashing, fleeing.

Her pounding heart urged *hurry, hurry!* But she carefully worked one arm and then the other out of the pack strap, then broke the twigs that held her by the hair, and finally got to her feet and listened.

She heard a distant yell that might have been a malediction. Then, "Ha!"—Damon, victorious. She ran towards the sounds. The dense growth grabbed at her. She sloshed through the mucky remains of a vernal pond. She leapt over a fallen log. She charged at a confusion of rocks. She sensed the gulf yawning beyond, halted so suddenly she lost her balance, and fell forward. Gasping for breath, horrified, she stared down at shattered boulders and deep water. One more step, or two, and she would have flung herself right over the cliff.

Nearby, two men snarled at each other. They struggled, flat on the ground, Damon on top. Jareth's right hand held a knife, and Damon's left hand kept the sharp edge away. Blood dripped from Damon's nose onto Jareth's face. Damon raised his right hand to pummel Jareth but smacked his fist into the ground instead. Jareth snapped at Damon's throat. The donkey, a few paces away, brayed in panic and yanked desperately at its tether.

Seth leapt at them and slammed her booted heel down onto Jareth's elbow. He bellowed and dropped the knife. She snatched it up and flung it away. Sunlight flashed on the blade, but its edge was dark with blood.

Seth jerked her knife from its sheath, crying, "Damon, hold him!"

The men flailed at each other. Damon didn't seem aware of her at all. His blows were going awry. His fist slammed into earth, and then it slammed into rock. Seth heard a dreadful, choking groan that twisted into her ears like a screw.

The assassin pushed Damon towards her, an ungainly, sprawling obstacle, with scarlet rivers flowing down his grimacing face. His eyes had rolled back. His limbs began to spasm. Seth's mind protested stupidly that what she saw was not what she saw.

She noticed, distantly, that Jareth had struggled to his feet and was taking a couple of staggering steps towards the donkey. Seth ran to the donkey and slashed the tether. "Run!" she shrieked.

But Jareth had gotten hold of the halter. The donkey reared. The stolen box, tied to his harness, jounced heavily. Jareth flung a leg over the donkey's back. Seth pushed him off. The donkey twisted between them, trying desperately to get away. He reared, and Seth went sprawling. Jareth scrambled to the beast's back and wrapped one foot in the harness. The donkey tried to buck and lost his balance. He stumbled backwards.

Jareth's eye widened. He was looking over the edge of the cliff. He yanked desperately, trying to free his foot.

"Trust the donkey!" Seth cried. But Jareth tried to fling himself off, with his foot still entangled. The poor, scrambling beast, hopelessly unbalanced, uttered a wild bray. "Imbecile!" Seth screamed. But by then she was screaming at no one, neither donkey nor man, and the awful thud and splash of their landing was already in her ears, awaiting her notice.

Seth stared at the empty space where man and donkey had been. To continue yelling seemed foolish, so she fell silent. She wobbled to Damon—to save him, to fix him. But he had no breath, no heartbeat; his body was vacated. Jareth's poison had killed him, and now no one could fix him.

The shadows grew long and the sea birds ceased their lonely calling. Seth roused herself to walk dully along the trail the men had smashed through the woodland. She found Damon's pack, with one of its straps torn from the seam, and found her own, still caught in the thorns. She dragged them carelessly back to the cliff's edge and used the last of the water to wash the blood from Damon's face. His body had become cold and rigid. He should be learning to grow flowers. He should be fathering a child for Seth to dote on. This ending was all wrong.

As the sun set, a solitary woodland bird began calling for company but received no answer. The water at the bottom of the cliff lapped and sighed. Distant waves boomed. A voice called.

Seth was roused by a dull new dread. Had Jareth survived the fall? Must she defend herself from him, or help him, or let him die?

She dragged herself to the cliff's edge. She saw why the water made so little noise here: before her lay a sheltered harbor. Its gently rippling surface burned to the west with the reflected light of the sunset. To the east the water lay in darkness. But in front of her, lights scooted across the water's surface. Oars splashed. A voice began singing, then a second and a third, each one singing a different song, but without discord.

These could be Jareth's fellow assassins, coming to meet him here by prearrangement. Seth peered down and spotted a dim human form lying among the boulders, half in water. His arm waved. She drew back from the cliff's edge, but she couldn't think of what to do.

When she peered over again, half a dozen empty boats bobbed in a cluster, lanterns burning, all tethered to one that still had an occupant. The other people climbed easily across the boulders. One paused, silhouetted against the bobbing lantern light, naked, or nearly so.

The people found the donkey and gathered around him. Seth heard the murmur of their voices, somber now. Poor donkey! How frightened he had been! She wiped fresh tears with her sodden shirtsleeve. One of the people called out and pointed at Jareth. As they converged on him, his arm continued to wave. Seth realized the movement came from the motion of the water. He was dead, then.

The one rower brought over the cluster of boats. The five people lifted Jareth's stiff body.

Seth cried, "Beware! There is poison!"

They all looked up and observed her solemnly. The rower began to step casually from one boat to the next, removing short ladders and a ball of twine, tossing these to the people on the rocks. They lashed these ladders into one, which they tilted to rest against the cliff. Seth could not imagine trusting herself to this rickety contraption, but a woman climbed up it briskly.

Her quick glance took in Damon's body, the two packs, and Seth. She called something to her fellows. Her words sounded like water.

The sunset had faded, and all colors had faded with it, but the woman's hair seemed to be a glossy black. It was tied back in a tail, in which were woven strings of small seashells. A skirt wrapped her hips, falling to the knee. She wore nothing else, not even shoes. She gestured gracefully and spoke to Seth.

Seth said, "Damon was my friend. He died protecting me. This is all wrong."

The woman said something quietly. Seth pointed over the cliff's edge and made an expression of revulsion. "Jareth was an evil man."

The woman grunted. Then she squatted down and used her hands to illustrate people, who walked each on two fingers across the dirt. They encountered each other, and began to bang together violently. Seth flinched. One fell, and then the other collapsed. Seth cried out.

She wept as the woman summoned some of her companions up the ladder. She wept as they wrapped Damon's body in a sling of fishnet and lowered him with ropes. She wept as they put him into a boat. But when the kind woman indicated that Seth also should climb down the ladder, Seth refused.

The woman spoke, gestured, implored. Finally, Seth made her hand into a person and walked it across the ground. Then she clasped a handful of dirt and pressed it to her cheek. "Earth blood," she said, "No boats—never! Not even for Damon!"

The woman pointed at herself, and made her hand walk on the ground also.

"Yes," Seth said. "If you don't mind. I don't know what to do."

Seth awakened many times that night. Once she awoke with her face wet and thought she had been weeping in her sleep, but it was a heavy fog that chilled her to the bone. She remembered the stolen box. It had gone over the cliff with the donkey. But even with dawn light rising she couldn't see beyond arm's length, and when she peered over the cliff's edge there was only fog, and she became dizzy from trying to look through it.

A hand clasped her shoulder. "Esset," said the water woman, a sound like water withdrawing from sand. It was her name for Seth, and Seth, who could not pronounce the woman's name either, was calling her Alila.

"I lost something over the cliff." She gestured into the fog.

Alila made a rowing motion, as if to remind Seth that the bodies had been taken away.

"It was a box. The donkey carried it."

Alila's face was difficult to see in the fog, but of course she didn't understand, and Seth couldn't explain through gestures. It didn't matter, for the donkey must have destroyed the box when he landed on it, and even if the box had survived, the sea had ruined whatever it contained. She let Alila pull her away.

They walked in fog all morning, pushing through invisible thickets, winding around trees they could not see until they loomed suddenly into their faces. Alila held Seth's belt, and Seth kept the cliff to her left, invisible but palpable, a yawning vacancy. This blindness seemed to last forever, but when the fog cleared abruptly, the woods and the cliff were unchanged, as if they had been walking in one place all that time.

For two days they traveled along this ledge. The harbor, which at first had grown wider, gradually narrowed. Across its quiet waters, boats sometimes journeyed, rowed by people like Alila. But often the entire harbor lay empty as far as Seth could see. She felt too dull to appreciate the beauty of the place, though few Shaftali had ever set eyes on it.

On the second night Seth saw lights reflected on the water—many lights, some dense and some scattered, spread across a great distance.

She heard the wailing of an infant, the barking of dogs, and a sweet, distant singing. She smelled wood smoke. The rising light revealed the village she expected to see, but she had never imagined that it would be floating. The house roofs were low and flat, and naked children played on the rooftops in the sun. Seth counted houses and stopped at a hundred. The houseboats were tethered in rows with lanes in between where rowboats passed, as wagons pass in a street. "Alila, is this where you live?" said Seth. She should be amazed, but felt nothing.

"Essikret," said Alila, gesturing at the town or at the people, or both. In the distance, three naked children fell off a roof, one of them just a toddler. Nearby adults continued their work—and then all three children reappeared, calling shrill taunts at a child in a boat, who also leapt overboard, along with a small white dog. They engaged in a splashing tussle and Seth's eyes told her they were drowning, though her ears could hear laughter and an occasional playful bark.

Seth and Alila began walking again. And now the water down below them became so shallow Seth could see sunlight on the sea bottom, and the flickering sparks of fishes. White birds chased them, hovering, splashing into the water, lifting up into the air, and splashing into water again. To the west, the water ended at a long, curving beach. The beach gave way to what seemed a vast hay field with hundreds of streams meandering through it, dividing and redividing like blood vessels, as far as Seth could see.

They reached a stairway cut into the living rock. Alila and Seth climbed down the cliff, holding ropes tied to steel spikes that were driven into stone. The ropes were flexible, with a texture more like leather than like hemp. They smelled like salt.

At the bottom of the path, Alila began to dance on the dark sand. The coarse cloth of her skirt wheeled around her, and her strings of shells flashed and glittered like many-colored jewels. A flock of long-legged birds nearly as tall as she watched her closely, and some began to dance also, solemnly bobbing their spear-shaped heads on long, flexible necks and taking high, bouncing steps with their backward-bending, willow-wand legs. Alila stretched her arms out to embrace the water, the beach, the sky.

The great birds began to run across the beach, each stride longer than the one before, and then were flying, their long necks stretched out ahead and their long legs trailing behind. Seth and Alila walked after them. When they reached the first of the many streams that flowed from the wetland to the harbor, Seth saw the sense of bare legs and stopped to remove her boots and her trousers. Alila drank from the stream, so Seth did also, and could scarcely taste any salt.

Ahead, rowboats cluttered the beach. There seemed to be a lumberyard or boatyard well above the highest tide mark, stacked with logs and resounding with the sharp sounds of adzes and axes. Here a group of young people, who wore the skirts shunned by younger children, were trailing scarves of bright silk in the air as they danced around an unlit pyre. High overhead, ravens and other scavenger birds wheeled, hungry for carrion but fearful of the scarves. The dancers' only instrument, a drum, was played by a girl with twisted legs. Some of them sang, shrill and discordant, and Seth wanted to cover her ears. Damon would love that peculiarly practical dance, though, were he alive.

People had noticed their arrival and were gathering: the sawyers with yellow wood dust stuck in their sweat, villagers in boats they dragged to the beach, others who didn't bother with boats, but swam. The beach smelled unpleasantly of decay. Seth took a dry, twiggy branch from the lumberyard's waste pile, lit it at the only fire on the beach, where a pot of stew was simmering, and brought it to the pyre. The wood caught quickly, popping and spattering from the fat they must have treated it with. Seth stood back, and from that slight distance, hazed with smoke, Damon looked very like himself, dressed in the plain work clothes Seth had purchased for him, with a love-knot tied in his hair.

A man began singing a song that seemed dreadfully sad. All the people joined in, and again many seemed to sing different songs that intertangled with each other in ways that were surprising to Seth's ears. She sat on the sand and, her heart empty, watched Damon burn.

For several days, Seth only watched. She watched the tide come in and invade the many streams with seawater. People in boats rode the tide inland, and when the tide turned, they returned with fowl, rushes, roots, greens, and fresh water. Alila cut her houseboat loose, and her neighbors helped tow it to shore, so Seth could climb aboard without having to swim or be afloat. The boat's deck was a workroom with table and stools. Three steps down a ladder was a cleverly organized one-room house, a kitchen complete with storage and fireplace, with beds that were like slings of canvas folded away in cupboards. Small holes in the roof were plugged with faceted glass that sprayed light everywhere; they had lanterns but never brought them below. It was a marvelous little house. But as soon as a wave made it shift and grind on the sea bottom, Seth fled for dry ground. There she sat on the sand and watched as the houseboat was towed back to its place. A cat sat on the rooftop, nonchalantly washing its face. Alila's three children sat with Seth, showing her how to suck living snails from their shells. They ate theirs raw, but she cooked hers in a pan, then couldn't eat them—they were awful—but a dog ate them, and followed her hopefully for the rest of the day.

The weather stayed calm, though the fog came and went, and Seth slept on the beach except for one cold night when she took shelter in the carpenters' town, where in a row of grounded houseboats the shipbuilders lived. Many were earth bloods, building boats they could not endure to travel or live in. In the chilly morning, the harbor steamed like a cauldron. An onshore breeze began to blow, and little swells sighed onto the beach. After the tide had turned, Seth heard a cry from the village. She saw bright silken scarves being waved by people on rooftops, as a single-masted ship sailed grandly towards them across the harbor. People crowded the rooftops, and the carpenters who had gathered at the water's edge gave each other congratulatory nods. Children cheered when the ship dropped anchor, and then there was a great launching of rowboats, and with much shouting and laughter the ship was offloaded. First came many baskets of fish, and soon on every houseboat deck people were hard at work with their gutting knives. Next large bundles were lowered from the ship to the waiting boats, and all of these were brought to shore. There began an impromptu fair. The oilcloth wrappings were spread out and the contents displayed: tools, fabric of silk and of wool, bags of corn, and tins of lard, sugar, and paint. Throughout the afternoon people admired the goods, before everything was distributed. Every household received something, and all the children were given nuts and candies and toys.

As darkness fell, a bonfire was lit on shore, and kegs of sweet ale were tapped. Drums, flutes, and stringed instruments were brought out, and the villagers danced. Seth watched from the edge of the salt marsh. Tomorrow, she told herself, she would ask for provisions and take her leave. She could not bear to go back to Basdown—she would go directly to Watfield and tell Emil what had happened. After that—oh, there was nothing Seth wanted any more! This was grief—she knew it well enough. And it was responsibility. She had not killed her friend, but she had put him there, between her and the poison, and if she had not done this, he would not have died.

"Esset?" Alila approached, with a young man Seth did not recognize, who must have arrived on the ship. Looking unhappy, Alila gestured to him and said a word—his name, Seth assumed.

She said politely, "Greetings."

The man said, "Greetings. Your people call me 'Silver.'"

Seth stared at him, openmouthed, until Alila spoke. The man squatted down and said, "This woman—Alila, you call her—is brokenhearted from your sorrow. She wants to give you a gift."

Seth clutched his hand in both of hers. "You must be the Speaker of the Essikret! Have you heard that there is a G'deon in Shaftal once again? Do you know—"

The firelit dancers beyond them were exuberant, but Silver was somber and said, "We will discuss these things later." He turned towards Alila. She held out a hand, in which was cupped a string of shells, which flashed with light in all colors.

"These shells are precious to the Essikret," said Silver. "A person must dive deeply, and only in certain places, to collect the shell with the living creature inside. It must immediately be treated or the colors will fade. Alila wishes you to have this necklace."

Alila poured the string of shells into Seth's hand, and spoke.

"She says, 'Remember our friendship,'" said Silver.

Seth looked at the shells in her hand, and fear stirred. When she looked up, Alila had backed away, and several muscular sailors had stepped forward.

"I am very sorry, Esset," Silver said. "You must come with us onto the ship."

Chapter 30

In pale dawn, with the sun not yet risen, Zanja awoke to unendurable restlessness, and, leaving her things in the woodcutters' camp, walked back to the river. The waterfall, invisible to her left, uttered a distant roar, but the water here seemed smooth as stretched silk except where it plunged over boulders. To her right, the river curved out of sight, into dense forest. In between the waterfall to the east and the forest to the west, there sat an ancient woman with her feet in the water, with the powerful current parting around her ankles.

The berthed boats of the water people were gathered here, pulled by the current, bumping each other hollowly as they strained against their tethers. Zanja felt she had a great deal in common with those boats: she need not even try to understand the current that pulled her, for she would go where it went, whether she understood it or not. She knelt upon the creaking mosaic of water-rounded tones. So she had once used to kneel before the na'Tarwein elders, but always on several layers of woven rugs. The patterns in those rugs had been complex, but not mysterious. These stones, though, seemed to have no pattern at all, nor were they comfortable to kneel upon.

Ocean held a large shell in her hands. Her fingers fit between the spines that ridged it, as though the shell had grown to match her hand. She sipped water from it as though it were a cup, and droplets spattered her bare knees. "Are you thirsty, traveler?" she asked.

She offered Zanja the shell. Perhaps it was foolish to accept a drink from a water witch, but Zanja sipped politely from the strange cup and handed it back to her. "I thank you, Grandmother."

The old woman dipped her fingers in the water and scattered droplets in the sunlight. "You may ask me one question, granddaughter."

Zanja said nothing. The water witch glanced at her—sardonic, amused, and possibly grateful. She uttered a laugh and splashed her feet in the rippling water. The shell necklace upon her breast flashed in the rising sunlight. "My brother of the lakes and rivers has taught you something!"

Zanja said, "I suppose he taught me that there are patterns I cannot see, and music I cannot hear."

The water witch flung water in a glittering arc over her head. She turned her face upward. Water splashed upon her face and became tears. She was a glyph: past within future, sorrow within joy.

Then she bent over and smashed the shell's pointed tip to the stones, and put the shell to her lips and blew. In a spray of water, the improvised horn uttered a gurgling, melancholy sound. Ocean blew again, and now the sound reverberated: clear and sweet.

Zanja heard a cry. She stood up, and turned. The Ocean People appeared in the distance, bounding among the saplings. Four of them held the handles of a wood-carrier, in which was suspended the gigantic stolen book. And now Zanja saw their pursuer, thundering upon them like an avalanche: Tadwell G'deon.

"A fool has attracted the rock man's ire," Ocean commented. Now standing ankle-deep in water, she watched what avalanched towards them with amusement.

"It was for you I stole the book," said Zanja.

"You desire the book. The rock man chases it. I do not care at all about books."

The swift-footed people had nearly reached the river. Tadwell pounded hard behind them—slow, relentless. To become trapped in a confrontation between the opposing elements of water and earth seemed very unwise.

"I think I should get into a boat now," Zanja said.

Ocean climbed into a skiff and set the oars into the locks. She pointed imperiously at the other bench.

Zanja undid the mooring, waded through water, stepped in, and sat hastily as the rocking skiff jumped forward on the swift current. Ocean's white hair made a frame of light around her aged face. Her hands crossed at the wrists and put the oars into the fast-moving water. The boat jumped into the swift current. Whooping, the Ocean People leapt into their bright red and yellow boats.

Tadwell's charge halted at the water's edge. The water lay between Zanja and him, an ever-widening barrier. Yet they were surrounded by earth, and earth even lay beneath them. A fool has attracted the rock-man's ire.

But now the shore fled out of reach.

In the other boats, the Ocean People were now yodeling mockingly and waving their arms or their scarves in farewell at the glowering earth witch. Zanja cried, "Tell them not to taunt him!"

"Hoo-hoo!" cried the old woman.

The skiff climbed a wave that flung it past a half-submerged boulder. The water witch dug her oars into air, teeth bared, and the rowers on either side of them shrieked. Zanja clenched the edge of the bench to keep from flying out of the boat. From shore, those waves had not seemed so high. Ocean's oars dug in and whisked them neatly up the side of the next wave.

They flew in a spray of water. A wave fractured into droplets, which hung suspended before Zanja's gaze. Each one contained the complete sky and the entire earth. Then the droplets coalesced, and became the wave again, and the boat was flying up a hill of water. Zanja felt something rising from her gut. She opened her mouth, and yelled exhilaration. They fell, and fell down the side of the wave.

"Oof!" The hard landing flung Zanja off the bench, nearly into Ocean's lap. Water gushed in on both sides. Ocean knocked Zanja on the head with an oar. She scrambled out of the way and wrapped her arm around the bench, amazed that she was still in the boat. Ocean's red-painted oars flashed in air, dipped in water. With her foot she indicated the bucket that was tied to the bench. Zanja let go and began bailing.

A breath hissed in the grinning woman's teeth as she steadied the boat, which jumped this way and that like a confused rabbit. The other skiffs nearby jumped about also. The shoreline on each side behaved oddly—not slipping past, but remaining still. Yet at the same time, it seemed to be rippling, and the water's surface rippled also, in an exactly contrary movement. Some of the Ocean People had been spilled into the water and were being hauled into boats again. Some were bailing, and others had stood up and were shouting a rhythmic chant while flapping their oars like wings.

Zanja looked wildly for Tadwell, but their mad voyage had left the angry figure planted on the bank out of her sight. The water grew more agitated. The witch cried a warning, and everyone shipped their oars and dropped to the decks. Zanja huddled in the cold water at the bottom of the boat, face to face with Ocean. The old woman's expression was terrible: grim and desperate.

Zanja said, "The Otter Elder told me that you must return me to my place...or die with me."

The water witch said nothing. The boat began to spin.

Zanja raised her head. A brown wave loomed over their spinning boat. Stones and logs flew along its crest as if from a catapult. The Ocean People were shrieking—a nearby boat flipped over.

Ocean reached one arm over the boat's edge. Muscles bulged as she dug her hand into the water. The spinning stopped, and the boat sluggishly turned its bow to face the enormous wave.

They flew up. Zanja slid under the bench, braced her feet on the stern, and then found herself nearly standing, looking up at the serene, dawn-pink sky. The water witch clung to the bow like a spider, her toes and fingers somehow holding to the boat's ribs. A dreadful thud of collision, and an entire tree flew past them. Stones rattled on the bow, and then it was raining gravel.

And now they were falling, and falling, and Zanja wanted to vomit, but there was no time for it. The jolt of their landing flattened her to the bottom. The boards warped. Water squirted through the cracks into her face. Then water poured in on both sides, and she struggled out from under the bench, lest she drown. The water witch already was rowing again. Zanja heard hoarse shouts and glanced at the shore. Sights flashed past, making no sense: a running man, flung up in the air like a toy; the trees of a woodland tumbling over like scythed wheat; the earth rippling as huge boulders were heaved up from the firmament; a cliff rising, or a valley sinking; dust rising like smoke into the rosy sky. She saw overturned boats, people clinging to floating logs in the swirling water. She saw water flow uphill. And now she saw Tadwell. They had somehow returned to where they had begun.

Ocean uttered a sharp command. Zanja shouted, "Take me ashore!" But the witch whacked Zanja's leg with the bucket. As she began bailing again, Ocean leaned over the edge, and more water poured in. She grunted with effort, and dragged aboard—not a drowning person—the lexicon.

The boat began to spin again. The shoreline now seemed to be rapidly becoming more distant, even as the boat spun in place. A huddle of Ocean People clung to each other, thigh-deep in water. A few other boats were still afloat but unoccupied. In the distance, water began to flow downhill again, boiling, frothing, thick with dirt. Zanja retched from vertigo. But Ocean caught the crazy current with her oars, and the boat steadied.

What had been a clear, fast-moving river now seemed more like the muddy bottom of a nearly dry lake. Far to the east, where the sun's red-flushed face had risen, Zanja could see what had been the harbor: the cliffs, the impossibly narrow entrance to the sea. Yesterday's neatly arranged village had now been torn to pieces, the boats scattered across the heaving water.

They had not gone over the waterfall. They had not been flung into that pocket of ocean. Thus, it should have been impossible to see the harbor at all. But—somehow—they now were on a level with it.

Ocean's boat ran aground.

Tadwell waded towards them through the thick water or thin mud and yanked Zanja out of the boat. Her shirt seams ripped. He dragged her through the cold soup, across shattered, sharp-edged stones, up a slope, the surface of which was cracked and fissured. He flung her down. He ripped the earring from her ear. He put his hands around her neck.

"You've done exactly what she wanted!" she gasped.

The hands closed around her throat. Zanja's dagger had gotten itself into her hand. As Tadwell strangled her, she would fight him. That dagger, forged by earth magic far more powerful than his, might even be able to kill him. She flung the dagger away in a spasm of revulsion.

Then she realized, with no little irony, that she would die a hero after all—though no one would know it.

While she thought these things, she fought him for her life. But it was hopeless—he had the power of Shaftal in his hands.

"Tadwell! Let her go!"

"What are you doing here!" the G'deon roared.

"What are you doing!" the other man bellowed back at him. "You tear the land to pieces! You make yourself a murderer! For what?"

The back of Zanja's head cracked on a rock. "Arel—go away," she said, for she could breathe again. But her voice was like the scratching of a cricket, and neither of them noticed her.

"For Shaftal!" Tadwell shouted.

"For Shaftal? Only a madman could expect that to make sense!"

"This woman's very existence threatens Shaftal! And yet I trusted—"

Zanja creaked, "Quiet!"

They both looked at her. Perhaps her rudeness had gotten their attention.

"Tadwell—kill me if you must. But don't talk about it. Not to him, not ever."

After a moment, Arel stepped back, and turned. He picked up Zanja's dagger. He stiffened with surprise.

While Tadwell was flattening the landscape to make the river flow in reverse, Zanja had been on the water—not a restful place, certainly. But Arel had been riding the bucking back of the earth—it must have been him she had seen being thrown into the air. He had landed like a katrim, of course, and had kept running, directly towards the center of the madness, while trees fell and boulders exploded out of the soil all around him. The man certainly should be beyond surprise.

"Bloody hell," Zanja said. "Nine curses of the nine gods. Shit." She would have cursed in the water language also, had she known how to do it. Her ear hurt as if it had been torn from her head; her ribs felt like they had been hit with a club; and now the rocks of the deranged earth seemed to be embedded in her skull. She'd have a G'deon's finger marks on her throat, too, if she survived this day.

Tadwell loomed over her, breathing heavily, his big hands poised to clutch her throat again. "Tad," said Arel quietly. "She threw her dagger out of her own reach, so she couldn't harm you."

The G'deon made an irritated movement, as if a fly were buzzing around him. Arel said, "She stole a book—this seems beyond doubt. But why? She can't sell it, and it contains no secrets. She is drawn to glyphs, but there are no obstacles to studying them. She could even have stolen a smaller book! What she did is no more reasonable than what you're doing."

Arel squatted, wisely keeping his distance. From head to foot he was covered with dirt. Zanja's dagger dangled from one hand, and she saw the ripples in the metal as if she had never set eyes on that beautiful weapon before. Karis had invented the technique of folding the steel and pounding it flat, fusing the layers, over and over. The best metal-smiths in Meartown had been unable to imitate her work. Two hundred years in the future, this dagger would still be unique.

"Fire logic compels," Arel said. "Its compulsions are beyond expla-nation. But they are never wrong."

Tadwell's head moved, just a small amount. He said to Zanja, "That old woman demanded the book?"

That old woman? At least Tadwell was belatedly guarding his tongue, but he had recognized his adversary. The water witch had delib-erately communicated her presence to him by sitting upon the stones of the riverbank. Tadwell's extraordinary rage had been inspired by Zanja, and by his anger at himself for trusting her. But only water magic could taunt an earth witch into such a massive act of destruction, and surely Ocean had known that.

Zanja said, "I was brought here so I would steal the book. But not because she wanted it. Because she wanted this—this cataclysm."

"Rock man!" cried a voice from the river.

Though Tadwell certainly did not understand the water tongue, he turned sharply. Arel hastily rose and helped Zanja to her feet, murmur-ing in their language, "Your warning was inadequate, my sister! Why did you take that book?"

"Because I wanted it," she said.

He uttered a strangled sound, as if the struggle between bewilder-ment and amusement were choking off his breath.

She took her dagger from him.

"That blade—!" he said.

"If Tadwell does kill me, bury my dagger in a place no one will find it."

She looked towards what had been the river. The water witch, standing in her rocking boat, was holding up the massive lexicon. Her necklaces flashed and glittered in the light of the rising sun. Other survivors of the catastrophe waded dazedly towards her, towing boats or carrying oars. A man who had already reached Ocean helped her to dangle the book over the confused, muddy water.

Zanja said, "Tadwell, the lexicon must be ruined already, for it fell in the water, when—"

He grabbed Zanja's arm, crushing flesh to bone. "The book has no value, then. It's a fair trade!" He took a step towards the water, hauling her with him.

"You need not force me, sir."

To her surprise, Tadwell let go of her and allowed her to turn back to Arel. A bleeding scrape on Arel's high cheekbone was caked with dirt. His warrior's braids, which Zanja had rebraided for him when she was imprisoned in his room, had begun to come loose from the bindings.

When Tadwell exiled her, as he certainly was about to do, she would never see any member of her tribe again. She felt the old loss, familiar, no more or less endurable: her people were gone, and had been gone, for nearly six years.

She said, "Farewell, my brother. The mountains shelter you, the waters nurture you, the gods remember you."

He replied as was customary, in the language of Zanja's dreams, and they embraced. He felt very real.

She turned away and walked beside Tadwell, back into the soupy mud. She stripped off the sodden Paladin's waistcoat and dropped it behind her. Tadwell, a walking boulder beside her, began to speak.

"I know I can't return here," she said, interrupting him.

He splashed forward two more steps. "You didn't tell him, did you?"

"Tell him what?"

"Perhaps I seem stupid—"

"Somewhat," she said.

He uttered a harsh snort. "Zanja na'Tarwein, your tribe is gone. I had wondered if it might be true, and now I'm certain. But you didn't tell Arel."

Each step Zanja took felt like sinking into a quagmire—there was no solidity here, just a morass. She said at last, "My people, these water people, the giants of the south, the other mountain tribes—the western tribes—we all will be extinct some day. For to be alive is to change, and to fail to change makes death certain."

"What is that? A poem?"

"It is a poem not yet written, by a poet people will always suspect might be crazy."

Tadwell snorted again. "Aren't all poets crazy?"

They were more than knee-deep in mud, now. Grandmother Ocean stood in her boat waiting for them. The boat's prow was gashed, scarred, and dented by the objects the maddened river had catapulted at them. The ancient woman gazed down at them without expression. The water man who held the bowline was mud-brown from head to knee. He grinned, and some of the mud on his face flaked away. Then he knelt, not in respect to the G'deon, but to offer Zanja his knee as a step into the boat. Tadwell stopped her with a hand on the shoulder. "The book first," he said.

Ocean's boat rocked as the book's great weight was transferred, from her arms to the kneeling man's hands to Tadwell's massive shoulder. The lexicon was not muddy at all—it didn't even look wet. Tadwell would take it back to its vault and lock it safely away, to be burned by the Sainnites.

Zanja stepped up onto the man's knee and stepped into the boat. Pain stabbed her side. Gasping, she stumbled to the bench. Holding her ribs, she turned to watch the G'deon return to shore, carrying the book on his shoulder.

All around him, the landscape seemed to be resolving its elemental confusion: the earth was settling out of the water, and the water was separating from the earth. Mudflats were appearing, crisscrossed by tiny, eastward-flowing streams and channels.

Arel met Tadwell on firm ground and offered his hand. Zanja thought Tadwell would not take it, but he did.

Ocean dug in her oars.

Chapter 31

The G'deon and the Speaker had disappeared from sight. Ocean rowed laboriously through the soupy water, until she seemed to find a sluggish current and shipped her oars. Though Ocean was an unbelievably old woman, Zanja didn't offer to help with the rowing. The chill lifted under the influence of the rising sun. The devastated landscape ceased to be amazing and become only wearying. The pain in Zanja's ribs grew worse, and she moved to the boat's bottom, seeking a position that eased the pain. Blood from her torn earlobe stiffened on her neck as it dried; it seemed too much trouble to wash it off.

With her head leaning against the boat's wooden edge, carefully positioned to avoid pressing the bruises in her skull, Zanja closed her eyes against the brilliant, dust-suffused sunshine.

"What did you do to me?" she asked, remembering the water she had drunk from Ocean's shell. She would have complied without being bespelled, had Ocean bothered to explain what she was doing. But perhaps water witches couldn't explain, like Karis couldn't. Earth bloods know what they know, and gods help anyone who gets in their way...

Zanja chuckled and woke herself up. Sunlight glared, and she shaded her eyes with a heavy hand. She still couldn't see Ocean. "Grandmother, why have you done these things? How will you recompense me?"

The boat creaked softly, the muddy water splashed heavily, and the witch gave no answer. The oars lay where she had placed them. Her bench was empty. Zanja was alone again—utterly alone.

She shut her eyes and slept.

Someone was calling. Zanja opened her eyes and sat up slightly. She saw a wide, smooth stretch of blue-green water that reflected the sun. Her unguided boat had drifted into the harbor.

"Traveler, the tide turns!"

She looked in the direction of the voice and found herself an arm-span from the tarred hull of the Ocean People's ship. A man dangled from the ship's side, one foot on a flimsy rope ladder, and the other heel hooked over the skiff's edge, tethering it. "Climb, traveler!"

She fought herself to her feet, breathing fast to diffuse the pain. Her wet clothing hung from her, and her boots were heavy with water. She discovered that the leather boot fastenings had become too gummy and soft to be untied, so she took her small knife out of the boot sheath, sliced the straps, hacked loose the sheath, and flung the boots into the puddle at the bottom of the boat. Holding the sheathed knife in her teeth, gasping with pain, she began climbing the rope ladder. The man's weight at the bottom of the ladder held it steady.

At the deck rail, she hesitated. The ship's deck was in such tumult that she feared another disaster might have occurred while she slept. The men below her on the ladder said, "We must hurry—the wind will soon turn." She heaved herself over the rail, lost her balance, and was crashed into by a running sailor. She clutched the rail, gasping. Her helper hopped to the deck and hauled in, rolled up, and stowed the ladder. He pointed towards the stern and gave her a push.

She went where he pointed. She found a place to sit among coils of line and bundles of canvas.

To the west lay a vast stretch of devastation. Dust floated over the churned landscape like brown fog. The new, far more distant cliffs looked raw and unfinished. Tracts of trees lay on their sides, their roots grasping at air. The lovely waterfall was no more. Upon the new shore, some of the water people were salvaging logs and cut firewood from the pileup of debris, while in an improvised pen, their youngest children rolled and shrieked in the mud. In the water, rowboats clustered around sinking houseboats, from which people threw everything they could salvage. On rafts of logs lay piles of rescued objects: cushions, baskets, barrels, and bodies. Zanja's heart hollowed out. What disaster had she brought upon these people with her passion for a book of lovely pictures?

A body stirred. Another rose up and staggered to a cask to get a drink. She shut her eyes, relieved. Ocean had warned her people, of course, and they had been prepared for the cataclysm.

The ship creaked like the knees of an old person climbing a stair.

Zanja opened her eyes to find that her view had shifted; the ship was turning on its anchor, and the sailors replied with an enthusiastic, bellowing chorus that resolved into a song. In clusters they began heaving at ropes. At the sound of flapping canvas, Zanja looked up and saw a sail being raised. The canvas sighed and then cupped like a hand. The ship came alive. Astonished, Zanja watched the wrecked village begin to recede. The ship moved like a living creature, but with muscles of wind. How quiet it was!

But as the ship neared the opening to the sea, the booming, pounding crashes of the waves against the rocks became deafening. A woman far aloft in the rigging screamed instructions. People yanked on a great wooden wheel. The ship plunged into chaos. It bucked and groaned, and the lookout's precarious perch swung wildly back and forth as the vessel wallowed in troughs and reared over breakers. Then they slipped through the fissure, and the ocean opened up before them.

Yesterday morning, from that very cliff, Zanja had observed the ship's arrival. Since then the earth had shifted its foundations, but her situation was in no way improved. The stolen lexicon had been taken from her. The water witch had disappeared, and Zanja was an exile. Karis and the rest of her family remained two hundred years out of reach. Zanja understood nothing.

Zanja did not know where she was being taken, but to travel like this was marvelous. She stood at the rail as they flew away from the grasping waves of the coastline. A stark, water-rounded stone island slipped past them, and several dozen gigantic, slug-shaped creatures raised their whiskered faces to bark at them like a pack of angry dogs. They passed a larger island, where dwarfed trees clung to bare rock. After that, there were no more islands; just open sea.

While Zanja marveled, some sailors set up a sunshade and went to sleep. Others worked on the rolling deck, checking and coiling the lines, mending fish nets and hanging them in the wind to dry, while some played a music game with tiny, piping flutes.

No one spoke to her. They did not seem oppressed by catastrophe, though perhaps their loud laughter was their own way of screaming at the elementals whose war had wrecked their peaceful village.

The land and landscape that had shaped Zanja's life began to seem small, and its remoteness made her feel quite unmoored. When the Sainnites first spotted—or would spot—Shaftal, it would look like this: a dark line of land, a promise that their terrible voyage would soon end. By the time they had realized—would realize—what a dangerous shore they approached, they would not be able to turn away, and most of their ships would be wrecked. They would resent and hate Shaftal for good reason.

The sun sank behind that deceptive promise, turning Shaftal gold, which faded to purple. The land melted into the sea. A sailor brought Zanja a supper of boiled fish and slimy seaweed. She lay on her back, floating in wonder as the universe filled up with stars.

She awakened to the sound of raucous whistling. A few sailors at the bow made that happy racket as the sun's edge lifted above the horizon. Others awoke, and some stamped a rhythm on the deck, and the stamping became dancing as the swollen sun escaped the sea.

One of the dancers was Grandmother Ocean.

Zanja stood up, then staggered like a drunk. The ship had begun to climb and descend steep swells that came at them from the northeast. But the dancers made the rolling deck part of their dance, and the old woman walked towards Zanja as if on solid ground.

"Where have you been, Grandmother?" Zanja asked. The water language had no words for greeting or farewell.

"I have been to a good salt marsh filled with birds, crabs, and clams."

"But your people—!" Yesterday's dreamy acceptance had dissipated. A pain struck Zanja, and she cried out, "My people—!"

"The ocean is great," the old woman said, irrelevantly.

The witch gestured, and Zanja looked across the restless waters, all the way to the horizon. The horizon made the edges of a vast bowl, filled to overflowing. Above it lay another bowl, the sky. The sun and this arrogant ship were the only sailors in two parallel seas without shores.

Zanja's gaze returned to the old woman, who continued to rock peacefully with the ship's tossing. "I admit I'm insignificant," Zanja said. "But—"

A sailor gave a shout, and people swarmed up the rigging as a wave rose up before them like a looming giant. The ship boomed hollowly, and water sprayed across the deck. Flung off balance, Zanja clung to the rail, baffled by this rough sea beneath the sunlit sky.

The water witch, who ignored all Zanja's important questions, answered a trivial one she had not asked. "The water feels a distant storm," she said.

Some people had drawn near, five bare-chested sailors whose muscular arms and shoulders belied the seeming ease of the ship's movement. "Throw her overboard," Ocean told them.

And they did.

Zanja came to the surface, gasping, in the hollow between two moving hills of water. One hill came at her and she slipped up its side. From the top, she saw the ship flying away from her on a freshening wind. Though its rigging was crowded with sailors, they were preoccupied. No one was even looking at her. Water splashed in her face, into her open mouth, and some entered her lungs. It burned. She began coughing helplessly. Sliding down the watery hillside, she went under. With a panicked kick of her legs she rose to the surface, where she again climbed a wave. This time she turned her face away from the crest so it would not break in her face. The ship sailed briskly out of sight.

Her belt hung from her hips, dragging her down. She unbuckled it and let it go: the two blades Karis had forged for her, the glyph cards Emil had given her in the early days when none of them even suspected how these new friendships would reshape their lives. How could she let these treasures go? But they were gone already. She tore off her clothes, her fingers already numb with cold. Naked but more buoyant, she climbed up and slid down the waves, over and over, until it began to seem like the waves were standing still, while she moved over them by a power she could not control. Soon she shuddered so violently from cold that she could scarcely continue to swim. She became desperately thirsty. Her legs hung from her, heavy burdens dragging her under, and she could not undo them and let them go.

A wave enveloped her. She emerged into a froth of wind-whipped water. Black clouds stamped towards her and let loose a torrent of harsh rain. A distant lightning bolt stabbed into the sea. Water mixed with wind; rain raised more water as it fell; and Zanja began to drown even as she swam desperately to keep her head in the air.

Thunder detonated on top of her and a bolt of white fire plunged into the water. Her light-blinded eyes retained an afterimage. A bowed shape? A boater pulling at the oars?

A curling wave shoved her into a quiet, cold darkness that asked only that she give her last breath in exchange for relief from the exhausting struggle. But she flapped her ungainly limbs and moved out of the black peace into the screaming wind, where she flailed her arms as though she could swim in the watery air.

A hand grabbed her wrist.

She looked into a pale, terrified, determined, and familiar face. A Basdown cow doctor.

Seth grabbed Zanja's elbow. She let go with her first hand, and then clamped it under Zanja's armpit. She jerked Zanja out of the water's muscular grip. They sprawled into the flooded bottom of a skiff.

"Zanja?" Seth gasped.

Zanja vomited seawater. Seth weakly pounded her back, and Zanja's vision went black, but when she came out of her swoon she could breathe again. A wave tilted the small boat sideways, and water gushed in. Seth shrieked, clutching wildly at the boat's rim. But Zanja, though stupid with cold and exhaustion, had noticed the old woman in the prow, who was guiding the four oarsmen with vehement gestures. Each stroke of the oars placed the boat in a safe place upon the violent water: up, in, through, and past the foaming waves. They would not drown.

The witch turned her face up into the torrent and shouted. A weighted rope flew out of darkness; the oarsmen passed it to Seth, who fumbled at the tangled harness, then tied it onto Zanja. She was hoisted high into the wet air in jerky alternations of movement and stillness. The hull of the ship swung close, then away. Now she dangled near the deck rail, the wind pushing her back and forth, and she saw three sailors leaning on a rope, their bare feet clinging to the wet, tossing deck as though they were attached to it by pegs. Zanja's rope was caught with a long-handled hook, and she was dropped to the heaving deck. Someone yanked off the harness, and she dragged herself to the mast, which swung through black sky, its fittings jangling, all but one sail tightly furled. The ship groaned with effort.

People clung to the rigging, wrestled with the ship's wheel, and huddled in shelter from the waves, ready to take action when it was needed.

These ocean people wore the same skirts and shell necklaces as before, but they were not the same people. This was an old, weathered ship, but it was larger than the first, and many of its fittings were of metal rather than wood: they jangled in the wind. It was not the same ship. Nor was this the same weather. When Zanja sank into the wave, the sun had been shining in a clear sky, but she had emerged into storm. Seth had come to her, but she also had come to Seth. Between sinking and rising, she had come home.

Two sailors dragged Seth to her, and one of them flung at them a length of rope. She couldn't hear what the sailor shouted, but it made sense to use the rope to tie both of them to the mast. As she knotted the rope around Seth's waist, she shouted, "How could they possibly get you on this ship? It must have been quite a fight."

Seth muttered hoarsely, eyelids fluttering. A wave broke over the bow. Seth cried out and clutched at Zanja. The rescue boat had been lifted into sight and dangled from ropes. The water witch and an oarsman still rode in it. The ship's roll brought the boat close, and the two of them leapt for and landed on the deck. Huddled sailors hooted appreciatively. The oarsman sauntered off.

Ocean turned and met Zanja's gaze.

Zanja understood: months ago, when the current sucked Zanja under the ice, Seth's hand had reached to save her from drowning, and for a moment it had seemed she would succeed. Zanja couldn't imagine how it had even been possible for Seth to be here at the crucial moment, to succeed in saving her after all, and so complete the pattern that the witch's intervention had interrupted.

The ship lifted its prow to meet a looming wave. Seth uttered a cry. Zanja put her arms around her as the ship rose up the side of the vast wave: sturdy, fearless, unsinkable. Zanja laughed out loud.

It was a glorious storm.

Chapter 32

Seth awoke and immediately wished she hadn't. The old terror, which had lost none of its power during two nights and a day at sea, clutched at her again. There was no certainty, no stability, no safety here. The unrelenting nausea overwhelmed her again, and she retched out a nasty-tasting mucus.

A hand was laid lightly on her shoulder. "We're going west," said Zanja, "Towards home."

"I can't endure—" Seth began, but stopped to retch again. Her muscles ached with vomiting.

"Only you could have saved me from drowning," Zanja said. "It had to be that way. And if you hadn't succeeded, the water witch would have died with me. That's why her people helped do this to you, and to me, because they need her magic."

"That makes me feel so much better," said Seth.

"Sarcasm! Well, I guess you'll live."

"I'd rather not."

"If you can bring yourself to look up, you should. It will make you feel better."

Seth shifted her head so she could see Zanja, squatting on the never-steady deck. Like the water people, Zanja now wore a loincloth made of spun seaweed, and her dark skin shimmered with white, dried salt. Her high cheekbones were a sharp ledge above dark hollows. Her ribs formed ridges in the surface of her skin and were marked by a large, black bruise. Her earlobe was torn open, revealing bloodless, shriveled cartilage.

"You don't look like the G'deon's wife," Seth croaked.

She sat up in increments. She turned her head. Sunlight blazed through a crack in the clouds onto the ship. The sailors shouted, and some flung themselves to the deck in a pantomime of relief and exhaustion. "These people are detestably silly," she muttered, and Zanja laughed.

The beam winked out, but through fresh rents in the clouds new beams appeared, casting patches of blinding light upon the agitated surface of the sea. Seth moaned and covered her eyes. Zanja nudged her. "Not that way. Look to the west."

Seth forced herself to look where Zanja pointed. A sunbeam revealed a distant stretch of rocky shoreline. Seth cried, "Shaftal!"

"Shaftal," said Zanja. "My Shaftal."

"How can you look like that? As if you belong on this cursed boat?"

Zanja said, "It's a habit, I guess—looking like I belong."

"But your disguise is incomplete." Seth dug into a pocket, where Alila's string of shells had been an uncomfortable lump, and offered Zanja the necklace.

Zanja put the necklace on and glanced with some bemusement at the bright decoration on her scarred breasts. Then the ship moved sharply and she fell onto her butt. Seth laughed, and then moaned. "Very pitiful," Zanja commented. She stood up and staggered away.

Seth fixed her gaze on Shaftal, the only thing in this world of water that remained steady. More sunbeams broke through the roiling clouds. The storm is over, she told herself. But it made no difference.

Zanja returned with Silver, who carried a small pottery bowl. "I went seeking a remedy for your stomach, and this man began talking to me in Shaftalese," Zanja said.

"My kidnapper," said Seth. She had been bitter, but now she was too exhausted for any passion, even anger.

Silver squatted down and offered her the steaming bowl, a cloudy broth with herbs floating in it. "Esset, drink this."

"You are mad."

"A small swallow," pleaded Silver. "A little drop on the tongue."

So Seth had often begged sick animals to swallow their medicine, hoping to avoid the struggle of forcing it down their throats. She took the bowl and quickly sipped from it. It was not entirely revolting: a fish broth, intensely flavored by herbs, a flavor she recognized. The herbs might settle her stomach, and they would certainly make her sleepy. Perhaps she could finish the voyage unconscious. She quickly drank it all.

Zanja said to Silver, squatting beside him, "I want to ask you some questions. Would that be impolite?"

Silver laughed. "Your people must be stiffer than mine."

Zanja looked sorrow-struck, as though she had lost her tribe only yesterday. And in fact she had, thought Seth. But she could not bear the disorientation of the thought and turned her gaze to the black line of cliffs.

She heard Zanja say, "How long has your tribe lived in this harbor, the place the Shaftali call 'Secret'?"

Seth's family had been in Basdown before history began, and it had not even occurred to her to wonder how long that had been. Silver said, "The Essikret used to live in Hanish Harbor, until the Shaftali waged war on us and drove us away."

Seth felt too dull to be shocked by this outrageous statement, but she looked at the two speakers in time to see Zanja sit sharply back on her heels. "But G'deons have protected the border tribes for four hundred years!"

"It happened long ago."

"Before Mackapee? Before the Law of Shaftal?"

"Long ago," Silver said once again, "but we remember."

· Zanja was silent. At last she said, "Because Grandmother Ocean remembers? Because she was alive when it happened?"

Seth's stomach gave a vile twist, and she said desperately, "Don't talk about her! Please!"

Zanja said in surprise, "Talking about water magic makes you sick? I'll be more careful."

Soon Seth dozed. She half awoke when Zanja and Silver discussed a long-ago time when the cliffs to the west of Secret Harbor had collapsed. Then she dreamed that a cliff fell on her, but its rocks became water, and a monstrous wave crushed her, and she drowned. When she awoke, night had fallen, Silver had left, no lanterns burned, and the ship's rocking seemed almost tolerable. No one moved across the starlit deck. Zanja stood leaning on the rail, though she must have been exhausted. She gazed northward, towards the mountains of her people.

Do you think I never felt responsible for someone's death?

Clement had said those words, when Seth thought she couldn't endure the horror of Zanja's sudden, icy death. But Seth had not understood then what Clement meant by responsibility. Clement had sent her friends to die, even though she knew those deaths served no good purpose. So she had lived most of her life, until just a few months ago, when she finally made the fighting stop. Seth understood now, for she had brought Damon with her, and he had been killed, and she continued to watch it happen, over and over, trying to undo it, to think of what she should have done to save him. Yet Damon continued to be dead. As Zanja stood watch, looking towards the far-away mountains that were said to hold up the sky, did she see her people dying, over and over? Did Clement see every death also, each one unforgotten, each one a scouring wound across her poorly armored heart? So the habits of war destroyed them, even when the war left them alive.

"No more deaths," Seth said. "Not even one." This was the determination that drove Clement, that drove Zanja, that drove Emil, and that must drive them all. Not desire for justice, not yearning for understanding, nor any other passion.

Zanja's head did not turn, yet she said, in that uncanny way of fire bloods, "If we are to desire anything, then we must accept failure."

Seth sat up cautiously, her head spinning. But the ship's deck had ceased its insane writhing and only moved gently. Seth lay her palms flat upon the oil-impregnated wood. This ship was made from the bones of trees, and the trees were made from earth. Here they floated, at the mercy of the sea and sky, on a ship that was Shaftal.

For two interminable days the ship lingered by the hazardous coast, waiting for the proper wind, tide, and light with which to enter the hidden harbor. In the meantime, the sailors cast their nets, gutted the catch, and preserved the fish in salt. Once, they brought in a single fish big enough to feed everyone on the ship, destroying the net in the process. Its red flesh tasted like nut paste.

The Speaker of the Ashawala'i and the Speaker of the Essikret talked with each other for hours at a time. Seth joined the fish-gutting crew, and then a sailor showed her how to mend nets. Every time a net was used, it must once again be mended, but Seth didn't mind: some tools, to be useful, must be fragile.

She drank a great deal of water, which tasted strongly of the oak casks. She even ate solid food. Sometimes nausea returned, but she could dispel it again by reminding herself of the solidity of the ship. She told Zanja about Damon, about his death, and about her guilty grief. She wept while she talked, and Zanja sat beside her, holding her hand, saying none of the stupid things that people usually say.

"I didn't save my people," Zanja said later. "I couldn't bear to do nothing, but knew I must. So I kept hesitating, torn between unendurable outcomes, until my time ran out."

Seth also tried to avoid saying any of the stupid things that people usually say. "Two hundred years before the massacre, what could you have done?"

"My people remembered things through stories. I could have told Arel a story, for him to tell the next Speaker, and so on for ten generations, until it came to me. The Speakers are always fire bloods, and they would recognize the story's importance. And perhaps when the story returned to me, I would realize it was a message to myself."

"But if you were to succeed in preventing that catastrophe," Seth said, "then you wouldn't become who you are, so the water witch would never take you—" She stopped, feeling distinctly woozy.

"And my people would still be massacred, for I wouldn't be brought back to tell that story." Zanja shook her head, seeming scarcely less disoriented than Seth was. "And yet every day we believe we are responsible for the future! I suppose the difference is that we're acting in hope, but not in certainty. Even Medric, when he dreams of the future, is only dreaming possibilities."

In bits and pieces like this, they each recounted events the other didn't know. To Seth, Zanja's adventure seemed mostly miserable, and largely unbelievable, but her injuries were convincing enough. Seth's own adventures had also been dreadful. As she recounted them to Zanja, she realized how uncertain she had been, and yet how stubbornly she had obeyed her common sense without any idea what she was pursuing. She had chased the stolen box, without ever knowing what it contained; she had reached out to grab the hand flailing in the water, without even suspecting it was Zanja.

And yet she felt, quite suddenly, that all this effort and heartbreak had been for a purpose, and that she had made progress. With the box destroyed and Damon dead, that sensation of progress was no easier to explain than Zanja's theft and loss of the lexicon, or the water witch's apparently deliberate goading of a G'deon into destroying her own tribe's safe haven. What had, after all, been accomplished?

They both declared they were heartily sick of viewing the raw coastline and exploding surf, though it was a perspective on Shaftal that few Shaftali ever saw. The incessant barking of the sea dogs began driving Seth to distraction. At night she woke up in startlement, thinking something was dreadfully wrong to make the cow dogs bark like that. The sea dogs, though, if they barked for a purpose at all, did it for a purpose known only to them.

At last the conditions were right, the sails were unfurled, and the ship's prow was pointed at the cliffs. Seth stood with Zanja at the rail, holding the wood so tightly it made her hands hurt. "How suicidal this seems," Zanja said, in a tone of amazement.

"You enjoy things no sane person should enjoy."

"I do," Zanja admitted. "And yet somehow I have survived."

Yet when the sailors had managed, by skill or magic or sheer good fortune, to slip between the rocks, and the ship's sails sighed and went limp as the cliffs blocked the wind, Zanja sighed also, like Seth, with apparent relief. "Karis would never forgive me if I were to drown so close to shore," she said.

Seth looked at her. The bright shells against Zanja's skin seemed even brighter, for her skin had darkened in the sunshine even as Seth's skin reddened. Her lean body stretched itself shoreward, though the cliffs were as forbidding here as they had been on the outside. Seth, too, yearned for solid land—but once she had achieved it, all the unresolved problems and difficulties would still await her: Basdown's easy turn towards hatred, telling Damon's lover he was dead, what to propose to the Peace Committee, how to save Clement.

"What?" Zanja murmured, and Seth realized she had given a start.

"I'm trying to save Clement," Seth said.

"Someone should," Zanja replied distractedly. "This harbor is huge! I didn't realize—it seemed such a disaster."

She fell silent, and they stood elbow to elbow for a long time, as the tide slowly carried them westward. The highest of the sails filled with wind once again, and even with the help of wind the sun was pierced upon a mast by the time the floating village came into sight.

"Oh, I see," Zanja breathed. She turned and looked back at where they had come, then forward, beyond the village, at the beach, the vast salt marsh, and the remote cliffs that were just a blur of black at the horizon. "Filled with birds, crabs, and clams," she said.

"You're being mysterious, and it's very irritating," said Seth.

Zanja raised a hand, and with a gesture she put the big, busy village into a kind of frame. "That village is four times the size it used to be. The people are thriving, and so I realize that before, they were barely surviving. Now they have land on which to collect wood, and they can float entire logs down the river. They have plenty of water, both salty and sweet. If they are trapped in the harbor by weather, they can survive, without going anywhere. They can survive."

Her hand, which had been framing each component of the Essikret's rich world as she spoke, paused now, a frozen gesture that contained nothing. "She rescued her people. All this was for them, to secure the future for them. She could have done the same for mine!"

She looked ill, Seth realized—ill with anger. But then she seemed to take control of her rage, and her breathing slowed. "By the gods, I'm weary with trying to understand that water witch!"

She turned then, so sharply she dug at Seth with her elbow, and didn't even seem to notice. She shouted something in the water language, something so shocking that every sailor on the ship stopped working and stared at her. Seth noticed this appalled, shipwide stillness as she turned. Then she saw the old woman, who had not been on the ship since the lifting of the storm.

The water witch now wore dozens of shell necklaces, and her skirt seemed new, as though she had merely gone home to put on fresh clothes. Yet she looked, Seth thought, years older. Skeletal, her shoulders had lost muscle; her skin and breasts sagged wearily.

The water witch spoke. Zanja cried, "What?" She turned back to the rail, digging Seth with her elbow again. Seth turned also, feeling the rigidity in the body beside her, frustrated that she understood so little. Zanja breathed heavily, openmouthed, staring intently at the beach, eyes moving rapidly, hands clenching the rail as Seth's had earlier. "Dear gods," she breathed. Her muscles jerked into movement, and she began to climb over the rail.

"Zanja, what are you doing?" Seth cried. She grabbed at her, but Zanja had already leapt off, and seemed to float, with her long, slim braid whipping through air, her seaweed skirt billowing, her necklace lifting up to hit her in the face. Then she was gone. Stunned, Seth leaned over the rail and saw the ship's shadow undulating far below. Foamy ripples marked the place Zanja had entered the water, and there she suddenly emerged, tossed her wet hair from her eyes, and began to swim.

Towards what? What had she seen? Seth looked where Zanja had been looking towards the beach. Sunlight flashed on water, nearly blinding her. But there was something lying on the sand, a shape—a person maybe, sculpted of sand, with shadowed folds that could be clothing, and a sunburnt shrub of hair.

Karis.

"That iron woman on the beach," Ocean had said, "is little wiser than the rock man by the river."

Zanja had not thought of how jumping into the water would feel like falling into a pile of boulders, or how pain in her bruised ribs would weaken her, or how swimming would call forth the fatigue that lingered after her last ordeal in the water.

A man laughing in his boat rowed to her and hauled her aboard, to sprawl among a half-dozen splint baskets that were black with age and smelled unpleasantly of fish. Zanja pointed towards shore, unable to catch her breath enough to speak. He began rowing in that direction, lazily.

The massive, sand-colored form on the beach had not moved. Karis lay on her side, as though she had escaped drowning, or suddenly fallen ill, or quite abruptly died. The boatman shouted at Zanja and she found she had begun to stand up. She squatted down again, and he commented reasonably, "Your hurry will only make you slower."

"That woman on the beach is my wife! How long has she been lying there?"

"It was dark when she arrived," said the boatman.

"What is she doing here? Seth said she's in the west! Why is she all alone?" The boatman shrugged. But, as sometimes happens, Zanja immediately knew the answers to her questions. Two hundred years and three days ago, she had dropped her indestructible knives into the sea. And now Karis thought that she had drowned.

"Row faster, can't you?" Zanja cried.

The boatman grinned. "You have been gone from your wife a long time?"

"Hundreds of years."

"Then you will survive a little longer," he said, and pulled steadily, no faster than before. Zanja peered over the boat's edge and saw the sea bottom, dark, glittering sand, patches of sea plants, flickering fishes, an odd and dangerous looking creature walking sideways on spidery legs. The bottom seemed scarcely an arm's length away. Zanja looked up again at her beloved's sprawled form, so close now, so close she could see scarlet blood on the bottoms of her feet.

She flung herself towards the shore, and she went under—the bottom was not as close as it looked. She came up, gasping, and the boatman had shipped his oars and gestured at her in good-humored exasperation. He began bailing—she must have swamped the boat.

She swam towards shore. The water felt thick as gruel. Her feet finally touched bottom, but that helped little. She fought the water, splashing high fountains around her, calling, "Karis! Karis!"

Karis still did not move.

In the more shallow water, Zanja tried to run and fell onto her face. When she got up, choking on salt water, Karis was lifting her head, turning, heaving herself to her knees.

Zanja splashed to dry sand and fell again, but this time Karis caught her.

When Zanja first knew she loved Karis, then, too, she had happened upon her, unexpected and unlooked for. Over a year after the massacre of her people, Zanja had felt something she thought forever lost to her: a centering, a certainty; not just desire, though that was powerful, but knowledge. With Karis, she might live with purpose again.

So she lay now as she had landed, and the hard ridges of a blacksmith's hand scraped her bare shoulder blade. Zanja felt the rise and fall of Karis's startled breathing several times before the G'deon of Shaftal stirred and murmured against her ear, "I told myself I would not despair of you—I need not think at all until I had rested. You began shouting though, and I thought I was dreaming."

"You're much too filthy to be dreaming," Zanja said.

"Oh, do I stink?"

"Very much."

"Tell me, dear wife, why are your knives on the bottom of the ocean?"

"Because I was in the ocean with them, and had to let them go, or drown."

Karis raised her head. Her fatigue-reddened eyes were glassy with tears. "You have become quite feral," she said quietly. "And this here— it must hurt." Her fingertips stroked Zanja's bruised ribs, and the pain went away.

Zanja caught Karis by the disastrous tangle of her hair and kissed her, and kissed her again. She felt a shudder in her wife's muscular back. "Will we make love here," Zanja began, "or—"

Karis pulled back from her. She set her roughly aside and got to her feet, staggering, showering sand from her clothing.

"Gods," Zanja muttered. She didn't have to look to know that the water witch was approaching. "Karis, she's older than your oldest powers! You're like a child to her!"

Karis hobbled needlessly towards the water's edge.

Out of patience with earth bloods, Zanja said to her back, "At least leave the firmament be!"

Karis paused. "What?"

A boat made a grinding in the sand. Seth tumbled out, crawled through the shallow water, and fell face down onto the sand with her arms flung out, as though she were trying to hug it. The water witch disembarked and stood in the water. The enraged earth witch seemed of little interest to her.

A wavelet washed over Karis's bloody feet. She uttered a cry and fell to her knees. Zanja ran to her, saying, "Get out of the water!" At least Karis heeded her now—she crawled to dry sand and huddled there, rocking with pain. "Fresh water!" Zanja cried. Silver leapt out of the boat and ran towards a wooden tank and a clutter of buckets.

Ocean commented, "The G'deons never like me."

"Have you done them any favors?" Zanja said.

"Many, many times," said Ocean.

Karis's voice, harsh with rage, smashed through the witch's melodic water words. "Does she think she isn't flesh? That I can't tear her limb from limb?"

Zanja rested a hand on Karis's tense, powerful shoulder. "Grandmother, what favor have you done this G'deon?"

"When you understand, traveler, so will she."

The ancient woman looked out at the vast wetland, and then she turned towards the vast harbor. How long had Ocean planned this extraordinary act of water magic? Only now did she seem certain of her success, now that she was there in the midst of it, with Seth and Zanja on dry land. And now she walked into the water, and when she was hip-deep, she dove. Light fractured, and when the pieces joined together again, the witch was gone.

"In another time, she is walking back to shore," said Zanja.

"It better not be in my lifetime," Karis muttered.

Silver arrived with a bucket of water, and Karis dipped a foot into it, hissing with pain. Seth, apparently unable to stand—perhaps feeling, like Zanja, as if the solid ground were swaying underfoot like the deck of a ship—crawled to Karis, yanking off her shirt for Karis to rest her wet foot on. "What have you done to yourself?" Seth cried. "Where are your shoes? Silver, can you get some bandages? And healing herbs?"

Karis sighed. "Dear heart—save me."

Zanja murmured, "She'll leave you alone sooner if you just let her fuss some. Then tell her how tired you are—that you need to sleep."

Tears of pain were leaking down Karis's cheeks—her other foot was in the bucket now. But her hand rested on Zanja's—warm, strong, hungry. "Where can we go?" she asked.

Zanja studied the stiff, waist-high grass of the wetland, thousands of green swords jammed by their hilts into the sand. But...even if they did cut Zanja, those pains would be worth enduring. "I'll make a house for us. It won't take very long."

"Then I'll come to you," Karis said. "If I must crawl on my belly."

Chapter 33

Karis uttered a hoarse cry. She had kept Zanja riding on the crest of that wave for a long time—but now Zanja plunged wildly over. In a tangle of limbs, hands, mouths, they both climaxed.

Zanja's fractured thoughts were slow to become coherent again. By then, Karis had fallen asleep. Her big, coarse, powerful hand lay between Zanja's thighs. Zanja could have sworn that her lover had orgasmed through her fingers, but to whom could she ever tell such a marvelous thing?

The grass walls of their trampled den rattled in a passing breeze. Karis lay still, breathing deeply, her fatigue-shadowed face having given up its sorrows. Zanja kissed her, and Karis smiled in her sleep. Zanja felt around for their scattered clothing and haphazardly covered them with it.

Later, feeling Karis awaken, she awakened with her. The sun was setting, and from the village could be heard friendly shouts and laughter. Closer, but still remote, an axe chopped wood, then fell silent. The grass rustled dryly, and a long-legged white bird as tall as Zanja stepped through the green blades and glanced around their trampled den in surprise. Its black legs were thin as twigs. It raised one foot and paused, as though considering, then it continued onward, stepping neatly between their legs and slipping into the grass again.

Karis let out her breath. "What a place!"

"It seems enchanted," Zanja murmured.

"It's too wet, though. And there's something unsettled about it."

"Tadwell ceded this part of Shaftal to her, the water witch. He didn't know it as her plan—he was trapped in his own anger and would have done anything to punish me."

"I see," said Karis after a moment. Her warm, rough fingertips stroked up Zanja's throat. "These bruises are his work?"

"Yes."

"And this?" Zanja flinched reflexively as Karis took her torn ear-lobe between her fingers, though her touch could not give pain, not now anyway.

"Yes."

"Shall I fix it properly? Or do you want a ragged earlobe?"

"You couldn't endure that," Zanja said.

"I couldn't. Not at all."

Zanja lay quietly, her head tucked in the hollow of Karis's shoulder. She felt a pressure on her ear, as though her flesh was being glued together like two pieces of wood. Somewhere in this salt marsh, the earring lay where Tadwell had flung it, buried in mud, tangled in plant roots, or decorating the home of a crab. "I pretended to be a Paladin," she said, "after I nearly froze and starved to death."

"And now here we both are, freezing and starving together."

"I'll go foraging," said Zanja.

She didn't have to forage far. At the entrance to their den were two buckets, one full of water, and the other containing several dried fish, a tin of hardbread, and a crisp wad of hairy seaweed. There also lay a pile of neatly folded blankets. They ate everything in the bucket, which then became their toilet. Wrapped in blankets, they talked until they slept again.

In dead of night, Zanja awoke to find Karis's mouth upon her breast. She tilted her head back and the wheeling stars filled her vision until they exploded.

Chapter 34

The sun was climbing rapidly up the western slope of the sky by the time Zanja felt inclined to get up and emerge from the grass den. For hours, the sounds of the Essikret village had imposed on her dreams: crying babies, ringing axes, shrieking children. Below these sharper noises flowed an undercurrent of laughter and singing, and the distant booming of the ocean. Now she saw the harbor, a blue jewel within which floated white clouds, across which people scooted in rowboats. The tide had pulled the water back, exposing a long stretch of black sand, upon which naked children roamed. Did Tadwell ever realize what a beautiful place he had created in his extraordinary fit of temper? Zanja took a breath of salty air and let it go: perhaps she could not think of these people of the past as dead, but she must accept that they were gone, and that these unanswered questions she had been left with would remain unanswered.

She spotted Seth, sitting cross-legged in the shade of the water tank, and walked over to her. Seth had combed her wind-tangled hair and tied it back so it revealed her face, sunburned and chapped by wind, and her eyes, red and puffy with weeping. Using a wooden needle, she was picking apart the seams of a longshirt and wrapping the salvaged thread around a spool she had improvised out of a small piece of water-polished driftwood. Zanja squatted beside her in the shade. "Thank you for the supplies last night. But you should have looked after yourself, after all you've endured."

"I'm fine," said Seth. And, despite the ravaging voyage and exhaustion of sorrow, she had a dogged look that Zanja knew well from seeing it so often in Karis: Seth would fix what was broken, or die trying.

"Is that your friend's shirt? Damon's?"

"It was, but now it will be yours."

Zanja glanced down at her bare breasts, glittering necklace, and seaweed skirt. "What, is this outfit not acceptable?"

Seth managed a smile. "You look rather good in it, but I want my necklace back. Is Karis still asleep?"

"Yes, and I hope she sleeps for days."

"Well, we aren't going anywhere until her feet heal. She might as well sleep."

"No, we'll leave much sooner than that, for she says that Paladins are chasing her. Once they arrive, they'll be able to carry her out of here. We must go to Watfield."

"Don't you mean Waet's Field?" Seth had reached the knotted end of the thread she was reclaiming, so she cut the thread with the knife that lay beside her. She set her project aside. "I want to show you something."

Zanja felt a movement within, a tidal shift. After all, would something be explained? She stood up hastily. Seth also stood up, saying, "Oh, you and Emil perk up in the same way! Like dogs hearing something important but too far away for ordinary people to hear."

She led the way through the boatyard, where busy carpenters greeted her by name. Beyond the boatyard, a cluster of dry land houseboats was tucked against the cliff. Their hulls were painted with stylized waves where the water level would have been, and the painted creatures that frolicked above and below the water were so strangely shaped and brilliantly colored that they hardly seemed like fish at all except that they had fins. One of these house boats had a door cut into its side at ground level, and Zanja followed Seth in. It was a tool shed, where hazy light that flowed in through open hatches dimly revealed rough shelves crowded with hand tools carefully wrapped in oilcloth. Here, an old man who was painstakingly sharpening a chisel scarcely seemed to notice them.

Seth said, "The water people took Damon's gear with them in their boats, that night. This is where I found his knapsack when I went looking for it this morning, to get that shirt for you." She squatted at a set of rough-hewn shelves that were crowded with indistinguishable bundles, took hold of a large knapsack on the bottom shelf, and heaved it out. Underneath it, half covered by adjoining objects, nearly invisible in the shadow, lay a very large box.

"The box Jareth stole!" said Zanja. "The one you thought was destroyed and lost!"

"But I couldn't get it out by myself—it's too heavy."

Even with the two of them working on it, removing the box was a tricky business: it was indeed heavy, and difficult to get hold of, and it was wedged in by other objects that themselves resisted being moved. Eventually they pulled it off the shelf and managed to carry it between them, outside into the light. They dropped it on the sand, and Seth rubbed at its dirt and salt stains with the tail of her shirt. The revealed wood gleamed as though it had been polished with wax. "It isn't even scratched," said Seth. She looked up at Zanja and added with concern, "You're panting."

Zanja's heartbeat was thudding in her throat, but not from the effort of freeing and moving the thing. She said, "There's never been a lock Karis couldn't open."

"We aren't going to wake her up!"

"Oh, she'll fall asleep again."

They carried the box in stages to the grass den. Karis lay naked, sound asleep, with a blanket pulled across her face to block the sunlight. The bright light cast curved shadows along the muscles of her back as though she were a breathing sculpture. Zanja's love, tested and tempered though it had been through these six years, rose up in her heart as fiercely as if it were brand new. Seth said in a hushed voice, "But look how tired she is."

"She'll wake up to eat, and be glad of it."

They left and returned sometime later, bearing a pan of fried fish, a salad of vinegared seaweed, and a basket of steamed buns that smelled unpleasantly like fermenting ale. Karis had awakened and was sitting among the blankets, wearing her filthy shirt, with the massive box pulled into her lap. "What an odd thing you've found," she said.

Zanja said, "That's the box the assassin stole from Seth's house."

"Stupid man. Is that breakfast?"

She reached for the frying pan scarcely before Zanja set it down, and began eating steaming fish with her fingers. Zanja tried a bite of the bread, which was gummy but tasted much better than it smelled. "Seth, tell Karis about the box—I told her only a part of its story last night."

While Seth recounted the adventures of the stolen box, Zanja and Karis ate everything but the fish bones. The story ended with Damon's death, and Seth began to weep, and Zanja saw that she couldn't speak of it without reliving it. Most memories become old and faded, but some do not—and this one, Zanja feared, would remain fresh forever. Karis reached out a greasy hand, then lowered it. She would not try to fix this pain: that lesson she had learned from what happened with Clement. Yet she had not learned it soon enough, for catastrophe seemed inevitable now. Clement might be made whole again, but Karis had squandered too much time in her mad rush across Shaftal, and now it was impossible for either repair or recovery to happen before the convening of the commanders.

Soon, Karis must tell Seth what she had done to Clement. It would be a good rehearsal for equally difficult explanations she must make in Watfield: to Gilly, Ellid, Emil, and, worst of all, to Norina. Then they must reconcile themselves to accomplishing whatever they could with whichever general was chosen instead of Clement. Although none of those commanders were as notorious as Heras had been, still it seemed likely they would find themselves again at war.

Seth wiped her face with her hands. "And what's in that cursed box? And how, in Shaftal's name, did it wind up under the guest bed at High Meadow Farm?"

Karis glanced expectantly at Zanja, for apparently she, too, knew the answer to Seth's question, though by her own less arcane methods.

Zanja said, "The Basdowners couldn't be convinced to live properly on the land and stop killing each other."

Seth protested, as she had before on the boat, "How can this be true? Nobody even remembers such a thing!"

Zanja continued, "Because of their intransigence, Tadwell was in Basdown, and Arel with him. Arel told me they had visited High Meadow Farm. The people of your farmstead were unforgiving and hot-tempered, he said to me."

Seth uttered a snort of disbelief.

"And I told Arel I had a friend from High Meadow, who's nothing like that. Do you understand what I'm saying, Seth? Arel thought I belonged in the past, not the future, but Tadwell knew the truth, and if Arel told Tadwell what I had told him, Tadwell would be able to—"

Seth gazed at her, blank-faced.

"—to leave this box there for me," Zanja said.

"What?" cried Seth.

Karis had put her hand on the box, which lay between her and Zanja, and now Zanja heard the quiet click of its latch popping open. She lifted the lid. There lay the lost lexicon, preserved by librarians, rescued from destruction by water magic, protected for two hundred years by earth magic.

It looked exactly as it had looked when Zanja first unwrapped it, outside of Kisha. Its leather-bound cover was still gilded with patterns of interwoven vines; the leather itself, though unbelievably old, was still soft to the touch. Zanja opened the cover, turned a few thick pages, and held the book open to the glyph that means Water. In the illustration, a woman leapt up joyously, flinging water from a shell. The water became waves, which curled around her, repeating in their curves the graceful curve of the dancer's back, arms, and flying hair. Water logic: beautiful, and beyond explanation.

Seth said in outraged tones, "You stole that book on impulse, Tadwell chased you because you had stolen it, that witch used him to save her people because he was chasing you, and then he gave it to you?" Her voice gained volume. "He left it for you at High Meadow, and Jareth stole it on impulse, then we chased him because he stole it, and he killed Damon? All this because you like pictures?"

Seth's version of events misrepresented a few things, but to correct her would not solve the problem.

"Throw that monstrous thing in the ocean!" Seth cried.

Karis said quietly, "That book may be the oldest thing in Shaftal."

"But how is it worth so much? It's unreadable—Zanja says so!"

"Oh, she'll read it eventually. She and the other glyph-obsessed people will not rest until they understand every symbol."

"But even if it makes a thousand people happy—"

"It might make us wiser," said Zanja.

"Will it give us what we really need now? Fairness, or justice, or peace?"

"Oh, don't you know?" said Karis. "The healers have created a tisane for that. We just have to steep some herbs and drink it down."

In a moment, Seth uttered a reluctant laugh. "Yes, I'm being unreasonable."

"It's the water glyph," said Zanja. "I should have known it would have a bad effect on you."

"You certainly should have known that!"

Zanja turned a few more pages of the lexicon, saying, "Well, this one will also befuddle you, but without making you angry. Look at these two illustrations." They were on adjacent pages, of course, for they were the glyphs East and West, and the illustrations were similar to those with which Zanja was familiar. In one, a woman in a rowboat fished in the ocean and the sun lay near the horizon, and in the other a man traveling in the mountains gazed towards the peaks and at the sun that rested upon them. Neither Seth nor Karis seemed to notice what was so strange about these, so Zanja tapped a finger on the glyph that marked the illustration known as West, and said, "This is the glyph for East. And this—" she turned the page, to the woman in the boat, "—this is West."

Seth and Karis stared at the pages as Zanja flipped back and forth from one illustration to the other. Finally, Karis said, "How could anyone not know which way the ocean lies?"

"A tired copyist made a mistake," said Seth doubtfully.

Zanja said, "But there are so many strange things in these illustrations, the copyist would have to have been tired all the time. Here's one odd thing I think I do understand, though it's very surprising. Do you remember, Karis, when I told Clement that her glyph-sign is Blooming?"

Karis nodded, and Seth said, "Clement mentioned it to me, but I'm not familiar with that glyph."

"Because I invented it." Zanja leafed through the massive book, then spread it open again. "But there it is!"

The kneeling woman in the illustration wore clothing that seemed to be a length of rich cloth that was wrapped and draped around her, leaving a breast exposed. Her hair had been coiled atop her head and was pinned there with an ornate comb. Seth said, "That woman never did any work, not in that outfit. How muddy that dragging hem would get in the rainy season! But she's outside in her garden." Seth examined the plants and vines that filled every bit of the illustration, the limits of which were defined by an ornate, arching arbor. "Each flower is stranger than the next!"

Karis also leaned over the book, which was upside-down to her, and they began discussing, arguing about, and dismissing as entirely fanciful every one of the illustration's blooming flowers. Then Seth said, "But this one is real." She pointed at the flower growing out of the woman's lovingly cupped hands: a long, graceful stem that dangled bright blue, bell-shaped blossoms. "It's that forced bulb Clement gave you, which smelled so marvelous. You put it in my room."

"It grows in every garrison, I think," said Karis.

"Damon told me the soldiers dig the bulbs every autumn and store them indoors. If they are left out in the cold they turn to mush by spring. I asked him how any self-respecting bulb could be so dependent on a gardener for its very survival. He said that it was a bulb from Sainna, where the ground never freezes. This picture—from four hundred years ago…!"

"Longer than that," said Karis.

They both became speechless. Zanja realized that for once she was sharing with earth bloods rather than with fire bloods the sensation of knowing without words, without reason, an inarticulate and momentous truth. All three of them stared at the alien woman in her alien garden.

"It's a Sainnese woman," said Seth. "It's a Sainnese garden. It's a Sainnese book."

Zanja said, "They brought this book with them, the first time they came to Shaftal—the first time they tried to conquer this land, only to be conquered by it. After that, they became Shaftali."

Karis and Seth both looked at her, still baffled. "The Sainnites became you, Seth," said Zanja. "They became you and everyone who looks like you. All Sainnites are Shaftali, as Karis said at the council—but it's also true that all Shaftali are Sainnites."

Once again, Karis slept. Seth declared she would not think any more impossible thoughts that day and returned to her mundane task of dismantling Damon's shirt. Zanja went into the water and swam out to the village, where a woman nursing her infant upon the rocking water pointed in the direction of Silver's boat. When Zanja had reached the correct row, people told her to climb up into a boat, and then she was able to walk from house to house, forging a trail of mirth as she balanced her awkward way from the edge of one boat to the next. Children, dogs, old people and young, all greeted her with friendliness, offering a joke, a song, a wagging tail, or food. Zanja's progress would have been much faster had she continued to swim, but during this inefficient journey she learned many new words.

"A warm day," she declared as she stepped into Silver's boat. "Too warm for work."

"Who is working?" asked the woman there, whose bare feet, tucked into loops of rope, supported a loom so simple that the weavers of Zanja's people would have found it as laughable as these people had found her sense of balance. Yet, with her hands free because the loom was also looped around the back of her neck, the weaver wove upon it at a brisk pace using a shuttle made of transparent bone.

"Where are you going?" asked another woman, who with one hand continuously plucked dried and shredded seaweed from a basket, while her other hand managed a spindle that dropped steadily from her fingers, spinning an ever-lengthening cord.

"I am where I am going, I think. If you're not working, then you are playing. Who is winning your game?"

"I am!" the women both said, and laughed. The spindle hit upon the deck and the spinning woman stepped up onto a stool, clinging to it with her toes, which these people used as nimbly as fingers. Almost immediately, the spindle hit wood again, and Zanja bent to pick it up and wind the yarn. Among her people yarn-winding had been a child's task, but despite the many years since she had been a child, her fingers remembered exactly how to do it so the spindle wasn't unbalanced. Then the weaver protested that Zanja's help was giving the spinner an advantage, so Zanja wound an empty shuttle with fresh yarn for her.

The door into the low house was of child's height, but when Silver appeared there, he climbed up from a much lower deck, so she first saw the top of his head. "Oh, Zanja, you have come visiting. Would you like to have some soup?"

"I am not hungry, but perhaps you can answer a question for me."

"Climb down, then," he said.

Entering the boat's interior was like climbing inside a piece of furniture. Light sprayed from glass prisms in the ceiling, and Zanja could see dim cupboards, from floor to ceiling and even overhead, and a swaying hammock in which hung a child-sized shape. A cat appeared in the shadows and gracefully climbed up the ladder into the bright light of afternoon. The windows all were propped open, and a sea breeze blew in through some, and out through others. The small room smelled of spices.

Zanja said, "You have a way to summon Grandmother Ocean, don't you?"

Despite the shadows, she could see Silver's eyebrows lift. "I thought you would inveigh me again to go with you to this city, Watfield, which I have already told you is too far from the ocean. But this question you ask I will not answer, Zanja na'Tarwein."

"I don't expect you to say anything that's forbidden. But I must speak with her before we leave this place."

Silver said, "I will not summon her, and she would not come."

Zanja squatted in the dim room. "She thinks she has managed her great project so the only alteration is the one that matters, but she is wrong. She has balanced the differences between present and past, but she has not balanced the differences between present and future. Her meddling has caused problems we can't resolve, which will lead to worse problems. I know this is true, because it affects a pattern that has been foreseen. What she has done will damage the future. Is that not important enough that you should summon her?"

"She left this with me to give to you." Silver opened one of the cupboard doors and took out a wooden vessel. He handed it to Zanja. It was a heavy container very like a barrel, with a cork in the flat lid. The liquid within sloshed softly.

Zanja pulled out the cork and sniffed the vessel's contents: Water. She corked it carefully.

"Are you satisfied?" asked Silver

"I am," she said.

Chapter 35

The Paladins arrived by boat, the falling tide pulling them eastward out of the wetland, just as the water people who went out the day before to meet them had been carried westward on a rising tide. Seth was sick to death of water and water logic, and gladly left behind the floating town, the lovely harbor, and the cheerful people. Soon their small company struggled through woodlands so dense they often had to cut a path for Karis's litter. The Paladins had chased after Karis with nothing but whatever they happened to be holding, and it was fortunate that one of them had been holding a hatchet.

At least Karis was behaving herself, Zanja commented during that first grueling day. The Paladins had chased their G'deon the entire width of Shaftal, and arrived with sore feet and raw tempers. Karis was apologetic and obedient, though in an obviously insincere and utilitarian sort of way. At the Han Road, when they finally reached it, two Paladins who had gone ahead by boat now awaited them, with the lexicon safely stowed in a wagon confiscated from a farm family. Karis meekly crawled into the wagon bed and lay down in the straw. "Deliver this baggage to Watfield in twelve days," she said.

The Paladins took turns driving the wagon, and the rest of them walked. This far south, the road was in terrible repair, and those who went afoot suffered much less than those who banged and bounced all day across displaced cobbles and through potholes. After two days of slow, bone-jolting travel, Karis sat up one afternoon. "What happened to the road?"

Seth, surprised out of a daze, noticed the smooth stretch of road before them. "Oh, we're in Basdown."

"Basdowners take good care of the highway."

"Of course we do. It's our only road."

Some time after sunset had given way to full darkness, Seth heard the High Meadow cow dogs begin barking in the distance, but when the small company reached the wagon track to the farmstead she was tempted to pretend she had missed it in the darkness. They turned down it, though, and the dogs rushed out and surrounded them. A horse kicked at an agile cow dog and missed, of course. "Hold up!" said Seth. "Land's sake!" The wagon rolled to a stop.

The lead dog immediately stood on his hind legs and began scrabbling noisily at the side of the wagon. "What is wrong with you?" Seth asked. "Tell the pack to let us in—we're hungry and our feet hurt!"

He barked excitedly at her. "Karis, he wants to meet you." Seth leaned over to boost him up into the wagon bed, and he rushed impetuously into Karis's lap, put his paws on her chest, and cried an eloquent welcome with his nose nearly touching hers.

"Greetings, sir," said Karis. "Your whiskers are quite tickley. Did you know you're a magical dog?"

The dog uttered a sharp bark, then returned to Seth to be hoisted out of the wagon. He and his pack sped into the looming darkness, barking with the kind of enthusiasm that was certain to bring out the entire household. Seth hoped they wouldn't stare at the G'deon of Shaftal as though she were a two-headed cow.

"Our dogs are magical?" said Seth as the wagon started down the track, which was too narrow to allow people to walk beside it.

"Get in," Karis said. Seth did so and encountered Zanja on the other side, doing the same. Every time Seth saw Zanja unexpectedly her heartbeat paused, for she would remember buying the longshirt and breeches for Damon, the shopping trip he had designated their first adventure.

"They won't offer us seaweed for supper, will they?" asked Karis, as Seth and Zanja settled beside her. The wagon bed, despite its carpeting of straw, smelled strongly of onions.

"No, sand porridge," said Zanja.

"Or roasted bugs," Karis retorted.

Seth supposed that these were private jokes. The dogs barked wildly in the distance. A branch scraped along the side of the wagon, and the Paladin who drove them muttered an apology, though she wasn't certain whether he apologized to the wagon or to the branch. The other Paladins trailed wearily behind them.

Zanja said, "Seth, what is it about the Basdown cow dogs that makes them famous?"

"They have very rigid ideas. I know what you saw in the past, but I can't believe the Basdowners once fought each other over their farm boundaries, for the dogs would never have permitted that."

Karis grunted, covered her face, and began rocking from side to side uttering muffled choking sounds.

"I guess I have made a mark on history," said Zanja.

"You two are conspiring to tease me."

Karis lowered her hands from her face. In a strangled voice, she said, "Tadwell resolved the problems in Basdown by working magic on the cow dogs. Those dogs have been herding the people of Basdown for two hundred years."

"What?" said Seth.

Karis seemed to have gotten her mirth under control, but Zanja was holding her breath. Seth supposed she should be offended and out-raged, but she felt something unexpected erupting in the hollow of her sorrow. "We need more dogs, then," she said. "A lot more. One for every person in Shaftal. To bite their ankles every time they misbehave."

Karis began heaving with stifled mirth again, then gave up. All three of them were roaring with laughter as their wagon trundled into the yard, where the entire family had come out of the house, and the children danced in the dirt with the joyful dogs.

Seth slept in her old bedroom, with her familiar old quilt and the cush-ioned bench where she had first put her hand on Clement's knee. She awoke in early dawn, hearing the creak of stairs as people began going out to milk the cows. Last night, Mama had agreed to bring the news of Damon's death to Ten-Furlong Farm, and Seth awoke to a sensation of relief. She also felt Clem's ghost awakening slowly in the bed beside her, blinking in sleepy surprise as though Seth were no more strange to her than the stranger inside her own skin. Perhaps, thanks to Karis, Clem-ent would always be a ghost: a hollow imbecile, a devastated wraith. In neither state could she have the peace she deserved.

For peace, thought Seth, is not merely an absence of war. It is all the things that war displaces, the things that war makes not merely unachievable, but unimaginable. Only peace makes peace possible.

She got up, dressed hastily, and went to the room that had the biggest bed, where a Paladin dozed in the hall. Zanja opened the door before Seth tapped on it. "I'm glad you're here. You can help put the mattress back on the bed."

"The bed wasn't big enough?"

"It was, except that Karis kept hitting her sore feet on the footboard."

Karis yawned prodigiously, sitting in a chair by the cold fireplace. Seth and Zanja wrestled the mattress back onto the bed frame. Karis, who seemed to find it a trial to watch others struggle to accomplish something she could have done easily, loudly reminded herself that she was just baggage.

"You're too unwieldy and willful to be baggage," said Zanja.

Seth said, "Karis, can you undo the magic of the cow dogs?"

"Why, when it has worked so well?"

"Because people who are accustomed to being herded become cows. When the Basdowners made me their councilor, they wanted peace with the Sainnites. Then Jareth came, and immediately they hated Sainnites and wanted war. People who just do what they're told aren't being good—they're being cows."

Karis began working her fingers through her hair, which every day seemed even more wildly tangled. Bits of straw and chaff floated from her head. "Maybe," she said finally. "Maybe it was Tadwell's error of mercy."

Zanja picked up the wooden water vessel she had carried with her from Essikret, and slung its seaweed cord crossways over her shoulder. "Ten days," she said.

Karis nodded.

"I'll tell the Paladins you're ready to go."

"I need to think about this," Karis said.

Seth realized Karis was talking to her. For a moment, she had been heeding something else, the creak of Clem's ghostly foot in the hallway.

Karis added, "Perhaps you're right about the dogs, but I need to fix my old mistakes before I start making new ones."

"The Basdowners have been like this for two hundred years," Seth said. "So there's no reason to hurry, I guess."

Seth's family had offered to load the wagon with fodder for the horses and food for the people, for by tomorrow they would be in the

Barrens. "I'll go make certain the wagon is ready," Seth said. She went out, following a ghost.

Clement is in her quarters. She sits on the bed. Occasionally, she can hear the soldier in the hall, shuffling her feet, clearing her throat. Some soldiers stand guard quietly. Some are never quiet. This room is frigid in winter and sweltering in summer. It contains a chest of proper size and shape, in which is stored everything Clement owns. On the windowsill are the remains of the bulbs she forced into bloom when the garrison was still buried in snow. The rest of her bulbs, Gilly told her, were planted at the correct time and are now breaking ground. Every year she has watched for that first growth. Why? She has been pondering this question for hours. She has not gone to the garden, and now it is dark.

Gilly ran to greet her, and then he did not smile. Ellid clasped her hand and called her "General." Ellid said that seven of the garrison commanders had arrived, then looked at Commander Euphan and her face became quite still. Euphan had talked to Clement a great deal during their journey to Watfield. She still could not remember why she had not trusted him.

Ellid said, "The rest are expected tomorrow. What are your orders?"

Sevan murmured to her. Sevan had not gone to Appletown Garrison—she had returned to Watfield with her officers. She said it was the G'deon's orders.

"Pardon me, General," said Ellid. "Of course you must rest."

"I must rest," Clement said. She is the general. She knows she is, for people address her as general. A general's duties are a general's duties. Now she waits in her quarters for someone to tell her what a general's duties are.

She hears something in the hall. The soldier clears her throat. She shuffles her feet. She says loudly, "The general is not to be disturbed!"

Why? Clement wonders. She stands up. Perhaps whoever is coming will explain why she has always looked at the garden every day to see if her bulbs have broken ground. She goes to the door and opens it. The hall is dark, and full of people.

"I'm sorry, General," says the noisy soldier. Her face is not right.

The soldier turns to the crowded people and begins to argue with them. Zanja na'Tarwein is talking to her. Zanja used to be dead. She used to be in history. She is not dead or in history any longer. Her voice is quiet and steady. "I understand this," she says. She is fluent in Sainnese, and this is a very useful thing. "However, this is Karis G'deon. She is your general's general. She goes where she pleases."

The soldier breathes. "I am ordered—"

"Commander Ellid's orders, I assume. Karis outranks her."

It is wrong for these people to arrive without warning. Clement feels certain of this. She looks up, and up further, for Karis has pushed the soldier out of the way, and it is proper to look into a person's eyes no matter how tall she is. Karis puts her hand on Clement's shoulder. Clement is in the room. She is walking backwards. Other people come in behind them. Clement is sitting again on the bed. Karis's hand is on her shoulder. Clement realizes that Karis has pushed her across the room, which certainly must be improper. She begins to object.

"Be quiet, Clement," says Karis. Clement's shoulder hurts. She is quiet. "Zanja, go find them."

Zanja puts something on the floor beside the bed and leaves the room. Several Paladins are here. Among them is Seth. Seth is breathing. She stands where she is. She is steady. Her hands are at her sides. It is not right for them to be here, Clement thinks.

"Wait in the hall," Karis says. She is not talking to Clement. The people leave the room. Seth stands where she is.

Karis says, "Seth. She has not asked for you."

Seth says, "Clem, do you want me to leave?"

Clement says, "It is not right for you to be here."

Seth breathes. She turns and leaves the room.

"It is not right for you to be here," Clement says.

Karis says, "I decide what's right, little though I like it." Her hand is on Clement's shoulder, and it is heavy. Her shoulder hurts. Her other hand is undoing Clement's buckles and buttons. Karis puts her hand inside, on Clement's skin.

Clement remembers Seth, how Seth was, how she was, how she could not hold her. And she cries out.

Norina Truthken enters the room.

"Don't let her—" says Clement. "There is a horror—"

She remembers. The pain. The thundering clock. The healer-torturer. She remembers. Gabian gazing solemnly at her, awaiting the answer to a question, his soft face against her breast. Will we be or will we not be, and will we be able to choose our lives? We will, Gabe, but I never will. She remembers. She cuts her friend's throat. Her friend's hot blood pours onto her hands. She watches her die, and loves her, and hates her. When she betrays the betrayer, she betrays herself. Loyalty is all she has, all she has ever had. Without loyalty, she will now betray them all. She has betrayed them.

The horror gnaws her entrails, and she screams.

"Drink this," says Karis.

"Talk to me," says the Truthken.

Norina and Emil had arrived with Ellid and Gilly and an officer Seth did not recognize. When Clement began screaming, they took the lamp that was in the hall and retreated to a room in which were stored several dozen soldiers' chests. They sat on chests, and Gilly put his hands over his ears.

Emil said, "Commander Ellid sent for us after Commander Sevan explained to her what had happened to Clement. We were meeting downstairs, trying to decide what to do."

Seth would like to have been there when Zanja appeared out of the shadows and said—she didn't know what she had said, probably something courteous and mundane.

After a long silence, Gilly said, "How long will take for them to fix what's wrong with her?"

Emil said, "I don't know."

"The time we have must be enough," Zanja said, "for we won't get any more."

Seth would rather have been in the room with Clement, fruitlessly holding her hand. At least that hollow, weary screaming wouldn't be echoing inside her head, yanking at her will: do something, do something, do something now. If Clement had been an animal, Seth would have ended her suffering already. Would that be an error of mercy?

"How much longer?" cried Gilly.

Seth sat down beside him and took his hand. He said, "I've nursed her through some painful injuries. Her mouth might draw tight, and if it was particularly bad, she might make a sound, like a grunt, very quiet."

"This is a different kind of pain, I guess."

Ellid said something in Sainnese. Gilly replied with harsh, barking words. Seth didn't know what it was about, but no one spoke in this way to a commander, certainly not a clerk like Gilly. Yet Ellid replied quietly to his angry words, and Gilly rubbed his ugly face with his hands and replied in reasonable tones. The other commander, Commander Sevan, spoke also. They were discussing how to solve a problem, Seth thought. She heard a name, Euphan, several times.

Zanja and Emil sat quietly with their arms around each other, not telling each other what had happened, not talking at all. Seth had never seen Emil so unworried.

She began to feel like she was alone in the room.

Clement's awful cries fell silent. The people waiting in the storeroom stopped talking. The flickering light of the lamp—a plain, practical object, like most soldiers' things—illuminated their faces but surrounded them in shifting shadows. Seth became aware of her throbbing feet, her aching legs, the dragging weariness of tension and travel.

The hallway outside their door heaved a sigh. Emil stood up hastily, then the door was opened, and Karis filled the door frame. "Emil, don't," she said.

"Don't what? Kiss you?" he said.

Karis let her breath out, and they embraced, and Emil murmured, "Oh my dear, you've done so well."

Seth had never found a family in Basdown, had never found a place she wanted to be more than she wanted to be in High Meadow, and she had not much wanted to be there either. Now she had finally chosen, and kept choosing and rechoosing the same thing, over and over, in all different kinds of ways.

Speaking over Emil's shoulder, Karis said, "Seth, she wants to talk to you."

Seth stood up and went out into the silent hallway. Then she turned back and said into the room, "Gilly, do you think she'll want Gabian?"

He bounded to his feet. She continued down the hall, to the door to Clement's room, which was ajar. The Truthken stood guard outside, where a soldier ought to be. Norina glanced at Seth without speaking. Her shoulders were resting against the scarred, unfinished plank wall. She leaned her head back, and shut her eyes. Whatever she had done in there had been exhausting.

Seth went in the room. Clement was standing, peering into a tiny metal mirror no larger than the palm of her hand, smoothing her cropped hair. Seth turned up the wick of the lamp that stood on the tabletop, and the barren room's shadows retreated. The vessel Zanja had carried from Essikret to this room now lay on its side on the floor, empty, its cork halfway across the room. It contained water, Zanja had said. And it contained time.

Clement turned. Before, she had looked healthy but lifeless. Now she looked drawn and exhausted, and her eyes were hollow with pain.

"Gilly's getting Gabian," Seth said.

"Will he remember me?" Clement looked around the room as though wondering how she had gotten there, or whether it was the right place. Then, she looked down at the wreck of her boots. She said, "They'll make me general tomorrow. What they needed me to prove, I've proven now. Bloody hell." She took a breath. "A while ago you were here, and I made you leave."

There was a silence. Seth said, "I wanted to be the one who tells you that I've let one of your soldiers be killed. Damon, of Prista's company."

Clement's mouth grew tight. She made a small sound, like a grunt. Out in the hallway, Norina stirred.

Seth said, "He was a kind, funny man, and I was lucky to be his friend. He was becoming a flower farmer. He died protecting me, but it shouldn't have happened."

"We need more people like him, not fewer." After a moment Clement added, "Very little has been explained to me yet."

"Probably because it would take hours."

There were voices in the hall. Norina said to someone, "Not yet."

Seth said, "I won't let go of you again."

Clement took a breath. "Seth—"

"I understand that you can't make room for me—I understand why that's impossible. So I'll make room for myself. I know how to help the Shaftali love soldiers, and how to help the soldiers love peace. And the Peace Committee will find other people to help, and there must be other soldiers like Damon. One day soon, you'll realize your people are safe. You'll notice that you've gone an entire week without worrying."

Clement turned away. Seth had said too much. She should have waited, waited for other things to be settled. The general put on her hat, which was clean, with its insignia polished to glittering brilliance, but destroyed by weather, so shapeless Seth doubted it could even be reblocked. Clement glanced down at her wrecked boots again.

She turned to Seth at last, and there she was: not the general, but Clem. But it was the general who said, "I'll give you whatever you need."

Seth nodded, and turned towards Norina, to tell her that the next person could come in. But Clem said, "Seth."

She turned back.

"It takes two to hold on. You'll have to teach me how, probably."

Seth went to her, and put her arms around her. She felt a surprise in that lean frame, then a relaxing. Clem's head became a weight on Seth's shoulder. Her hat fell off. The back of her tunic was damp, sweat-soaked from her ordeal. Seth felt Clem's arms lift, felt her hands take hold of her. They held on.

Chapter 36

Clement, Gilly, and Ellid walked with them to the gate, and Gabian chortled sleepily in Clement's arms. Occasionally, he seemed to notice anew that his mother had returned to him, and he would utter a loud announcement: "Yow!"

"Very strange," Clement would reply to him. Or she would ask him a question, such as, "And how exactly have you managed to become twice as heavy as I remember?"

The wagon awaited them, with the horses hanging their heads, shifting their weight from side to side. Karis said to one of the Paladins, "I'll walk."

Zanja put a hand upon the Paladin's arm before he could begin a pointless protest. "Master Paladin, she's finished with pretending to be manageable."

He uttered a snort, the first sign of humor in any of these grim Paladins. At Zanja's side, Emil said quietly, "If you please, Farber, drive the wagon."

"Of course, Emil," he said.

Karis and Emil began the tedious bidding of farewell, a Shaftali custom Zanja could participate in if she had to but would never understand. The Ashawala'i had merely bidden each other farewell, and only made a ritual of it when they knew they would never see each other again. Perhaps this was the custom of a people who expected every day to be their last. And when the Sainnites encountered it in this distant land, they had not recognized it as their own.

Clement took Seth's hand and spoke to her, bidding her a private farewell, Zanja thought. But they looked into each other's eyes, and then Seth turned her head to say over her shoulder, "I'll come to Travesty in the morning. Would someone call the Peace Committee together for breakfast with me?"

"I'll do it," said Zanja.

"That won't be necessary," said Gilly. "The committee is here in the garrison, all of them, scattered in various companies. I'll send some notes around and have all of them meet you somewhere."

Seth stared at him, and then looked at Emil, as if to ask whether it was really true. Emil said, "I'll have Garland send over some decent food for you."

"It took those two long enough," Karis muttered, as they started into the city behind the rattling wagon, with the other Paladins walking close to her. Her bandaged feet were in slippers that someone at High Meadow Farm had hastily made for her. She was not limping, though she was walking very carefully. Her feet had bled all over Shaftal in the last few months, and many a farmer would soon be surprised by the inexplicable fertility of fields she had crossed.

Emil took Zanja's elbow. A lamp burned on a nearby corner, and she saw tears shining on his face. "Gods know you've got plenty to weep about," she said.

"Saleen," he said. "Of course he's dead. But I still expected to see him."

A raven must be killed and fed to the general so she will continue to live in agony. A tribe must be sacrificed to guarantee the survival of all tribes. The present moment comes to us through unnoticed actions of the past—too many to count, mostly unknown and unnoticed, and sometimes unavoidably terrible. We give ourselves up to the future, one drop of blood at a time, whether we choose to do it or not. That is the truth, Zanja thought, little though we can endure it.

Karis said, "I might have sent for you right away. I might have stayed with Clement when I thought Zanja was dead." She was talking, Zanja realized belatedly, to Norina, who walked beside her.

Norina said, "I'm tired, not angry. You are the G'deon. You did what you did."

They took several careful steps, and the Paladins behind them, too exhausted to pay proper attention, began to outpace them, then realized what they were doing and fell back. Fortunately, their ineffectual protection was not necessary.

Norina said, "If you had been more rational, we'd have had the same outcome, though perhaps with less anxiety and effort."

"You're wrong," Zanja said.

"And the correct answer is?"

"Only this moment can be changed, Madam Truthken."

"You're both right," Karis said. "At my next irrational moment, I'll endeavor to behave rationally."

Travesty came into sight, so extravagantly lit up that Emil missed a step, perhaps appalled by the expense of all that lamp oil. Karis said, "Garland's been baking, do you smell it? And J'han is with Medric and Leeba, waiting by the door."

Zanja said, "Well, let her run to you—running is what she does best."

The watchdogs began a glad barking, and Paladins rushed out, and a little girl came shrieking down the road into her mother's arms. Medric, close behind her, clutched Zanja's hands, crying, "What have you learned?" Then he turned around, ran to the wagon, and flung himself into it.

Zanja turned to Emil, who was wiping his face on his sleeve. "Do you suppose that the people who believe the Sainnites are a blight on Shaftal will be surprised to learn that they themselves are Sainnites? Oh, and there's a glyphic lexicon in the wagon."

She added after a moment, "I don't think I've ever seen you speechless, my brother. Is your heart still beating?"

"I truly don't know. By Shaftal—" With tears still on his face, but laughing, Emil went to the wagon, and Medric shoved the lexicon into his arms.

Epilogue

One day she realized Jareth was dead.

She had been waiting for him for so long—ten days longer than the longest she had expected to wait.

For months she had not thought about that night, had not thought what it meant. She had done her part, and after that she survived, as she had always survived, with her paints.

Jareth was dead, though. And Senra, Charen, Tarera, and Irin were dead. And they had failed.

She felt a moment of abject grief, and then terror. What if—? What if—!

Her son.

She was painting a new sign for the tavern, applying one last coat of lacquer. She did this work outdoors, in the alley behind the building, all alone. She lay down her brush. In a moment she looked at the sky. The afternoon was well on the way to becoming evening. A tree that bloomed in a nearby yard cast its petals across the rutted dirt. Spring was ending, and summer would come, and then what?

She had expected to die. When she didn't, she expected something else to happen—a plan, a message, something. She knew what she must not do, but was she to continue in this way forever? What if he didn't know what to do? What if he had forgotten about her? What if her son—

She could not think that. Must not.

A flower petal had floated into the lacquer, and she carefully picked it out.

A raven flew past, and she watched, her heart pounding, until it was gone.

If Jareth is dead, well then, he is dead, she thought. There were others—she could find the others, couldn't she? Or send someone a message? Not to him of course, but to someone else.

She was not to do that. He had said—he knew—he was—

What was wrong with her, that she was thinking such things? She would finish the sign, then she would decide what to do. She could wait for Jareth one more day. She could offer her services to the tailor, whose shop sign was practically blank, just a shadow and a few flecks of blue.

The tree cast more petals her way. She looked up again, and saw another raven.

The world is full of ravens, she thought.

Acknowledgments

One February day, a porch rail collapsed under me and I fell sixteen feet onto concrete. I broke seven bones, including a shattered vertebra, and when I regained consciousness I couldn't inflate my lungs. I was passing out again due to lack of oxygen, but I remember my wife, Deb Mensinger, talking to me very, very calmly. Then she began breathing for me. Without her breath this book wouldn't have been written—and I hope you appreciate reading it as much as I appreciate being able to write it. Thanks also to the hundred or so friends, relatives, and strangers, who stepped forward to keep my crisis from becoming a catastrophe, a few of whom were Don, Gretchen, and Rod Marks, Ellen Klages, Ellen Kushner, and Judy Goleman. The members of my writer's group, Delia Sherman, Didi Stewart, and Rosemary Kirstein, steadily offered insightful and incisive commentary on my less-than-coherent first draft, which helped me to produce another, better draft for them to comment on, and another one after that, while, amazingly, their interest and intelligence never flagged. Additional friends of this book include Calie Voorhees, Anita Roy Dobbs, Jeanne Gomoll, Gesine Kernchen, Elizabeth LaVelle, Donna Simone, and Widget, my Welsh corgi. Finally, I have been more than fortunate to find an agent, Shana Cohen, who knows her business and yet manages to remain cheerful and humane; and my editors, Kelly Link and Gavin J. Grant, who from the day they said "yes" made it clear that they valued a lot more than my words.

About the author

Laurie J. Marks (lauriejmarks.com) is the author of eight novels including the first two Elemental Logic novels, *Fire Logic* and *Earth Logic*. She lives in Melrose, Massachusetts, and lectures at the Department of English at the University of Massachusetts, Boston.